Sweet Release

by
Pamela Clare

SWEET RELEASE

Kenleigh-Blakewell Family Saga, Book I

Print Edition
Published by Pamela Anne Clare, 2012

Cover Design by Seductive Designs
Cover Photo by Jenn LeBlanc of Studio Smexy™

Originally published March 2003 by Dorchester Publishing Co., Inc.

Reprinted by Dorchester Publishing Co., Inc. in November 2008.

Copyright © 2003, 2011, 2012 by Pamela Clare

ISBN-10 0983875952
ISBN-13 9780983875956

ACKNOWLEDGMENTS

Special thanks to Marie Force for her encouragement and help. Without you, Marie, I never would have taken on this project.

Additional thanks to Benjamin Alexander, Michelle White, Ronlyn Howe, and Stephanie Desprez for proofreading the manuscript and helping me to chase out all the little scanning glitches. I couldn't have managed this without your help.

Thanks, too, to Natasha Kern, my agent, for helping me to rescue my rights to this novel.

DEDICATION

This edition of *Sweet Release* is dedicated to the two people who have tirelessly stood by me for many long years as I've worked to write the books that are in my heart: my beautiful sister Michelle, who has been my best friend since the day she was born, and my younger son Benjamin, who was 4 when I started this book and who is now about to graduate from college.

Mikki and Benjy, I do not know what I'd do without you. Thank you for helping me work toward my dreams. I am so lucky to have you in my life.

Prologue

London
March 8, 1730

Alec Kenleigh tossed back the last of his brandy and savored its heat as it scorched a path to his stomach. There was nothing to be done about it. Nothing—not a warm meal, nor a woman's body, nor drink—seemed to ease his mind this night.

He shifted his gaze from the crackling fire to Isabelle, who sat at her gilded French dressing table, brushing the tangles from her long, dark hair. She always went straight from the bed to her mirror.

How utterly absurd.

"What is it?" she asked, looking as much at her own reflection as at his.

"Hmm?"

"You are staring." She stopped brushing long enough to fix him with a practiced, seductive gaze. At one time that look would have made him ache. Now it had no effect on him at all.

"You please me," he replied.

It was what she expected. She laughed, as he had known she would, then resumed brushing.

God's love, she was a beauty. That, at least, was the truth. Alec let his gaze linger on the delicate features of her face, slender throat, and full, creamy breasts, which swayed with each stroke of her gold-handled brush, their dusky red nipples taut with arousal even now. He'd never met a woman as given to sex as Isabelle.

She smiled coquettishly, evidently mistaking his perusal for desire.

Aye, she was physically flawless. Experienced. Charming. So why had he begun to lose interest? He wasn't perturbed by her other lovers.

He had known about them from the beginning. Nor did he care that she spoke endlessly of trivial matters—fashion, parties, London's latest scandals—for he'd never known a woman whose thoughts did not revolve around such things. Except Elizabeth, of course, but his sister was the exception among women. The truth was that Isabelle St. Denis, with her French accent, her late husband's wealth, and her matchless beauty, inspired only lust. Although he appreciated the joys of lust, Alec had come to realize he wanted more.

The clock in the parlor below struck one. He rose and began to dress. Never during the five months they'd been lovers had he stayed the night. Both of them preferred it that way.

"Leaving so soon?" Isabelle put her brush aside and rose to meet him. Embracing him, she pressed her breasts against him and ran her fingers through the hair on his chest. Her wet tongue teased his nipple.

"I'm afraid I haven't been very good company tonight." He placed a kiss on the end of her upturned nose. Her skin was heavy with the scent of French perfume.

"Can't I persuade you to stay a bit longer?" She stroked the length of him through his breeches.

Alec closed his eyes for a moment, enjoying her expert touch, then pulled her hand away, ignoring his hardening cock. She turned away abruptly, her lips pressed into a disappointed frown. Grabbing a white silk dressing robe from the nearby settee, she shouted for her maidservant. "Mary!"

Ignoring her, he tied his hair back with a velvet ribbon, forgoing the more complicated *ramillie* for a simple queue, then reached for his shirt.

What a perfect way to end the day. His mistress was shrieking like a banshee, and after their confrontation this morning, Philip no doubt hated him. He'd dealt harshly with his brother, Alec knew. But, by God, Philip was no longer a boy. It was time for him to cease his debauched ways and take on manly responsibilities.

There was more than enough work for him at the firm. If Philip wanted money to spend on whores and gambling, he'd have to earn it. Alec yanked impatiently at an uncooperative button on one of his cuffs.

"*Mais, merde alors!* Where is that little *putain*? Mary!" Isabelle strode like a half-naked queen to her mirror and began brushing her hair again with quick, agitated strokes. "English servants are so lazy. In Paris she'd not be treated with such leniency."

"Then it is good Mary was born in England and not France."

Isabelle responded with a derisive "humph" and muttered French profanities that would have stung the ears of the most hardened men. Refusing to be baited, Alec smoothed the frills of his embroidered jabot, slipped into his waistcoat, and began to feel under the bed for the soft leather of his boots.

Hurried footsteps approached from the hall, and Mary's pale face poked through the door. Although he had never asked her age, he was sure the girl was no more than sixteen—about the age of the girl Philip had destroyed. Alec thrust one foot into its boot, then the other.

"Mistress?"

"See to it Monsieur Kenleigh's carriage is brought around. *Rapidement!*"

The girl scurried away.

"Thank you for your charming hospitality, Isabelle. I can find my own way out." He was in no mood to endure a display of temper.

"Alec, wait!" Isabelle rushed into the hall and wrapped her slender, pale arms around his waist, her rouge-stained lips bowed in a perfect pout. "Don't be cross with me. What am I supposed to feel when you no longer want me?"

"There are more than enough randy young studs in London eager to take my place." He lifted her chin and kissed her lightly on the lips. "You'll not even miss me."

"Oh, but I will," she said, looking up at him sulkily from beneath dark lashes. "You may know how to please a woman's body, but you have much to learn about a woman's heart."

Alec laughed. "Would you have me believe you love me, chérie? You're simply displeased it is I, not you, who has decided to end things."

End things? He hadn't thought about it before, but as soon as the words were out of his mouth, he realized that was exactly what he wanted to do. He watched surprise, then rage flash in Isabelle's eyes.

Her lips spread in a coy smile. "You'll be back."

He kissed her lightly on the lips, then turned once more toward the darkened staircase, leaving her to sulk as she chose.

Downstairs in the foyer he found his greatcoat laid out next to his hat and gloves. The light patter on the window told him it was raining again.

"Sir?"

He looked to find Mary standing behind him, her thin face lit from beneath by the candle she was holding.

"Might you be needing anything else, sir?"

"No, thank you, Mary."

She curtsied and stepped back to await his departure. Isabelle would have her skin if she failed to lock up behind him. He put on his coat and went to the door. Moisture on the rain-spattered window prevented him from seeing anything outside, but he'd be able to hear his carriage arrive. He wanted to get home to his own bed, to forget this entire day.

The look on Philip's face had been one of total disbelief, though it was not as if Alec were cutting his brother off entirely. Philip lived in his home, ate at his board, made use of his servants, grounds, and stables. Alec had merely placed a condition on Philip's rather generous allowance. Their father's will specified that Alec was to manage his brother's financial affairs as he saw fit until Philip's twenty-fifth birthday, a scant year away. Given the sorry state of things, Alec had neglected his duty far too long.

Mary sneezed and curtsied sheepishly in apology.

Alec smiled in what he hoped was a reassuring manner. What a burden it must be waiting hand and foot on a woman like Isabelle, he thought, noticing Mary's chapped lips and the dark circles under her eyes. He had seen enough bruises on her face to know Isabelle occasionally struck her. He had offered more than once to help Isabelle find a French servant, hoping she would release Mary into his care. With five children to tend, his sister would welcome the extra help, and there was no doubt Elizabeth would be far kinder to Mary. But Isabelle had become jealous, mistaking his concern for something less honorable, and had jealously refused to let the girl go.

Mary shifted nervously under his gaze.

Alec looked away. From the street outside came the clack of hooves against wet cobblestones. "Good night, Mary. Get some sleep."

"Good night, sir. Thank you, sir."

He welcomed the blast of cold rain against his face, as it stole' his breath and blew away the cloying scent of Isabelle's perfume. Pulling up the collar of his greatcoat, he descended the steps two by two, then climbed into the dry warmth of the richly appointed carriage. He sank into the claret cushions, closed his eyes, and let the rocking of the coach carry him away. Still, his mind would not rest.

What could he have done differently? He could have taken Philip to task years ago, before things had gotten so out of hand. He could have forced Philip to join the military, where many younger sons found both discipline and their place in society. At the very least he could have waited until Philip had slept and was sober. Instead he'd confronted his brother the moment Philip had staggered through the door this morning. The sun just up, Alec had heard the door slam, heard Philip's footsteps in the hall, and had followed him upstairs to his rooms.

Philip had taken it much harder than he'd imagined. His voice still rang in Alec's ears, the images fresh in his mind.

"You bastard!" Philip's boyish grin faded abruptly into an angry grimace. Then, fists clenched, he swung.

Alec stepped easily out of his path, and Philip crashed onto the Persian carpet in a drunken heap, his powder-white wig askew.

"My God, Philip. Look at yourself." Alec turned away, the stench of tobacco and alcohol overpowering. "Obviously I have been remiss in my responsibility. I should have done this long ago. I might not have cared quite as much if you were intent on destroying only yourself, but I won't let you take others down with you."

Philip rose unsteadily to his feet, his face rigid. "She was a whore."

"She was sixteen!"

"It was her own damned fault! I didn't tell her to—"

"No! She was your responsibility!" Anger burned like hot iron in Alec's gut, and he fought the urge to slam his fist into Philip's insolent face. "Had you any sense of decency, you would have offered to provide quietly for her and the babe. Instead you abandoned her, and she died trying to rid herself of your get."

Philip stood for a moment, his hard brown eyes gazing unflinchingly into Alec's. Then he looked away and his expression softened.

"I regret what happened, of course." He tossed his wig onto his large four-poster bed. "Had I known what she intended to do . . . You can't seriously mean to let one mistake come between us, Alec. We are brothers."

An apologetic, boyish grin spread across his face.

"You can't charm your way out of this one, Philip. You will live according to my terms, or you won't see another farthing."

Philip's nostrils flared, and his smile grew fixed. "You won't get away with this."

"I already have."

The coach struck a rut, jarring Alec back to the present. It was strange to think he'd once been envious of his brother. Philip, as the second son, hadn't been burdened with learning the intricacies of the shipbuilding trade. That duty had fallen to Alec. As the firstborn son, he had inherited the vast Kenleigh estate, including the business his great-grandfather had started. While he had suffered the attention of joyless and unforgiving tutors, Philip, who was six years younger, had spent his childhood doing whatever pleased him. Their father, who had ignored Alec except to chasten him, had found Philip amusing and had indulged him in his antics, allowing him to break every rule without consequence.

Now Alec's envy had turned to pity, perhaps even contempt. Philip lived in a hell of his own making. He was almost always drunk and had fallen deeply in debt. His friends, if one could call them that were harlots, drunkards, and braggarts. If one of them didn't kill him, surely the pox would. Then there was the alewife's daughter.

Socrates had answered the back door in the middle of the night to find her, weak and bleeding, on the step. Alec had sent for the surgeon immediately, but the doctor had said there was nothing to be done. The girl had died within the hour, her life leaking from between her legs in a pool of scarlet. While the good citizens of London blamed her for her own death and were happy to forget her, Alec could not.

The carriage jolted to a halt, nearly throwing Alec from the seat. He waited for the motion to resume, but the carriage remained still.

What the devil?

Had an axle broken? And where was Edward? Had the driver, whose inconstant temper was a mystery, decided it was no longer his duty to keep his master informed?

"Bloody hell!" Alec pulled up his collar and threw open the carriage door.

Icy, wind-driven rain bit into his face.

The first blow took him by surprise. It exploded against his skull, knocking him to his knees on the wet cobblestone. Through a haze of pain, he looked up in time to see the butt of a musket arcing through the air toward him. Deflecting the impact, he grabbed the weapon and tore it from its owner's hands.

But the third blow came from behind.

Pain shattered Alec's thoughts.

A flash of red.

Darkness.

*F*rom the shelter of a doorway across the street, an old man, drunk and unable to sleep in the cold, wet weather, watched the two thieves as they dragged the unconscious man into the alley from which they'd sprung. He heard them shout at one another, but the wind and rain drowned out their words.

Ten minutes later they appeared again, carrying the man stiffly between them. They dropped him facedown next to his coach.

"Poor bloke." Still, he didn't mind if rich folks got robbed now and then. They had it coming.

As soon as the thieves vanished again into the darkness of the alley, the man stumbled over to the still form. Perhaps there was a bob or two the thieves had missed. A glint of gold on one finger made him gasp with delight, and he reached out to claim his prize. No sooner had he touched the man's hand than he jerked back.

The hand was as cold as the draft from a tomb.

The old man staggered away, looking anxiously about to make sure no one had seen him. If anyone had, they'd surely blame him for the killing and he'd find himself swinging from the end of a rope. Still, that gold ring would bring him enough ale and bread to fill his belly for many a day. His belly growled, and he inched forward again.

The ring slid off easily. Feeling braver, he tried to search the dead man's pockets. Thieves who would miss a gold ring could easily have left behind a shilling or two. But no matter how he tried, he could not reach the pockets from behind. Tugging on one of the dead man's arms, he managed to pull the body over onto its back.

What he saw sent him retching to his knees.

Gasping for breath, the old man tottered to his feet, dropped the ring, and fled, sobbing, down the street.

Chapter One

His Majesty's Commonwealth of Virginia
Lancaster County, on the Banks of the Rappahannock River
May 18, 1730

*C*assie Blakewell watched the sluggish craft struggle upriver against the current, her stomach knotted. Of all the things she had to do to keep the plantation running, from caring for the sick to squishing dratted hornworms, dealing with soul drivers was the thing she dreaded most. Soul driver. The words alone lent a chill to the otherwise warm spring air.

"Let me do the talking." She nervously smoothed her skirts and fluffed the muslin ruffles that edged the bodice of her gown. "We don't want trouble."

Micah nodded his head and wiped away beads of perspiration that trickled down his wrinkled forehead from the tight salt and pepper curls on his head. The frown on his dark face told her he was far from happy. Small wonder. Until last year he'd been the one to make all decisions regarding the buying and selling of bondsmen and slaves. Last summer her father, who knew how to deal with troublesome strangers and nosy neighbors, had become ill. White folks had been suspicious of free-born Negroes before last year's slave uprising, but they'd become positively hostile since. Although a free man and the best overseer in the county, Micah was now safer pretending to be a slave when around strangers. It was a lot to swallow for a man who had once owned his own farm.

Somewhere in the distance a wood thrush and its mate exchanged a honeyed song. Cassie inhaled the scent of pine and tried to calm the fluttering in her stomach. She loved this river and the land that cradled it. Let everyone else move to the noisy streets of Williamsburg in search of wealth and adventure. She would remain here, surrounded by the only riches that mattered.

She shielded her eyes against the glare of sun and water, watching the small boat creep closer to the pier. The spring freshet had the river running high and fast.

"He's gonna cheat you blind." Micah was only goading her, but she felt her temper rise just the same.

"I know what I'm doing. Didn't I get Tom at a good price?"

Tom was the newest bondsman on the plantation, and she'd felt quite lucky to get him for only eleven pounds.

"That's because there ain't nobody else wants to buy a half-blind blacksmith. You got robbed."

"He's very skilled. You said so yourself."

"Maybe so." Micah shrugged and grinned.

"What about Nate and Rebecca? They've worked out well." Just because she was young and female didn't mean she couldn't make good business decisions.

"Yes'm, they have. But you'll be paying to feed another mouth in a few months. Most folks don't take in redemptioners whose wives are expectin'."

"Most folks are just plain silly, if you ask me." She crossed her arms, refusing to be baited further.

"Yes, Miss Cassie, that's the truth." Micah chuckled.

The schooner drew alongside the pier. She tucked a wayward curl under the confection of silk roses and taffeta that sat upon her head. Normally she had no use for the handiwork of a milliner, but right now she was pretending to be a proper young lady, and this silly bonnet was a necessary prop.

"Do you think they'll have bondsmen this time?" Cassie didn't really expect an answer. How should Micah know?

The flow of bondsmen from England had slowed to a trickle by the time she was a young child. Nowadays there were mostly convicts and slaves, and she hoped to avoid buying either. Oh, it was true her father owned slaves. These days it was impossible to run a large estate without them. But it sat no better with her than it did with her father.

"Ho, there!" A fleshy, red-faced man stood on the deck and waved to her.

Two slave boys dropped the gangway onto the pier, came ashore, and secured the craft.

Cassie fought a momentary wave of nausea as the stench hit her. Boats carrying human cargo seemed to have their own particular odor— the smell of sweaty, unwashed bodies combined with excrement, disease, and death. She took a perfumed kerchief from her satchel and held it to her nose, willing the nausea to pass.

The rotund man who had hailed them disembarked and walked toward her, wheezing and glancing about as if trying to find someone— a husband or father.

"Good day, Miss." He bowed, removing his hat to reveal a dirty wig that barely covered his shaved head. "Is the owner of this estate nearby?"

"I'm afraid my father is away on business. He left me to trade with you in his stead."

The pudgy man's eyebrows shot up in momentary surprise, but he quickly recovered. "The name's Sylas Edwards, Miss...Miss...?"

"Blakewell."

"Miss Blakewell." He bowed again, his eyes fixing on the lace fichu she had lucked into her décolletage for modesty's sake. She felt a shiver of revulsion and involuntarily raised a hand to her bosom.

He smiled, exposing a row of half-rotted teeth.

"I'm sure you're eager to get on your way, Mr. Edwards, so if we could get down to business, I'll not keep you from your journey."

"I'm a dealer in slaves and bondsmen, Miss." He motioned to a member of his crew to bring the human merchandise forward.

At the clinking of chains, Cassie's heart fell. Only convicts and slaves wore fetters. She exchanged a knowing look with Micah and turned to see several miserable creatures, linked by neck and ankle, shuffling down the gangplank and onto the pier. Five were slaves. One appeared to be English. All were filthy. All stank. She covered her nose with the scented cloth, quelling another wave of nausea.

"I've got here five prime African bucks, all of them young and strong," Sylas walked toward his chattel, riding crop in hand.

Most of the slaves stared at the ground. The tallest one, however, boldly returned Cassie's gaze. His chest bore long, fresh scars, she felt certain he was being sold by a former owner who'd found him difficult.

"I've also got a convict straight from Newgate."

As if on cue the Englishman, who seemed twice as filthy as the rest, moaned and swayed. The tall slave, who was chained beside him, reached out, hands in wrist irons, to steady him. The soul driver went on as if nothing had happened.

"Considerin' what he's guilty of, I doubt if your father would want the convict around, not with a beauty like yourself to protect."

With a warning like that, she couldn't resist asking. "What are his crimes?"

"He's a defiler of womenfolk." Sylas gave a satisfied grin at her gasp. "Aye, they'd have hung him, but he had coin aplenty and bought off the judge, he did."

She looked closely at the wretched man's face, or rather what she could see of it. His face and beard were caked with dirt and blood. Dark hair was matted to his head with sweat. His eyes were all but closed, and had it not been for the kindness of the tall slave next to him, she was sure he would have collapsed. He was gravely ill.

"They'd all make good studs, if your father's looking for breed stock."

Breeding stock? Cassie gasped, her gaze fixed on the convict's face.

But Sylas was talking about the slaves.

"Pardon me for bein' so blunt about such things, Miss Blakewell, but your father did leave you to do a man's job."

"Of course." She felt her cheeks burn.

Suddenly the convict's legs gave way entirely, and he slumped toward the ground. The entire line of slaves was forced by the chains to squat to avoid choking either him or themselves. Sylas fell upon the prostrate convict, shouting and kicking the man in the ribs with his boot.

"No!" Forgetting the horrible odor emanating from the captives she rushed forward and forced herself between the soul driver and the fallen man. "There is no need to strike him. This man is ill. He needs a doctor."

Sylas laughed, his round face spreading into a sneer, and raised the riding crop.

"My job is to sell him, not to coddle him. Stand back."

"Mr. Edwards, you can't possibly mean to beat him. He is unconscious." The poor soul hadn't collapsed on purpose. "If you want him to fetch a good price, you'd best see he receives care. Surely even you know this."

"Move out of my way, woman." The slave peddler's watery eyes bulged in his angry red face.

She swallowed hard, willing herself to match his menacing glare. The soft crunch of boots on pine needles told her Micah had come forward and stood directly behind her. Reassured by his presence, she spoke in a firm, unwavering voice.

"This is my father's estate, Mr. Edwards. I speak for him. As long as you stand on our land, you will respect our wishes. No one hits a defenseless man here, even if he is a felon."

Sylas wavered for a moment, looked over her head at Micah, and slowly lowered the riding crop.

The convict moaned again, then mouthed unintelligible words.

She knelt down and touched his forehead. "He's burning up."

"He needs water," said the tall slave.

"Yes, of course. Micah, bring me some sweet water from the wagon, please."

"Missy, I know what you're thinkin'," Micah whispered. "Forget it. You don't know what you'd be gettin' into."

She could tell by his voice that Micah was genuinely alarmed. "Water, please, Micah."

They'd never had a convict on the plantation before.

"Do you know this man?" she asked the tall slave.

It was uncommon to see a slave show concern for a white captive. It was even more uncommon to witness the reverse.

"No."

"You seem to care what happens to him. Why?"

The slave met her gaze unblinking. "No man deserves to die like a dog."

She stood and faced the soul driver again, her decision made. "How much for these two?" She pointed to the prostrate felon and the slave who had shown him compassion.

Both the slave and Sylas looked at her with surprise. Micah erupted into a spasm of coughing and came rushing back, her request for water forgotten.

"Forty pounds. Thirty for the slave and ten for the convict."

"Miss Cassie," Micah said in a strained voice. If the situation hadn't been so serious, the expression on his dear face would have made her laugh. "Your papa won't be happy if you come home with a trouble slave and a half-dead convict. Don't—"

"Forty pounds is robbery, Mr. Edwards. This convict will probably die. Ten pounds is far too high a price for one so sick." She looked at the slave. "This one has lash marks. No doubt his former master found him troublesome."

She was surprised to hear how calm she sounded. Inside she was quaking like a leaf in a storm. "I offer thirty pounds. Twenty-five for the slave, five for the convict."

What if he refused her offer? She hadn't much more to bargain with.

Sylas shook his head. "Not a pound less than thirty-eight." His gaze dropped to her bosom.

"Thirty-five," she said on impulse. "Plus this bill of lading. I'm afraid if you can't accept that, then you shall have to take your cargo and continue on your way without a sale." She took the bill from her purse and held it out for his inspection. "And I shall have to tell my father how rudely you behaved toward me. I'm sure he'll spread the word to our friends and relations upriver." Never mind that they had none. The soul driver couldn't know that. "My offer is more than fair, Mr. Edwards. I suggest you accept."

The unconscious man moaned again. Trying not to show feminine weakness, she ignored him.

Sylas took the bill and read through it with obvious difficulty.

"That bill gives you possession of ten pounds of my father's best sweet-scented tobacco. You need simply to present this bill to my father's factor in Williamsburg to collect it."

Sylas tucked the bill under his belt. "And the thirty-five pounds?"

She opened the strings of her purse and placed the precious coins in Sylas's upturned palm.

"These two go with her," the soul driver bellowed over his shoulder, motioning to a slave boy, who quickly unlocked the selected men's collars and fetters and led the rest away. "Here's the convict's papers, Miss. If you're lucky, he'll die."

She took the packet of papers and sighed with relief as the odious man turned and walked back toward his vessel.

"You shouldn't have done this, Miss Cassie," Micah said. "We got enough to worry about without keepin' an eye on some convict!"

"Aye, Micah. You're right." He *was* right. There was tobacco to plant, merchants to pay. There was her father, not to mention Jamie. Her little brother seemed to need constant watching these days. And her father? Heaven only knew. "What else could I have done?"

Micah placed a reassuring hand on her shoulder. "You got to learn that you can't save everybody." But his eyes held no reproach. "Let's get 'em home."

Micah and the new slave, who said his name was Luke, lifted the unconscious man and carried him to the wagon. Cassie opened the convict's papers and glanced over the first page.

Nicholas Braden, known also by the name Cole Braden. In black ink were scrawled the words *Convicted ravisher and defiler of women.*

She shuddered. What had she done?

E very muscle in his body ached. Alec struggled to focus on his surroundings, but the room continued to spin and his head to throb, forcing him to close his eyes again. *Damn!* He felt as weak as a newborn pup.

He remembered arguing with Philip, Isabelle's shouting, leaving in the rain. After that he could recall nothing but random images. A ship. Darkness. The fetid stench of filth and illness. Incessant pain and thirst. Strange faces. Men like Socrates with skin as dark as night. A witch, or so she seemed, with gray hair and a dark face covered with strange markings. He shivered involuntarily. Could it all have been a nightmare?

There was one other face. He remembered a woman with hair the color of polished copper in sunlight, startlingly green eyes, and the voice of an angel. Her cool hands had given him comfort. He had tried repeatedly to reach for her, only to watch her fade into nothingness.

He lifted a hand to his throbbing temple.

Chains.

Although his hands were now free, he remembered being in fetters. Had he been kidnapped? Alec tested his feet, relieved to feel that they, too, were free. Whoever still held him captive obviously felt he posed no threat now. That was the truth. In this condition he doubted he'd be able to stand, much less escape.

He heard children playing outside, someone singing, the clang of a blacksmith's hammer, and he smelled pine mingled with the scent of newly fallen rain and lavender soap. Wherever he was, it was an odd place to keep a hostage.

He opened his eyes again, willing the dizziness to pass. He appeared to be in a one-room shanty. Light trickled through cracks in a small, shuttered opening that served as a window. Next to the bed stood a crudely built pine table holding several candles that had melted low. Next to it stood a rough-hewn chair. On the opposite end of the room was a small hearth, but no fire. Strange that he did not feel cold. Springtime in England was not known for its warmth.

He tried to sit up. The ache in his skull forced him to rest on his raised elbows. He was completely naked beneath the thin blanket, his clothes nowhere in sight. Whiskers tickled his chest. Alarmed, he reached up and felt a full growth of beard on his face.

Several weeks must have gone by, much more than he'd first imagined.

No wonder he felt so weak.

Rage coursed through him, making his head throb anew. Elizabeth and Matthew must be beside themselves with worry. Perhaps even Philip was distraught. But who had done this? And why? Perhaps the pitiful souls who called this hovel home were holding him for ransom. But even this life was better than the hangman's noose that awaited the culprits at Old Bailey. And hang they would. He would see to it personally.

From outside he heard the approach of voices, one of them distinctly feminine, the other deeper. The voices stopped at his door, and the hinges squeaked. He sank back into the pillows, closing his eyes.

"Thank you, Zach," the woman said.

There was something about her voice....

"Pleased to help, Miss Cassie," a man answered. "Would ye like me to stay?"

"That won't be necessary, but thank you. I'm sure I'll be quite safe. He's too weak to harm a flea."

*C*assie stepped from the heat of the midday sun into the cool darkness of the shanty. Careful not to tip the serving tray and spill Nan's good chicken stock, she shut the door behind her. The convict's fever had broken yesterday afternoon, much to her surprise.

Takotah had tried to feed him last night, but he'd been too exhausted to take more than a few sips of broth. Perhaps now he'd be hungry. Whoever had transported him had treated him horribly. With broken ribs, a broken nose, bumps on the head, and lash marks on his back and chest that had festered, he'd seemed destined for the grave. But he'd survived, thanks to Takotah's healing skills—and his own stubborn refusal to die.

Giving her eyes a moment to adjust to the darkness, she placed the serving tray on the table next to his bed. She hated to wake him, but he needed to regain his strength. The man who slept so peacefully now bore no resemblance to the filthy, broken soul she'd brought home a week ago. Despite the thick beard, this man was devilishly handsome, with dark brown hair that fell just beneath his shoulders, indecently long eyelashes, and gentle features marred only by the yellowish tinge of fading bruises and the thickening where his nose had been broken.

She crossed the room and opened the shutters to let in more light. She turned back toward him and felt her footsteps falter. The blanket had slipped below his waist, revealing a broad, muscled chest covered with soft, dark curls that tapered down a flat abdomen. It had been easy to ignore his body when he'd been ill. He'd been merely an assemblage of parts, each needing attention in its turn. Now those parts had healed into a disturbingly masculine whole.

She sat next to him on the bed, ignoring the tickle in her belly. Hesitantly she placed her hand on his chest. His skin felt warm and alive, and his heart beat steadily beneath her palm. She touched his forehead and smiled, pleased to feel the fever had not returned. Asleep like this, he hardly looked a dangerous criminal.

She gasped and would have screamed, had the arm that encircled her throat not cut off her breath.

"Who are you, woman, and why do you hold me prisoner?"

Chapter Two

*T*he convict's voice was ragged, his beard rough on Cassie's cheek. One arm held her tightly against his bare chest. The other threatened to choke her.

Cassie tried to pull free, but her struggles only made her need for air more acute and forced her deeper into his lap until she felt his . . . She froze.

His grip around her throat tightened. He was going to kill her.

"Scream, and I'll break your lovely neck. Do you understand?"

She nodded frantically, mouthed *aye*. Slowly he released the pressure on her throat. But he did not free her.

Cassie drew in gulps of air. "Let me go!" She'd meant to sound undaunted, but her mouth had gone dry, and the words came out in a squeak.

"Answer the question."

"My name is Catherine Blakewell." Her voice was shaky. Her heart slammed sickeningly in her chest. "For the next fourteen years you shall serve my father as his bondsman by right of His Majesty, King George. Regardless of the crimes you have committed, my father will treat you fairly, though he would kill you if he knew of this!"

"What are you raving about, woman?"

The arm that encircled her throat drew tighter.

"You've been ill for some time. I've brought broth.... Please! You're hurting me!"

"What place is this?"

"You're at Blakewell's Neck in Lancaster County, Mr. Braden—"

"Lancashire? In the north country?"

"Lancaster County. Virginia."

The convict reacted as if he'd been struck by a fist, releasing her just as suddenly as he'd seized her.

Cassie leaped up from the bed and backed away until her back met the clapboard wall. Her hands rose protectively to her throat, her body shaking uncontrollably. Whatever she'd expected when he awoke, she certainly hadn't imagined this bold assault. She'd not underestimate the threat this man posed again.

"What is the date?" The convict's voice was strained, his face pale.

"It is the twenty-fifth of May. You've been fighting a fever for a week now. I've tended your wounds—"

"May? My God!"

"Surely you remember, Mr. Braden."

"Braden?"

Did he not even remember his own name?

"You were transported to the colonies," she said, trying to prod his memory. "My father bought your indenture."

For a moment the convict's eyes held raw fury. Then he moaned, clasping a hand to his temple. Slowly he slumped, unconscious, back onto the pillow.

Cassie watched as he sank deeper into the bed, her heart still pounding. Arms crossed protectively over her bosom, she inched forward. "Mr. Braden?"

His features were peaceful, his breathing deep and even, but he'd feigned sleep once today already. She would not be so easily tricked again.

London

*T*he crystal goblet shattered on the wall next to Lt. Matthew Hasting's head, missing Alec's favorite painting by inches. Matthew tried not to look startled. To do so would only give Philip satisfaction.

"I will not allow you to run this business behind my back!" Philip strode menacingly toward Matthew through the disorder that had once been Alec's office.

Empty bottles lay on the mahogany desk. Clothing, half-eaten plates of food, and crumpled parchment mingled with wine stains on the plush Persian carpet.

"Someone has to take charge."

"You have no right to make decisions for me!"

"If you were capable of making decisions, I'd gladly step aside."

Philip stopped, his face inches from Matthew's, his brown eyes dark with fury. "I am the heir to this estate, and you will respect me as such!"

"Respect you? You are a debauched fool. A worthless drunk. Not even the lowliest clerk in this office respects you."

For a moment Philip looked as if he would explode. Then the fight visibly drained from him. He turned away, ran his fingers through his unwashed hair, and reached for a decanter of brandy.

"A debauched fool? A worthless drunk?" Philip faced Matthew again, forcing a smile. "Well, that's a bit harsh, even if it is true." He emptied the glass with one swallow. "Do you know that Alec hated me? Never a kind word to spare. Do you hate me too, Matthew? I hope not."

"Alec never hated you."

Philip laughed. "I suppose he told you that? 'Poor Philip! I do so care about him, though I—'"

"Do *not* ridicule your brother in front of me." Matthew struggled to rein in his temper. "If you lived a thousand years you'd not become the man he was. The least you can do is pull yourself together and try to live up to the responsibility Alec passed on to you."

Startled, Philip said nothing. Then his face tightened into a grimace.

"I am the heir to the Kenleigh estate," Philip said at last, his voice unsteady. "It is my right to take my brother's place in London society."

"Inheriting his titles, his possessions, is one thing. Taking his place is quite another. If you want respect, you must earn it."

"Will you . . . help me, Matthew?"

Nothing Philip could have said would have surprised Matthew more. The beseeching look in his eyes was something Matthew had never seen before.

He stepped forward to where Philip stood about to pour himself another drink and placed his hand over the top of the glass. "Don't. For Alec's sake. For your own sake."

A muscle worked in Philip's jaw, and for a moment anger flared in his eyes. Then he put down the decanter and turned away. "Leave me! I wish to be alone."

Taking the decanter with him, Matthew strode from the room and closed the door. Back in his own office he sat down wearily at his desk. It was only noon. The spring sun rode high in the clear sky, and pigeons were busy tending their brood of chicks outside his window. He'd have to bring the children in so they could see the baby birds. Little Anne would be delighted.

He watched the pigeons feed their young and rubbed his right thigh. Since a ball had shattered his leg at the Battle of Malplaquet some twenty years ago, pain had been his constant companion. He'd grown so accustomed to the discomfort that it rarely registered in his conscious mind. If it hadn't been for Elizabeth, who loved him despite his physical disfigurement, he might have found it impossible to accept. As it was, so many good things had happened in his life that the loss of his limb seemed trivial.

Poor Elizabeth. He'd never seen her so distraught. He would never forget her tears and sobs of grief when she'd heard that Alec had been murdered. Thank God she'd been spared seeing his body. Whoever had killed him had gone out of his way to be cruel. Even in his years on the battlefield, Matthew had seen nothing like it. Alec had been stabbed in so many places the wounds were impossible to count. His face had been hideously mutilated. His eyes had been cut out. Had it not been for the clothes he wore, his dark hair, and the signet ring the murderer had dropped in his haste to flee the scene, Matthew never would have recognized him. Even Philip had been shocked by the brutality. His face had gone pale, and he'd dropped to his knees, sick and shaking.

The investigation was proceeding slowly, with little evidence and no suspects. Matthew himself had questioned Alec's mistress, Isabelle St. Denis, but she'd had little of worth to say. Alec had been tense that night, she'd said. He'd been in a hurry to leave, refusing to bed her a second time. Isabelle had apparently taken this as a personal slight, but Matthew doubted she would have killed Alec. Adultery, not murder, was her habit. Matthew had discovered this when Isabelle had reached out and cupped his testicles the moment he'd finished questioning her.

Meanwhile, the constable had taken an old beggar into custody after he'd been found in the streets ranting madly about a corpse with no eyes. They'd hoped once he was sober and calm he might prove to be a witness, but the poor fool had died of gaol fever within a week.

Matthew rubbed the ache at the base of his skull. It was odd so little of Alec's blood had been found at the scene. Though it had been raining, nothing could have washed away that much blood. The driver had been killed too, his throat slit from ear to ear. There'd been blood aplenty around him. None of it made sense.

Matthew had hoped that Alec's death would bring about a change in Philip. At first it seemed he'd been shocked into mending his ways. But after Alec's funeral, Philip had hit the bottle again, staying out all night, paying little heed to the estate that now belonged to him. He'd ignored Elizabeth's entreaties to cease his foolishness.

Instead he now spent money at an even more immoderate rate, throwing it away on gaming and extravagant nights of drinking and whoring. He'd even brought one of his prostitutes to the office, tupping her on what had once been Alec's desk, his indecent moans so loud that Matthew had heard from across the hallway.

It had seemed like a desecration.

Perhaps there was still hope. Philip had never asked for help before. Matthew would do his best to encourage Philip on this new path, praise him for his slightest accomplishment, and indulge his desire for admiration. But would Philip stay the course?

Matthew closed his eyes and prayed.

*C*assie gently buried the roots of the last parsley seedling in the dark soil and stood, brushing the dirt from her fingers. Shielding her eyes from the morning sun, she looked across the rows that made up the kitchen garden and smiled with satisfaction at what she'd accomplished.

"Oh, hush," she answered the magpie sitting on the fence, piercing the day with its discordant squawk.

The bird, its black, blue, and white feathers gleaming in the sunlight, looked at her with one shiny black eye and screeched again in defiance.

"You're rude."

Evidently insulted, the bird squawked once more, then flew away. Why had God given such a beautiful bird such a very unpleasant song?

The strawberry plants were already in blossom, their tiny white flowers drawing scores of bees. The onions she had planted around the edge of the garden to discourage insects were nearly a foot tall.

Cucumber vines with small yellow blooms vied with larger squash plants for space on the ground, while bean and pea seedlings crept skyward, slender tendrils grasping for purchase on tall wooden stakes. If she could keep the deer and insects from eating the fragile plants— and the children from trampling them underfoot—she'd be finished planting the kitchen garden by the end of the week. Of course, that meant fixing the rickety worm fence that an angry sow had knocked over in January. Most of the bondsmen and slaves were working under Micah's direction, preparing the hills for the tobacco seedlings that would be ready for transplanting from their seedbeds with the next rain. The men couldn't be spared for other work. Zach, the only sawyer, had more than enough to do. She would have asked Luke to rebuild the fence days ago, but he was guarding that troublesome Mr. Braden.

The scoundrel was recovering rapidly. Nan said he was eating well and would soon be up and about. Cassie was glad the cook had volunteered to attend to him. After her terrifying encounter yesterday, she wanted nothing to do with him. He was altogether too . . . alarming. She had decided it best not to tell anyone—not even Nan, who'd been with the family for as long as she could remember and whom she trusted completely—what he had done when he'd awoken. Everyone was worried enough as it was, and though she'd been nearly frightened out of her wits, no real harm had been done.

Since she'd registered the convict in Fredericksburg, as the law required, objections had been pouring in from neighbors who, understandably, didn't want a dangerous felon living in their midst.

The Carters and the Lees, who rarely agreed about anything, had both voiced their disapproval. Even their nearest neighbors, the Crichtons, who owned several convicts, had sent a letter to her father complaining that Blakewell's Neck was not secure enough to contain a man who preyed upon women, especially with her father away. It wasn't only Mr. Braden the Crichtons objected to, she knew, but also her father's liberal attitudes and his "blackamoor" overseer, as Master Crichton shamefully called Micah.

She adjusted her apron and breathed in the fragrance of herbs in blossom: lemon balm, rosemary, lavender, pennyroyal, and more. Her mother had taught her to identify them all by scent alone when she was just a little girl. Standing here in the morning sunshine surrounded by the excited buzz of bees, she could almost hear her mother's voice.

Marjoram for a maiden's blush, hyssop for cleanliness. Speedwell for fidelity, cocklebur for thankfulness...

Her reverie was interrupted by the squeals of a half dozen children, who bounded around the cookhouse and headed straight for the garden. As usual, Jamie was in the lead.

"You can't catch me, you bloody pirates!" he yelled, turning on his pursuers and bravely wielding an imaginary sword.

His foul language made Cassie cringe. Still, she couldn't fault him for it, not when he'd learned it from her.

"Oh, no, you don't, captain!" She caught the towheaded four-year-old from behind in time to prevent his treading on the feathery green tops of newly sprouted carrots.

The ragtag band of bloodthirsty pirates who'd been pursuing her little brother came to a halt and looked up at her sheepishly, their faces—brown and white—sticky from Nan's blackberry preserves.

"Even pirates know how to take orders." She looked sternly at Jamie. "I've told you more times than I can count not to play near the ovens or the garden."

Jamie shifted under his sister's gaze but said nothing.

"Now off with the lot of you before I have to lock you all in chains belowdecks."

The gaggle of children erupted into cries of imaginary terror and dashed off toward the apple orchard.

Perhaps Zach should fix that fence today. If there was one thing living with small children had taught her, it was that pirates quickly forgot. She shook the loose mud from the hem of her skirt and started toward the sawmill.

The humid morning breeze shifted, carrying with it the rich scent of baking bread. Her mouth watered. Nan made the best wheaten bread in the county. Of course, it was the only wheaten bread in the county. Everyone else was too busy growing tobacco to spare the labor necessary for growing wheat—or anything else, for that matter. Laws had been passed long ago mandating that farmers grow a certain amount of corn each season. Without those laws, the population would likely starve to death come winter. Even Micah had thought her crazy when she had suggested putting in wheat.

"Too much work," he'd said.

Then he'd tasted Nan's bread.

On the grassy lawn beside the great house, Nettie was hanging out freshly laundered sheets, the white linen a marked contrast to the brown of her skin and the red of her skirts. She gave Cassie a guarded smile. Cassie smiled back. She and Nettie had been best friends as children, but that had changed when they'd gotten older, put away their cornhusk dolls, and assumed the roles of slave and mistress. Girlish giggles had been replaced by reserved smiles, shared confidences by delegated duties. An impenetrable wall had arisen between them. It was the way of the world, Cassie's father had told her.

Perhaps it was. But that didn't mean Cassie had to like it.

Behind the whitewashed cookhouse, Rebecca, her swollen abdomen outlined by the white of her apron, struggled with the butter churn.

"A good mornin' to you, Miss Cassie," she called, out of breath but smiling, her round cheeks rosy from exertion. Since she'd taken over the dairying, they'd had more butter, milk, and cheese than ever before. She stopped to brush a long strand of dark hair out of her face.

"Let me help." Cassie took the paddle. The fence could wait awhile longer. "How are you and the babe faring this morning?"

"Fine, bless you, mistress. The child grows stronger and more restless each day. Nate says it's a boy, but I think we've got a daughter, and a wild one at that."

The happy glow on Rebecca's face gave Cassie a momentary twinge of regret. How wonderful it would be to have children of her own. But with her father so ill and a little brother who was all but an orphan, she could not leave to start her own family, even if by some miracle she managed to find a man she cared for enough to marry. Her father had asked her to protect his honor and Jamie's inheritance, and she would.

"Have you asked Takotah?" Cassie inquired, trying to shift her thoughts. There was no use in longing for what could not be. "She has the gift. She can tell the sex of a babe long before it's born."

Rebecca's sunny face suddenly grew grave, her hands dropping protectively to her belly. "Nate says I'm not to go near her. He says she's a witch."

"Oh, rubbish! Takotah might look frightening, but I have yet to see her be anything but gentle. Nate is filling your head with superstitious nonsense."

"Aye, mistress." Rebecca didn't look convinced.

Cassie knew better than to press the issue. Many of the servants, even some of the slaves, were afraid of Takotah, who had stumbled weak and wounded out of the forest one day long ago. Cassie's parents had nursed her back to health, ignoring those who advised them to kill her or risk finding a knife in their backs one night.

When she had recovered, Takotah, whose full name was too difficult to pronounce, had asked to stay with them to repay what she saw as a life debt. Her people, the Tuscarora, had been all but annihilated by settlers. Everyone she knew, including her husband and children, had been killed, leaving her no one to return to.

Cassie, only three at the time, had always thought of her as magical. The black tattoos on her dark face seemed a part of that magic.

"Miss Cassie! Miss Cassie!" The shrill voice rose above the clang of the blacksmith's hammer and the rhythmic rasp of Zach's saw.

Cassie grimaced. She didn't have to look to see who it was. She had purchased Elly's indenture almost nine months ago and still hadn't found a chore the young woman, whose head seemed to be forever in the clouds, was willing to perform without complaint. Rebellious and contrary, Elly fought Cassie at every turn. Of late, Elly had been assigned to help with the cooking, much to Nan's dismay.

"Yes, Elly?" Cassie tried to conceal her annoyance.

"It's the convict! He's shoutin' at Nan and swearin'—"

Cassie dashed toward the slave cabins. If that knave had frightened or injured Nan, she'd turn him over to Sheriff Hollingsworth and be done with it.

She could hear the shouting long before she entered the cabin. Luke stood silently in front of the door, arms crossed, a slight grin on his face. Although she knew little about the taciturn slave, she had already come to trust him implicitly.

"Damn it, woman, I don't want to eat! I wish to speak with your master!"

Something crashed to the floor.

"Now there's a fine mess," she heard Nan say in a bored voice.

Cassie stepped through the doorway, resolved to show no fear this time. "My father is not available, Mr. Braden, but you may speak with me."

Then her eyes adjusted to the dimness, and she gasped.

Chapter Three

"Mr. Braden!"

The convict stood naked at the side of his bed, his maleness covered only by a corner of the sheet he'd pulled across his hips. The room was a shambles. The chair had been knocked over, the cornmeal mush Nan had brought splattered across the floor and up the far wall, the wooden spoon and bowl thrown into the corner.

Nan, rather than looking frightened by the beastly display, stood mere inches away from him, arms akimbo, the expression on her round face that of an annoyed mother about to scold an ill-behaved child. But Cole Braden was no child—that Cassie could plainly see. He was ill-behaved, however, making no attempt to cover himself, as any gentleman would have done in the presence of women. Still, if Nan could ignore his lack of clothing, so could Cassie.

"I have urgent business with your father." His voice was cold.

Cassie tried to keep her eyes focused on his face, not his hard, corded thighs or the well-defined muscles and scattering of dark curls on his chest.

"My father is in England on business, but you may relay a message to him through me." She smoothed her skirts, feeling strangely aware of the dirt clinging to her hems, and the stains on her apron.

"This is no matter for a girl to handle."

She stiffened. "Be that as it may, you will have to speak with me, as my father has left me to manage his affairs."

The convict's eyebrows rose in surprise and his gaze traveled over her, his blue eyes showing nothing but contempt. She fought not to look away.

"Very well." He paused. "A crime has been committed. My name is Alec Kenleigh, not Nicholas Braden—"

"I don't care if ye're bloody King George!" Nan glared at him. "Ye need to eat if ye want—"

"I own a shipbuilding firm in London. I have no idea how I came to be in this godforsaken land, but I need your father's help in alerting the authorities so I may return to England as soon as possible."

For a moment Cassie could not grasp what she had just heard.

"Do you mean to say you've been spirited? You're not a convict?" She couldn't help laughing. "There are rumors that such things happen with small children, Mr. Braden—"

"Kenleigh."

"But to a man of social standing? Surely that's impossible."

"Nevertheless, it has happened. If you inform your father, I'm confident he will find the time to help amend this unfortunate situation."

"You expect me to believe you?"

"I don't care what *you* believe. You simply need to deliver my message. If you would allow me to write a letter to my brother-in-law, the matter will be easily resolved."

Cassie bristled at his easy dismissal of her.

"You may send your letter, Mr. Braden, or whatever your name is. But be warned, I shall read it. I can't have you calling a pack of river pirates down on our heads to help you escape." She noted with satisfaction the convict's raised eyebrows. He'd thought her illiterate. Many women in these colonies were. "I shall also demand your vow that you will not try to escape. Promise me you will serve my father as his bondsman until you have proved your tale true. I spent my father's good coin to save your life. If you are a gentleman, you'll want to repay him."

Silence stretched between them. For a moment she was sure he would refuse.

"Don't worry," he said at last. "He'll get his due." It sounded more like a threat than a promise. "May I ask how much I cost?"

"Nearly ten pounds."

"Ten pounds?" He laughed bitterly, shaking his head as if ten pounds were nothing.

"Do I have your word?"

"Aye, Mistress, on my honor." He bowed his head slightly in a mock display of submission, an icy smile on his lips. "You shall have your ten pounds from my flesh. And more, I'm sure."

"Good." She felt herself relax, though asking a lying felon to keep his word did seem futile. "I shall also send a note to the county sheriff. He should be able to help us learn the truth. Nan, could you fetch pen, ink, and parchment? And send Elly to clean up Mr. Braden's mess."

"Yes, Missy."

The plump cook turned to leave, giving the convict one last disgruntled look. No one dumped her food on the floor without first tasting it.

"I should also like to shave and be fitted with proper garments. Unless, of course, it's the custom here for young ladies to stare at naked men."

Cassie involuntarily raised her hands to her cheeks, feeling them flush with anger and embarrassment.

"Indeed, you shall have clothing, Mr. Braden. In Virginia, we are civilized. It is your decision to stand there improperly exposed. As it is, I barely noticed."

"Is that so?" The arrogant smile that played across his face told her he'd seen through her lie.

"I've lived on this plantation my entire life, Mr. Braden. I've cared for both sick men and sick animals. Men differ but slightly from horses, bull, boars, and … and cocks!"

"Cocks? Then may I suggest you haven't looked closely enough?"

"I was referring to the way men preen and strut about, Mr. Braden."

She strode toward the door, forcing herself to appear calm. Inside she seethed. The man was insufferable! The smug way he'd smiled at her—how dare he suggest she enjoyed seeing him naked! She'd as soon look at the back end of a pig!

"As soon as Mr. Braden has been fitted with clothes, he will be free to walk about the grounds," she told Luke between gritted teeth as she passed. "Keep your eye on him. If he tries to escape, you have my permission to strangle him."

"Yes'm."

She caught the slight smile that flitted across Luke's face. But there was nothing funny about this. Nothing at all.

"Sure and 'e's got a temper," observed Nan as Cassie overtook her.

"See that he gets clothes, please. Preferably something woolen and itchy." Cassie stomped on ahead, her skirts swishing.

"Got yer goat, did 'e?" Nan called from behind her with a chuckle.

Cassie stomped into the great house. The nerve of that arrogant man! She'd saved him from certain death on that slave peddler's schooner and offered him a new life, only to have him act like a pompous ingrate.

She sat with an exasperated sigh at her father's desk and penned a note to Sheriff Hollingsworth, who lived a long day's journey upriver. No need to mimic her father's script this time. Everyone believed he was still in England chasing down prime horseflesh and perhaps a new wife. Sometimes the situation demanded she forge letters in her father's hand. Other times it meant making up stories about his latest adventures communicated to her in letters no one else saw. Cassie told herself that maintaining one big lie was no worse than telling dozens of small ones, as she would otherwise have been forced to do to conceal her father's condition and whereabouts.

It was, after all, the only way to keep her promise to him.

Some had been scandalized by his decision to leave his daughter in charge of his estate, but most viewed it as further proof of his eccentric nature. Master Carter had offered to help should Cassie need it, but she was determined to do without his assistance. A woman could manage an estate as well as any man, and she would prove it.

She finished the letter, folded it, then sealed it with a few drops of candle wax. What if the convict's story were true? The thought gave her pause. What if Cole Braden were not Cole Braden at all but an innocent man who'd suffered a horrible injustice at the hands of greedy traders? His speech was refined and suggested a genteel upbringing. But surely no one would attempt to kidnap and sell one of the gentry in these modern times when regular shipping kept both sides of the Atlantic in such close contact. The kidnapper would be caught. These days nothing scandalous happened in London or Williamsburg without news of it being spread to the other side of the ocean a scant two months later.

No, such intrigue was too fantastic to be true. Besides, no one as handsome and smug as Mr. Braden could possibly be innocent.

*A*lec pulled up the plain linsey-woolsey breeches the cook had brought him and tied them at his waist. Weak, thinner, and scarred by the lash, the body he was dressing did not feel like his own. At least he'd been allowed to shave.

Wincing at the protestations of his healing ribs, he pulled the shirt over his head and tucked it in. Although the garments were plain, they were clean and well made. Dressed like a peasant, his feet bare, he decided he must look much like the castaway in that story by Daniel Defoe, another book he'd never had time to read. He remembered complaining once to Elizabeth and Matthew that he'd like to see the Americas, though he had never imagined it would be under these circumstances.

If Miss Blakewell were true to her word, his letter to his sister and brother-in-law was already on its way to the county sheriff with her own dispatch. The sheriff, she'd said, was a trustworthy man who would see to it that his letter made its way quickly and safely to port.

Yet, despite her assurances, Alec felt uneasy. Blakewell and his lovely daughter stood to gain fourteen years of hard labor at his expense if he failed to regain his name. It was not in their best interests to aid him, and he could not be entirely certain they hadn't been in on the plot to kidnap him in the first place. Everyone knew how desperate planters were for able-bodied men. Their peculiar institution of slavery had arisen from just that need. If the master's daughter had to work in the fields, as the mud on her gown had suggested, Blakewell's Neck was more shorthanded than most farms. Besides, what kind of man would leave his daughter to run his estate?

Shielding his eyes against the daylight, Alec walked out the door and into a strange and unfamiliar world. If what she'd told him was true, he'd been cooped up in that blasted clapboard shanty for more than a week now. It felt good to be outdoors again. The sun warmed his skin, and a sticky breeze tickled his nostrils with unfamiliar smells.

When his eyes had grown accustomed to the light, he saw that he stood in what appeared to be a small village. Children, white-skinned and brown-skinned, ran back and forth, laughing and playing together in the rows between clapboard cabins similar to his. Women went about their daily chores, some tending small garden plots, others sweeping and cleaning. He surmised these must be the quarters for slaves and indentured servants. Though small and crudely built, the cabins were clean and in good repair.

In the distance, the blue line of sky met the jagged silhouette of forest. Pines taller than any he had seen thrust upward in search of sunlight. The twitter of birds, their songs foreign, filled the air. A flock of yellow-green birds lifted off the roof of a nearby cabin, all flapping feathers, and swept across the sky, flashes of orange-gold gleaming in the sunlight.

He was so far from home.

With the giant who'd been assigned to guard him following silently behind, he made his way slowly through the cabins toward what appeared to be stables and barns, silently cursing his stiff muscles.

"My name is Alec Kenleigh. If you're going to follow me around all day, we might as well introduce ourselves."

"Luke," the big man said, lapsing into silence once again.

Alec could see newly healed lash marks peeking out from under Luke's shirt. What transgression had he supposedly committed to earn them?

Stories Socrates had told him—tales of whippings, maimings and torture—sprang into his mind. Socrates had been born and raised a slave until Alec's father, in need of assistance during a visit to Jamestown, had purchased him. Freed when they'd returned to England, Socrates had stayed to serve first Alec's father, then Alec, as his valet. After Alec had taught him to read, Socrates had become even more proper and English than the king himself. He'd been Alec's only real link to his father, showing him affection when his father would not. As a result, Alec had endured Socrates' admonitions to sit up straight, to straighten his jabot and keep his waistcoat buttoned without complaint, eager for the praise that always followed.

What would Socrates think if he could see Alec now, barefoot and dressed in coarse clothing? The thought made Alec smile.

A pretty young woman, her belly swollen with child, stepped from the front door of one cabin, only to rush back inside as soon as she saw him and slam the door behind her. He became aware that, with the exception of the children, who seemed oblivious to his presence, everyone was staring at him. Like the petite, flaxen-haired maidservant who'd brought him clothing and a razor and had cleaned the gruel from his cabin floor, these people's eyes held a combination of fear and suspicion. Considering what they all believed him guilty of, he could not blame them.

Miss Blakewell had shown him the indenture papers she claimed were his when she'd come to take his letter. Nicholas Braden, ravisher and defiler of women. After the way he'd treated her on their first encounter, Miss Blakewell had every reason to think him capable of such a heinous crime.

Past the dairy barn, stables, and animal pens he found a smithy, a sawmill, and several massive warehouses. He poked his head inside one to see what it contained.

"The dryin' shed, this is."

Startled, he turned to see a bare-chested, fair-haired young man covered with sweat and sawdust.

"Drying shed?"

"For curin' tobacco." The man pushed past him and opened the door wide. "After it's harvested, we hang it from those racks till it's dry and ready for prizin'."

Alec looked in to see an enormous space divided by scaffolding that rose to a ceiling crisscrossed by wooden beams.

"Right now all we got in here is empty hogsheads and bats." The man smiled, then whistled loudly into the cavernous space.

The ceiling crawled. A few winged inhabitants, roused from sleep, flew loose from the rafters, then resettled among their kin.

"They don't harm anyone, but they do keep the little 'uns away. The name's Zachariah." The man extended his hand with a warm smile. "Friends call me Zach."

"Alec Kenleigh."

Zach's handshake was firm. "Kenleigh? So it's true. Elly said ye're claimin' to be some kidnapped London gent."

"Aye."

Their gazes locked for one long moment.

"Gentleman or felon, it makes no difference to me. We all turn to dust in the grave." Zach stepped around the corner of the warehouse to a rain barrel. He dipped his shirt into the water and, with a robust groan of pleasure, squeezed it out onto his chest. "You'll find most of us— most redemptioners, that is—have an open mind. The colonies have given us all a new start. All that matters is what a man does here and now."

Though casually spoken, the words were laden with warning.

"It's returning to my life in England that concerns me."

"'Tis the safety of the children and womenfolk at Blakewell's Neck that concerns me. Harm any one of them, and I'll break yer neck with my own hands."

Though the sawyer was a few inches shorter than Alec, a life of physical labor had given him the body of an ox. Alec had no doubt he was fully capable of carrying out his threat.

"Thanks for the warning."

"Don't mention it." All traces of suspicion vanished and were replaced by a huge, dimpled smile. "Look at me. Here ye are standin' one leg barely out of the grave, and I'm threatenin' to put ye back in. Let me show ye 'round."

Zach gave Alec a tour of the outbuildings, pointing out the stables, the brick smokehouse, the cooper's shed, the carpenter's shop, and the tannery, which, fortunately, stood on the periphery, downwind from the rest of the buildings.

"Under that willow is the cemetery." Zack pointed to an enormous tree that must have been standing since long before the first European landed on these shores. A small iron fence surrounded a plot dotted with a dozen or so weathered tombstones. "A mile or so beyond this forest is the Rappahannock, home of the biggest fish you'll ever see."

"Rappahannock." Alec tested the unfamiliar word, memorizing this bit of geographical information.

If Miss Blakewell and her father refused to help him, he would need it to escape. He had given his word, aye, but he would keep it only if Miss Blakewell kept hers.

"On the other side of this pasture is an apple orchard. They brew cider here that can put a grown man down so fast, all he can remember the next day is the first swig."

The rueful laugh and shake of his head told Alec that Zach spoke from personal experience.

"Where does the river flow?"

Zach eyed him cautiously for a moment. "Into the Chesapeake."

The Chesapeake Bay, Alec knew, flowed into the Atlantic. Then something caught his eye. "What in God's name is that?"

A small hut stood by itself some distance away from the rest of the buildings on the edge of the dark pine forest. Made of branches, it was like nothing Alec had ever seen. A thin line of smoke curled from its roof.

"Takotah," Zach answered.

"A ta-ko-ta? What is its purpose?"

For some reason Zach found the question amusing, and his face split into a wide grin. "Takotah is a woman—the old Indian healer."

Alec felt goose bumps creep along his spine. A memory of gray hair, black eyes, and a dark face scarred with black designs flitted through his mind.

"She's saved my life, aye, and she saved yers. But she's got a face that could scare the feathers off a chicken, so she does." Zach laughed. "Ye and me, my friend, we're lucky. Master Blakewell and Miss Cassie, they're as fair and hardworkin' as any ye'll find in the colony."

Alec, remembering Luke's scars, rather doubted that.

"The trouble with planters is that too many of them forget they were bondsmen once themselves. Take Fancy-Pants Crichton," Zach continued. "His granddaddy was a redemptioner, but that boy is so full of himself..."

He shook his head in disgust, seemed to catch himself, and laughed. "Ye'll see for yerself soon enough, I'm sure. Now let me show you the gristmill. Built it stone by stone, we did, just last summer. Even King Carter doesn't have one of these."

Alec had no idea who King Carter or "Fancy-Pants" were, but he knew he'd never seen anything like Blakewell's Neck before. It was like a small village. Nearly self-sufficient, the estate, enormous by English standards, supplied most of the needs of those who lived and worked on it. But, if he understood Zach correctly, Blakewell's Neck, although large at nearly sixty thousand acres, was far from being the largest. That honor went to King Carter, who, if Zach was telling the truth, owned more than 250,000 acres. For one moment Alec felt he could understand what attracted men to this wild land. Estates of this size were unheard of in England, and the possibilities were staggering.

But if the land was vast, the buildings were shockingly primitive. Of all that he had seen, only four were of stone—the mill, the smokehouse, the whitewashed cookhouse, and Blakewell's house. Everything else was made of the same clapboard as his cabin. The great house itself, which stood separated from the cookhouse by a cobblestone courtyard, was surprisingly small for a holding so vast.

Two stories high with a porch, an upstairs balcony, and glass windows, it was elegant, but exceedingly simple. Vines clung to its sides, and rosebushes, dotted with red, pink, white, and yellow blooms, entwined themselves along the porch railing. It looked like a quaint English country inn, not a manor house. By the time Zach excused himself—the mistress had asked him to fix a fence, he explained—Alec was more than ready to return to the cabin he'd cursed so vehemently only an hour ago. His head ached, and his legs felt as weak as straw.

As he rounded the stables on his way back toward the cabins, with Luke trailing silently after him, he heard a woman's melodic laughter and saw Miss Blakewell leading a bay mare out of its stall and into the courtyard. He felt his body tense.

Although she was fully clothed in fashionable, if rather out-of-date, riding attire, the red-gold curls that spilled freely down her back to her hips reminded him of Lady Godiva. When they'd spoken this morning, he'd called her a girl. But everything about her, from her full, pink lips to the gentle swell of her breasts, to her delightfully rounded bottom, bespoke her womanhood.

Just then she saw him, and the laughter died on her lips. Her eyes momentarily widened. Was she afraid of him? He couldn't blame her.

"Mr. Braden," she said icily. Her greeting to Luke was noticeably warmer.

Alec was so intent on Miss Blakewell, he didn't notice the horse. As she passed, he realized the mare she had saddled was one of the finest he'd ever seen. With the sleek lines of an Arabian, such an animal would make a welcome addition to the finest stable in England. He reached out with one hand and stroked the mare's flank. Whatever else he might be, Blakewell was an excellent judge of horseflesh.

"She's a beauty." He didn't realize he had spoken until he heard his own voice.

Miss Blakewell stopped and glared back at him, her cheeks pink. "You'll not speak about me in such an improper manner."

"I was referring to the mare, Miss Blakewell. She's lovely." He stepped closer and scratched the mare's withers.

The animal nickered in appreciation and looked at him with a soft, dark eye.

Miss Blakewell's blush deepened to scarlet. "I suppose, being a gentleman, you know a great deal about horses?" Her tone of voice implied that, since he was really just a felon, he knew nothing.

"Aye. Horse breeding is one of my passions. I've got four mares descended from the Darley Arabian, and a stallion whose great grandsire was the Godolphin Barb, though I never got to ride them as much as I would have liked."

There'd always been too much work to be done.

"And my mother was descended from Queen Elizabeth."

Alec ignored her sarcasm and bent to examine the mare more closely, ignoring a wave of dizziness. "She's got clean limbs and good bones."

A horse inside the stables whinnied, and the mare lifted her tail.

"She's in season. Have you bred her?"

"I refuse to discuss such matters with you, Mr. Braden." She turned and led the mare away.

Yes, indeed, the mare's owner was a beauty as well.

Alec watched Miss Blakewell mount and ride toward the forest. Her decision to sit astride the horse on a man's saddle would have caused a small uproar at home. What a creature she was.

Another wave of dizziness threatened to engulf him. He continued on his way, eager to reach his bed before his legs gave out entirely.

He'd been thinking about Miss Blakewell all morning. Since the moment she'd laid her hand against his chest yesterday, he'd been unable to rid his mind of her. She possessed none of the qualities that usually attracted him to women. Where Isabelle and the others before her had been petite, buxom, and blatantly erotic, Miss Blakewell was tall, coming nearly to his nose, rather thin, and seemingly innocent. While Isabelle's beauty had been suited for the drawing room and bedchamber, Miss Blakewell's was meant for fresh air and sunshine.

Despite her flaws, Miss Blakewell was perhaps the most captivating female he'd ever seen, with wide eyes, translucent skin, and lips full enough to tempt the archbishop of Canterbury. When she'd come to his cabin this morning, clad in that muddy blue dress, dirt smeared on her cheeks, and her hair spilling in curls around her face, she'd looked like a milkmaid who had been caught behind the barn with the stable boy. But, lord, what a milkmaid. Though she spoke like a well-bred Englishwoman, her unruly red-gold hair, together with her startlingly green eyes and quick tongue, made her seem as wild as the land on which she'd been raised. The man who would first teach her the ways of passion would no doubt find her a delightful pupil.

What in the world was he thinking? He entered the cool darkness of his cabin, cursing himself. He should be thinking of his family and the firm, not daydreaming about some colonist wench, the daughter of a slave owner, the daughter of the man who *owned* him.

His life had been stolen from him, and Miss Blakewell stood between him and his freedom.

Alec sank onto his bed, damning his weakness, and stared at the clapboard ceiling. He, Alec Kenleigh, a man who had built ships for kings, was now another man's property. Though the state was temporary, the very notion galled him.

He'd always opposed slavery, but he'd never given indentured servitude much thought. He'd always viewed it as the natural station for those who broke laws, fell desperately into debt, or lacked coin but sought a better life. And it was, wasn't it?

Yet it was now Alec's lot, as well. Subservience might suit others, but it did not suit him. He must get home soon, before Philip ran the firm into the ground. Before his family gave him up for dead.

He began to review what he'd learned of the land today, but exhaustion soon overtook him. He drifted into a sleep troubled by the scent of lavender and a pair of emerald eyes.

Chapter Four

C assie sat in her father's study, adding the column of figures for the third time. Frustrated, she dropped the quill on the desk and massaged the painful knot in her neck.

Some days it seemed hopeless. Even if this year's tobacco harvest were as plentiful as the last, she wouldn't be able to pay off her father's creditors. It would take five such harvests at last year's prices to get the plantation out of debt. The chances of that happening were slim.

Even if the new tobacco-inspection law stabilized prices, there were any number of natural disasters that could destroy an entire harvest. Hornworms could ruin the leaves. Too much rain at the wrong time could drown the plants or make the harvested leaves rot before they finished curing. Too little, and summer heat could kill the seedlings or make cured leaves crumble into useless dust. And right now what they needed was rain. The seedlings could not be transplanted to the fields without it.

The biggest threat to Blakewell's Neck came not from nature, but from other planters. If anyone found out about her father's condition, everything he had fought for would be lost. She had considered the possible consequences at least a thousand times, always arriving at the same conclusion. While the creditors seemed more than happy with the large sum she had sent them in her father's name last October, they would be far less generous if they were to discover that the head of the household, who had no grown son, was no longer able to manage his own affairs. A guardian would be appointed to manage Blakewell's Neck in her father's stead, and the guardian would start selling land to pay the debts.

The first to go would be the north quarter, which, because it was ideal for growing sweet-scented tobacco and not the more common

Orinoco variety, was the envy of all planters in the county. More than one had tried to take it from her father by less than honest means. Next, the old and weak among the slaves would be sold to make room for younger, stronger bodies. Families would be divided. Old Charlie would find himself at a slave auction, mocked by planters who found his age amusing. Cassie felt her temper rise at the thought.

But, she was ashamed to admit, what worried her the most was knowing a guardian would immediately arrange her marriage. Her father had promised to let her wed the man of her choice. A guardian would not be so kind. That she was still a maid at two-and-twenty was unusual. Most young women were mothers at her age, some several times over. But she had turned down more than one offer of marriage, waiting, foolishly some said, for love.

If a guardian were given control of her life, she wouldn't even be consulted. In the blink of an eye she would find herself the chattel of some planter, bound by oath and law to do as he bade, to surrender her belongings, her body, her soul to please a man she did not love, might never love. While her father had tolerated and encouraged her desire for independence, even hiring tutors to teach her arithmetic, reading, and writing, a husband might not be as understanding. Laws permitted a husband to beat his wife should she disobey. She had seen enough bruised women to know that there were more than a few men who availed themselves of this barbaric husbandly prerogative.

Oh, Father, please, come back to us.

She closed her father's ledger and tucked the bright red book next to the others on the shelf. Worrying would accomplish nothing. She rose and walked across the study to the open window, hoping to see a storm brewing on the horizon. A defiantly bright and cloudless sky stretched as far as she could see. Though more sunshine was not what they needed, it was a beautiful day. Cassie closed her eyes and let the warm breeze wash over her. The sweet scent of her mother's roses—roses her father had brought from England as a gift for his new bride—filled her with determination.

Either the harvest would be plentiful, or it would not. She'd done everything she could think of to make Blakewell's Neck less dependent on tobacco, planting wheat, barley, even hemp. It made no sense to fret over something she could not control. And as for the rest? She could only do her best, and God willing…

Below in the courtyard, chickens pecked at the cobblestones. Rebecca sat on the cookhouse steps squeezing the whey from newly formed curds. A gaggle of children sat on the porch steps enthralled by another of old Charlie's tales, this one about Pocahontas and Capt. John Smith. Odd that Jamie was not among them. No doubt he was in the cookhouse pestering Nan for treats.

"Are the Indians going to chop off Cap'n Smith's head, Charlie?" asked wide-eyed Daniel, Nettie's son and Jamie's closest playmate.

The two had been born but days apart and had been inseparable since they'd learned to walk. Nettie had never told anyone who Daniel's father was, refusing to speak of him even to Cassie. But the boy's light skin and the light brown of his soft curls were evidence his father was a white man.

"Maybe," the old man answered, drawing out the suspense.

"Nah, silly. They're gonna eat 'im," replied ten-year-old Peter.

"Or burn 'im," added Beth, already at age five as incorrigible as any lad.

"They have to burn 'im first to eat 'im. Right, Charlie?"

Heads turned expectantly to old Charlie, who whittled in silence.

Cassie stifled a giggle. He would not finish the story until the children were still once more. So it had been when she was a child. Her eyes were drawn away from the children toward the sound of masculine laughter. Her breath caught in her throat.

The convict, on his way to the well with Zach and Luke, had shed his shirt and was clad only in sweat and breeches. After a week of working in the hot sun, the gentlemanly white of his skin had begun to darken to bronze, and the red scars on his chest and back were fast fading. As she watched him stride with cougar-like grace across the courtyard, she realized she'd never seen a more beautiful man.

It was a disturbing revelation. She had, after all, met many handsome men. Men from honorable families. Decent men with the manners, pale skin, and soft hands of gentlemen. Yet she'd felt nothing remotely akin to this primitive leaping of the heart that seemed to afflict her every time she set eyes on Cole.

The first time she had seen him clothed and on his feet, his face newly shaven, she'd found it difficult to breathe. The heavy growth of beard had concealed a shockingly handsome face with full lips, high cheekbones, and a firm chin. She flushed with renewed embarrassment as she remembered the humiliation she'd suffered that afternoon. How was she to have known he was talking about her horse? Then a thought struck her. Perhaps she was not really attracted to him at all. Maybe she was simply afraid of him. The man was in all likelihood a convicted felon whose crimes would have brought him a brutal death at the gallows had he not been transported. Any young woman in her right mind would fear such a man. Even Sheriff Hollingsworth, who'd said in his reply that he would come to question the convict as soon as he was able, had warned her to be ever vigilant.

Aye, that must be it. She was afraid of him.

But try as she might to fool herself, Cassie knew the truth. What she felt was nothing less than attraction. She watched as Cole drew a bucket of cool water from the well, the muscles in his arms and chest shifting with each pull of the rope. Water spilled from the tin cup as he drank, trickling down his neck and over his chest. He handed the cup to Zach and wiped the water from his lips with the back of his hand.

Cassie shivered.

More than once she'd allowed herself to daydream about those lips. She'd imagined that Cole was telling the truth, that he really was a wealthy shipbuilder, a gentleman who'd been beaten and sent abroad against his will. In her daydreams, she'd helped him regain his name, and he'd kissed her. Overcome with love, he'd renounced his life in England and stayed to court her with flowers, sweet words, and picnics in the forest, where one day he'd asked for her hand. With her new husband as Jamie's guardian, they'd been able to protect her family's interests from the comfort of their own estate nearby.

It was a ridiculous, romantic fantasy. She ought to be ashamed for permitting herself such silly, useless thoughts, especially when they revolved around a man like Cole Braden. Were other women afflicted by such musings? She hadn't the courage to ask. For any woman to think in such a manner about a convict was disgraceful. But in her daydreams he'd been a true gentleman, irresistible, not the half-naked, lash-scarred rake who stood looking up at her with cold blue eyes just now.

Cassie leaped back from the window so quickly she struck the back of her head against the sash. She'd been staring at him shamelessly, and he'd seen! Worse than the pain of the blow was the mocking smile that played across Cole's arrogant features. He was laughing at her!

"Ooh!" She paced the study furiously, rubbing the lump that had begun to form on the back of her head. *That bloody, rotten cad!* How she'd like to wipe that grin off his face!

Nettie poked her head into the room. "What is it, Missy?"

"Nothing, thank you, Nettie," she answered, trying not to take her bad temper out on Nettie.

Micah had been right, Cassie thought as she sank into her father's favorite armchair with a frustrated moan. Cole Braden was far more trouble than he was worth. And she'd actually allowed herself to daydream about... about *that*...with him! Geoffrey had already offered to buy the man's indenture from her. Although she had immediately dismissed the notion, knowing the harsh treatment that would await Mr. Braden at Geoffrey's estate, the idea suddenly seemed to have its merits.

But no. That would never do. The Crichtons had earned the reputation of being the cruelest masters in the county. She'd seen the senior Master Crichton strike a slave child once for simply bumping into him. Regardless of what Cassie thought of him, Cole had done nothing to deserve such abuse.

Well, almost nothing.

*A*lec rose from the bench near the cookhouse where he'd eaten his midday meal of cornbread with butter and cool apple cider. He stretched. Although his ribs still ached on occasion, his body had healed beyond his expectations. His muscles, weakened from illness and unaccustomed to physical labor, had at first protested these long days in the sun. But now he was no longer sore. In fact, he'd grown stronger.

He'd been assigned to work with Zach cutting lumber, probably to keep him nearby and under Zach's watchful gaze. Angry at first to find himself relegated to such menial labor, he had been surprised at how much he enjoyed working outdoors. In some ways it was preferable to sitting behind a desk all day approving schedules, checking designs, and negotiating contracts. Although he'd tried on occasion to work with the men in the shipyards when he was younger, genteel society looked down upon physical labor, and his father had not allowed it. No son of his would work with his hands. A gentleman's work was accomplished with his mind, not a hammer and saw.

Alec swallowed the last of his cider and made his way toward the stables, eager to get a better look at the mare he'd seen last week. Luke and Zach were still finishing their meal, and he doubted they'd notice his absence. And if they did, he really didn't give a damn. He'd keep his word, but he'd not play the compliant prisoner.

In the courtyard, the cook was chasing a worried young hen that seemed to stay one step ahead of her, much to the amusement of the children sitting on the porch steps.

"It's goin' to be a pleasure puttin' ye in me stew pot, ye silly bird!" Nan lunged with a grunt, only to have the hen spring to the left in a squawking mass of flying feathers.

The children shrieked with laughter. Alec had a feeling that the cook could have caught the chicken had she really tried, but that would have brought the performance to an abrupt end, disappointing her young audience.

After working in the sticky heat, he found the coolness of the stables a welcome relief. The pungent odors of manure, horses, and hay pricked his nostrils. This, at least, was familiar, reassuringly so. Though he was starting to feel more adjusted to his surroundings, he still felt himself a stranger in a very strange world. The flowers, the trees, the birds, even the scent of the wind were completely foreign to him. He did not belong here.

That would soon change.

When his eyes adjusted to the darkness, he was surprised to find not only Miss Blakewell's mare, but several other sleek horses, the kind one might expect to see on a wealthy estate in England. Although they had clearly not been properly groomed or exercised for some time, he would not have hesitated to breed any of these animals with his stock at home. How someone in the remoteness of this new continent had managed to obtain such animals was beyond him. One of the horses, an enormous chestnut stallion, rolled his eyes and snorted a warning.

"I'd give a chest of sterling to see your dam, old boy." He patted the velvet of the restless animal's nose. "Easy now."

The horse stomped nervously in its stall, tossing its head and nickering. Miss Blakewell's mare returned the nicker from several stalls down.

"So that's the trouble." He patted the stallion's neck and scratched its withers.

The animal quieted under his touch.

"You're close enough to smell her, but too far away to do anything about it."

He understood the stallion's plight far better than he cared to admit. For all that he disliked her, Alec found himself unable to ignore Miss Blakewell. His body had nearly healed, and its response to her presence was becoming more and more pronounced. Even hard physical labor was not enough to make sleep come quickly at night. What he needed, he decided, was a woman.

Nearly three months had passed since that last night with Isabelle, and his body understandably yearned for sexual release. But while the other bondsmen on the estate sought their pleasure with servant women, he would not even consider it. He found none of them, not even Elly, the

little minx who so captivated Zach, alluring, and he'd not risk getting a
woman with child when he had no intention of remaining in the colonies.

More than once he'd tried to conjure up an image of Isabelle's face,
only to be thwarted by a vision of red-gold hair, green eyes, and full,
rosy lips. Still, he'd sooner become a monk than bed Miss Blakewell.
Not only did he find her far too outspoken and proud for a woman, but
right now her father *owned* him. How could a man suffer that and remain
a man? Besides, a liaison with her would probably lead him straight to
the whipping post, if not the gallows, and he was in enough trouble as
things were.

"Women."

The stallion whinnied and nodded his head in agreement.

Alec was walking toward the mare's stall to get a closer look when
he noticed a pair of eyes spying on him from between the wooden slats
of an empty stall at the end of the walkway. "A good day to you."

A small, flaxen-haired boy barely old enough to wear breeches
climbed slowly up the planks of the stall door.

"What's your name, lad?"

The child eyed him suspiciously. "Jamie."

The boy's hair and clothes were covered with straw and more than
a little dirt. Cake crumbs clung to his lips.

"Good day, Jamie." He stroked the mare's silky neck and addressed
her. "And what's your name?"

Aye, she was a beauty, though not half so lovely as her owner.

"Andromeda," the boy answered on the mare's behalf.

"Andromeda?"

The lad nodded.

"And the big stallion?"

"Debaron."

Alec pondered the name for a moment before he realized the child
was trying to say "Aldebaran."

"He's dangerous." The boy eyed the stallion fiercely.

"Who told you that?"

The boy shrugged. "Everybody."

"Then it must be true."

"Are you a pirate?"

Alec chuckled. Barefoot and shirtless in loose cotton breeches, with his hair tied back in a simple leather thong, he must surely look like one. "No, but I build ships. Big ones."

The boy's face lit up. He jumped down from the gate and ran toward Alec, holding out a small wooden ship for his inspection. "Old Charlie whittled me this one. It's a warship."

Although tiny, it was expertly crafted, with hemp rigging and sails.

Alec crouched down in front of the boy. The child's eyes were a dazzling green.

"Charlie carved this?" Alec had no idea who Charlie was, but he didn't say so. "He did a fine job."

The boy's face lit up.

"I bet you use it to chase down pirates."

Jamie nodded.

Such green eyes. They haunted Alec's dreams. The boy must be hers. His curls were light blond, hers reddish gold, but the resemblance was uncanny. No wonder she was still unmarried. Bastardy had ruined many a maid's chance of a good match.

"If you want, mister, Charlie can whittle one for you."

"I'd like that." Alec suddenly missed his nieces and nephew with a fierceness that nearly took his breath away. They would have grown so much by the time he was finally home again, he could only hope they wouldn't have forgotten him.

"What's your name, Mister?"

Alec hesitated, fighting back the wave of homesickness. "People here call me Cole."

There was no need to confuse the child with the truth.

The boy's other pocket began to squirm, and Alec heard a tiny, muffled meow.

"What have you there, lad?"

Jamie pulled out a fuzzy gray-and-white kitten so young its eyes had not yet opened.

"What a pretty kitten. But this little one needs her mother."

"She's mine." Jamie clutched the kitten possessively to his chest.

"Aye, she's yours, but she's still too little to leave her mother. Without her mother's milk, she'll die."

The boy looked at Alec, then down at the kitten, curls bobbing.

"Where did you find her?"

Jamie wrapped a dirty hand around one of Alec's fingers and led him toward the stall from which he'd appeared.

*C*assie was both relieved and disappointed to see that Cole had left the courtyard when she went outside a short time later. The lump on her head still ached, but not half as much as her pride. Twice she'd made a fool of herself in front of that dreadful man. It would not happen again. It would not.

Charlie had finished his story about Pocahontas and was telling another about Captain Kidd and Skeleton Island. Jamie, who would never willingly miss the telling of this tale, was still nowhere to be found. Apprehension quickened her steps.

"Nan, have you seen Jamie?" She entered the cookhouse, where Elly stood grumbling over a washtub of dishes, while Nan plucked the chicken that would become the family's evening meal.

"Nay, Missy. I haven't seen him since he came by to wheedle a tart out of me about an hour ago. Run off again, 'as 'e?"

"Aye, he has." How could it be so difficult to keep an eye on one tiny child? "Have you seen him, Elly?"

Elly shook her head peevishly.

"Eleanor!" Nan snapped.

Elly's spine stiffened at the sound of her full, Christian name. "What?"

"Work is a blessing, child," Nan scolded her. "Idle hands brew trouble. Now run and find Master Jamie."

Elly nearly flew out the door.

"Teach that girl her place, I will," Nan grumbled.

"If anyone can, Nan, you can." Cassie laughed. "I'm going to check with Takotah. I found Jamie asleep in her lodge last time he disappeared."

"Then you'll want to take some bread and cider for your father." Nan laid the chicken aside, then rapidly put together a basket of victuals and handed it to Cassie.

Cassie hurried to Takotah's lodge, calling for Jamie as she went. Inside, Takotah was hanging bundles of plants upside down to dry.

"He is not here," she said before Cassie could ask. "Did you check the cookhouse?"

Takotah knew Jamie well.

"Aye, but Nan hasn't seen him either." Cassie was genuinely worried now. She placed the basket of food next to the hearth. "How is Father?"

She'd been so busy, she'd not been to visit him in two days.

"He is unchanged. He talks to your mother's spirit, but he eats well."

It was the answer Cassie had expected, but hoped not to hear.

"How is the new man?" Takotah asked.

"The convict?" Cassie sniffed in annoyance. "He is the most awful, bothersome man I've ever known."

Takotah smiled, the tattoos on her cheeks and chin seeming to come alive as she did. "He is also very handsome, is he not? And strong."

Cassie stammered for a response, wishing she could disagree, but the direction her thoughts had taken lately made an honest answer impossible.

"Micah says he is not to be trusted, and I agree." She failed to mention that Micah had been surprised and pleased by Cole's quick learning and his willingness to work.

Takotah smiled, but said nothing.

If she hadn't been so worried about Jamie, Cassie would have been irritated by this. But, genuinely afraid now, she barely noticed and turned to leave with a muttered farewell.

Even before she reached the cookhouse, Cassie could see something was terribly wrong. Micah stood in the courtyard holding his flintlock, deep in conversation with Zach and the other men. Nan was pacing to and fro, wringing her hands on her apron. Elly was fidgeting nervously. Redemptioners and slaves stood together, whispering among themselves. Then they saw her and grew silent.

Her skin crawled.

Nan ran toward her as fast as her plump old legs could carry her. "Oh, Missy, he's gone!"

Chapter Five

*C*assie's heart stopped. "Jamie?"

Dear God, what did Nan mean by "gone"?

"No! Well, aye!" the cook stammered. "But the convict is missin', too! He's run off, he has!"

"Oh, God!"

Her brother was lost, and now no one could find the convict? If anything had happened to Jamie, she would never forgive herself. It was she who was entrusted with the boy's care, and it was she who had brought the felon to live among them. Why, oh, why had she taken such a risk?

"Most likely he'll be usin' the boy as a hostage," Micah said, looking a decade older than when she'd last seen him this morning. "Luke says Braden was with them till the noon meal. When he and Zach finished, the convict was gone."

"I can't believe Cole would hurt the boy," Zach said.

"He won't." Everyone looked toward Luke. The man had hardly spoken since his arrival on the plantation. "He's not that kind of man."

"Where have you looked?" The steadiness in Cassie's voice belied the panic that flowed through her veins like poison. Her brother could be killed—or worse. She had heard stories of men who did things to children, indescribable things. If Mr. Braden had no qualms about ravishing women, then perhaps . . .

"We've checked everywhere, Missy," Nan said.

"He can't have gotten too far. Zach and I are goin' to saddle up and ride with the men along the riverbank," Micah said. "It's harder to make good time through the forest, especially with a child. If he's as smart as he seems, Braden will use the river to keep his sense of direction. He'll be headin' for a port town. If we find no sign of him, we'll check along the road to Fredericksburg."

"I'll do that," Cassie said.

The men stared at her but said nothing.

"You can't expect me to sit here while some convict drags Jamie through the countryside. Besides, we can't afford to lose time."

"What're you gonna do if you find him?" asked Micah.

"I'll take Father's pistol. I know how to use it."

"Miss Cassie..." Micah shook his head.

"I have to do something. If no one will join me, I'll go alone, but I'll not sit by while Jamie's life is in danger!"

"I'll help," Nate called from somewhere in the crowd.

"Count me in," Tom added from behind her.

Other voices called out their willingness to join her. The sound of an approaching rider interrupted them.

"Oh, no." Cassie felt her heart sink.

Of all the times he could have chosen to call ...

"Bloody hell," Zach grumbled none too quietly, echoing her thoughts.

Micah, who by law could not carry a firearm, handed the flintlock to Zach.

Geoffrey Crichton rode up on his roan gelding and pulled to a stop in the courtyard. The powdered wig he'd chosen to wear over his blond hair looked positively silly. He hopped down from the horse and strutted through the crowd toward Cassie, his exaggerated gait an ill disguise for his limp.

"Catherine." He bent to kiss her hand. "Is something amiss?"

She hated to involve him in Blakewell affairs. The less he knew, the safer they all were. Not that Geoffrey was a bad sort, really. He simply didn't know how to mind his own affairs. He'd never approve of her running the estate, and Cassie had gone to great lengths to keep him from discovering the truth. He'd made it clear many times that he believed docility in women a virtue. But there was no way to keep her brother's disappearance a secret, not when they'd be crossing other planters' lands to find him, and she had an obligation to warn the neighbors that the convict was at large.

"Jamie is missing." She braced herself for his reaction. "And the convict is gone."

"Indeed." Geoffrey calmly flicked the lace at his wrists. "It's no surprise. My father and I were afraid something like this would happen, especially with your father away."

"Micah is taking some men along the river. I will lead a party along the road to Fredericksburg."

Geoffrey looked at Micah with open contempt. She knew he viewed all men with dark skin as slaves. In his mind there were no exceptions.

"If your blackamoor would provide me with a fresh mount, I will gladly lead the second party. This is no job for a woman, and I do have some experience in tracking runaways." He adjusted his leather gloves. "If you could dispatch a messenger to Crichton Hall, I'm sure my father would gladly lend you the use of his hounds and some of his men."

Cassie bristled at his thoughtless dismissal of both her and Micah but said nothing. Now was not the time. She needed Geoffrey's help. Her brother's life was at risk.

"Thank you, Geoffrey." One of the field hands took Geoffrey's gelding and led it to the stables.

Geoffrey began barking orders to the assembled men.

"Missy! They're in here!" the field hand shouted, motioning to the stable.

Cassie lifted her skirts and ran, sickened by the taste of her own fear, oblivious to those who followed her.

"Jamie!" she cried.

Inside, she saw Cole and Jamie emerging from the far stall. If he had touched so much as a hair on Jamie's head . . .

But Jamie looked unhurt, unafraid. Cole looked puzzled, his brows drawn together in a confused frown. Rather than holding a homemade knife or some other crude weapon to her brother's throat, as Cassie had expected, Cole was cuddling a newborn kitten against his bare chest. Astonished and unable to breathe, Cassie could do nothing more than stare.

*A*lec had just begun to explain to Jamie how cats bathed their kittens with their tongues when the stable doors had burst open and a crowd had rushed in. Foremost among them were Miss Blakewell, who looked wan and frightened, Micah, the overseer, Zach, who was carrying a flintlock, and an absurdly dressed man who strode into the stable as if he owned it.

"What in the hell is going on?" Alec looked from one angry face to the next.

"That's what we're wantin' to know." Zach's face was grim.

"I'll ask the questions." The overdressed fop glared at the sawyer, as if this were a play and Zach had stolen his line. "Come here, felon, and don't touch the boy."

Comprehension rushed through Alec, leaving him stunned. He felt his gorge rise, willing himself to speak with a calmness he did not feel. "We'll talk more about ships and kittens another time. Move along, lad."

Slowly, so as not to alarm anyone, he placed the kitten he had been holding in the straw, where its nervous mother quickly retrieved it.

"Guess what! He builds ships. Real big ones!" Jamie seemed unaware of the tense drama that centered on him.

Alec watched as the boy raced to his mother, who scooped him up and hugged him as if her life depended on it, silent tears spilling down her cheeks. He felt something twist in his stomach.

"Only a monster would hurt a child." Alec wanted somehow to comfort her. He met her gaze and held it. Her eyes were as green as a meadow in spring, and he found himself reaching to brush a tear from her cheek.

The sharp sting of a riding crop across his chest stopped him.

"Keep your distance from Miss Blakewell, convict!" The fop glared at him, riding crop gripped tightly in a gloved fist.

It took every ounce of will Alec possessed not to strike the man in the middle of his pretty face.

"Geoffrey Crichton!" Miss Blakewell stared wide-eyed at the bewigged fool. "Here, we do not strike our servants."

"Of course." The dandy bowed stiffly. "Forgive me."

So this was Fancy-Pants. No wonder Zach disliked the man. He was a pompous ass. Alec exchanged a knowing glance with Zach, who rolled his eyes and shook his head.

"I'm sorry, Mr. Braden. Master Crichton sometimes forgets himself." Miss Blakewell sent Crichton a scathing look.

Alec saw a muscle twitch angrily in the fop's cheek as her comment struck home and felt a grudging respect for Miss Blakewell. No doubt many men cowered before this fool, yet she had insulted him without worry.

"I'll get salve for your wound." Her gaze met his and she turned to go.

He looked down to see an angry red welt spanning his chest. "Thank you for your concern, Miss Blakewell, but it's nothing."

The worry in her lovely eyes seemed genuine. It was almost enough to make him forget for a moment who she was, who she thought *he* was. Almost.

"Everybody back to work." Micah led the curious gawkers away from the stable. "Everything's fine. Just a misunderstandin'. Back to work."

"Nan, take Jamie to the cookhouse, please," Miss Blakewell gave the child one last hug and kiss before putting him down. "And this time, young man, stay where I can see you, or I'll take a switch to your backside!"

"Eleanor!" The cook turned and glared at the younger woman as they walked away. "I thought ye said ye checked the stables."

"I did!"

"Ye did a bloody poor job of it!"

Alec heard Zach's laughter as the sawyer followed the object of his affection out of the stable, teasing her along the way. Slowly voices faded, leaving only Alec, Miss Blakewell, Luke, who was standing guard again, and Fancy-Pants, who was looking Alec up and down as if he were some sort of exotic animal.

"I'm sorry, Mr. Braden. We thought … that is, Jamie was missing, and when we couldn't find you, we thought … " Miss Blakewell stammered apologetically.

"I know what you thought." Alec spoke more harshly than he'd intended. "You were wrong."

Crichton was still staring at him, disdain on his face.

Alec met Crichton's gaze, then looked at Miss Blakewell again. "Am I your new prize stud to be displayed before curious neighbors?"

Although he'd addressed Miss Blakewell, who started at the vulgarity of his words, the comment had been aimed at Crichton. When the riding crop was raised this time, Alec was ready for it and caught Crichton's wrist in midair.

Miss Blakewell gasped. "Geoffrey, no!"

"Miss Blakewell said they don't hit servants here." Alec's gaze locked with Crichton's. A full head taller than the younger man and of a bigger build, Alec knew he had the physical advantage despite his recent injuries. He smiled icily at the fear and surprise that showed on the other man's face.

"Stop it, both of you!"

Finally Crichton relaxed and lowered his arm, nostrils flared, gray eyes cold with hatred. "You'll live to regret this, convict."

And Alec knew he had made an enemy. It was a strange feeling for someone whose disagreements with others had been limited to business disputes and drawing room debates.

"If you'll excuse me, Miss Blakewell, I am needed elsewhere."

Cassie watched Cole leave, feeling ashamed for having jumped to so hideous a conclusion. She'd expected to find him holding Jamie hostage or worse. Instead he'd been cradling a kitten, a sight she found strangely unnerving. Not that she trusted Cole Braden now, but she was sure he had not meant to harm or frighten her brother. The shocked expression on his face when he'd realized what they believed him guilty of was enough to convince her he'd never considered hurting Jamie.

Geoffrey stepped back, flicking the ruffles at his wrists and throat. Cassie could tell from the ticking muscle in his cheek that he was furious. A heavy silence stretched between them.

"Are you sure you don't want to sell his indenture now that you've had a taste of what might happen?"

"No, Geoffrey. Thank you. This incident was a misunderstanding, nothing more. It was our fault for not checking the grounds more thoroughly." The admission was not easy to make. She'd talk to Elly later.

Geoffrey eyed her doubtfully. "Very well. But I'm going to take the liberty of sending over one of our most trustworthy men to help keep an eye on him."

"He is already under guard—"

"And has already managed to elude your darky once. I'll listen to no objections, Catherine, not when your safety is at stake. I'll send him tomorrow. I hate to think of you here unprotected."

Cassie started to object but was interrupted again.

"Assign my man whatever task you like. He'll be yours to do with as you choose. I know your father left you in charge. Despite whatever I might think of his . . . unusual decision, I will respect it. But enough of that. I came by to give you this." He reached inside his waistcoat and removed an envelope.

She opened it to find an invitation to Geoffrey's twenty-third birthday party, to be held, as usual, the last weekend in June.

Geoffrey took a deep breath and smiled at her, the anger having left his face. "I hope you and Jamie will be able to attend. I don't think you've missed my birthday celebration since we were small children. It wouldn't be the same without you."

Cassie felt a twinge of regret for having admonished him in front of the others. Although it was inexcusable for him to have struck Cole, he had done so in a misbegotten attempt to protect her. Though she often disliked the severe man Geoffrey had become, it was hard for her to forget she had once adored him.

"Thank you, Geoffrey. Of course we'll come."

The smile that now brought dimples to Geoffrey's handsome face reminded her of the boy she'd grown up with.

"Would you stay for tea?" she asked, remembering her manners.

She tried not to seem too relieved when he declined.

*A*s soon as Blakewell's Neck had disappeared behind him, Geoffrey let out an exultant whoop. The horse beneath him broke into a gallop. He finally had a plan. With Henry's help, he'd have Catherine at the altar before winter. And then . . .

The thought of bedding her was intoxicating.

He wouldn't tell his father about this. He'd surprise him instead. His father would be proud of him, proud that he'd been a man and taken action on his own. He'd wait until his father had gone to Williamsburg for the season, and then Catherine would be his.

As for the convict, Braden would pay dearly. Not just for humiliating him in front of servants and slaves, although that in itself was reason enough. There was something about the way the felon and Catherine had looked at each other that had made him want to kill the man. Clearly the knave's story about being kidnapped had captured Catherine's overly romantic imagination in some way. Geoffrey's anger flared anew as he remembered the way her eyes had softened when she'd seen him. He kicked impatiently at his horse's flank with his good leg, driving the animal beneath him to a frenzied pace.

No matter how unconventional she might be, he loved Catherine. His father wanted the match so he could acquire her dowry—fifteen hundred acres of riverside land. They'd be able to build the wharf they'd always talked about and have direct access to the river like the other good families. But Geoffrey wanted only Catherine.

He'd decided long ago to make her his wife. He'd been six then, she only five. She'd come to visit him as he lay in bed recovering from the accursed fever that had left him lame. She'd shown him kindness when his own father, sickened by the sight of Geoffrey's infirmity, had refused even to enter the room. Her beautiful green eyes wide with concern, she'd lifted herself onto her toes and kissed him on the cheek.

"Feel better, Geoffey," she'd said, calling him by his pet name and putting a single wilted rose on his pillow.

He'd known from that moment he loved her. Surely she'd turned down all her previous suitors because she was waiting for him. Yet she seemed to go out of her way to avoid him, rejecting his advances, however mild they might be. Why?

One thing, however, was certain. The moment he had control of Blakewell's Neck, he would make Nicholas Braden regret the day he was born.

Chapter Six

"*I*'ve told you everything I remember."

Candlelight danced on the brick walls of the darkened cookhouse, over the copper pots that hung neatly on their hooks and across the faces of the two men sitting opposite each other at the table. The sheriff seemed to Cassie to be enjoying himself, having devoured three bowls of Nan's oyster stew, several slices of cornbread, and most of a jug of cider. Cole, who'd not yet eaten, sat back lazily, his arm draped over the back of the chair beside his, the tense line of his jaw the only sign he was under any strain.

For three hours Cassie had watched and listened from where she stood near the hearth as Sheriff Hollingsworth had relentlessly interrogated the convict on the details of his supposed kidnapping. Her feet hurt. Her lower back ached from standing motionless for so long.

The sun had long since set. The beating of slave drums and the pulsing song of katydids floated on the warm night air. So far, the sheriff's efforts had yielded naught. Cole held firmly to his account and was so convincing she would have believed him had he but one shred of evidence to bear out his claim.

"Now back to your journey." The sheriff buttered the last piece of cornbread. Crumbs littered the linen tablecloth around his bowl. "You were at sea for at least six weeks, yet you claim to remember so little of the voyage. Perhaps—"

Cole slammed his fist on the table and sprang to his feet. "Damn it, man! Must we continue this useless interrogation?"

The room was so still, Cassie could hear her own heart beat. The only movement was that of trembling candlelight.

Then the sheriff's young deputy, remembering his duty, stepped timidly from the shadows and aimed a cocked and loaded pistol unsteadily at the convict's head.

Sheriff Hollingsworth, seemingly unaffected by the convict's outburst, broke the silence with a belch and, wiping cornbread crumbs from his stock and waistcoat, motioned for Cassie to refill his cup. Only then did she realize she had been holding her breath. She did as he directed and went back to stand by the hearth.

Cole glanced at the pistol, rolled his eyes in seeming disgust, and slowly resumed his seat.

"Suppose what you've told us is true." Sheriff Hollingsworth packed his pipe with tobacco and lit it with a bit of kindling he'd touched to flame. Drawing deeply on the aromatic smoke, he sent a series of white rings floating toward the ceiling as if he hadn't a care in the world. "Who in bloody hell would want to ship you here? Surely the culprit would know you'd fight to reestablish your name. Why not simply lop off your head and be done with it?"

Cassie nodded. This part of the convict's story made no sense.

"I don't know." Cole shook his head. "For money. Or perhaps the kidnapper thought I'd die on the journey or perish before I was seasoned to the colony. Then there'd be no body in England to give the crime away."

"Who would want to kill you?" Sheriff Hollingsworth asked.

"I've no idea."

"Your heir, perhaps?"

Cole seemed to consider this for a moment, then shook his head. "Philip has many flaws, but he's not capable of this."

"You've no enemies?"

"None."

"Business rivals?"

"Several, but none who would stoop to kidnapping or murder. Of course . . ." Cole paused.

"Out with it, man. If you've anything to convince me what you're saying is true, you'd best tell me now. You must know I don't believe a bloody word you've said tonight."

"There are a few irate husbands in London who would not be heartbroken were I to vanish suddenly."

The sheriff guffawed, slapped his knee, and gave Cole a conspiratorial grin.

Cassie did not bother to hide her look of censure. *Men!* That a sheriff and a felon could find common ground when it came to violating the sanctity of marriage spoke volumes about their sex.

*E*lly felt a hand slip over her mouth, her surprised gasp cut off by a man's callused hand.

"What have we here?" Zach whispered in her ear, his lips caressing her cheek. "Ye wouldn't be eavesdroppin', would ye, Elly?"

"Shhh!" She turned her attention back to the conversation in the cookhouse.

Despite the infernal slave drums, she'd been able to hear almost everything from her hiding place beneath the window near the woodpile. When the convict had jumped to his feet, she'd gasped out loud. She didn't want to miss a moment of this.

She felt Zach's lips touch the back of her neck, sending warm shivers down her spine. She ignored him. Then his lips nibbled at her ear and traveled down the side of her throat.

"Zach! Stop it!" She fought not to laugh.

"Never mind me." His hands moved near her breasts. "Spy to yer heart's content."

His lips and tongue caressed her nape. She started to protest, but the words never left her mouth. Before she could speak he had turned her toward him and captured her lips with his. She would have pushed him away had the feel of his mouth on hers not driven all thought from her head. She felt her arms slip behind his neck in surrender and invitation. Something deep within her ignited as he probed her mouth with his tongue. With one of his hands he pressed her body against his. With the other he cupped her breast, teasing an already taut nipple through the cloth of her dress and chemise. She felt her knees weaken.

It was happening again, and she did not want it to happen. Not with him.

"Stop!" She pushed his hand away and turned her face from him, struggling to regain her poise.

Zach released her. "I love ye, Elly."

His brown eyes said all that and more, a wistful smile on his lips. Moonlight played across his blond hair and sun-bronzed skin. And she couldn't deny she desired him.

"Oh, hush." Her heart still beat wildly, and her skin tingled where he'd touched her. "You'd best forget all your silly ideas right now, Zachariah Sawyer, for you must know I'll never marry you."

His real surname was Bowers, but she called him Sawyer to remind him—and herself—of what he was and why she could not spend her life with him. She tried to ignore the shadow that passed over his handsome face. She was destined for something better than this. She'd not waste her life cooking, cleaning, and bearing children for a man who could barely provide a roof over her head and a meal for her belly. Even if that man were Zach.

"Still dreamin' of Fancy Pants, are we?" His lips brushed her throat. "I can make ye forget him."

He claimed her lips fiercely this time. Despite her resolve she found herself embracing him, her fingers running over the smooth muscles of his bare back, returning the kiss with a fervor equal to his.

"I know ye want me, Elly." His voice was hoarse, strained.

She moaned in defeat and let her head fall back. His lips brushed the tops of her breasts. Liquid warmth spread throughout her body, gathering between her thighs. Her fingers pushed through his hair and pressed him against her. The scent of newly cut pine, sunshine, and male sweat filled her head.

She felt him lift her skirts and nearly gasped when he cupped her bare sex with his hand and began to caress her slowly. Her body, craving what he had to offer, moved rhythmically against the pressure of his hand. God help her, she *did* want him.

"Oh, Zach." She moaned, arching against him. He was driving her mad.

The musky scent of her desire made Zach's head spin. He gripped her bare bottom, pulling her mound against the swell of his breeches. The contact sent heat through his loins. She whimpered in response and spread her thighs for him, leaning against the cookhouse for support. He lifted her, sought the silken folds of her womanhood. She was hot and wet and cried out softly as he slid a finger first over her swollen bud and then inside her.

"Elly!" He throbbed as much from the sight of her awakened passion as from his own need. Her eyes were half-closed, her lips parted, her golden hair spilling in a disorderly, shimmering mass over her shoulders. Her breath came in heated gasps. God above, he wanted her. He wanted her so badly it hurt.

But this wasn't right. If he didn't stop now he was going to tup her up against the cookhouse as if she were a common whore. He reluctantly pulled his hands to her face and rained kisses along her nose and lips. She moaned with frustration. Aye, he wanted her, but not like this. It was her first time. She deserved better.

"Let me come to yer cabin tonight, Elly."

Her eyes fluttered open, and she looked at him with undisguised longing. For a moment he thought she would say aye, but then the passion fled her face and was replaced by fury. "No!" She stepped away from him and smoothed her skirts into place.

She'd almost allowed Zach to take her here next to the woodpile. Nay, she'd almost begged him to. How could she expect to find a proper husband if she were no longer a virgin? Her body was all she had to offer a man. And certainly a gentleman like Geoffrey Crichton would expect his bride to be untouched.

"No." She ignored the lingering ache deep within her. "I can't give myself to a man like you."

Zach's expression hardened.

She looked away, unable to meet his eyes.

"I love ye, Elly. Maybe one day ye'll come to your senses and realize that ye love me, too."

She watched his back as he walked away, trying to fight off the emptiness that had engulfed her. The breeze that had felt so warm just moments ago made her shiver. She had not meant to hurt him, but she had to make him understand. No matter what she felt, no matter what her shameless body wanted, she could not marry a sawyer. She'd watched her mother fade away caring for a brood of fourteen, the wife of a fisherman nearly twice her age. If there was one lesson she had learned, it was that a woman's happiness and that of her children depended on the coin in her husband's coffers. Zach had nothing.

Voices intruded into her thoughts. It seemed the sheriff was about to leave. She slipped into the shadows and back toward her cabin.

"I'll do what I can for you. I'm not saying I believe you, mind, but stranger things have happened." The sheriff stood and stretched, his enormous belly threatening to pop the brass buttons on his jacket. "Until I find proof you are not Nicholas Braden, 'tis Nicholas Braden you shall be. You'll do as your master bids without argument. You'll cause no trouble. If you attempt to escape, Master Blakewell will be within his rights to see you hunted down and flogged and your indenture extended. Harm anyone, and I'll see you hanged."

"So I've been told." Alec looked pointedly at Miss Blakewell, who refused to meet his gaze. "I've already given my word."

"The ship you arrived on, the *Easy Mary*, has long since gone, probably off to the Indies. There's no way of knowing when she'll return. As for the soul driver, 'twould be impossible to track him down. The best I can do is to check the *Mary's* papers, see who was listed as cargo. Perhaps there were others on board who saw or heard something suspicious."

The sheriff poured the last of his cider down his gullet and wiped his mouth on his sleeve. "I sent your letter to Williamsburg two days after receiving it. I took the liberty of writing one myself to the magistrate at Newgate. He ought to be able to clarify this situation, if anyone can. We can expect a response in late summer or early fall."

Late summer or early fall?

Alec swore under his breath. Though only a matter of months, it might as well be an eternity. Every day he remained in this place was an injustice. Didn't these people understand he had a family and a thriving concern to return to? No, of course they didn't. They thought him a liar and a criminal of the worst sort. The look in their eyes—loathing mixed with fear—made their feelings plain. To them his words meant nothing. Now his entire future rode on a letter.

He'd be lucky if he ever saw England again.

Standing up slowly so as not to alarm the trigger-happy fool of a deputy, he watched as Miss Blakewell bade the sheriff good night. "Next time you write your father, tell him he's lucky he missed me. I'd have cleaned his pockets. I'm feeling lucky tonight." The sheriff laughed heartily.

"I'll tell him." She smiled innocently.

"I'm off to Crichton Hall for a game or two of whist. Old Crichton owes me fifty pounds, and I aim to make it an even hundred." The sheriff laughed at his own joke. "Young Master Crichton fancies you, girl, and one day I expect he'll finally ask your father for your hand. It would make a fine match."

So that bastard Crichton wanted to marry her. *Fine. Let Crichton have her.* Alec certainly didn't care. Why, then, did he feel gratified at the look of distress that flashed across Miss Blakewell's pretty face before she managed to hide it beneath a polite smile?

"Geoffrey and I are just old childhood friends, Sheriff, nothing more. Good night."

She shut the door and turned to face Alec.

"I'm sorry."

Everyone else had gone. Candlelight caressed her face, and Alec felt an insane urge to take her in his arms and kiss her. "Sorry?"

"You haven't had your supper yet."

How absolutely beautiful she was. Her unruly red-gold hair had begun to slip free of its pins again and hung in long, curling strands around her face. More than once he had wondered what it would feel like unbound in his hands. Though she had tucked a muslin kerchief in the top of her bodice, as fashion and modesty demanded, the cleft between her breasts made a dark shadow he found more than a little distracting. Truth be told, she was playing havoc with his senses.

"I'll survive."

"Nonsense. Sit down and have something to eat. We've more than enough to share, and there's something I've been meaning to discuss with you."

She moved to the fireplace, the muslin of her gown rustling as she walked, and stirred the remainder of the cook's stew, which had been kept warm over a low, glowing fire. The scent made his mouth water.

She quickly filled a bowl and placed it on the table with a spoon and a cup brimming with cool cider. From the shadow behind a large mixing bowl on a shelf she removed a loaf of bread wrapped in cloth and cut a thick slice. A warm, yeasty smell tickled his nostrils. It was wheaten bread.

"We have to hide this when the sheriff comes," she said somewhat sheepishly, placing the bread next to his bowl and pushing the butter crock to his side of the table.

"I can see why."

Alec sat, giving in to his hunger and, not waiting to butter the bread, took a bite. He tried not to groan aloud. Since he'd arrived, he'd eaten only cornmeal, with occasional greens and a bit of salted pork or beef now and again—corn bread, corn muffins, boiled corn mush with bacon. He tasted the stew and had to force back another satisfied moan. He would never have imagined such simple fare could seem like a feast.

"As you must have noticed when you were in the stables yesterday, the horses have not been tended properly for some time," she said, smoothing her skirts unnecessarily. "We have need of a groom to curry and exercise them."

"You'd like me to take on those duties."

"In addition to your other tasks, aye. You claim to be experienced with horses."

So he was being put to the test. She was clever. If she could not verify his identity, she could at least check into parts of his story. "As I said, horses are one of my passions."

"You may begin in the morning."

"As you wish, mistress."

"Very well, then." She reached for a broom that stood next to the hearth and began to sweep the redbrick floor. Though she acted as if he were not in the room, Alec could tell his presence made her nervous. Her movements were awkward, and she stayed on the other side of the table, refusing even to glance in his direction.

As the stew took the edge off his appetite, he felt himself afflicted with hunger of another sort. Bent slightly at the waist, the curves of her lovely *derrière* rendered nicely by the fall of her skirts, she presented a delectable picture. He felt a tightening in his loins and cursed himself. He was a grown man, for God's sake, not some randy youth who got a cockstand every time he saw a pretty face.

He tried to shift the direction of his thoughts. "The stew was delicious. Thank you."

"You're welcome." She swept yellow cornbread crumbs into the fire. Then she turned toward him. "I know you had hoped the sheriff would be able to do more for you tonight, but rest assured, Sheriff Hollingsworth is a man of his word. If he says he'll investigate, he will."

"You'll forgive me if I remain skeptical."

"You've no need for concern. If your story is true, you'll be released. It's only a matter of time."

"Time that benefits you and costs me greatly." He stood.

"You must understand we cannot simply release you because you wish it. We have an obligation to the Crown—"

"Aye, an obligation to the Crown. And a need to get every shilling out of my hide you can. I understand all too well, Miss Blakewell."

She abruptly placed the broom next to the hearth and faced him, her hands on her hips, her cheeks flushing a tempting shade of pink. "You were sick, dying! I bought your indenture to save you the indignity of dying in chains, but more than once I've regretted that decision."

"Have you?"

The convict mocked her! With that tone in his voice and the lazy smile on his face, he mocked her! Cassie fought the profane retort that flew to mind. She was trying to make up for having suspected him so unfairly yesterday, offering him a chance both to prove himself and to do what he claimed to enjoy, and he was responding by baiting her. Oh, the arrogance!

"You may go now, Mr. Braden."

"Aye, *Mistress.*" He turned to leave.

His voice made her skin tingle. It was deep and husky and as intimate as a touch.

"Why must you do that?"

"Do what?"

"Address me in that fashion."

"Is 'mistress' not the proper form of address?"

"Aye, but the way you say it . . . it's all wrong."

"How do I say it?"

"You speak with too much...familiarity."

"I beg forgiveness, Mistress." His handsome face was the picture of contrition, though his tone was anything but sincere. Dressed in plain linsey-woolsey breeches and a white cotton shirt that contrasted sharply with his dark hair and tanned skin, he looked like the quintessential rake—dark, dangerous, and breathtakingly male.

She turned and began clearing the table, effectively dismissing him. She wished he would stop watching her and go. Her hands trembling, she dropped the empty cider jug onto the brick floor, where it shattered. Cursing silently, she bent to pick up the broken pieces.

"Let me help." Cole knelt beside her.

"No, thank you, Mr. Braden. I can take care of this myself." Why couldn't he leave her in peace? "It is my carelessness that caused it."

"Aye, but I provoked you." He began to gather broken crockery.

"Provoked me? Rude behavior from you is hardly enough to provoke me, Mr. Braden." She hurriedly picked up several of the knife-sharp shards.

Dropping the fragments with a pained gasp, she stared at her bleeding palm in surprise.

Cole reached for her hand. "Let me see."

She rose and pulled away from him. "It's nothing."

Cole ignored her protests, taking her hand in his. The contact startled her, sending frissons of warmth from the tips of her fingers to her belly.

"It's deep. We need to stop the bleeding." He took a clean napkin from the table and pressed it firmly to the wound.

She winced.

"Am I hurting you?"

Tantalized by his nearness, Cassie couldn't answer. He smelled of leather and sunshine and something that could only be the natural fragrance of his skin. How could she be so affected by this one man? Other than those whose bodily odors were overpowering and offensive, she could not remember noticing a man's particular scent, much less feeling drawn to him because of it.

They seemed to stand there for an eternity, Cole holding her hand, she looking anywhere but at him. She heard the steady inhale and exhale of his breathing, felt hers quicken. She ventured an upward glance and felt the deep blue of his eyes penetrate her composure.

"That should slow it. Have you any salve nearby?"

"On the second shelf above the worktable."

In two quick strides he'd found the jar and was back, holding her hand and carefully spreading the ointment over the cut, which now bled only slightly.

"Does it sting?"

"Aye." Her voice caught in her throat.

His touch was gentle, disturbingly so, as he made delicious, slow circles on her skin. Pain from the cut mingled with pleasure, creating an excruciating sensation that left her nearly bereft of breath and thought.

"I suppose your Indian medicine woman made this concoction."

He wrinkled his nose.

"Takotah?" Cassie couldn't help laughing at his reaction. Takotah had created many a smell far more unpleasant than this one with her herbs and potions. "Aye, but she's not mine. She can leave the plantation anytime she likes."

"Why do you suppose she stays?"

"Her people were all but wiped out by settlers. Her husband and children were murdered. We are the only family she has."

Cole seemed to consider this, then nodded his head thoughtfully.

What a strange man he was: gentle one moment, harsh the next. The image of him holding that kitten against his chest leaped unbidden to her mind once again, causing her heart to beat faster.

Since yesterday afternoon, she'd watched him play with the children. Following Jamie's example, they had bombarded him with questions about pirates and sailing vessels. So far, he'd indulged their every query with surprising good humor. Yet she'd also seen the way he sprang from his seat tonight, his expression that of a man ready to kill. She remembered the terrifying strength of his arms as he'd cut off her breath and threatened to break her neck not so long ago.

That he was dangerous was clear. But he was no common felon. That much was also apparent.

"Is that better?" His voice was deep and soothing, his blue eyes warm.

Cassie nodded, afraid to speak.

He reached for another napkin and carefully wound it around her hand. Dark lashes cast shadows on his cheeks, and he frowned slightly as he worked. The day's growth of whiskers made the skin on his chin and cheeks appear dark and rough. She resisted the urge to stroke his face.

"This should do it." He tucked one end of the napkin under to create a temporary bandage.

His gaze captured hers and held it unwavering. He should have released her hand by now, but he did not. Nor did she try to take it from him. Then, ever so slowly, he turned her hand over and, without breaking eye contact, brought it to his lips.

Entranced by the deep blue of his eyes, she could at first do nothing but marvel at the warm sensation his lips created when they touched her skin. She'd been kissed this way a thousand times before, but never had this simple act made her pulse quicken. What she had once viewed as a polite form of greeting was with him an act of intimacy. She gasped and snatched her hand from his grasp as reality replaced surprise.

"You've no cause to fear me."

"I'm not afraid."

"You're trembling."

"It's the night chill."

"You're lying." He smiled.

She started to protest, felt her face flush. *Damn him!* Why did he delight in humiliating her?

"Either you're afraid of me, or you want to be kissed as badly as I want to kiss you."

His eyes darkened with an emotion some primitive part of her recognized. Her heart hammered wildly. She knew she should flee or call for help, but her feet refused to move. "You go too far, convict."

"Do I? Or do I, perhaps, not go far enough?"

Chapter Seven

C ole tucked a finger gently under her chin, and Cassie knew he was going to kiss her.

Though her mind told her she must stop him, her lips tingled in anticipation, and her hands, which should have pushed him away, moved to rest lightly on his chest. She closed her eyes. His breath moved over her face as he bent toward her. One strong arm encircled her, pulled her against his warm, hard body. Then she felt the first tentative brush of his lips against hers, warm and soft. Her heart had nearly ceased beating when she heard the door creak behind them. She jumped away from Cole as if burned.

"Beggin' your pardon, Missy." Nan appeared. "I saw the candle still lit and thought someone might be needin' my help."

"No. Thank you, Nan." Cassie felt her face flush and struggled to compose herself. Her heart was still pounding, and her lips burned.

Nan looked from Cassie to Cole to the broken crockery on the floor, concern plain on her round face.

"I was just clearing the table when I dropped the jug and cut myself. Mr. Braden was good enough to bandage the wound for me."

"With your permission, Mistress, I'll retire now." Cole stepped back.

She forced herself to meet his gaze. His face was a stone mask. The passion she'd seen there only moments ago had vanished.

"Aye. You may go." She tried to sound indifferent. How could she have lost her head so?

He walked past Nan and out the door.

"You, too, Nan. You're always up with the sun. I can take care of this mess."

"Now, don't go thinkin' ye can pull the wool over these old eyes." Nan bent her heavy form to pick up the scattered shards. "Somethin' happened in here, all right."

"It was nothing, really." Cassie joined her, careful this time to avoid the sharp edges. "He missed supper, so I gave him some stew. We had a bit of an argument, and I dropped the jug. That's all."

"A tiff, eh?"

"He was just bandaging my hand."

Nan looked anything but convinced. She rose with a grunt and carried the shards to the tin bucket containing the evening's oyster shells, "Do ye think he's cobbin' us all, Missy?"

"I don't know."

One minute it seemed obvious to her he was lying in an effort to escape his sentence. The next she was almost certain he was telling the truth. How was she to know for sure?

"Don't ye think ye should find out before ye fall for 'im?"

"Fall for him? Me? Oh, Nan, surely you don't think I would..."

The cook's eyes showed that she did. Cassie started to object.

"Well, I'm puttin' these old bones to bed."

"Nan!"

"Good night, Missy." Nan took the steps carefully and shut the door behind her.

Cassie stomped and swore. This was all his fault. He'd known what he was doing. Why else would he have taken his time bandaging her hand, practically seducing her? He'd probably planned to kiss her all along. She had played into his hands so easily. Now Nan, whose instincts Cassie had always trusted, was suggesting she was becoming enamored of the knave. Was she?

Of course not! Though she had to admit his being a convict and as handsome as he was made him fascinating in a beastly sort of way, he was hardly the kind of man a woman would choose to love. But then she remembered the heat of his gaze and the softness of his lips as they brushed fleetingly over hers—and she wondered whether a woman could fall in love against her will.

A lec followed the sound of the drums, letting the pulsing beats drown out the pounding of his own heart. What was happening to him? He'd lusted after women before. He'd even thought himself in love once or twice. But never had he lost control of his own actions.

He had not meant to kiss her. But then he hadn't expected to find the feel of her skin so tantalizing. He hadn't planned on being bewitched by her emerald eyes or enthralled by the sound of her voice and the scent of her skin. When he'd seen the effect his touch had on her, something in him had snapped.

This was insane! He was acting like a stag in rut. Of all the women in Virginia, why did he have to lust for the one he could not have, the one he could never trust, the one whose father *owned* him? Perhaps he wanted her simply because he could not have her. Perhaps it excited him to court disaster. He'd not been himself since he landed on these shores.

Or perhaps she was simply the most enchanting female he'd ever met.

Regardless, he had to put her out of his mind for good. The sooner, the better. He could ill afford the consequences should his appetite for her become common knowledge. While even King Carter would have considered him an exceptional catch had Alec wed one of the land baron's daughters with his name intact, pursuing Miss Blakewell as a convict put at risk his own life and her reputation, though he suspected the latter was already tarnished because of her son. Who was the boy's father? The man deserved a sound thrashing for abandoning her and the boy.

Ahead, he could see slaves gathered around a bonfire. Women were singing and dancing to the beat of the drums. The rhythm and movements were like nothing Alec had ever seen. There seemed to be no discernible pattern of steps, as with the dances he knew. Instead figures moved about in a combination of leaps and slower, more sensual motions, shouting and singing. All English accounts he had read of African tribal culture described the ceremonies as primitive, but Alec brushed that term aside. Their dancing and singing under these circumstances seemed an act of defiance, of spirit.

He spied Luke sitting just beyond the light of the fire and headed toward him. Rather than returning his greeting, Luke eyed him suspiciously and stood. The drumming and dancing ceased, and Alec realized the slaves were staring at him, even the children.

"I apologize. I didn't mean to interrupt. I was enjoying the music." It had not occurred to him he might not be welcome among them. Though Alec was aware that many of the indentured servants did not like Africans and disliked having to live and work with them, he had not realized the slaves felt the same way about the English. Certainly Socrates had never pushed him away. "Please continue. Forgive my intrusion."

Somewhere in the crowd, hushed words were exchanged in an unfamiliar tongue. As he turned to go, someone placed a hand on his shoulder.

"Stay." Luke motioned for him to sit on a tree stump.

Alec looked from Luke to the other faces, illuminated by the light from the fire so their dark skin seemed to glow. Their eyes held suspicion and curiosity, but not the outright hatred he'd glimpsed in some of the bondsmen. He sat. The drumming resumed, the dancing and singing with it.

Luke smiled. "You are a strange one, Cole Braden."

"Do bondsmen never join you around your fires?"

Luke laughed loudly. "The white servants would rather choke to death than sit with a slave."

"But they work beside you all day."

"That's why they hate us. They're ashamed to work same as us, to live same as us. They know they're gonna be free again one day and we won't. See for yourself." Luke pointed.

Alec glanced across the field toward the cabins to see redemptioners staring at him, surprise and disgust etched on their faces. He had obviously violated an unspoken rule everyone here accepted without question. He'd always believed Socrates had embellished his stories of cruelty and bigotry to make them more exciting, but now Alec was beginning to think Socrates had been restrained in the telling.

He dismissed the bondsmen and turned his attention to the dancing women. Their bare feet kicked up dust. Their limbs glowed with sweat. Their sensual movements did nothing to calm his overly stimulated blood. Someone tapped him on the shoulder and handed him a cider jug. Welcoming the chance for a drink, he smiled his thanks, tossed back the jug, and swallowed deeply. Unholy liquid fire burned its way down his throat and into his stomach, making him gasp for air and causing his eyes to water.

Luke and the men around him laughed. This was not fermented cider, but the strongest, most lethal whiskey he'd ever tasted.

"Satan!" He shook his head, feeling like a young lad given his first taste of Scotch. "You might have warned me."

Luke grinned and shrugged.

Not willing to be outdone, Alec took another swig and, apart from a slight grimace, managed to control his response.

"Where'd you learn to make that?" he asked hoarsely, passing the jug to Luke, who swallowed it as if it were water.

"Old Charlie say the master taught 'im."

"The master?"

"In the old days he used to come and share a jug with us." The elderly man Alec assumed was Old Charlie gave him a wide, toothless grin. "But Miss Cassie, she don't know 'bout it. It seems she thinks corn ought to be for eatin'."

The men around him burst into laughter.

Alec smiled at their good humor, pondering what he'd just learned. The master used to drink with his slaves.

"I've never met Master Blakewell. What kind of man is he?"

Someone cleared his throat. Old Charlie looked at the ground.

"We're just his slaves," one of them said at last.

It was a strange response, almost is if... They were hiding something.

The whiskey made the night air seem even warmer. Alec accepted another swig, then sat back and watched the dancing. The young woman he recognized as Nettie seemed to have her gaze on Luke. She was tall for a woman, with long, coffee-brown limbs, a slender waist, and pert breasts that swayed provocatively beneath her dress, which she had lifted to give her feet more freedom. Her hair was wrapped in a flowered scarf. Whenever she faced in their direction, she looked directly at Luke with large brown eyes that glittered with excitement. Her invitation was unmistakable.

Luke, however, seemed not to notice.

"She seems to favor you," Alec pointed out.

Luke frowned, the humor that had danced in his eyes only moments gone. "She's young. She don't know what she's doin'."

"She seems to know perfectly well what she's doing."

For a moment Luke said nothing. When at last he spoke, his voice was so low that Alec might not have heard him had he not been sitting beside him. "I had a wife once. We had us a child—a girl. But the master, he died. His son, the new master, had himself a rotten heart. He wanted my wife. He took her."

Luke reached for the whiskey and drank deeply, then spoke again, his voice devoid of emotion. "I came back from the fields to find her cryin', her face bruised. I ran to the house and demanded to see the dog, but he kept hisself hid. I warned him, tellin' him I'd kill him if he touched her again.

"That night I broke the blade off a bucksaw, made her a knife. The next mornin' the master had the overseer flog me for threatenin' him. I didn't care, as long as he stayed away."

Alec's gaze dropped to the lash scars peeking out from under Luke's shirt.

"But he came again, and she cut him. Gave him an ugly scar across his face. He broke her neck."

"I'm sorry." Alec struggled to comprehend what he'd just heard. Then the horrifying question came to him. "Where is your daughter?"

"He done sold her. Then he sold me."

"And you have no idea where she is?"

"I wouldn't be here if I did." Luke motioned toward the bondsmen with a jerk of his head. "Now you see why they hate us. Someday they're gonna own land, and that means they're gonna own slaves. If they're good to us now, they can't treat us like animals later."

Redemptioners huddled with their families around cookfires near their cabins, sending Alec disapproving glances.

Luke stood, then walked out of the circle of firelight into the darkness of the forest.

Nettie follow him. She returned moments later, disappointment on her face.

The dancing ceased. The slaves broke into groups, as families and friends spoke to one another in low voices and returned to their cabins for the night.

Alec thanked the men who'd shared their devil's brew with him, stood, and walked toward his cabin. In the distance he saw dim light spilling from the upstairs windows of the great house, and his mind returned to Miss Blakewell, whom he had desired so fiercely just a short time ago. Now she seemed repulsive to him. She lived, if not in outright luxury, then in comfort, while outside her door, men and women lived in squalor as her chattel. How many men and women worked each day to support her family?

One hundred and fifty? Two hundred? The majority of them would do so until the day they died, as would their children and their grandchildren.

There was no way under heaven to justify it. No way at all.

"Ye've got a taste for darkies?" A grizzled old Scotsman stepped into Alec's path. His small, piggish eyes glared at Alec with undisguised contempt, work-roughened fingers scratching at the stubble of his beard.

"Have you got something to say to me, man?"

"Ye'd be wise to stick with yer own kind. True, some of their lasses are pretty enough to make a man fair burst his codpiece—" Alec grabbed the Scot by his collar, cutting his words short, and lifted him until only his toes touched the ground.

"Watch your mouth, old man, or I'll knock the few teeth you still have down your miserable throat!" With that, he pitched the man into the dirt and walked off.

"Ye'd best watch yer back!" the Scot yelled.

Alec ignored him.

"Cole!"

Alec walked on.

"Blast it, Braden!"

"What do you want?" Alec spun around to find Zach following him.

Zach threw up his hands in a mock gesture of surrender, a grin on his face. "I'm not fixin' to fight."

"That bastard's lucky I didn't smash his skull in."

"This is how it is here," Zach said. "There's nothin' ye can do about it except get yer fool head knocked off."

"Is that a threat?" Alec took a step toward Zach, knowing full well the ham-fisted young man could easily break his neck.

"No. I'm against slavery, too. But in most places these days it's harder bein' a bondsman than a slave."

"Why do I find that hard to believe?" Alec turned and resumed walking toward his cabin.

Zach fell in beside him. "Slaves are worth a sight more than servants, considerin' they belong to their masters forever."

Alec snorted in disgust. "I fail to see your point."

"Bondsmen serve their masters for seven years, slaves for a lifetime. When a slave takes sick, his master pays to doctor 'im. He feeds his slaves well and hopes they'll breed. But a bondsman isn't worth as much. If he takes sick, the master is just as apt to let 'im die as nurse 'im to health. If he can save coin by feedin' 'im less, even if it means starvin' 'im, he will. A bondsmaid found with child is likely to be flogged and forced to serve longer, even if it's the master's babe she's carryin'."

Alec shook his head in disgust, stopping in front of his cabin.

"Like I said, Braden, we're lucky. Miss Cassie and her father are fair to slave and servant alike. They've been mighty good to you. I've heard most convicts are kept in shackles and chained to their beds at night."

"This is barbaric."

"You'll pardon me for sayin' so, but it isn't that different from jolly old England."

"What do you mean by that?"

"I knew what I'd be facin' when I came here, but I came anyway. I was tired of bowin' and scrapin' to gentlemen who weren't worth their own weight in dung."

Alec felt his temper begin to rise again. "Owing deference to one's superiors can hardly be equated with slavery."

"I say it is slavery."

"Luke's wife was raped and killed by his master, Zach. In England, the bastard would have been hanged for it. Here, no one looks twice."

"Aye, he'd have swung—if the court convicted him. But how often are gentlemen made to account for crimes against the common folk? You claim to be a landed gent. How many women spread their legs for you because they felt they had no choice?"

Alec's fist connected squarely with Zach's face, knocking Zach flat on his back in the dirt. "Goddamn you, man, I've *never* used my station to force myself on *any* woman!"

The pain in his knuckles was nothing compared to the rage that surged through his veins. Then he thought of Philip and the alewife's daughter. Rage was replaced by a vague sense of nausea.

Zach sat up with a moan, massaging his jaw. "God's balls! Ye pack one hell of a wallop, Braden—or whatever yer name is. I'll give ye that one, because I earned it. But don't do that again. I don't want to have to hurt yer pretty face." Zach laughed heartily, his eye already beginning to swell.

Alec helped him to his feet, feeling enraged with himself, with Miss Blakewell, with the whole insane situation. "That was poorly done."

"Don't go givin' me none of that gentleman shite. Like I said, I earned it." Zach slapped him on the back. "What kind of concern did ye say ye owned back in England?"

"A shipbuilding firm."

"Who buys your fine vessels?"

Alec did not understand the change of subject, but he was too tired to care. "Most of our contracts are with the Royal Navy. But we also sell ships to merchants."

"To merchants?"

"The East India Company, traders to the Baltic and the Levant, long-distance merchants in Liverpool and—"

"Slave traders?"

Alec felt as if he'd been kicked in the stomach.

Chapter Eight

*C*assie barely heard the thunder that disturbed her dreams, snuggling deeper into the softness of her bed.

"Do I? Or do I, perhaps, not go far enough?"

Cole's arms encircled her and pulled her against him. The smell of his skin and the feel of his hard body were intoxicating, but not nearly as exciting as the feel of his lips as they took hers. He kissed her with a tenderness that turned her body to liquid and flooded her with desire. "Cole!" she whispered against his throat, entwining her fingers in his thick, dark hair.

"Don't you think you should find out if he's telling the truth before you fall for him, Missy?" Nan asked as she washed dishes somewhere behind them.

The truth? Yes, the truth. The truth was she wanted him to keep kissing her.

His lips possessed hers as his hands worked gently to free her hair from its pins.

Rolls of thunder pierced her sleep completely.

It was raining.

Rain.

Cassie sat upright, suddenly wide awake. It was finally raining!

She leaped from bed, ran to her balcony doors, and threw back the curtains. Though it was past dawn, the overcast sky gave the impression of daybreak. Quickly she donned an old chemise and an underskirt, delighted to be free for at least one day of the infernal tightness of a corset and the silliness of stockings. Why women should have to wear such uncomfortable clothing in the first place, she didn't know. Her old yellow dress, although tight around the bosom and a bit too short, would be perfect for what lay ahead.

She had just pulled the threadbare gown over her head when a knock came at her door. It was Rebecca.

"Micah said to wake you, Missy, but I see you're already up," she said with a curtsy.

"I'm on my way. If you could help Nan today, I'd be grateful. I'm taking Elly to the seedbeds."

"Aye, Missy."

The two women shared a conspiratorial smile. Elly was going to hate this.

Cassie decided to forgo wearing shoes and, grabbing a frayed ribbon, followed Rebecca down the stairs, tying back her hair as she went. From the hallway she saw that Jamie's bed was empty. He was no doubt already playing in the puddles. He'd always been an early riser, though usually he crawled into her bed and waited for her to wake up before going outdoors.

The rain was heavy and cool and brought with it a sense of giddiness even as it soaked her dress and hair and trickled down her skin, leaving goose bumps. Since she was a small child she had loved planting days. Not only was the normal routine abandoned, but propriety was tossed to the wind. Mud became the fashion. Master, servant, and slave worked together in an air of celebration—at least on Blakewell's Neck—putting in the crop upon which all depended for survival. Although few planters these days actually worked with their servants, her father had maintained the practice even when the need no longer existed, saying it reminded him of the old days when slaves were scarce, and planter, slave, and servant slept in the same house, ate the same food at the same table. Cassie, who'd been allowed to work in the fields, intended to uphold his tradition.

She crossed the courtyard to the cookhouse.

Elly greeted her with a look of defiance. "I'm not goin' out there."

"Yes, you are." Cassie realized she'd been looking forward to this moment for a very long time. To see mulish Elly Lanham covered head to toe in mud would bring her great joy. It wasn't very Christian of her to delight in another's misery, but she'd never claimed to be a saint.

"This isn't proper work for a lady!"

"Here in Virginia it is."

"But other women are staying behind!" Elly motioned toward the cabins, where women bustled about preparing the food that would be brought to the fields at midday.

"Only the older women and those with small children are spared from the fields on planting days, Elly, and they work just as hard as the rest of us."

"Eleanor!" Nan was bent over the hearth stirring porridge. "Do as your mistress bids."

Within five minutes Cassie had gulped down her breakfast and was on her way to supervise planting at the east seedbeds, Elly trailing unwillingly behind. Micah, with Jamie's "help," was already directing workers at the beds behind the drying shed. On a clear day the walk would have taken her a mere ten minutes. But in the mud, with Elly straggling behind her, it seemed to take forever. Cassie had half a mind to send the girl back to the kitchen, but to do so would reward the bondsmaid's petulant behavior.

Cassie looked for Cole as she walked along but did not see him. She had not forgotten for one moment what had passed between them last night, though how it could have happened, she still did not understand. Nan was right. To think of him as she had allowed herself to think of him—to allow him to kiss her!—before she knew the truth about his identity was sheer folly. And dangerous. The man was most probably a liar—a liar and a convicted seducer of women, who was trying to wile his way into winning his freedom or at least a night in her bed. He'd admitted to the sheriff he'd bedded married women. How honest could such a man be, convict or gentleman?

Certainly she should thank the cook for her timely intrusion, though how she'd bring herself to tell Nan the truth she did not know. She had to get control of her feelings before she compromised everything that mattered to her. Gaining the respect of the bondsmen and slaves, who were not predisposed to taking direction from a woman, had been difficult enough to start with, even though she'd had help from Zach, Micah, and Nan in winning them over. She could not afford to lose any ground.

Yet even as she swore never to let it happen again, she remembered how gently he'd touched her, how warm his lips had been as he kissed her hand. Though his actions had at first surprised her, there'd been no force or coercion. That was the worst of it. She'd *wanted* him to kiss her. She'd dreamed about it all night.

Had he? He'd seemed as affected as she, his eyes blazing with an intensity that made her insides knot up even now. Why, then, had he looked at her as if he were made of granite just moments later? Clearly the kiss had meant nothing to him. He was merely toying with her.

"Mornin', Miss Cassie." Zach gave her a dimpled grin. He was drenched, his hands full of seedlings. His right eye was bruised and swollen.

"What happened?" Cassie and Elly asked almost in unison.

Elly stood on tiptoe and touched her fingers to his cheek, making him wince.

"Nothin'." He pushed Elly's hand away.

"Does it hurt?" asked Elly.

"Did corn whiskey have anything to do with this?" Cassie demanded. "You know I don't approve of that vile brew. Or brawling for that matter."

"It's not what you think."

"Does it hurt?" Elly asked again.

"Who hit you?" Cassie would see the culprit punished. "Don't bother trying to protect him. I'd wager he looks a sight worse than you do. It won't take much to find him."

"Would ye let a man speak?"

Chagrined, Cassie realized they'd been hurling questions at him without giving him the chance to answer. Elly stood beside her, arms akimbo, glaring up at him.

"Last night I was talkin' with Braden, and my mouth got the best of me. That's all."

"Cole hit you?"

Of course. It had to be. No other man on the plantation would have dared to strike Zach.

"Aye, and a good one, too." Zach smiled and rubbed his cheek. "But don't worry. I deserved it, so I didn't hit him back."

"You *let* the convict hit you?" Cassie would never understand men.

"Well, I didn't let him exactly."

"Very well." She'd have to talk to Cole later. Or perhaps Micah could do it. Right now she didn't want to be anywhere near the convict. "Would you care to teach Elly how to transplant tobacco?"

Zach was sweet on Elly. This would give them a chance to be together, and it would get Elly out of her hair.

Zach's smile vanished. "I think she'd rather have someone else teach her."

Cassie caught a quick exchange of glances between the two, who now faced each other as if they were carved from stone. "Well, I'm sure I don't know whom she could have in mind. You're more experienced than most."

"That's what I keep tryin' to tell her." Zach grinned.

Elly turned beet red, looked away.

Cassie got the feeling she was missing something. "Go with Zach," she ordered, her patience gone. Why was everything about this morning proving to be difficult?

"This way, Miss Lanham." Zach turned and strode toward the fields, Elly following sulkily behind him.

Glad to be rid of the quarrelsome girl, Cassie turned toward the seedbeds, acknowledging the greetings of those she passed. She joined Takotah, who was busy unearthing seedlings and passing them to waiting hands. Despite her age, which no one, including Takotah, knew for certain, Takotah worked tirelessly. Even though she'd often questioned the English obsession with growing large amounts of tobacco only to put it on ships and send it halfway around the world, she nonetheless treated its cultivation with great respect. It was sacred to her people.

"Good day." Takotah gave her a quick smile.

Cassie took up a trowel and began unearthing the tiny plants. Her palm was stiff and sore where she'd cut it, forcing her to dig with her left hand. Despite the awkwardness of it, she quickly established a rhythm. Muddy hands took up the seedlings as fast as she and Takotah could dig them up.

If racing to and from the fields, tiny plants in hand, was tiring, working on one's knees in cold mud digging up seedlings was utterly grueling. Soon her fingers grew numb from the cold, and her back began to ache. She put these small discomforts from her mind, knowing this was only the beginning of a very long day. Planting usually lasted until late in the evening, only to begin again the next morning if the rain held.

The leaden sky concealed the passage of time. Only when she ran out of seedlings did she realize it must be close to the noon hour. She stood stiffly and stretched. Three seedbeds identical to this one awaited her, mere footsteps away. The rain still fell softly, and a cool southwesterly breeze brought a chill to the damp air.

She wiggled her stiff fingers, urging them back to life, and moved down to the next seedbed.

She hadn't been working for long when a cheer went up around her. The hands that had been eagerly taking seedlings from her turned into feet running the other direction. She looked up to see Old Charlie driving the long-awaited lunch wagon toward them. She, too, felt famished. The seedlings would have to wait. A crowd had already converged on the wagon, and Old Charlie and Nettie were trying to turn chaos into an organized food line.

"Now, hold on. Nobody's gonna starve. There's plenty. I said back off, you ragamuffins! You heard me!" Charlie was waving a ladle at some of the more boisterous young men who were trying to climb over the sides of the wagon.

Raucous laughter filled the air as one of them fell backward and landed on his posterior in a puddle. Then, without warning, a shoving match broke out between Cyril, one of the younger slaves, and Henry, the old Scotsman Geoffrey had sent to help.

"I said whites first." Henry pushed his way to the front.

Cyril clenched his fists but stepped away from the wagon, making room for the line of hungry redemptioners, who had no qualms about taking advantage of Henry's bullying.

"There is no pecking order here!" Cassie had to shout to pierce both the din of the storm and the chatter of the hungry workers, repeating herself twice before she had their attention. She pushed through the wet, muddy bodies to the wagon. "Everyone will get his fill, slave and bondsman alike."

She took a water jug and poured the clean liquid over Cyril's hands. "Nettie, feed this man, please. He's hungry."

Nettie nodded and handed a surprised Cyril a tin bowl heaped with steaming corn porridge, a biscuit, and a tin cup brimming with hot cider. As Cyril passed her, the smell of the porridge made Cassie's mouth water and her stomach growl impatiently. The women had tossed in salted pork as an extra reward, and she could almost taste it.

Men and women passed, one by one, rubbing their hands together under the thin stream of water she provided. Henry scowled at her as he passed, his displeasure with her clear. She and Micah had both made it plain to him when he arrived that things were different here and bigotry would not be tolerated, but it was obvious he respected neither of them enough to obey. If he didn't listen, she'd send him back to Geoffrey.

The problem was forgotten the instant she saw Cole approaching. Wet, his dark brown hair looked as black as a raven's wing. He'd managed to keep it tied back despite the rain and physical labor. His white shirt clung to his body, outlining the muscles his arms, abdomen, and chest with disturbing clarity. His breeches, which stuck to his strong thighs like a second skin, were muddy. He looked like an English squire who'd been caught in a downpour while hunting on his estate. Even had he been coated in muck, Cassie suspected his proud bearing and refined features would still lend him the appearance of gentry.

But if he looked like gentry, she must look like the poorest of peasants. Mud coated her from her feet to her bosom and was caked under her nails. No doubt it was also smeared liberally across her face. And her hair, of course, was only partly contained by the ribbon in which she'd tied it this morning. It stuck to her cheek and neck, disappeared under the mud on her bodice. She had never managed to look as beautiful and ladylike as Lucy Carter and her sisters or the other Northern Neck planters' daughters. They never worked in the fields. Their hair was always neatly coifed on top their heads and seemed to stay in place. Their gowns were cut the latest fashions from England and France. It had never really bothered Cassie before, but now that she'd made the comparison, she found herself severely lacking.

She silently cursed herself for her silliness and resolved to put such thoughts from her mind. As Nan was fond of saying, work was a blessing. If Cassie looked like she'd been working hard, she had no reason to be ashamed. If she wanted to, she could stay inside all day, chatting about fashion and beaux and worrying about the size of her waistline. She didn't want to. Besides, who was Cole Braden that she should care what he thought of her appearance.

When Alec had first seen her this morning, he'd not recognized her. Bent over in the dirt, her wet hair hanging in limp curls to her hips and tied back by a single frayed ribbon, she appeared at first to be another servant. Alec had noticed her curves, the way her work dress clung to her back and hips. He'd noticed her pink toes peeking out from underneath her where she'd tucked her feet. He'd noticed the curve of her shoulder, the shapeliness of her arms. He'd wondered how he could have missed such a jewel in a relatively confined space. Then he'd seen her face.

Her cheeks smeared with mud, raindrops rolling from the tip of her nose, her brow furrowed with concentration, she had seemed not the domineering plantation mistress he knew she was, but a charming peasant wench. She had not noticed him, although more than once she'd placed tiny seedlings in his hands. He'd sworn last night he'd not let himself be deceived by her physical charms. For although he could not condemn her for her lifestyle without also condemning himself, he knew she was not to be trusted. Not when she continued to gain from his loss of freedom. Not when her very presence shattered his self-control.

When she'd waded into the argument between Cyril and the grizzled Scot—the same man he'd thrown in the dust last night—he'd been surprised. He hadn't expected her to care. But then, she *had* intervened on his behalf when Crichton struck him. She'd fed him at her own table. Of course, all this really proved was that she—and her father, if the man really existed—were kinder masters than most planters. That was faint praise at best.

As they drew nearer the wagon, Alec noticed Nettie watching Luke, though he still stood behind several men in line. Nettie smiled warmly at Luke, who ignored her and stepped to the front of the line. Miss Blakewell poured a thin stream of water over his hands, acting as if she did not notice Alec. Luke nodded his thanks and accepted a bowl and mug from Nettie without acknowledging her. Nettie frowned ever so slightly.

"How's the hand?" Alec asked, rubbing his palms together vigorously under the clean water.

"Fine, thank you." She seemed to make an effort not to meet his gaze.

Had she thought about last night as much as he had during the past several hours? Then he caught sight of her bosom and felt heat rush to his loins. Somehow she'd managed to squeeze herself into a dress made for a woman with half her natural endowments. Streaked with mud, the rounded tops of her breasts swelled above the bodice. Her nipples, taut from the chill, strained against the cloth of dress, and her skirts clung to her legs, giving an enticing outline of her thighs. Even spattered with mud, she looked disturbingly desirable.

Half forgetting what he was doing standing here in the rain, he accepted a bowl of porridge from Nettie and, spilling a bit of the hot cider on his hand, managed to extract himself from Miss Blakewell's presence.

*B*y the time Cassie had managed to eat, everyone else was already finished and back at work. Using her biscuit to scoop up the last of the warming porridge, she quickly finished and helped Charlie and Nettie secure the contents of the wagon. It was piled high with crocks, bowls, jugs, and pots. It looked as if the women had raided every cabin on the plantation in search of enough bowls to feed them all. Now they'd have the dishes to contend with.

Cassie joined Takotah at the seedbed again. The afternoon passed slowly. Her hands and feet again went numb from cold, but she distracted herself by listening to the gossip of the bondswomen working nearby.

"Rebecca is near as big as a barn. She'll not find it easy to birth that babe of hers."

"Since when is birthin' ever easy?"

The women laughed ruefully.

"Me mother always said to drink a tankard of ale each mornin'. It keeps the babe small. And I've given birth to nine so far."

"Did you do as your mother said?"

"Aye."

"And did it work?"

"Nay. But it helped me keep me sense of humor."

The women's merry laughter made Cassie smile. She did not notice that the cut on her palm had reopened and was bleeding again until Takotah took her wrist and turned her hand over.

"It's nothing." Cassie began to dig again.

"It will not heal well wet and filled with mud. You should clean the wound and let someone else take your place."

"Over something as silly as this?" Cassie wasn't used to dawdling while others toiled.

Takotah seemed to read her mind. "There are many here who can do this work. Show some sense, and take care of that cut."

Cassie swore under her breath. In a battle of wills, she knew she stood no chance against Takotah.

Reluctantly she stood and stretched. She wandered toward the fields, eager to see the results of the day's hard work. Already they'd emptied half of the second seedbed. If the rain continued they'd be finished by tomorrow night. It certainly showed no sign of letting up. The storm clouds continued to thicken, and the sky was dark. She found herself longing for a hot bath and clean, dry clothes.

Rather than walking all the way to the tobacco field itself, she decided to cut through the forest to a nearby hill. From its grassy crest, she'd be able to see all the fields at once. Accustomed to walking barefoot in the forest since she was a little girl, she stepped neatly through the foliage, avoiding nettles and sharp stones. The rain fell gently under the cover of the ancient pine boughs, and the trees gave her shelter from the wind. Birds whistled and chirped in an untrained chorus, their jumbled melodies punctuated by the occasional dissonant croak of a raven. A doe, flushed out of hiding, bounded in front of her. She watched as it leaped gracefully over fallen logs and ferns and disappeared into the trees. It was probably trying to lure her away from a fawn it had hidden in the grass.

The forest had always been her favorite place. Though others feared its darkness and the creatures that roamed among the trees, she had always felt at peace here. Since she was small, she had come alone to its enfolding greenery to daydream. Here, whatever she could imagine became reality. She slowed her steps, inhaling the scents of rain-soaked pine, pungent undergrowth, and wet earth. It was easy to envision a unicorn with a silver mane and tail stepping out from the bushes in front of her. Or a knight in brazen greaves and a chain-mail shirt riding his destrier through the trees on some sacred quest. Or a handsome and dangerous highwayman—

"Taking a stroll, mistress?"

Chapter Nine

*C*assie spun around, startled.

Cole stood not far behind her, leaning lazily against a tree trunk. Where had he come from? She'd thought herself completely alone.

"Wh . . . what are you doing here?"

"I didn't mean to frighten you." He turned to leave.

"You didn't frighten me." She couldn't have him thinking that she was afraid of him. "I was merely . . . startled."

He stopped and faced her, his gaze locking with hers. It occurred to her she was, at this moment, quite unprotected. If he really was the man they claimed he was, he could attack her now. No one would hear her screams. She knew she should be concerned, but she was not. She felt no fear, sensed no malice.

Not that the man didn't look dangerous. The damp shirt clinging to his skin made her intensely aware of his virility and strength. Before she could catch herself, her eyes moved from the muscles of his chest, where his flat nipples stood like dark circles beneath the wet cloth, down his abdomen. Moved by some force she could not name, did not even want to consider, she took a step toward him. Then another.

"The cut on my hand was bleeding. I had to stop." Feeling silly, she sought for words to fill the silence.

His gaze moved over her body, stopping briefly as he perused her breasts and thighs. His gaze was so intimate, he might as well have touched her. The intensity in his eyes when they met hers again made her breath catch in her throat. As if in response, her nipples tightened against the worn fabric of her damp dress. It seemed to Cassie he looked upon her as a starving man might look upon a holiday feast. She involuntarily moved a hand to shield herself.

This time, it was he who stepped closer.

"I saw the black eye you gave Zach." She reached for the safety she felt in authority. As the person who owned Cole's indenture, she was in control. As a woman, the object of his desire, she was vulnerable.

He smiled rakishly. "And you intend to reprimand me?"

"Yes."

"Very well, but don't be too hard on me. I've already apologized, though I must say the man deserved it."

"My father does not tolerate fighting among the men." Her voice carried none of the reproach she'd intended to convey, but in truth, speech had become most difficult.

If his eyes revealed desire, they were a mirror for the torrent of emotion that sprang from somewhere deep within her and flooded every part of her body.

"And well he should not."

"Wh...what are you doing here?"

"The rain reminds me of England." There was sadness in his voice. "What are *you* doing here, Mistress?"

"I wanted to climb the knoll, look out over the fields."

"You should be careful. There could be predators about." He reached for the hand that covered her bosom, gently brought it to his lips, and placed a lazy kiss on the inside of her wrist. She could not help the thrill that passed through her body when his lips touched her skin.

Alec knew he was a fool to do this, but damned if he could make himself just walk away. He had tried. As God was his witness, he had tried. Then she had spoken and come toward him, looking like some wild forest sprite from a pagan legend. The rain had washed most of the mud from her face and arms, and her wet dress hung limply on her body, outlining her breasts, her hips, her thighs. Even dressed in muddy rags, her long hair in wild disarray, she put Isabelle with all of her fine silks and careful grooming to shame. Her wide green eyes held none of the practiced seductiveness he'd seen in the women he'd known. Instead her eyes gave play to every emotion that passed through her—wariness, confusion, the stirrings of desire.

With a frustrated groan he slipped an arm behind her back and pulled her to him, capturing her lips with his in a fierce kiss that shattered what was left of his self-control.

Rain.

Warm honey.

He ran his tongue over her lips, urging them apart. He felt her stiffen with surprise, then felt her relax, her tongue joining tentatively with his.

Her arms slipped behind his neck.

"Cassie." He kissed her forehead and cheeks.

She gazed at him from under half-closed lids, her eyes dark with arousal.

"God, woman, you're driving me mad." He returned to her lips with a growl, overcome by an all-consuming hunger that defied logic and made a mockery of his attempts to control it. He felt her arch against him, molding the soft curves of her body to his. A small whimper escaped her. He bent to taste her throat, raising goose bumps along her wet skin. Her shy responses told him that, though she had borne a child, she was still unpracticed when it came to sex. For some reason the thought was exhilarating.

He buried his face in the thickness of her hair, pulled loose the ribbon that still held most of it prisoner, and took the heavy mass of wet curls in his hands. He felt her kiss his throat, timidly at first, then boldly, her lips hot against his skin.

Was this worth getting his neck stretched?

Some rational part of him fought for his attention. Her tongue traced a path across the sensitive skin on his neck. Her hands cautiously explored the muscles of his chest.

Sweet Jesus, yes.

Cassie felt as if she might faint. This was like nothing she'd imagined. What he was doing with his tongue had never been a part of any daydream. Did people really kiss like this? His arms held her even tighter, his hands pressing into the flesh of her back, the heat of his rigid sex startling her as it pressed against her belly. He was so hard and warm, and he tasted of salt and rain. She let her hands explore the planes of his back through the irritating obstacle of his shirt.

What was she doing?

His lips and tongue explored her throat and cheek, his kisses leaving a trail of heat. Some small part of her knew she should flee. She was practically making love with a man whose identity she could neither disprove nor confirm. A man who could be a dangerous convict. A man she'd sworn only hours earlier to avoid.

"Stop! I . . . we can't."

He released her, his face now hard, the gleam in his eyes the only sign that he was feeling anything at all. "You play a dangerous game, Mistress."

She watched him walk away.

He was right. She *was* playing a dangerous game. What if she'd suddenly found herself on her back, her skirts lifted to her waist, his hands around her throat? No one would have felt the slightest sympathy for her. In the eyes of society, women who allowed themselves to be alone with men deserved whatever they got. But no. He'd had his chance to violate her, but he hadn't. If he hadn't exactly been gentle, well, he certainly had not hurt her.

What if she had lost herself completely, allowed him to take her just now? Would it have been as pleasurable as his kisses? Would she have enjoyed it? Would he have started a baby growing inside her? Something in her blood ran hot at the very thought. Still, however she might long for children, the public humiliation of bearing a bastard was not a price she wanted to pay. If anyone discovered the child's father was a convict, she'd be dragged through the streets, perhaps flogged. It had happened more than once. It was said no woman could lie about the identity of her babe's father while suffering the pangs of childbirth.

What had she done? The future of the plantation and all who lived on it depended upon her keeping a level head. If only her body wouldn't betray her like this. She wrapped her arms around her waist to still her trembling.

*A*lec slowed the galloping stallion to a walk and smiled with satisfaction at the powerful animal's instantaneous response. He'd been working with Aldebaran every day for two weeks and was pleased with the horse's progress. Though initially stiff from lack of proper exercise, the stallion was daily improving in both speed and stamina. With continued training, there'd not be a horse in the entire colony that could outrun this creature.

He patted the animal reassuringly on its withers as Aldebaran jerked on the reins, signaling his eagerness to run again. "We'll go even farther tomorrow. I promise."

He'd ridden Aldebaran through the fields and down a muddy and rutted wagon road toward the Rappahannock. Pine forest now gave way to brackish marshland and sandy beaches—and the grandest river he had ever seen. He stopped for a moment to breathe the salt-tinged air and watch the dark waters roll toward Chesapeake Bay. Gulls drifted on air currents or bobbed on the surface of the river, their cries carried aloft on the humid breeze. Water lapped against the sandy shore, where sandpipers scoured the shallows for their midday meal. Mosquitoes, revived by the recent rains, gathered in hungry, buzzing swarms in the shadows. In the hazy distance, he saw the opposite shore, a blurry dark line against the cloudy sky. These waters had brought him here, and they would take him home again—one way or another.

How simple it would be to ride off on Aldebaran and not return. He could plunge into the current, where dogs could not follow his scent, and swim with the horse to the other side. Then he could ride upriver to Hobbes Hole or head over land and river toward Williamsburg. Once the horse was in top form, he'd be able to stay far ahead of any pursuers. With any luck he'd be able to join the crew of a ship bound for England before the reward posters and word of mouth caught up with him. The plan had its flaws, but sitting astride Aldebaran and watching the river flow toward the Chesapeake and freedom, he was sorely tempted to try.

But he had given his word, and he would keep it. For now. The sheriff had sent a message several days ago saying he'd soon be arriving with two convicts who'd come over on the *Easy Mary* and claimed to have met Nicholas Braden in Newgate. There was no sense in Alec's risking the dangers of an escape when he could be a free man any day. He reluctantly turned the stallion's head and, with the slightest movement of his heels against the animal's flank, brought Aldebaran to a canter.

He let the wind rush through his hair and tried to clear his mind. It had been a fortnight since his foolhardy tryst in the forest with Cassie ... Miss Blakewell, he corrected himself, eager to force whatever distance he could between himself and his damnably lovely "mistress." How could he have been so stupid? It was not like him to be led about by his cock. He'd never lost his head over anything, much less a woman. Yet, had Cass... Miss Blakewell ... not objected, bringing him back to reality, he would have taken her then and there, consequences be damned.

She had apparently kept the incident to herself and seemed as eager to avoid him as he was her. She spent her days tending the garden and helping the cook in the kitchen. He took long rides around the plantation and worked in the stables. When they were forced to be near one another, as they had been when he'd saddled her mare earlier today, he found his craving for her as overwhelming as it had been on that rainy afternoon in the forest.

Where had she gone this morning? Riding out at roughly the same time each day, she always left carrying a basket laden with food and drink far more than one woman could eat alone. No explanations were given. When he'd questioned the cook, Nan had made up a story about Miss Blakewell taking Jamie for a picnic, yet Jamie had remained near the house all day. There seemed only one explanation: She had a lover. Perhaps the very man who'd fathered little Jamie, only to forsake her and the boy.

Why should it bother him? Isabelle had had other lovers. Most of Alec's lovers had been married women who returned to their husbands' beds after warming his. Never once had he cared. But the thought of Cass ... Miss Blakewell making love with another man ate at him until he found himself plotting like some jealous husband to follow her. One glimpse of her slender throat, one whiff of her skin, one moment's contact—even the sound of her voice—and his balls began to ache. When he went to bed at night, his mind was filled with her: her scent, the feel of her skin, the image of her—eyes closed, lips parted and swollen from his kisses. Not even old Charlie's lethal corn whiskey drove her from his thoughts. He wanted her. He wanted her beneath him, bared to his touch, moaning with unbridled pleasure. He wanted her to cry his real name as he brought her to her climax and found his own within her.

Alec shifted, uncomfortable in the saddle, and cursed. To imagine such things only made his predicament worse. To have her was impossible, or at least a very bad idea. Miss Blakewell was nothing but trouble.

He was so caught up in his thoughts that he didn't notice the man hiding among the trees watching him.

*C*assie stood in the doorway of the cookhouse and sighed with pleasure as, at last, a sticky breeze caught her, bringing some relief from the almost unbearable heat. The morning's rain had left the ground muddy, the air heavy and humid. Though the cooking fire in the hearth had burned itself low since midday, the kitchen was a furnace. She'd worn her pale green cotton gown, the lightest one she owned, and still she was uncomfortable. Standing over steaming dishwater, as she had been for the past twenty minutes, only made matters worse.

"I'd wager even Satan thinks 'tis hot today." Nan sat at the table, peeling potatoes.

"Aye." But Cassie was only half listening.

The slow *click-clack* of a horse's hooves on cobblestone grew louder. She withdrew into the shadows, where she could not easily be seen and watched as Cole led Aldebaran through the courtyard toward the well, Jamie following behind. The past two weeks had taught her he had not been lying when he'd said he was skilled with horses. She'd made a point of checking up on his work at night and had been both pleased and surprised with the results. The stables had been cleaned and reorganized; the tack cleaned, oiled, and hung; broken boards and shingles replaced. The horses had been groomed from forelock to heel, and several had been reshod. Aldebaran, the only horse of which Cassie had ever been remotely afraid, had responded to his handling like a frisky but harmless puppy. It seemed she was not the only living creature rendered pliant by this man's touch.

As if he knew she was thinking of him, Cole glanced her way before tying off Aldebaran's reins and lowering the bucket to draw water. She stifled a gasp as he looked directly at her, but his eyes passed lightly over her, as though he did not see her. He looked so like an English country gentleman, with his proud bearing and long, graceful stride. Alec Kenleigh. She allowed herself to whisper the name, testing it. For what must have been the thousandth time since receiving the sheriff's dispatch, she found herself hoping Cole was telling the truth. It would assuage her guilty conscience greatly to know she craved the touch of a gentleman and not a lying felon.

And crave his touch she did. She could no longer deny it. She thought of Cole every waking moment. Not a night had passed this week or last when she had not lain in bed and remembered, in tantalizing detail, what had happened between them. She'd been burning with questions since then. Was it always like this between men and women? Was she a loose woman for having wanted it so? Was it possible to make these feelings go away?

But whom could she ask?

Not Nan. The cook might, out of fear for her safety, tell Micah, and then Cole's indenture was as good as sold. Besides, Nan had never married and wasn't supposed to know about such things.

Not Rebecca. Though Rebecca was a married woman with a child in her belly, Cassie was her mistress and could ill afford to lose her respect. If news of her feelings for Cole became common knowledge among the redemptioners, they'd have nothing but contempt for her.

The only person left was Takotah. Cassie knew Takotah would take her secret to the grave. Still, Cassie couldn't bring herself to tell anyone what had happened. How could she possibly explain it when she did not understand it herself?

She was about to return to washing dishes when she saw Jamie clamber up the stone side of the well to pat the stallion on the head. She started to scold him and tell him to climb down when Aldebaran shrieked and reared.

The reins went taut and caught Jamie's legs.

Cassie screamed and ran toward him.

In horror she watched as Jamie toppled backward into the well.

Chapter Ten

"*J*amie!"
Deadly hooves slashed through the air around her, striking wood and brick. Heedless of the danger, Cassie dashed past the screaming horse and looked over the well's rim.

Her heart stopped.

Somehow Cole had managed to catch one of Jamie's ankles. Below Jamie loomed darkness.

"Cut the reins!" she heard Cole shout.

The stallion shrieked and reared, jerking at the bonds that restrained him.

Cassie darted back to the cookhouse, where Nan stood, mouth agape in horror, and grabbed the potato knife from her hands. Sharp, hard hooves were everywhere, chipping wood, masonry, cobblestone.

Not even thinking, Cassie dashed back, grabbed the reins, and cut through the tough leather.

Aldebaran reared once more, his dark eyes rolling in his head, then galloped away.

"I won't let you go." Cole spoke to Jamie, his voice soothing.

Jamie's frightened whimpers echoed from below.

Cassie peered over the rim, unable to breathe, as Cole slowly pulled Jamie up.

"I've got you." Cole slowly lifted Jamie over the edge and into his arms. "Take him."

Cassie grabbed for her brother, hugged him to her, and carried him to the cookhouse steps, where she sank in a trembling heap.

"Praise the Lord!" Nan cried. "Bless ye, Cole Braden! Bless ye!"

"It's all right. It's all right." Cassie did her best to reassure Jamie, but couldn't stop the quavering of her voice. "You're safe, love."

Was that Jamie crying, or was it her?

She kissed him over and over on his downy curls, holding him tightly. "Don't ever climb up there! And stay away from that stallion, do you hear me?"

Fear made her words sound angry. She held him tighter, stroking his hair.

In her arms, Jamie whimpered.

"It wasn't the stallion's fault."

Cassie looked up to see Cole doff his shirt and hurry toward them.

"That animal nearly killed all three of us! Jamie didn't do anything to frighten—"

"It wasn't Jamie's fault, either."

It was then that Cassie saw the angry red welts on his chest, arms, and abdomen. "Oh, Cole!"

"If I were you I'd get indoors," he said. "I think those hornets are feeling spiteful."

Then Cassie heard it—a faint buzzing sound.

"Hurry!" Nan scolded. "I'll nae have those devils swarmin' into me kitchen!"

Gathering Jamie in her arms, Cassie stood and stepped quickly inside, Cole behind her.

"They've made a nest in the mortar." He closed the door behind them. "We'll need to smoke them out before we can seal the crack." Cassie sat Jamie on the table and searched his skin for welts.

"Did they sting you, love?"

Jamie shook his head, sniffing back tears.

But more than a dozen angry red blotches stood out against the skin of Cole's chest, with more on his arms and belly.

"I'll go find some mud." He moved toward the back door.

"Nonsense." Cassie took a jar of soda from the shelf. "What good will mud do? Sit down."

"Yes, mistress." Cole grinned.

"Should I fetch Takotah?" Nan asked.

"No need." Cassie ignored Nan's curious expression. "Find Zach and tell him about the nest. I don't want anyone else to get stung."

"Aye, Missy. Come along, lad." Nan picked Jamie up, settling him on her ample hip. "I'll nae be lettin' ye out of me sight again. Gave me old heart the fright of my life, ye did. I've a notion to tan yer backside."

*W*hat felt like a hundred white-hot needles pierced Alec's skin, burning and itching. He watched as Cassie poured a small amount of the white powder into a bowl and added water from the nearby pitcher, making a thick paste. She scooped the paste onto her fingertips, stood before him, and dabbed it onto the swellings. The paste was cool against his skin, her light touch soothing.

"Don't they hurt?" Her eyelashes cast shadows on her cheek, and her forehead was knitted with concentration.

He reached out to touch a wayward curl, but caught himself and pulled his hand back. "Aye, they sting."

She stopped and looked up at him, her green eyes wide. Tears had left tracks on her cheeks. "How did you manage to hold on?"

Alec remembered Jamie's terrified little face as he fell, Cassie's heartrending scream. "I wouldn't have let go for anything."

He brushed his fingertips over the smoothness of her cheek. It was a mistake.

She moved away from his touch as if scorched. Finished with his chest, she walked behind him. She worked quickly now, smoothing paste over the welts on his back and shoulders as if she couldn't wait to be rid of him.

"There." She stepped back. "That should calm the itching and bring the swelling down."

Remarkably, it already had. Only the welts on his thighs bothered him now.

"I believe I've some on my legs."

Cassie looked down at his thighs, her eyes resting for a moment on his groin. Her cheeks flushed pink, and she looked up at him with something akin to horror in her eyes.

Alec couldn't help but laugh. "I can handle that part myself." He took the small bowl from her. "If you'll excuse me, I'll tend to myself and then find Aldebaran."

He had reached the back steps and was about to leave when she spoke.

" I . . . don't know how to thank you. What you did was—"

He turned to find her watching him, her hands twisting nervously in the folds of her skirts. "We were lucky."

He stepped outside and walked toward his cabin, certain she was still watching him.

*T*he hornet's nest was the object of much curiosity for the rest of the afternoon. Children watched from a distance as the men examined it, built a fire beneath it, and flushed the bothersome insects from their hiding place.

The acrid scent of smoke still hung in the air when Cassie stepped from the cookhouse, where she had been chopping carrots and leeks for their dinner of turtle soup. She needed to find Cole. She hadn't seen him since he'd left this afternoon, and she needed to see how he was faring. That was what she told herself.

She'd mixed up more soda paste for his welts in case he needed it. But truth was, she needed to talk to him properly. He had saved Jamie's life, and he hadn't let her thank him.

When she caught up with him, he was settling the horses with their evening oats.

"Mr. Braden." She had no notion of how to begin. Her feelings became jumbled when he was near. She breathed in the scent of horses and sweet, fresh hay, willing herself to be calm. She was no silly girl who lost her wits whenever she saw a handsome face.

He turned his head, glanced at her, then started brushing Aldebaran without so much as saying good day.

She frowned, smoothed her skirts. " I . . . I wanted to thank you."

He stopped brushing and at last faced her.

"Jamie is very fond of you." She tried not to notice that the ties of his shirt had come undone, revealing his throat and a good portion of his chest. Or that the scent of the forest still clung to his skin. Or that her heart began to pound when he looked directly at her.

"As I am of him. It must be very frightening for you to be raising the boy alone."

"Aye." Her throat was suddenly tight.

"You've done an admirable job."

His compliment surprised her. "Thank you. When he was born, I was sure he would die. And when he didn't... I couldn't bear it if anything happened to him."

Those had been lonely days, and hard, but she wasn't sure why she now felt the sting of tears behind her eyes. Nor did she want to consider why she had just shared her feelings on such a private matter with a man who was practically a stranger. She had not been herself lately.

She felt the first hot tear slide down her cheek. He stepped closer, caught it, and gently wiped it away, his thumb leaving a trail of heat on her cheek. His gaze caught and held hers.

"You must know," he said softly, "I'd never let anything happen to your son."

"My son? Jamie?" Cassie laughed after a moment, her sorrow forgotten. "Jamie is my brother."

"Your *brother?* But…" Cole looked genuinely confused.

"Aye, my brother. My mother died four days after his birth. And my father … my father has not been himself since. I've raised Jamie since then."

"I see." Cole shifted awkwardly. "I misunderstood."

"You thought he was *my* child?" The idea was amusing, if a bit embarrassing. Cassie smiled, and found that Cole, too, was smiling—a silly, sheepish sort of smile. Then it hit her.

Fury replaced mirth. Before she realized what she was doing, she slapped Cole soundly across the face and stomped toward the door, swearing.

"Whoreson! Lecher!" She hadn't taken three steps when strong arms gripped her from behind and spun her around.

"Will you please explain yourself, Mistress?" He glared down at her, a bright red palm print on his left cheek.

"You thought me a fallen woman, and so ripe to your use! Admit it!" The toe of her shoe connected sharply with Cole's shin.

"*Ouch!* Blast it, woman!"

As he bent to massage his shin, Cassie saw her chance and dashed toward the door. But he was quicker. He pinned her arms to her sides and drew her so closely against him she could barely move.

"If you would but calm yourself, and give a wounded man the chance to speak in his own defense . . . or shall I hold you thus?" His voice became husky. His thumbs made tantalizing, slow circles on her flesh.

She felt the muscular length of his body pressed intimately against hers and ceased struggling. This was certainly not the position she wanted to find herself in.

He released her slowly. "You are correct that I thought you no longer a virgin—"

"Then you confess, you bast—"

Before she could say another word, he had pulled her against him again and had covered her mouth with his hand. "—as a woman can hardly bear a child and remain so. But you imply that my attraction is based solely on my mistaken belief that you had been bedded before. You underestimate your beauty, sweet mistress. Had I wished for someone truly experienced, I would have lost all interest in you the first moment we kissed."

Cassie began struggling furiously, her shouts muted behind his hand. How dared he insult her!

"My interest in you has little to do with the status of your maidenhead and everything to do with your charms, which, if I may say so, are sorely lacking at the moment." With this, he released her.

Carried forward by her own struggling, she pitched face-first into the straw. For a moment she lay facedown and motionless, too mortified to move. Then, slowly, she rose, brushing away straw that clung to her clothes and hair and smoothing her skirts. Her hair had come loose and hung in a disorderly mass. Her apron was soiled where her knees had pressed into the dirt, and her gown hung crookedly from her shoulders.

He had admitted to thinking her loose. He'd treated her roughly and had even criticized her kisses. She would not give him the satisfaction of seeing her cry. She turned to face him, adjusting her gown as best she could and hiding her trembling hands in her apron.

She lifted her chin and looked him directly in the eye. "I came only to thank you, Mr. Braden. You may return to your work."

"As you wish, Mistress."

Alec watched her walk away, cloaked with all the dignity she could muster, and fought the pricking of his conscience. She looked like she'd just been attacked. But, by God, she was the one who'd attacked him! He'd had to use strength to make her listen. It was her own damned fault. He wasn't the one who'd suddenly gone insane. She'd slapped him, scratched him, kicked him. All he had done was to protect himself. Why should he feel so blasted guilty for that?

Then something else crossed his mind.

Miss Blakewell was a virgin, after all. Not that he cared. Unlike those men who found excitement in deflowering maids, he had carefully avoided them no matter how alluring they might have been, preferring widows and wayward wives, who were more mature, more experienced, and less likely to make demands on his already sparse time. No demands. No expectations. No bonds beyond the bedroom.

But then he remembered the look in Cassie's eyes when he'd bandaged her hand, the way her body had come alive when they'd kissed. To fan the flames of passion and awaken her desire might well be worth it.

But whom had she met in the forest this morning? What did it matter? He would be leaving this land before long. In truth, the sooner the better. He had obligations. There was work to be done—ending the sale of Kenleigh ships to slave traders, for one, something he'd vowed to do as soon as he returned. His life was waiting for him far from this place, far from Miss Blakewell's charms—and her temper. God only knew what was happening back home. Had Philip bankrupted the firm yet? Had his family given him up for dead? He retrieved the curry comb from where he'd dropped it in the hay and immediately went back to brushing Aldebaran with a sense of urgency, determined to put Miss Blackwell from his mind.

Alec did not see her again that afternoon. It was a good thing, too, as he was in no mood to put up with another display of temper. He secured the stable doors for the night and began walking toward his cabin. The evening air was cool and carried the chirping and buzzing of insects, the smells of a dozen cookfires. Candlelight and the high-pitched giggle of a child spilled from the open windows of the cookhouse off to his right. It was not on his path, but he found himself walking toward the window anyway.

Inside, Cassie was giving a wriggling, splashing Jamie a bath. A fleet of wooden ships floated on the water before the boy, and, like an all-seeing lord high admiral, Jamie pitted them one against the other in a very wet and decisive battle. His sister finished rinsing lather from his hair, careful not to get the soapy water in his eyes, then sat back on her heels and listened with rapt attention to his accounts of mayhem and victory. She might be the child's sister, but she made a wonderful mother.

"Time to come out and dry off, little one," she said. "You're turning into a fish, I'm afraid."

"Can't I play just a while longer?"

"Nay. Look. You're growing scales." She lifted one of Jamie's feet from the water and pointed to his wrinkled toes.

"Those aren't scales!" He paused, looking uncertain. "Are they?"

"That's what Takotah always told me."

Despite Jamie's protests, she drew him from the water, quickly dried him, and pulled a nightshirt over his head. The boy rubbed his eyes sleepily and, rescuing a toy ship from the water, climbed into Cassie's lap, where she sat next to the hearth in a rough-hewn rocking chair.

"The drowsy Night her wings has spread, like sable curtains 'bout each head and born ye weary limbs to bed..." she sang as she rocked, her voice soft and sweet.

Something twisted in Alec's gut. It was a common English lullaby. Why should the sound of it make him feel so desolate?

"And she her pretty Faeries bring, and in your fancy dance their ring..."

Perhaps he missed his nieces and nephew even more than he'd realized. Certainly he had never longed for children of his own. Being an uncle had always been enough for him. Owning a thriving concern meant a life consumed by work and political matters. He'd seen his mother suffer the inattention of her husband and did not want to marry and beget offspring, only to leave his wife and children alone for days and nights on end. Besides, he'd no desire to brave the scheming mothers of London and endure the guile of their daughters. They cared only for the size of a man's estates.

As for true love, he gave no credence to such foolishness. His father and mother had rarely spoken, much less cared for each other. How they'd managed to have three children was something of a mystery to Alec, since his father had seemed to spend his seed solely on his mistresses. He would have thought the lot of them bastards had they not all resembled their father so closely. Elizabeth and Matthew were the only husband and wife Alec knew whose affection for each other seemed to grow each year rather than diminish. He'd leave matters of marriage and children to them.

Zach gave Nan a big kiss on the lips, deftly sneaking a handful of tarts off the table and hiding them behind his back.

"Don't think ye can charm me, Zachariah Bowers." The cook glowered sternly, but her round face flushing with color nonetheless. "I know well enough 'tis my tarts ye favor and not me, so save yer kisses for someone who wants 'em."

"Ah, come, Nan. Don't tell me ye don't like it when a handsome man steals a kiss," He stealthily handed the treats out the door to Jamie, who scampered away, giggling, Daniel in tow.

"A handsome man? Nay," she teased. "But stealin' a kiss is one thing. Stealin' me tarts — that's somethin' else, mind. Ye might as well take one for yerself. Ye must be hungry after all that thievin'." She pointed with plump flour-coated fingers toward the remaining tarts on the serving tray.

"Have you seen Elly?" He sat on a nearby stool and sank his teeth into the tart's strawberry sweetness.

"Aye, I have." Nan nodded with her head toward the great house while her hands busily shaped dough. "She's inside servin' tarts and cider to young Master Crichton."

"Fancy-Pants? Hell!"

Zach's good humor vanished. He had no doubt Elly was doing her best to catch the fop's eye. If she wasn't careful she'd find herself on her backside playing the trollop for him while he took some rich planter's daughter to wife. He'd use her, and when her belly started to grow big and round, he'd pretend he'd never seen her before. Zach had seen plenty of men like Geoffrey Crichton back in England. None of them could be trusted.

"He's been waitin' here for Miss Cassie for an hour now."

"An hour! Has Elly been in there with him the whole bloody time?" He rose so abruptly he knocked over the stool. In an hour, Fancy-Pants could have shagged Elly four times over and still have time to spare. Zach fought the urge to barge into the house and drag her out, kicking and screaming if need be.

"Aye, Zachariah, but not alone. Calm yerself, lad. She might not know it yet, but 'tis ye she loves, though what she sees in ye I don't know."

He snorted in disgust and paced across the room. They'd not been together since the night by the woodpile. She'd smiled at him, even said a few sweet things since then, but Zach knew she felt bad about how she'd treated him that night. He didn't want her pity.

"Master Geoffrey has got a convict with 'im, he has. A woman. And Sheriff Hollingsworth should be here with another any moment now."

"Does Braden know?"

"Nay, he's taken one of the horses out for a ride."

"Where's Miss Cassie?"

"Out to visit the master."

At the sound of a closing door he looked up to see Elly walking, serving tray in hand, down the porch stairs and toward the cookhouse. Even from ten paces he could tell her cheeks wore an excited glow. If he'd been a free man and she no longer a bondsmaid, he would have knocked the tray from her hands, kissed her so hard she wouldn't have been able to argue with him, and carried her off to the nearest church. There'd be no more of these Fancy-Pants shenanigans. But they were neither of them free to do as they pleased, so he stood in the doorway, watched her approach, and said nothing.

She spotted him. "If you were a gentleman, you'd offer to help me, Zachariah."

If she expected him to tend to her like some lovesick puppy while she flirted with another man, she was daft.

"Aye. And if you were a gentlewoman, you'd not trifle with the first fop to sniff at your tail, Elly, my sweet." Gratified by the stunned expression on her face, he walked back toward the sawyer's shed, whistling.

*C*assie rode along the river after bidding her father farewell for the day, stopping when she came to her favorite spot. She often came to this small, hidden cove when she needed to think. Giving Andromeda a chance to drink, she secured the mare to a nearby evergreen, slid off her shoes and stockings, and, holding up her skirts so as not to get them wet, stepped into the cold water. Though the day was hot and humid, the wind coming off the river was cool, and the chilly water licked at her calves, bringing at least some relief from the heat, bolstering her sinking spirits.

Her father had not improved. Not that she'd really expected to find that he had. More than two months had gone by since he'd recognized her, and she had to face the possibility that he would never be himself again. While it terrified her to know that sooner or later the truth would come out and life at Blakewell's Neck would change forever, no fear or sorrow matched that of watching her father slowly fade away. The man who had been Abraham Blakewell was gone. What remained was merely his body. Battling a growing sense of gloom, she kicked up a spray of water, watching the drops fall. There was nothing she could do for her father now but pray.

On the other side of the inlet an enormous heron walked in the shallows on ridiculously long legs, hunting for anything unfortunate enough to move. It eyed her warily but did not hide or fly away. A small blue crab, scared up from the bottom by the motion of her feet, scuttled into deeper waters. Off to her left, a splash and an expanding ring of ripples told her that a fish, perhaps a young spot or a bass, had just leaped up to catch an insect.

When she was a little girl Takotah had often brought her to this inlet on hot summer afternoons, and let her shed her clothes and swim in the water. The current was not strong except at the mouth of the cove, and the water teemed with life: fish, grass shrimp, crab, oysters, diving ducks, muskrat. For a curious little girl, it had been paradise.

She sat down on a large rock in the shade at the water's edge and let her feet dangle. Perspiration trickled between her breasts and down her back. How she would have liked to be that carefree little girl now, to undress and splash about, to float on her back and watch birds cross the backdrop of blue sky. But she was far too old to get away with swimming naked.

Wasn't she?

Temptation began to prick at her. There was little chance of anyone happening along and seeing her. There were no fields nearby and no workers. No one but Takotah knew she was likely to come here. Because the banks were high and the trees grew thick, the cove was well hidden from passersby, should there be any. No craft was likely to sail close enough to the cove for its passengers to see her. But she hadn't been naked in the open since before her body had begun to change from a girl's to that of a woman, and the very idea of romping about unclothed was more than a little frightening. If she wasn't completely undressed and didn't linger, perhaps it wouldn't be too out of order.

Before she was able to admit to herself what she was about, she had hopped to the sand and was lifting her gown over her head. She tossed it carelessly over a tree branch. Afraid of losing hairpins in the water, she removed them one by one and put them in a pile on a rock. She loosened her underskirts and let them fall to the ground in a heap. Removing her stiff corset proved a bit more complicated, but with a bit of tugging and pulling she at last managed to free herself. How she'd get it on again unassisted was a bit of a mystery, but she'd worry about that later.

She moaned with pleasure as the cool breeze penetrated the thin cotton of her shift and brought immediate relief from the heat. Unable to get herself to remove the shift, she stepped into the water, first only up to her knees, then to her hips, then at last to her chin. She laughed out loud, exhilarated by the feel of the cool water against her skin, giddy from her own recklessness. The water was so clear she could see her feet treading through the eelgrass and silt on the bottom. She held her breath and dove, propelling herself downward.

Cool and quiet, the world below the surface was completely different from the world above. It had been so long since she had been underwater that it all seemed new to her again. The light filtering to the bottom made everything appear a dappled shade of green, even her skin. The bigger fish had fled, but smaller fish and tiny grass shrimp darted through the thick, undulating vegetation, seemingly indifferent to her presence. Oysters, some half buried in the silt, littered the riverbed. Then, out of the corner of her eye, she spotted two tiny blennies fighting over the shelter provided by a small, empty crab shell. The ferocity with which the little fish battled was almost comical, considering their size. She watched until she thought her lungs would burst, then swam back to the surface.

She could not dally here. The sun would burn her skin if she remained in the water too long, and there was much to be done today. The kitchen garden needed weeding. Some of the herbs and vegetables were ready to be harvested and replanted. Rebecca was nearing her time and needed help with the more strenuous dairying chores. The tobacco, which now stood knee-high, had to be protected against hornworms and would soon need to be topped. But surely the plantation could survive without her for another ten minutes.

She had just spotted an eagle soaring high overhead when an enormous splash shattered the silence and made her gasp. She righted herself in the water, only to get a glimpse of a riderless horse on the bank and the form of a man gliding toward her underwater. Driven by raw panic, she turned and swam desperately toward the opposite shore. But before she had gone more than five feet, an arm closed around her waist.

She screamed and lashed out desperately with fists and feet. He had two hands on her and was pulling her nearly weightless body toward him through the water. "Let me go!"

She managed one good kick to the groin, then recognized him. "Mr. Braden?"

He doubled over in pain and sank beneath the surface.

Chapter Eleven

Cassie watched Cole's still form beneath the water and worried for one heart-thudding moment that she had knocked him out and he would drown. But when he rose to the surface a second or two later quite alive, the fury in his eyes sent her scrambling around him to the riverbank.

"Have you gone completely insane?" He glared at her from where he stood, waist-high in the water, his voice strained.

"Me? Perhaps you'd like to give me an explanation!" she shouted back, the salty breeze raising goose bumps on her wet skin. "You nearly frightened me out of my wits!"

"I thought to save your life, though I can see my concern was wasted." He moved slowly toward the shore in obvious discomfort. He wore no shirt, having discarded it carelessly on the sand. Rivulets of water traced paths down the skin on his chest and abdomen. His dark hair, normally tied back in a leather thong, hung, wet and dripping, just below his shoulders, the thong evidently lost in the water. Breeches clung to his thighs and groin like a second skin, leaving no detail to the imagination.

She watched him rise from the water, wet skin and muscle, and found it hard to breathe. "Save my life?" She shifted her gaze away from him and ignored the strange fluttering sensation in her abdomen. "My life was not in danger until you jumped into the water and nearly scared me to death!"

"I saw you floating and thought you drowned."

"Drowned?"

"Obviously I was mistaken." He came to stand before her. "And for that mistake, I've been all but unmanned."

"I thought I was fighting for my life." Why should she feel the need to defend her actions? She'd reacted in the only way she could under the circumstances. How was she to have known it was he?

"Fighting for your life. Against me? If I had intended to kill you, I would have done so long ago and spared myself endless trouble."

"Trouble? Trouble? I've treated you with every kindness, only to be rewarded with humiliation and ingratitude. Don't talk to me about trouble, Mr. Braden!"

He started to say something, but the words never left his mouth.

Cassie saw the change in his eyes, felt his gaze slide over her body. To her horror she saw proof of his growing arousal. The large bulge at the apex of his thighs was unmistakable. Following his gaze, she looked down at herself, shrieked, and darted behind the nearest tree. She might as well have been naked. The wet white cotton of her chemise clung to her skin and was so transparent every inch of her body was clearly visible.

He chuckled and walked toward Boadicea, the mare he'd abandoned on the bank.

"I don't know what you find amusing, Mr. Braden." Her voice was unsteady. "But if you'd kindly mount and leave me to dress, I'd appreciate it."

"You must forgive me if I refuse, Mistress."

"What? You cannot mean to stand there?"

"Aye, I do. Boadicea needs to drink and rest in the shade. I'm soaked to the skin, and, even if I wanted to, I doubt I could sit a horse just now, thanks to you. I'll turn my back, if you like, but I won't leave."

"But... but you're . . . you're . . ." She pointed, too abashed to actually finish the sentence aloud.

Didn't he understand she could not trust him when he had obviously let lust get the best of his body already?

"Aroused? How kind of you to notice." He gave her a jaunty grin, seemingly unashamed and making no effort to hide the evidence. "It seems you haven't quite unmanned me after all."

She felt heat rise to her cheeks. "You mock me."

"Mock you, Mistress? Never."

"Then I bid you to leave me in peace."

"I already said I'll leave when I am so inclined."

"Oh, you are a horrid man!"

"Are you going to stand behind that tree all day?"

"At least have the decency to turn around."

With a shake of his head and a smile, he turned and led the mare to water.

She darted out from the shelter of the pine and hastily donned her underskirts, all the while keeping a wary eye on Cole, who, to his credit, remained standing with his back to her, speaking in hushed tones to the horse. She grabbed her stockings and, ignoring the rough sand that clung to her feet, pulled them over her legs and tied them in place. Next came her shoes. But, as she had expected, the corset presented a problem. While it was laced she could tug it over her head but could not put her arms through and pull it over her shoulders. She tried unlacing it, putting it on backward, then lacing it and turning it around, but it was either too tight and wouldn't budge or too loose and slid out of place.

"Let me help."

"I don't need your help, Mr. Braden. I am perfectly capable of dressing myself."

"As you wish."

She could hear the smile that crept into his voice and was sure he was enjoying her frustration. She tried pulling the corset over her head once more, but managed only to pass her head and one arm through. She had almost decided to forgo wearing the hateful undergarment, when he suddenly turned and, with a curse, strode over to her.

"Turn around," he ordered gruffly, grabbing the corset from her and beginning to unlace it.

Biting off a retort, she reluctantly complied, covering her breasts, all too aware of his presence behind her. She heard the snapping sound of the corset strings being pulled impatiently through the eyelets. He'd had lots of practice at this, she realized sourly.

The corset was thrust abruptly in front of her by a tanned hand. "Put it on."

Cassie hastily wrapped the garment around her ribs, tucking it just beneath her breasts. For a moment nothing happened. If she had not been able to hear his breathing, she would have thought he no longer stood behind her. Then, stifling a gasp, she felt his fingers brush the skin of her back and neck as he gathered the wet mass of her hair to move it out of his way. She then felt small tugs as he began to pull the corset strings back through the tiny eyelets. But his fingers, which had so deftly unlaced the undergarment, now seemed awkward and slow. More than once he brushed against the wet fabric of her chemise with a knuckle or the back of his hand, each time flooding her body with heat and making it almost impossible for her to breathe.

She realized she wanted him to kiss her. An image of him, wet and nearly naked, his lips pressed to her neck, leaped uninvited to her mind. Shivers ran from her buttocks to the nape of her neck.

"How tiny does my mistress wish her waist to be?" His voice was a caress.

"Not too tight, please." She was surprised she could still speak.

With two quick tugs on the laces, he tied the corset fast.

"Thank you." Her words came out in a whisper.

He did not answer, but neither did he walk away.

Nor did Cassie turn toward him, sure her face would reveal the nature of her thoughts. She closed her eyes, wanting him to touch her, willing him to touch her, but also wanting him to ride away. She could not stop a quick intake of breath when at last she felt his hands cup her shoulders and slide slowly down her arms. Nor could she keep herself from leaning back to rest against him, her shoulders pressing against the cool, damp skin of his chest. When finally he bent his head and kissed the left side of her neck, she couldn't help moaning.

His hands at her waist, he slowly turned her to face him. His blue eyes no longer held the mirth she'd seen just moments ago but revealed a darker, more primal emotion. She should have been afraid, but she was not. How could he mean her harm when his touch brought such blinding pleasure?

And then he kissed her.

She closed her eyes at the first brush of his lips and felt him trace a scalding path across her lower lip with his tongue. She heard herself whimper and found herself reaching up to return the kiss. With one hand she delved into the tangle of wet, dark hair that fell over his shoulders and down the back of his neck. With the other she tentatively explored his bare chest, her fingers tracing the crisscross of scars. How soft the dark curls felt against her palm. She felt the muscles of his abdomen tense as she brushed a smooth, flat nipple with her fingertips.

"You don't know what you're doing to me," he whispered, his voice hoarse.

She looked into his eyes, eyes that held all the anguish of a man condemned, and felt a momentary thrill of victory. Was it possible that her touch affected him the way his affected her? She smiled and touched a hand to his cheek.

He growled, pulling her against him in a crushing embrace. When his lips met hers again all gentleness was gone, replaced by something untamed and ferocious that left her breathless. He moved to kiss the rounded tops of her breasts just above the lace of her chemise, and she heard herself cry out, stunned by the heat between her thighs. Arouse him though she might, she was still very much an amateur at this game. And when he moved a hand to cup her breast, his thumb caressing an already taut nipple, she thought she might melt.

"Cole." Husky and sensual, the voice that came forth from her throat did not sound like hers.

His hands stilled. He released her and stepped away. "Is that really who you think I am?" His voice was ice, his eyes slate. "Get dressed."

For a moment she could not believe what she'd heard. When he turned his back to her and walked to the water's edge, she realized he'd meant it. Confused and trembling, she quickly retrieved her gown and pulled it over her head. What had she done to deserve his ire? Torn between anger and wounded pride, she fought the tears that gathered behind her eyes.

Lifting her chin, she walked over to Andromeda and took the mare's reins.

"I don't know what I've done to merit your rage, Mr. Braden, but I am not some alehouse trollop to be used and dismissed at your whim." The trembling of her voice betrayed the torrent of emotions inside her.

He turned toward her and fixed her with an unyielding gaze. "What kind of woman would want to make love with a man she thinks is a rapist?"

Comprehension flooded her, and she felt the color drain from her face. She understood the question and its horrible implications. "You are not a free man yet, Mr. Braden. I pray for your sake you remember that." She climbed into Andromeda's saddle. "Your insolence could be your undoing."

"How right you are, Mistress."

*A*lec gave Cassie a good ten-minute head start before he mounted and began the ride back, sure she wouldn't want to arrive home in her disheveled state with him at her side. That would undoubtedly spawn awkward questions and unkind rumors.

When he'd first spied her, she'd seemed a vision of Ophelia, floating lifeless and beautiful on the river. He hadn't realized until she had begun to thrash and kick at him that she was alive. And that was one moment too late, he thought ruefully, shifting in the saddle.

Though his dip in the river had cooled his skin, the sight of her clad in that wet chemise, the curves of her body outlined in transparent white, had given rise to heat of a kind that no amount of cold water could douse. If he'd had any sense he would have brought an end to this torment by giving them both what they needed. Had she not spoken his convict name, bringing him to his senses, he would have. If he was going to make love to her, he would make love to her as Alec Kenleigh, not Cole Braden.

Deep down she believed him. He knew she did. But for some reason she would not admit the truth, not even to herself. She would not have allowed him to kiss her and touch her the way he had if she truly believed him a felon. Nor would she have kissed him back with such fervor, touched him so boldly.

He could still feel her fingertips moving over his chest, taste the sweetness of her lips as she opened her mouth to his. And the way she'd smiled when she'd seen the effect she had on him… it was the smile of Eve, of a woman just discovering her primal power.

Damn! He shouldn't be attracted to her. She was not the sort of woman he wanted. She was bossy, too assertive for a female. She had a hellish temper. She kept slaves.

Slaves carried over in Kenleigh ships.

The mare began to prance uneasily beneath him, jerking at the reins.

"It's all right, girl," Alec crooned, tightening his grip.

Boadicea stomped, snorted, and rolled her eyes in fear.

Alec felt the horse's muscles bunch as if to rear.

Timber groaned and cracked. Alec jerked his gaze toward the sound, kicked in his heels, and gave Boadicea her head. The mare sprang forward. With a crash, the tree hit the road behind them, missing them by a yard.

Alec muttered reassurances and pulled the reins hard, trying to slow the spooked horse. "Whoa, girl. We're fine. Good you were paying attention."

The whites of the horse's eyes flashed, but she began to settle under Alec's firm handling. Still, they were a good quarter mile down the road before Alec could safely dismount and retrace his route to check out the accident that could easily have spelled his death. From a distance he could see it was an old tree, enormous, its branches dead, its exposed wood whitened by sun and wind. For a moment he thought it had simply collapsed from age and decay. Then he saw the chop marks of an ax on its stump, fresh wood chips in the grass.

He glanced around but saw no one. Depressions in the grass around the tree told him someone had been there moments before. But who? And why? Mounting again, he rode through the trees looking for answers.

When he neared the plantation outbuildings a frustrating hour later, Alec glimpsed two carriages in the courtyard, one pulled by a matching pair of bays, the other by a team of dun geldings. Recognizing the latter as belonging to Sheriff Hollingsworth, he brought Boadicea to a gallop.

Freedom had arrived at last.

Hitching the mare to the porch rail, he took the steps to the great house two at a time and was met at the door by Nettie, who led him down a hallway to a simply but elegantly furnished sitting room. He'd barely had time to register the seated forms of Cassie and the sheriff, to note Geoffrey Crichton's overdressed presence at the window, when a strange woman detached herself from the background and walked toward him.

"Well, 'ello there, Cole." Her smile revealed broken and missing teeth, her tone openly sexual. Her face, though perhaps once pretty, was wrinkled and scarred from the pox. "Miss me?"

Alec saw the blood drain from Cassie's face, saw her hands clutch the arms of the chair. "Who is this woman?"

"A fellow prisoner from Newgate who has just confirmed that you are, indeed, Nicholas Braden, felon and liar." Crichton turned toward Alec with a triumphant sneer.

"That's impossible."

"You'd best give up this ruse, convict, for it will bring you nothing but the lash." Crichton rested one hand on the back of Cassie's chair and gave a limp wave with the other. "One would think from the look of your scarred hide that you'd had enough of that to last a lifetime."

Alec had never been accused of lying, and had he been at home in England, he would have called out any man who dared to do so. It was by the slimmest margin that he now managed to keep his temper in check.

"I speak the truth." He addressed the sheriff, who sat on a green brocade settee, his enormous form taking up space intended for two. "My name is Alec Kenleigh. I've never seen this woman before today."

"More lies!" Crichton snarled.

"Sally, you'd best take another look. A man's life is riding on this," the sheriff said to the bondswoman. "We already know you're a thief, a whore, and a liar. Consider yourself under oath. If we learn you're lying about this, you'll stand in the pillory, and I'll personally cut off your ears."

For a moment the bondswoman's face turned a sickly white. Then she stepped closer to Alec, inspecting him from head to toe. Her brown hair was heavily streaked with gray and hung in dirty strands to her shoulders. She stank. How could any man, no matter how long deprived of the pleasures of a woman's body, pay to tup such a repulsive creature?

"You claim to have known Nicholas Braden in prison?" Cassie rose. Dressed in a pale blue gown, her hair freshly coifed, she looked every bit the genteel plantation owner's daughter, not at all the type to swim in her shift alone in a river. Her face was impossibly pale. Her hands were trembling.

"Aye, I knew him, if you get my meaning, Missy." Sally gave Cassie a lewd grin. "He had a big appetite for the ladies, 'e did. The gaoler gave me to 'im more than once."

Cassie's eyes widened, and Alec saw hurt and remorse fill them. She looked away.

"Cassie, she's ly—"

"He's hung like a bloody stallion, though 'tain't how big it is, mind." Sally laughed. "'Tis what a chap does with it what matters."

"Quit your indecent prattle, woman." Crichton looked at the bondswoman with a menacing glare that made her visibly shrink. "Miss Blakewell is gently bred and needn't hear such filth."

"Is this or is this not Nicholas Braden?" The sheriff shifted impatiently.

The room was silent. Sally's gaze darted to Crichton before resting on Alec. "Aye."

"Who is forcing you to lie?" Alec grabbed the old woman's wrist and forced her to look him in the eye. "Is it someone in this room?"

The woman's brown eyes grew wide with fear, and she began to stammer incoherently. What at first was only a hunch, Alec now knew to be the truth. Someone was coercing her to lie about him. Someone here had so terrified Sally, she had risked mutilation and public humiliation to avoid his—or her—wrath. Inspiring such horror hardly sounded like something of which Cassie was capable. But if not she, then who? Crichton, perhaps? The fop hated Alec, for certain, and the old whore seemed afraid of him. But then his contempt for all beneath him was palpable. The sheriff? What motivation could he possibly have?

Filled with pity and disgust, Alec released her. There seemed to be little point in further questioning the woman. He felt certain that whoever had put her up to this was in the room, watching. She'd reveal nothing more.

"Murphy, what say you?" asked the sheriff.

Alec noticed for the first time a wiry, middle-aged man with an unusually long nose. He stood off to one side, holding his hat in his hands. Dressed in a plain cotton shirt and breeches, the man examined him carefully, one hand stroking the stiff gray whiskers on his chin.

"I can't be certain," he said at last. "Braden was a tall man, for sure, and his hair was dark. But the nose is all wrong, and he was big and soft around the middle, not the hale sort at all."

"What about my voice." Alec's hope kindled. "Surely you had occasion to speak to the man. Was his voice like mine? Was his speech refined?"

Murphy considered this for a moment. "I can't say for certain. Braden always used pretty words, sir, but the voice . . . It has been so long. Beggin' yer pardon, sir. I just can't remember."

"Is there anything else you two can tell us?" The sheriff looked as frustrated as Alec felt. "Did anything unusual happen before you sailed? Did you see or hear anything?"

Sally shook her head, looking at the floor.

Murphy rubbed his whiskers, then nodded. "Braden took sick with gaol fever afore we sailed. He was shakin' and shiverin' when they brought him aboard. Couldn't walk, eat, nor hold up his head. I thought they should've just left him in the gaol to die in peace instead of sendin' him to this place." '

"Get on with it, man." Crichton motioned impatiently with his hands. "Just tell us the parts of the story we need to hear."

"Some of the men swore Braden died the night afore we sailed. They said they saw him starin' open-eyed at nothin', blue as the sea and not breathin'. Since his shackles was empty that mornin', I believed them. But the next I knew, a fellow the crewmen said was Braden was makin' such a noise on the other side of the wall, captain had him flogged, not once, but two or three times. I member thinkin' that the fever must have destroyed his mind."

Alec closed his eyes. Broken images flashed through his memory. His wrists bound painfully above his head. Darkness. Throbbing pain in his head. A foul-smelling rag in his mouth. Unrelenting thirst. The agony of the lash as it bit into his flesh again and again.

"That was not Nicholas Braden. 'Twas I."

"So you awoke one morning to find Mr. Braden's shackles gone and were told he was dead?" Cassie asked, some of the color back in her cheeks.

Murphy nodded.

"And the next day the sailors told you that he was in the bed next to you?"

"Aye, Missy."

"Did they tell you why they had moved him or why they'd beaten him?"

"Nay, Missy."

"Did you see him again after—"

"This proves nothing." Geoffrey strode across the room to stand between Cassie and Murphy. "The mutterings of a filthy whore. The ramblings of a thief. This entire effort has yielded nothing."

Sally shrank against the wall as he looked in her direction. Murphy gazed at his own feet.

Sheriff Hollingsworth stood. "I'm afraid I agree with young Master Crichton. Though certainly suspicious, what we have here is neither enough to warrant releasing you from your indenture or enough to prove your words lies, Braden. I'm afraid we shall have to wait for word from London before this matter can be put to rest. Until then, Nicholas Braden you remain."

Alec's hopes disintegrated. He struggled for control as fury surged white-hot through him. "Damn it, man! Nicholas Braden died, and I was put in his place. It's obvious."

"Perhaps. But I still need proof." Sheriff Hollingsworth's tone was final. Then he turned to Crichton, the entire matter apparently forgotten. "Come, Geoffrey, the cook has baked some of that wheat bread of hers. She won't be able to hide it from me this time. I can smell it."

With a hearty laugh and a slap on the younger man's back, the sheriff made for the cookhouse after instructing both convicts to wait for him by his carriage.

"I'll be watching you, convict." Crichton's flat gray eyes peered menacingly out from under his white wig. His upper lip curled with contempt.

"Go to hell." Alec turned and strode from the room.

Chapter Twelve

*C*assie strolled with Geoffrey toward the crowded cookhouse, surreptitiously watching Cole lead Boadicea to the stables, trying to respond politely to Geoffrey's inquiries despite the turmoil raging within her. First the prostitute had convinced her Cole was nothing but a scheming, lecherous liar. Then Murphy, who seemed to be the more trustworthy of the two convicts, had raised enough doubt in her mind to convince her again that Cole might be telling the truth. The events Murphy described on board ship certainly were odd.

"Catherine? Have you heard anything I've said?"

"I'm sorry, Geoffrey. Do go on." She gave him her warmest smile and tried to look like a woman who had nothing more on her mind than playing hostess to her father's guests.

"I said my favorite bitch has dropped another litter of pups. I was wondering if Jamie might want one."

"How very kind of you, Geoffrey. I'm sure he'd love a puppy."

"It's settled then. They should be weaned by my birthday celebration. You can pick one and take it home with you."

Shouting poured from the cookhouse.

"I know it's here, woman. I can smell it!" The sheriff stood nose to nose with Nan—or rather belly to belly—arms akimbo in the center of the kitchen.

"It's tarts ye smell, old man."

"The only tart around here is standing in front of me! Where's the bread?"

"Grow yer own wheat, and I'll happily teach yer cook to bake it herself!"

"Come, Nan." Cassie put the butter crock and a pot of honey on the table in hopes of getting the sheriff and Geoffrey on their way as quickly as possible. "We've more than enough to share. Please, Sheriff, Geoffrey, sit and refresh yourselves. Nan, fetch some of Rebecca's cheese, please, and some cool cider. I'll go get a loaf of fresh-baked bread, piping hot from the ovens."

Nan's mouth dropped open, but she said nothing.

Cassie looked to where Elly sat at the table, one eye on her sewing—and one on Geoffrey. "Perhaps you can take your work outside, Elly."

"But it's goin' to be rainin' any minute." The bondsmaid had made a fool of herself every time Geoffrey had stopped by since Christmas.

Though Cassie had meant to discuss Elly's behavior with her, she had yet to do so. Perhaps now would be a good time.

"Is it rainin' now, child?" Nan gave Elly a grumpy frown, obviously not happy at having to share her bread.

"Nay." Elly rose and stomped out the door.

"Let me help you." Cassie took the sewing basket from Elly, eliciting another surprised look from the cook. She followed Elly down the back steps and waited for her to take her place on the bench that sat in the shade behind the kitchen. Cassie lowered her voice. "You really must stop making eyes at Master Geoffrey, Elly. It's most unbecoming. You're acting like a lovesick nanny goat!"

She plopped the sewing basket on the bench next to the speechless bondsmaid and walked toward the ovens.

By the time she returned to the cookhouse with a warm, crusty, brown loaf wrapped in her apron, the sheriff and Geoffrey were deep in conversation, the question of Cole Braden long since forgotten.

"Three have already died on the Walker plantation, all children, and none of them seasoned to life in the colony. They say business in Jamestown has nearly come to a halt," said the sheriff. "Aye, 'tis the dyin' time," Nan said gloomily.

Cassie set the bread on a wooden slab on the table. "The ague?"

She knew the answer.

"The ague." Sheriff Hollingsworth took the knife Cassie offered and cut himself a generous slice of warm bread. The yeasty aroma filled the small space.

Cassie's stomach sank. Each summer hundreds died from the devastating fever.

"Have the Walkers no quinquina?"

"Aye, of course they do. But who wants to use medicine on bondsfolk when you might be needin' it yourself soon?" The sheriff's callousness made Cassie stiffen.

She said the first words that came to her mind. "I'm sure the mothers of those three children feel comforted knowing their children died so their masters might sleep better."

"Govern your tongue, young miss. What would your father say if he heard you speak like that to one of his guests?" The sheriff cast her a sharp glance.

"He'd likely agree with her or say something even more absurd." Geoffrey gave Cassie a dimpled smile. "You know what a radical he is."

In his own way, Geoffrey believed he was protecting her by defusing the sheriff's ire. Still, Cassie could not force herself to smile back. He actually agreed with the sheriff on this matter, and that infuriated her. Medicine ought to be available to all who were ill, just as the gifts of the earth were for all to share. So Takotah had taught her, and so she believed.

"Aye, he's a strange one." The sheriff spoke with a full mouth. "Abraham has always been full of womanish ideas and a fondness for the wretched of this colony."

Outraged, Cassie held her tongue. If she had been a man, her father's heir, she might have spoken her mind. As a daughter she could do nothing but see to her guests' comfort. Oh, how she wished they would hurry up and go away.

Outside the cookhouse on the bench, Elly stabbed at linen with a needle and fought the urge to throw the cloth on the ground and stomp on it. If anyone was acting like a lovesick nanny goat, it was Miss High-and-Mighty Blakewell herself. Elly couldn't have been the only one to notice how flustered and rosy-cheeked Miss Cassie was anytime the convict was nearby. Miss Cassie might be a gentlewoman, but Elly was willing to bet her dinner that Miss Cassie had feelings for Cole Braden—the same kind of feelings she herself had for Zach.

Elly jumped as the needle pricked her finger. She stuck her finger in her mouth and tasted blood. The rasp of the pit saw in the distance told her Zach was hard at work. He'd be covered with sawdust and sweat already. Zach was kind and sweet. And when he kissed her...there was nothing better than that. But he was a bondsman, a sawyer, and he'd never be much more than one meal away from a hungry stomach. She hadn't come all the way to Virginia to go hungry. It really didn't matter what she felt for Zach or what he felt for her. No matter how many times he told her he loved her, he could never give her the kind of life she wanted her children to have.

She took her finger from her mouth and pulled out the note she'd hidden in her corset.

"Why haven't you responded to my letters?" Geoffrey had asked her earlier.

"It's not proper for a lady to write notes to a gentleman, sir." She'd been afraid to tell him she could not read and had no idea what was in the three messages he'd sent her.

"You're absolutely right, Eleanor. And, please, do call me Geoffrey. I think I should like to call you by the Italian—Eleanora. Or perhaps the Greek—Helena. Have you ever heard of Helen of Troy?"

She'd shaken her head.

"It is said she was so beautiful her husband sent a thousand ships to retrieve her when she was taken from him. It is a fitting name for you, my love."

She'd felt her face flush and had not known what to say.

"Please, Eleanor—Helen—come and sit. Share the tarts with me. It's shameful the way you are made to work. One as delicate and beautiful as you should have your own house, slaves and servants to care for you."

"No, sir, I don't think—"

"Come." He patted the settee beside him. "I'll not take no for an answer. There is no one here to see."

That wasn't true. The old woman he'd brought with him sulked in the corner, and Nettie lurked in the hallway, her disapproving gaze following Geoffrey's every move. Still, Elly had been unable to resist Geoffrey's dimpled smile or the tarts that sat on the table before him, so she'd sat. She had sat next to him that way for quite a long time before the others had arrived. They had talked, mostly about Blakewell's Neck and the convict. He'd asked a lot of questions.

She'd told him that she was afraid of Cole Braden—it wasn't true, but she knew he didn't like the man—and he'd assured her he'd do all he could to keep her safe. Then he'd asked her to meet him in the forest. Shocked, she'd shaken her head without thinking. Geoffrey had immediately begged for her forgiveness for asking her to do something so improper and asked her to come with Miss Cassie to his birthday party. Then the sheriff had arrived.

Miss Cassie could believe whatever she wanted to believe, but Master Geoffrey fancied Elly.

Elly resumed her sewing and went back to her daydream of banquets, beautiful gowns, and idle afternoons. Someday it wouldn't be just a dream. Then Miss Cassie and Nan and everyone else on Blakewell's Neck who thought of her as nothing but a bondsmaid and a silly child would be forced to treat her with respect.

"Eleanora." She repeated the name—a name more elegant than her own—and smiled.

*C*assie sat in the formal dining room, picking at her food. Three candelabras filled the room with a cheerful light that contrasted sharply with her mood. Though the sheriff had left once the bread was eaten, Geoffrey had lingered until she'd been forced to ask him to stay for dinner. He'd insisted on taking the meal in the great house, not the cookhouse, and Cassie, loath to anger him, had given in.

"More wine, my dear?"

"No, thank you."

Nettie entered the room, which was rarely used these days, and placed a warm apple pie on the table before them. The scent of cinnamon tickled the air. Dessert.

"Thank you, Nettie. We can serve ourselves."

Cassie couldn't eat another bite. Nan had outdone herself in an attempt to please Geoffrey, putting together the kind of feast that Blakewell's Neck saw only on holidays. Geoffrey hadn't seemed to notice the food or appreciate the effort made on his behalf. Her father had always said that wealth made men blind to life's pleasures, and if Geoffrey was any example, her father had been right. Filling and refilling his plate and his glass, Geoffrey had spoken endlessly of his plans for his estate once he'd inherited it. It was almost as if he wished his father would hurry up and die.

Not that Cassie could blame him. His father was a heartless man.

Cassie had never forgotten how Master Crichton had refused to visit Geoffrey when he'd been a little boy sick with fever, how he'd seemed to loathe his son when he'd heard Geoffrey might not be able to walk again. Geoffrey had surprised them all by walking within a month, but the permanent limp he'd acquired became the butt of his father's jokes. Geoffrey worked hard to hide it, but his father still made sport of him in front of other people. The elder Master Crichton was the cruelest man Cassie knew.

"It will be wonderful." Geoffrey took his last bite of pie.

She hadn't heard a word. Wine had made her sleepy, and the conversation had left her feeling dull. "Yes, of course it will be."

"I want to share it all with you, Catherine." He lifted her hand to his lips, his gaze never leaving her face.

Cassie felt strangely unsettled by his gesture. She drew her hand away. "Of course you shall share it with me, Geoffrey. We shall always be friends."

The clock struck ten.

"It's growing late, and I can see that you are tired, my dear." He stood, holding out his hand.

Relieved, she took his arm and walked with him outside to his carriage.

"How is Henry working out?" he asked.

"There was a little trouble at first, but he's come around."

"Trouble?"

"Aye. He was behaving in a quarrelsome manner toward the slaves."

"Ahh." Geoffrey nodded and smiled. "Even a man of his lowly station knows there is an order to the universe, Catherine. Still, if he disobeys, send him back. He knows what awaits him at Crichton Hall should he fail you."

Cassie swallowed a tart reply, determined now not to send Henry back, no matter how troublesome he became.

The carriage driver, a young man, scrambled up to his seat and took the reins.

Geoffrey turned toward Cassie. "Do you know that I've loved you since I was a boy?"

She looked away, uncomfortable. The song of katydids filled the silence. Fireflies flitted and glowed. "We were close as children."

"I love you still, Catherine, and I intend to have you as my wife."

"Geoffrey, I—"

"I do not mean to press you for an answer. In fact, I did not mean to mention it. But being so near you like this, I could not help it."

Cassie searched for the right words, eager not to hurt him but needing him to know her feelings. "Geoffrey, we cannot marry. We think nothing alike, you and I."

Even in the darkness, she could see his body grow rigid. "Of course we think nothing alike. Since when do men and women think alike? You say the strangest things." There was an edge to his voice.

She felt her irritation with him begin to swell. "I have no wish to marry."

"That is your father's doing. He has placed notions in your head that are not in keeping with a woman's station."

She started to speak, but he cut across her.

"I know you disagree, Catherine, but centuries of human history have shown that a woman's place is at her husband's side. It is the natural order. You will come to love being my wife. I will cherish you, protect you, provide for you. Our children will live like royalty."

She fought to keep her anger under control, but the evening had worn her patience to a single thread. "I will not marry you, Geoffrey. I do not love you."

The muscles of his jaw twitched. "I know more about you than you realize, my dear. When I truly ask you to marry me, you will eagerly consent, I assure you. Now wish me a good night."

Abruptly Geoffrey's arms encircled her, and his lips pressed hungrily against hers.

Cassie was so surprised she did not fight him, her mind registering only shock and a vague sense of revulsion.

His arms pulled her close, and his tongue thrust clumsily between her lips.

She twisted her head and tried to push him away. Pulling one arm free, she slapped him across the face with all her might. "Stop!"

"Don't fight me, Catherine." His grip tightened. His breath stank of wine and onion. "You can't win in the end. Let me show you how much I love you."

He bent his head toward hers again.

"I believe the lady told you to stop, Crichton."

Chapter Thirteen

C assie's breath caught in her throat.

Cole stood in the shadows, leaning lazily against the carriage wheel.

"You've no right to interfere in the affairs of gentlemen, convict!" Still, Geoffrey did not release her.

"You are no gentleman, Crichton."

"It's all right." Cassie recovered her voice. "Geoffrey was just leaving."

She felt Geoffrey's hesitation, sensed the hatred surging between the two men.

Geoffrey's grip began to loosen. He stood back and, lifting her hand to his lips, kissed it in farewell. "Good evening, Catherine. Remember what I said." He climbed into the carriage. "What are you looking at, boy?" he shouted to the young driver.

The carriage lurched forward and disappeared into the darkness.

"It seems I owe you another debt of thanks."

Alec could see she was trembling. "You shouldn't be alone with him."

The words came out more harshly than he'd intended. He'd come to demand the truth from her, not to rescue her. But when he'd seen Crichton forcing himself on her, all of that had been forgotten. It had taken every ounce of restraint he possessed not to beat the bastard to a pulp.

"Don't tell me what I should and should not do." Her chin shot up defiantly.

She wanted to fight? Good. So did he. "You're perfectly capable of protecting yourself, is that it? Or did you *want* him to take advantage of you?"

"Like you do?"

Alec laughed. Slowly he walked toward her, a predator stalking his prey, until he stood mere inches away. "I don't seem to remember you objecting to my kisses or my touch. Shall we test your resolve, compare his kisses to mine?"

"You've been drinking. I can smell it on your breath."

"You're damned right I've been drinking. And I want some answers." All evening anger had been a viper coiled in his gut, whiskey adding sting to its venom. It was time for him to strike. "I want the truth from you. Now."

"What truth?"

"Did you force the old woman to lie about my identity?"

"Of all the ungrateful—"

"Answer the question."

"You're being ridiculous." She turned and began to walk toward the great house.

He stepped in front of her to block her path and lifted her chin, forcing her to meet his gaze. "Answer me."

"Of course not! I don't know how you could even think such a thing! Why would I try to keep you here when I've come to dread the very sight of you?"

"I can tell by your eyes when you're lying. Did you know that?"

"Then you know I'm telling the truth."

"About the old woman, yes. Why do you lie about your father?"

Her eyes widened in surprise. She blinked it away. "You know nothing about my father."

"I know no one has seen him for months. I know he leaves his daughter and his only heir unprotected while he supposedly looks for breeding stock for his stables. I know he lets his daughter manage his affairs as if she wore breeches."

Cassie stiffened. "What difference does it make that I'm a woman? Or perhaps you think women should have nothing on their minds beyond needlework and frippery."

"Running an estate is men's work."

"Why? Why must it be so? A woman once ruled all of England, yet Englishwomen aren't even allowed to rule themselves."

"Women rule in their own way. They raise the children, run the household—"

"While men run everything else."

Alec could tell she was truly angry with him now and felt his own temper rise. "I've no wish to debate civilization's finer points. One day you'll marry and discover the joys to be found in serving a husband."

Were those tears in her eyes?

"If ever I wed, it will be to a man who treats me as his equal."

"Better to rule in hell, Cassie?"

Her voice quavered. "My life is none of your affair."

"Very well, then. You don't trust me. I don't trust you. But I don't have your life in my hands. It is the reverse, in fact, and I detest it!"

"Your life was in my hands, and I saved it, if you'll remember. Perhaps living like a bondsman will do an arrogant fool like you some good!" She pushed past him and walked inside, slamming the door behind her.

For the second time in recent memory, Alec found himself feeling like an ass.

"Come, Daniel, be brave. You must drink," Cassie urged, cradling the child's damp head.

How could she explain to a four-year-old that his survival depended on the vile concoction she now held to his lips? Having tasted the bitter quinquina once, the boy was reluctant to drink again.

"You want to get well, don't you?"

He nodded weakly, his tiny body racked with chills.

She swallowed the lump in her throat. It could just as easily be Jamie lying here.

"Then you *must* drink, sweetling."

The boy reluctantly parted his fever-parched lips, and, with a grimace, slowly drank the contents of the cup.

"That's a good boy." She lowered his head gently to his pillow and smiled reassuringly to Nettie, who stood next to the bed, her face a wan mask. "Bathe him with wet cloths to cool him. Let him drink if he becomes thirsty. I'll be back to give him another dose this afternoon."

The ague had hit Blakewell's Neck early that morning, sending four field hands and two slave children, including little Daniel, to their beds with high fevers and violent chills. Awakened just before dawn by Nettie's frantic knocking on her bedroom door, Cassie had found her hands full all morning helping Takotah tend the sick.

Those who were able to keep down the medicine, which had a miraculous effect on the fever, would be on their feet within the week. Cassie prayed, not for the first time this morning, that Daniel would be one of them.

She closed the small leather pouch in which Takotah stored the lifesaving red powder and gave the little boy one last kiss on the cheek, but he had already lapsed into a feverish sleep.

"He's a strong boy," Nettie said, more to herself than to Cassie.

"Aye, he is strong. And he has us to care for him." Cassie rose and took Nettie's hand with a reassuring squeeze. Her throat was tight. "We will not let him die."

"Thank you, Cassie." The tears Nettie had been denying all morning streamed down her face. It had been years since Cassie had heard Nettie use her name.

A light knock on the door told her that Luke had returned with the water she'd sent him to fetch a few minutes ago. English physicians, with their strange ideas about illness and medicine, did not permit those with fevers to drink, but Takotah had taught her that to refuse water to the sick was not only cruel, but might also be harmful. She would take Takotah's wisdom over the pompous blusterings of a physician anytime.

She opened the door and stood back to admit Luke, who was carrying two large jugs brimming with sweet water. Barefoot, his broad, muscular torso slick with perspiration, he carried the jugs as if they were empty, placing them lightly on the wooden table next to the bed. He had been hovering about the cabin all morning doing whatever he could to help. He'd even brought in a load of kindling and firewood, despite the obvious fact that it was nearly the end of June and the cabin was more than warm enough. Cassie hadn't realized how fond he was of Daniel.

"If you need anything, I'll be outside," he told Nettie, his deep voice strangely soft.

"You gonna stand in the sun outside my door all day?" Nettie asked, shaking her head and smiling for the first time all morning She sniffed and wiped the tears from her face with the corner of her apron. "Don't be a fool. It's much cooler in here. Sit down. Daniel will want to see you when he wakes up."

Luke glanced at the boy in the bed and back at his mother before sitting down somewhat awkwardly on an old milking stool far too small for him.

"Send for me if anything changes," Cassie said.

No one seemed to hear her.

"You must be thirsty." Nettie poured water into a cup and handed it to Luke.

Luke nodded his thanks and drank deeply, his eyes never leaving Nettie's face.

So that's the way of it, thought Cassie, feeling chagrined for having been so blind. Luke had taken a liking to Daniel's mother. She left, closing the door quietly behind her.

Though the sky was overcast, the day was already oppressively hot as she made her way toward the cookhouse, where the noon meal and a few moments' respite were waiting for her. Heavy clouds lay over the land like a suffocating blanket, and the air, thick with the smell of wood smoke and manure, was hot and sticky, without the slightest hint of a breeze. Perspiration trickled between her breasts and down her back. Despite the playful shrieks and giggles of the children, who chased one another through the rows of small cabins, she felt overcome by a sense of foreboding. First Geoffrey. Now the ague. Though she had purchased a large amount of quinquina when she was last in Williamsburg, she knew there might not be enough to go around should the ague spread. Heaven help them.

Aching for sleep, she longed to crawl into bed and let her dreams carry her far from worry and disease. Rest had been long in coming last night. She'd lain awake until late in the night, restless and troubled. Geoffrey had behaved so strangely. All that talk of marriage. He knew full well she would never marry him.

She lifted her sleeve to her lips as if to wipe away the memory of Geoffrey's unwanted kisses. How astonishingly different was her body's reaction to Cole. Geoffrey's touch had made her feel queasy, while Cole's . . . Could it be only yesterday she and Cole had stood on the riverbank kissing? It seemed ages ago.

What kind of woman would want to make love with a man she thinks is a rapist?

His question had haunted her all night. She had no answer. If she truly believed him a felon, why did she yearn for his touch?

Yet if she believed he was telling the truth, why did she treat him like a servant?

Though she could not legally release him from his indenture without the approval of a magistrate, she could at the very least relieve him of doing manual labor and ask him to employ his business sense on her behalf. He did claim to own a vast estate. But would he help her? Or would he belittle her? Like every other man Cassie knew, he did not approve of her running things. He'd made that clear last night. She could imagine him looking through the ledgers, a disapproving frown on his face, condescension in his voice as he criticized every decision, every unconventional idea.

Running an estate is men's work.

The memory of his words made her bristle.

In the cookhouse, she found Nan just sitting down to eat.

"Daniel... is he—"

"He's asleep, but he still has a powerful fever."

"Oh, look at ye, love." Nan rested her hands on her ample hips, looking Cassie up and down. "Ye must be famished. Sit down and let old Nan fetch ye a thick slice of bread and some cheese."

Cassie sat and gratefully accepted the food, only to discover she had no appetite.

"What is it, love? I can see in yer eyes something's wrong. Ye're not feelin' feverish too?" The cook felt her forehead.

"Nay, I'm fine. Just tired." Cassie forced herself to take a bite, then chewed and swallowed. Nan had enough to worry about. Cassie would tell her about Geoffrey's strange behavior some other time. She started to take another bite, but never got the chance. The door flew open.

"Miss Cassie!" Nate was out of breath, his freckled face red from exertion. "It's Rebecca!"

"The baby?"

It was still early, but babies rarely seemed to appear when one expected them.

"No." He shook his head, a shock of red hair falling into his eyes. "Fever. She's burning up!"

Cassie stood, gathering the leather pouch. "Nate, fetch water from the well. I'll bring cider and all the clean cloths we can spare."

Nate stood wringing his hands. "Do you think she'll ... "

"We'll do all we can." Cassie placed a reassuring hand on Nate's arm. "Nan, find Zach or Cole. Tell one of them to fetch Takotah and bring her—"

"The witch?" Nate shook his head. "I won't have her anywhere near my Becky!"

Cassie ignored him. "—to the tanner's cabin."

Nan nodded and was gone, hurrying as fast as her legs could carry her toward the pit saw, where Zach and Cole were cutting lumber.

"No!" Nate shouted again.

"Listen to me," Cassie met Nate's gaze. "Takotah might not live the way we do, but no one knows more about healing than she. I would trust Takotah with my life. Aye, and Jamie's, too."

She ignored the incredulous frown on Nate's face and hastened toward the cabins, leaving him behind.

"She wasn't able to save your mother, now, was she?" he shouted after her.

Cassie felt her step falter. "That wasn't Takotah's fault."

If Cassie had stayed to help, as Takotah had asked her to, her mother might have lived. But her mother had been in so much pain. Cassie had not been able to bear the sight of such suffering. Like a scared child, she had fled.

"It's said she has a drink that will curdle a man's seed in his wife's body and make it useless. I even hear she has a poison that will kill a babe in its mother's womb. She's a witch!"

"Nonsense!" Cassie turned to face him, her patience at an end.

She'd not waste her time explaining the necessity for such potions. These were women's secrets, not to be shared with any man. "Your wife and child need you. You can either stand here arguing with me, or you can help them. Which will it be?"

*A*lec stepped through the low entrance to the Indian woman's lodge. When his eyes had adjusted to the darkness, he realized she was not home. There was no reason to feel tense, he told himself. She was just an old woman. An old woman who had saved his life and who was now desperately needed by another.

The scent of wood smoke and strange herbs tickled his nose. Quickly taking in his surroundings—a small fire in an open hearth at the center of the room, plants, roots, and berries hanging from the ceiling, a bundle of animal hides stowed carefully in the corner—he turned to leave.

He froze, suppressing a gasp. He had not heard her approach, but the Indian woman stood just inside the doorway, looking up at him, assessing him with eyes so dark they might as well have been black. Her thick gray hair hung nearly to her waist in two slick braids. Her wrinkled face, as dark as that of any slave, was covered with strange black tattoos. She was clothed in an Englishwoman's blouse and a skirt of tanned animal skins. Whatever he had imagined she would do next, he did not expect her to smile and pat him on the arm. The simple gesture at once put him at ease.

"You are strong again."

"Aye. Thank you. I'm told you saved my life."

"I think you must have wanted very much to live." She brushed his thanks aside. "Now, let's go to Rebecca."

"How did you know?" Chills crept down his spine. He hadn't told her his reason for coming.

"About Rebecca?" Takotah grinned. "Maybe the wind whispered it in my ear. Or maybe her husband has a very loud voice."

In the tanner's cabin they found Cassie already administering the first draft of quinquina powder to Rebecca, who lay pale and shivering on the bed in the center of the tiny room, her dark hair clinging to her damp face, her arms wrapped protectively around her heavy abdomen.

Nate stood at the foot of the bed, shouting. "I tell you I won't have that savage anywhere near..."

He blanched and his words fell abruptly into silence when he saw Takotah enter.

Apparently oblivious to the ill will borne her by the tanner, Takotah went at once to Rebecca's side.

Rebecca's eyes widened in fear, and she recoiled.

"Don't touch her!" Nate lunged forward.

Alec caught Nate with a shoulder to the chest, knocking the air out of him and driving him back against the wall, where he held him fast. He had no doubt Nate would have thrown the old woman from the room had he not restrained him.

"Rebecca, Takotah is here to help because I asked her to come." Cassie took Rebecca's trembling hand and spoke in a calm, even voice. "She is the only one who can help you and your baby. Will you let her try?"

No longer the inexperienced maid Alec had kissed yesterday afternoon nor the hot-tempered planter's daughter, Cassie spoke now with the confidence and composure of a woman accustomed to managing a large household, reminding him for one unexpected moment of Elizabeth.

Rebecca's gazed moved back and forth from her husband, who swore and struggled fruitlessly with Alec, to Takotah, who sat calmly next to her on the bed.

"Aye." Her voice was so weak Alec was not sure at first she had really spoken.

Nate sagged against Alec with a resigned sigh, yielding to his wife's wishes.

Takotah closed her eyes and settled her open palm on Rebecca's swollen belly. "Your child is alive and healthy. She moves."

"She?" Rebecca smiled weakly through chattering teeth.

Alec wondered what kind of power Takotah possessed to tell so much from a simple touch.

"We must drive this sickness from you." Takotah motioned to Cassie to pour water into a tin basin next to the bed. Dipping a cloth into the basin, Takotah wrung it out and placed it gently on Rebecca's forehead.

"Come, friend," Alec said, loosening his grip. "Let's leave the women to their work. I've a notion we'll only get in their way."

He placed one hand firmly between Nate's shoulder blades and propelled him toward the door, feeling oddly satisfied by Cassie's grateful smile.

Chapter Fourteen

*A*lec swallowed another foul mouthful of whiskey and cursed. Distracting Nate was not proving at all easy. Enlisting Zach's help, he had at first managed to keep the distraught husband busy cutting lumber and, later, when that task was completed, playing cards.

But just before sunset Cassie had appeared, her face pale and drawn, with bad news. Rebecca had gone into labor, her weary body apparently eager to rid itself of its extra burden. One look at the frantic expression on Nate's freckled face, and Alec knew there was only one thing they could do for the tanner—get him good and drunk. And no man wanted to drink alone.

Old Charlie had generously donated a jug of his strongest whiskey to the cause, though he himself did not join them. Now Nate sat in front of a dying bonfire, with Alec on one side and Zach on the other, far beyond pain. They were far enough from the cabin so Nate could not hear Rebecca's agonized cries, which at first had driven the father-to-be into a frenzy, but close enough so that the distressed man could see the cabin's door. Not that Nate could actually *see* the cabin, with his eyes half closed and his head rolling limply about on his shoulders, Alec realized foggily. He handed the whiskey jug to Zach, who contemplated it for a moment as if he did not know what it was before clumsily accepting it and taking a swig.

So it had been when his sister had given birth to her children, the fifth no different from the first. Alec and Matthew had sat below in the drawing room, drinking Scotch in silence, both of them flinching with each pained moan that reached them from the floor above. Strange that men, who were supposed to be the stronger sex, who were supposed to protect women from suffering, became so completely useless when it came to childbirth, a suffering for which they were to blame.

Zach hiccupped and went to hand the whiskey to Nate, but Nate was no longer there. Or rather, he was no longer upright, having flopped over backward, unconscious, into the grass.

Zach struggled to his feet and looked down into Nate's placid face. "I think 'e's had 'nough."

"Aye." Alec felt dizzy himself.

Zach took another swig and handed over the jug.

Alec's stomach lurched. "No, thank you very much. Nate is quite uncon ... uncon ... uncon .. . he's out. We needn't drink another drop."

It was very hard to think.

"Suit yerself." Zach took another swallow and dropped the nearly empty jug into the dirt with a belch.

Alec found himself wrenched to alertness. Someone was calling for him.

"Mr. Braden?"

The call came again.

He stood up, willing his legs to be steady, and turned to find Nan hurrying toward him. Her face was pale, her hands clutching nervously at her apron.

"A fine bunch ye are." She cast a scathing look at the three of them.

"Aye," Alec managed in reply. The ground was very wobbly.

"Nate's keeled over for the night, I see. A lot of good he'll do his Rebecca in this state. Zach might as well be. Zachariah!" the cook bellowed.

The sawyer, who'd been staring blankly into the fire, jumped to his feet, staggered, then fell to his knees. "Yes'm? Pardon me, sweet Nan, but I'm a wee bit . . . um . . . drunk."

"Don't 'sweet Nan' me, you big lout." Nan planted her hands on her hips. "And look at ye, Mr. Braden, barely able to stand. Shame on the lot of ye, bein' worse than useless when the mistress needs ye!"

For a moment Alec felt like a young boy who'd been caught stealing sweets from the pantry.

"I do 'pologize, but we merely did what we could to console young Nate." He fought to clear his head and tried to remove the effects of the alcohol from his speech. "If there is aught I can do to help, please let me know."

The cook snorted derisively, her gaze moving from Nate to Zach and coming finally to rest again on Alec.

"I suppose ye'll have to do." She turned abruptly and headed back toward the cabin. "Come. We have need of yer strength—if ye have any that ye haven't squandered on drink, that is. Piss and wind. That's menfolk."

He fell in beside the cook, the brisk walk helping to clear his mind.

"The babe is not turned right, and Rebecca is too sick to sit on the birthin' stool, too weak to push, God bless her." Nan sounded near tears. "Poor Miss Cassie! This is so hard for her, though ye'd never know it. She'd never complain, but I see the fear in her eyes. She was eighteen when her mother died. Blames herself for it, too, she does."

"Blames herself?"

"She tried to stay by her mother's side, she did, tried to help Takotah, but she couldn't stand watchin' her mother suffer. Out the door she ran, pale as a ghost, out into the forest. When she came back she found her new baby brother alive, her mother dyin'. The master was so beside himself with grief when his dear Amanda finally passed on, he never saw how Miss Cassie tortured herself for it."

A muffled cry in the distance interrupted the cook and caused them both to hasten their steps.

"Then when she began to lose the master, too … " The cook suddenly fell mute.

Now alert, Alec willed her to continue, but Nan remained stubbornly mute.

She had almost said too much, and she knew it.

*C*assie tried to ignore the ache in her arms and shoulders. She must hold out for Rebecca's sake. She sat in the bed behind Rebecca, whom she had pushed into a semi-sitting position to ease the birth. Normally the birthing mother would squat on the bed or sit on a birthing stool, but Rebecca was too delirious from pain and fever to do either. Nor was she able to lift and part her knees on her own. Martha, a bondswoman who'd herself given birth nine times, supported one leg, while Takotah, who sat on the bed where she could easily reach under Rebecca's gown to check her progress, supported the other. Cassie had wedged her back against the wall for support, but she hadn't enough strength to hold Rebecca up for long.

She could see from the look in Takotah's eyes that things were not going well. The babe was coming into the world feet-first, and the birth waters Rebecca had passed were murky instead of clear. Takotah had tried to turn the babe, but that had only increased Rebecca's bleeding.

To make matters worse, Rebecca had been unable to keep the quinquina down once her labor had begun, and now, exhausted, she lay shivering with fever in Cassie's aching arms, conscious only when the pains came.

At the sound of the opening door, Cassie looked up, relieved, expecting to see Nan followed by Nate. Instead Nan entered with Cole.

"He's passed out, he is, Missy. Drunk—they're all dead drunk." Nan glared at Cole, more than a little disgust in her voice.

Cassie looked questioningly toward Cole, who apart from a slight flush looked reasonably sober.

"I believe I've enough wits about me to help," he said.

"Very well, Mr. Braden."

Rebecca moaned softly, turning her head to and fro. Nan quickly took Rebecca's other leg from Takotah, leaving the Indian woman two free hands. Gradually the moan grew louder and more frantic until it became a wail, and Rebecca's eyes at last flew open. Cassie fought for the strength to hold her up.

Cole was already at her side, taking Rebecca's weight and sliding into the bed behind her. "I've got her."

Though his breath smelled strongly of whiskey, his movements were smooth, his touch as he adjusted Rebecca's weight on his chest gentle.

Cassie bathed Rebecca's contorted face with a cool cloth, silently chiding herself for the weakness she felt inside. Silly emotions had no place here. Her sympathy for Rebecca's suffering would only make matters worse if she allowed herself to be overwhelmed. She had already learned that lesson.

The pain neared its peak. Rebecca sobbed and clutched frantically at the sheets. Cassie felt her own heart beat faster, and closed her eyes against the burning of tears. The parish priest had told her after her mother's funeral that women were meant to suffer in childbed as God's punishment for the sins of Eve. She hadn't believed it then, and, looking into Rebecca's anguished eyes, she refused to believe it now.

Such a god could only be a despicable tyrant.

She looked up to find Cole gazing at her as if he could read her thoughts. Hastily she looked away.

"Strength, Rebecca. Strength." Takotah spoke in a voice gentle yet as strong as iron. "You and your baby can survive this."

Cassie looked toward Takotah for proof she believed what she had just said, but saw nothing but worry on Takotah's face.

Slowly Rebecca's cries subsided, and she went limp once again.

"Poor lamb." Nan shook her head.

"A man ought to be good for more than spillin' his seed in a woman and causin' her such misery." Martha shared an understanding glance with the cook and glared at Cole, who opened his mouth as if to speak in defense of his sex, but said nothing.

"We must get her to drink." Takotah rose from the bed and poured water into a tin cup.

"Rebecca." Cassie took the cup from Takotah and urged Rebecca to consciousness. "Rebecca, you must drink."

Rebecca looked at her through glazed eyes, seeming not to comprehend. Cassie put the cup to her lips, but after taking just a sip, Rebecca turned her head away, slipping into unconsciousness again. Water spilled onto Cole's forearm and the sleeve of his shirt.

"Sorry," Cassie grabbed a cloth and wiping up the rivulets that ran down his arm.

"It's only water." Cole gave her a lopsided grin.

"Nate?" called Rebecca weakly, turning her head toward the sound of Cole's voice. "Nate?"

Takotah nodded to Cole, who looked puzzled for a moment before responding, "Aye, Rebecca."

"He calls her Becky," Cassie whispered.

"Nate?"

"Aye, Becky."

Cassie refilled the cup with water and gestured to Cole to speak again.

"You must drink, Becky. The babe...uh...needs water," he said, looking sheepish.

"Here, love," said Cassie, smiling at the embarrassed flush that appeared on Cole's cheeks. "Drink this."

Rebecca responded, swallowing the contents of the cup sip by sip before lapsing into a troubled sleep.

"When the next pain comes, ask her to push." Takotah held the baby's tiny feet. "If she thinks you're her husband, it might give her strength. The sooner this child is born, the better for both of them."

Cole nodded, though the look on his face showed he was more than a little uncomfortable.

The next contraction came almost immediately, building slowly until Rebecca began to cry out and call desperately for her husband.

"I'm right here, Becky. I'm here. Take my hands."

Rebecca released the sheet she had been clutching and grasped Cole's hands.

"The babe is ready to be born, but you must help it. You must push, Becky. Push."

For a moment Cassie was afraid Rebecca was too delirious to understand or too weak to push despite Cole's comforting presence. Then she lifted her head and began to bear down.

"Strength, Rebecca," Takotah crooned. "I can see your baby's feet."

"That's it, Becky." Despite whatever embarrassment he felt, Cole seemed to understand what was needed.

Rebecca cried out as the contraction passed its peak, then sagged against Cole, remaining only half-conscious.

"Rest, Becky," he murmured. "It will soon be over."

"I love you, Nate."

The chagrined look on Cole's face nearly made Cassie laugh out loud.

After two more contractions Cassie could see little legs. After three, Takotah held the baby's limp body in her hands. It was, as she had predicted, a little girl.

"Come, Becky, your daughter's nearly born," Takotah crooned as the next contraction began to crest. "Push her into the world where you can hold her."

Rebecca moaned through gritted teeth, and her bloodcurdling scream pierced the air as at last the baby's head emerged. The pain finally gone, she lapsed again into unconsciousness.

Cassie watched, hardly daring to hope, as Takotah massaged the baby and cleared fluid from its throat, speaking softly to the infant in her native tongue as she worked. Seconds seemed to stretch into eternity as, unable to breathe, Cassie waited with the others for some sign of life.

Just when it seemed sure that Takotah would be unable to coax life into the child, there came a little cough, followed by another, followed by the tiniest cry Cassie had ever heard. The baby's skin changed from bluish gray to bright pink, and Cassie knew from the smile on Takotah's face that she would live.

The room filled with laughter.

"Saints be praised!" Martha shouted.

Cassie felt relief wash through her and thought for a moment her knees might buckle. The room seemed to spin. Two strong hands grasped her shoulders, and Cole's concerned face swam before her eyes. "Are you well, Cassie? Perhaps you should sit for a moment."

" I . . . I'm fine." She willed her feet to be steady. "Just a bit tired, I think."

His hands felt warm through the linen of her dress, and the salty scent of his skin filled her nostrils. She fought the urge to sink against him, instead pushing past him to place a cool cloth on Rebecca's brow. The new mother lay back on her pillow where Cole had placed her, shivering in her sleep, the battle for her life still far from over.

Takotah had tied off and cut the cord and was giving the baby her first bath, which, from the sound of the baby's cries, she did not appreciate. After drying the infant and wrapping her in warm blankets, Takotah handed the baby to Martha.

"Aye, Rebecca will have her hands full with this one." Martha gave the baby a kiss before passing her on to Cassie.

Nearly four weeks early by Takotah's reckoning, the little girl was the tiniest babe Cassie had ever held. With only the faintest red fuzz on her head, tiny red lips curved into a furious frown, and dark blue eyes that already seemed to examine the world around her, she was a miracle.

It was then that Cassie realized she was laughing and crying at the same time, her vision blurred with tears that rolled down her cheeks.

"She's so . . . tiny," Cole said from beside her.

"Aye." Cassie smiled.

The baby began to root at her breast.

"And hungry." Cole chuckled.

Cassie felt color rush to her cheeks. "Would you like to hold her?"

His eyes widened in surprise. " I . . . that is to say ... "

She took advantage of his hesitation. "Support her head like this."

Ever so carefully he took the baby into his arms. When he finally looked up to meet Cassie's gaze, she thought her heart had stopped. His blue eyes held a warmth she had not seen before. The smile that now spread across his face made her breath catch in her throat. For a moment it was just the three of them—Cassie, the baby, Cole. She found herself wishing this were her baby, and Cole its father.

"Until Rebecca is strong again, the baby will need a wet nurse." Takotah had delivered the afterbirth and was now cleaning up.

"Aye." Cassie shook off her fantasy and gently took the babe from Cole. "I'll take her to Sarah. Her son is now three months old. She ought to have milk to spare."

Takotah nodded in agreement.

"And I'll go wake the father." Cole grinned.

*A*lec's self-appointed task was more easily said than done, as he quickly discovered. Nate refused to budge, even after a few firm kicks to his posterior. Zach, who might have helped, was now facedown in the dirt, snoring. There was only one solution.

Alec knelt over the tanner and, slinging him over his shoulder as he might a sack of grain, lifted him off the ground. Nate was lighter than he had expected, and he had no difficulty carrying him across the courtyard to the horse trough. He dropped Nate into the water and waited.

For a moment nothing happened, and he feared Nate was so drunk he would drown.

Then the tanner rose, coughing and sputtering, to the surface. "What... who ... aack!"

Alec took the floundering man by his collar and hoisted him to his feet.

"What. . . where am I?" Nate slurred.

"It's the middle of night, and you're standing in the horse trough, my friend."

Nate looked down at his feet, which were still submerged, and stepped clumsily out of the water. "I think I'm going to be sick."

With a moan, he doubled over and emptied the contents of his stomach into the dirt.

Alec left him and, carrying a bucket of water, walked back to Zach.

"Son of a ... !" Zach howled when the cold water hit him. Shaking his head, he lurched to his feet. "What the hell do you think you're doing?"

"Waking you up." Alec easily sidestepped a clumsy punch.

Zach landed on his knees in the din, then looked up at him. "Cole?"

"Aye. Rebecca's had her baby. I need help getting the new father on his feet."

"Baby?"

"A healthy wee girl."

"Where's Nate?" Zach staggered to his feet, clutching his head.

"On his knees, retching in the dirt." Alec pointed to the figure huddled on the ground nearby. At the mention of the word *retch*, he saw Zach's face turn white.

"Not you, too."

Zach sank to the ground, gagging.

Come to think of it, Alec wasn't feeling too well himself. He quickly turned and walked ten paces away, gulping in deep breaths of fresh air as he went, closing his ears to the foul sounds behind him. This was going to be a long night.

Chapter Fifteen

*T*wenty minutes later, Alec had both men on their feet and walking in the same direction. With their stomachs thoroughly purged, they seemed to feel much better.

"You're sure she has red hair?" Nate clawed at the mosquito bites on his arms. The nasty insects had preyed heavily upon him as he slept.

"Aye, I saw her with my own eyes."

"And Rebecca?"

"Asleep when I left."

By the time they reached the cabin, Nate was running, Alec and Zach following behind.

"Rebecca?" Nate opened the door and stepped to his wife's side.

"She's sleepin', and don't ye wake her." Nan eyed the three of them disapprovingly.

Martha was gone, leaving only Nan, who was busy tidying up the tiny cabin, and Takotah, who was folding several small skin pouches into a leather bundle.

"Will she ... live?" Nate asked Takotah, stroking his wife's cheek.

"She is still very sick, but we have come this far," Takotah smiled. "If she keeps down the red powder I just gave her and does not bleed too much, she should be well soon."

"No thanks to you." Nan glared at Nate. "While you were facedown in the dirt, Takotah—aye, and Cole, too—was busy savin' yer wife and babe."

Nate looked questioningly toward Alec, who shrugged, then Takotah. "I'm sorry. I called you a witch and worse, curse my tongue. I just didn't think that a ... a heathen could know the ways of healin'."

Takotah accepted the apology with a graceful nod.

"Now if only she had a cure for this headache." Zach stood near the hearth, holding his head in his hands.

Takotah patted Zach on the arm as she passed, her dark eyes twinkling with amusement. "What you need is sleep and a bit of sense."

She left the cabin, closing the door behind her.

"Sense? That'll be the day." Nan wiped her hands on her apron and plopped her heavy form down in the rocking chair. She'd offered to tend Rebecca through the night, and Takotah, with other patients to tend, had agreed.

Alec was about to leave to follow Takotah's advice and seek his bed when Cassie entered, carrying a tiny bundle. There were dark circles under her eyes, but her cheeks were flushed with excitement. When she looked at him, her smile was so full of life that any fatigue he might have been feeling vanished.

"Care to see your wee daughter?" She presented the little bundle to Nate, who stared down at the sleeping infant in wonder.

"Can I hold her?"

"Aye." Cassie laughed softly. "You needn't ask me. You are the babe's father, are you not?"

"Aye." He took the baby in his arms.

"Be sure to support her head," Cassie instructed. "No, like this."

Alec watched as she showed Nate how to hold his baby, lost in wonderment of his own. He'd never seen a baby born before, and didn't quite know what to think. It had been both terrible and wonderful, the pain and suffering all resulting in the tiny miracle Nate now held in his arms. Men were so proud of their physical strength, boasting of their feats to one another, but the kind of strength it took to withstand childbirth was something no man would ever be able to comprehend.

Cassie laughed softly again, smiling at him. Alec smiled back, though he'd been too lost in his own thoughts to know why she was smiling. If she was exhausted, she hid it well. The circles under her eyes were the only sign she'd risen before the sun. She exuded a vibrancy that seemed to fill the room with light, and everyone in the tiny cabin seemed to draw strength from her presence. Alec watched as she took the baby from its nervous father and kissed its downy head. It was obvious she loved children. He found himself hoping for her sake she would one day be able to raise her own. The sharp regret he suddenly felt knowing he would not be the man to father them surprised him. He'd never wanted to be a father before.

Did he really desire her that badly? Aye, he did. That was the hell of it. He'd vowed to himself time and time again to stay away from her, at least until his identity had been restored. But his vow didn't make his need for her go away. Seeing her like this, cradling a new life against her breast, her green eyes sparkling with happiness, he wanted her more than ever. But giving in to this hunger now might end his life and would certainly ruin hers. Though a night with her beneath him might be worth a trip to the gallows, he wouldn't ruin her life to gratify his lust.

Suddenly the cabin seemed much too small. He needed air. He bade Cassie a hasty goodnight and found the door. He'd made it almost all the way back to his own cabin when he heard her call his name. She had followed him outside and was hurrying to catch up with him. He stopped and turned to face her.

"I just wanted to thank you." She smoothed her skirts. "You may have saved their lives."

He found the praise both pleasing and disturbing. "You'd have been fine without me."

He turned and continued on his way.

She fell in beside him. "Have you ever seen a babe born before?"

"Nay, though I was home when my sister gave birth to her five children and saw them soon after."

"You're an uncle?"

"That I am. Four nieces and a nephew."

"Their names?" She acted as if she were testing him, but there was a playful smile on her lips.

She was teasing him, he realized—flirting. A small voice in his head told him to end this conversation. A rude retort would surely do it. But he batted the voice away as one might an annoying insect."

"Are you testing me again, Miss Blakewell?" He leaned against a rain barrel that sat beside his cabin and counted on his fingers. "Emily is thirteen and wants very much to be a lady. Victoria is ten and cares only for horses. Little Matthew is seven and detests being called 'little Matthew.'"

Cassie laughed, and Alec couldn't help laughing with her.

"Charlotte is five and adores me."

"So you've charmed her, too?"

"Aye, I have that effect on women."

They both laughed at his jest, Cassie tilting her head shyly away from him.

"The baby, Anne, is now seventeen months old." As he spoke his youngest niece's name, a pang of homesickness struck him hard in the chest.

"You must miss them very much." Her gaze had softened, her words almost a whisper.

He nodded, afraid to speak lest his voice fail him. The truth was, he missed them horribly.

Crickets chirped in the background, filling the silence.

"You'll be home with them by Christmas." She laid her hand gently on his arm.

He couldn't tell if she was sincere or not. She spoke as if she now believed him. And yet …

Did she know how beautiful she was? Even here in the light of a quarter moon, her hair mussed, dark circles under her eyes, she affected him. "You smell like lemon."

"It's the balm Takotah makes to keep the mosquitoes at bay." She shifted under his gaze. "I've tried to get everyone to use it, but most are afraid of anything she makes. The scent is quite strong, I'm afraid. I'd be happy to give you some."

"No, thank you. Mosquitoes rarely bother me."

"You may find that colonial mosquitoes are not as polite or discriminating as their English cousins." She stood there for a moment, lips slightly parted, as if she were waiting for him to kiss her.

He took her hand and gave it a gentle squeeze, fighting the urge to do more. "Good night, Miss Blakewell."

He turned and entered his cabin and closed the door behind him.

"Ouch!" Cassie grabbed the silver-handled hairbrush from Elly and massaged her stinging scalp. This experiment was turning into a disaster. "I can manage from here, Elly."

"But, Miss Cass—"

"You've done quite enough for now, thank you. You may go."

Elly gave her one last beseeching look, then left, closing the bedroom door behind her.

Cassie gazed into her mirror and began to comb her hair, or what was left of it. Elly hadn't given her a moment's peace in a week, alternately fawning over her and sulking, clearly desperate to accompany her to Crichton Hall. At first Cassie had refused to consider it, sure that Elly would make a ninny of herself over Geoffrey and embarrass them all.

But Cassie could remember the first time her mother had let her stay awake late enough to watch the ladies dress. She'd been dazzled by the bright colors of their silken gowns, the sparkle of their jewels, the heady scents of their perfumes. It had seemed a fairy tale, and she'd gone to bed with a head full of romantic dreams.

Perhaps she was being too hard on Elly. She could understand the girl's eagerness. Virginia's finest attended this event. It was the first large social gathering of the summer, the last before the wealthy planters would leave their estates for the opening of the House of Burgesses in Williamsburg. The only place one could see more colonial pageantry was at one of King Carter's affairs, or the annual Governor's Ball.

Still, what function scatterbrained Elly could serve at Crichton Hall eluded Cassie. She couldn't help in the kitchen—not without starting a rebellion among the cooks—and Cassie didn't trust her to look after Jamie. The only other possibility was for Elly to serve as her dressing maid, a task Nettie usually performed. Cassie had been willing to let Elly try, but the experiment had thus far proved to be more painful than she'd imagined.

She brushed the few remaining tangles from her hair and began to twist it into a simple chignon. It was not the style, but she was only going riding. And her hair, curly as it was, did not readily submit to being piled and pinned tightly to the top of her head. It always seemed to escape. She pinned the thick coil of hair into place, pulled free a small lock over each temple, and let the curls fall. She might not be blessed with obedient tresses, but at least she didn't have to spend hours burning her hair with a hot iron to create curls.

The dark circles had begun to fade from under her eyes, she noticed, examining her reflection. There'd been a lull in the fever outbreak at Blakewell's Neck, and she'd finally gotten a few nights' sleep. They'd been lucky so far. In all, seventeen had been stricken with the ague, and all had pulled through, thanks to Takotah and the quinquina powder. Daniel was himself again, and Rebecca, though weak, was now able to nurse her tiny daughter herself. Nate was boasting of the baby—they'd named her Catherine after Cassie—to anyone who would listen, portraying Takotah as a miracle worker.

Cole's part in the birth had not gone unnoticed either. Cassie could mark a change, especially in the women, who no longer, seemed to fear him but smiled and called to him as he passed.

Some of the young, unmarried bondswomen had even begun to flirt with him, their witless giggling grating on Cassie's nerves. Not that she was jealous. Far from it. She was grateful for the polite distance that had sprung up between her and Cole since little Catherine's birth.

She had been touched that night, more than she cared to admit.

Cole's gentleness and his willingness to help had surprised her. The way he'd held Rebecca's hands and whispered encouragement in her ear had made Cassie wonder what it would be like to be his wife, to bear his children. Would he hold her hand? Would he fret for her safety? Would he gaze with awe on their newborn children as he had little Catherine? The thought had left her with a longing she dared not name.

As to Cole's true identity, she was more convinced than ever that he was telling the truth, however implausible his story. Or perhaps the gaol fever had destroyed his mind, and he truly believed he was someone else. Regardless of his true name, she was now certain Cole Braden was not the kind of man who could deliberately hurt a woman. Seduce, aye. She herself was all but proof of that. But ravish and harm? Nay. No man could feign the kind of compassion he'd shown for Rebecca.

There'd been a change in him after that. Now his eyes held neither hunger nor hostility when he looked at her. Those emotions had been replaced by a distant sort of courtesy. Cassie had no idea what might have caused the change or what it might mean. The question of her father's whereabouts still hung between them. But whatever the cause for the change in him, he seemed no longer to desire her. For that she was honestly grateful. That was as it should be.

And these tears? Where did they come from? Perhaps she was just weary of illness and heat, she decided, refusing to consider any other possibility.

She stood and smoothed her riding skirts, forcing her thoughts elsewhere. There were only two short days before she would leave for Crichton Hall, and much remained to be done. She could not afford to waste time thinking about a man who neither wanted her nor had a place in her life.

*A*lec watched from beneath a stand of pines as Cassie rode past in the distance. He'd watched her ride in this direction every morning for most of a month now and was determined to discover her secret today.

This had nothing to do with jealousy, he told himself for the third time. It mattered not one whit if she was meeting secretly with a suitor. What mattered was restoring his name, and there were simply too many unanswered questions at Blakewell's Neck. Following her, as distasteful as it was, might provide some answers.

She rode with the confidence and skill of a man, and he couldn't deny feeling some odd sort of pride in her abilities. Of course, her habit of sitting astride would have been ill-tolerated in England.

Urging Aldebaran forward, he stayed close enough to be certain of her direction but not so close that her mare could sense the stallion's presence and give him away. Her tracks were easy to spy in the soft, damp earth of the forest floor. Even had he not been able to see them, he'd followed her this far before and had a general sense of where she was heading.

Alec relaxed in the saddle. It had rained again last night, leaving the air as fresh as when the world was new. Frogs sang cheerily from their hidden puddles in the forest bog, while birds called to one another from their perches among the trees. Their songs still sounded exotic to him as they echoed through this inconceivable expanse of wilderness. There was a vastness to this land that threatened to swallow a man, quite literally. Every Englishman knew the story of Roanoke. Fifteen hale men had vanished from Roanoke Island, leaving nothing behind, not even skeletons, to tell of their fate. Some believed they'd gone to live with the Indians or had become some tribe's dinner. Others thought they'd tried to sail for home and had been lost at sea. Alec was sure that, should the colonists ever cease to beat back the forest with ax and flame, it would engulf them, quickly reclaiming its own and wiping away any trace that Englishmen had once lived here.

That this new continent held unseen dangers was beyond dispute. Yet, despite the subservient nature of Alec's position at Blakewell's Neck, there was a freedom here he'd not experienced before.

There were no appointments to keep, no wigs or stifling apparel to wear, no dull dinners to sit through while pretending to be entertained. There were no conniving would-be mothers-in-law to guard against, no slithering MP's trying to sniff out his politics, no obsequious clerks trying to fawn their way into his good graces. Ironic as it might be, he was a freer man as Nicholas Braden than he'd been as Alec Kenleigh. But such responsibilities were the burden of a gentleman, and the sooner Alec returned to tend to his obligations the better.

A small brown rabbit darted out from cover just ahead of Aldebaran's hooves and fled deeper into the forest, its white tail disappearing in a bush. For a moment Alec feared the horse would whinny in alarm, alerting Cassie to his presence, but Aldebaran responded instantly to Alec's firm hand and kept his head. The stallion was in top form, and Alec was certain it could easily best any animal in the colony.

"Aldebaran—the follower," he whispered, reflecting on the irony of the racehorse's Arabic name. He doubted Master Blakewell knew what the word meant. "Don't worry, old boy. The other horses shall follow you."

He was looking forward to the race at Crichton Hall. He'd heard of the long-standing rivalry between the Crichtons and the Blakewells when it came to horse racing, and he was looking forward to the choked look on Crichton's face when his mount ate Aldebaran's dust. Of course, Cassie had not yet asked him to accompany her or to race Aldebaran. But then, he didn't plan on waiting for her invitation or her permission.

The ground began to slope downhill, and he slowed his mount, his gaze fixed on Cassie's form in the distance. This was where he'd lost her before. At the bottom of the hill, he knew, there was a heavily wooded marsh. Though he'd been able to follow her into it, he hadn't been able to track her once she'd gotten inside. Water and muck had swallowed all tracks, and the dim light made it virtually impossible to keep her in his sights. He had been forced to turn back before he lost his sense of direction and found himself spending the night in a swamp.

This time he'd be more careful.

*C*assie reined Andromeda to a stop and listened, tingles racing down her spine. Ever since she'd entered the marsh, she'd had an odd feeling someone was watching her. She bent over her mare and pretended to examine its leg for injury, using her position to look covertly behind her. She saw no one. It was the third time in a fortnight she'd felt eyes upon her in this marsh. She waited a moment longer, listening. Mosquitoes buzzed around her, and a raven called overhead, its throaty squawk echoing through the trees. Andromeda nickered softly, as if to question the delay. The mare knew the way to her father's cabin and was eager for the treat of apples she would receive there.

Cassie urged the horse forward again, chiding herself for letting her imagination get the best of her. She was not fond of these dark marshlands, to be sure. With their snakes, insects, and spiders, the marshes seemed unfit for human being or horse. Worst of all was the air. Thick, humid and smelling of rotting vegetation, the marsh air was known to carry the illnesses that made life in this colony so difficult. Her father had built the family's home far above the marshes, ensuring that the bad air would dissipate before reaching the estate's inhabitants. Even so, summer had always been a time of sickness. She considered it nothing short of a miracle that her father, who now lived in the middle of this, had been spared. The air didn't seem to bother him. He'd gotten the fever only once or twice in his lifetime. Even the voracious mosquitoes seemed to leave him alone. Cassie thanked Takotah's lemon balm for that. In the distance she saw the sandy rise that marked her destination.

Takotah had discovered this island long ago. Only six people knew of its existence, including Micah, Zach, and Nan. But only Takotah, Cassie, and Micah knew how to get here and back. Surrounded by dense marsh, it made the perfect hiding place, an oasis of solid ground and sunshine in a dark and murky swamp. Once she was safely on land, Cassie dismounted and led Andromeda to the makeshift shelter that served as a stall. It was a relief to be in sunlight again.

Leaving the mare contentedly munching on apples, she carried the basket of food toward the house. Nothing more than a clapboard shanty, the structure resembled a slave cabin, but it held back both rain and wind and kept her father safe. He had built it himself when he'd felt his wits begin to leave him. She had begged him to stay at the great house, but he had refused even to discuss it, leaving with only a change of clothes and a loaf of bread as soon as the tiny dwelling had been completed. "Father?"

She stepped through the door to find him standing with his back to the window. His gaze moved over the walls as if he were searching for something. Takotah said he was listening to spirits, but Cassie thought he seemed terribly lost. His shirt and breeches were wrinkled and askew from having been slept in, and his white hair hung in tangled curls around his shoulders.

"I've brought breakfast, Father. I hope you're hungry."

Her father did not answer. She had not expected him to. He gazed at the walls, his eyes darting back and forth. She placed bread and cheese on the table, and took her father by the arm. Only then did he notice her, giving her a glassy look that said he did not know her. Still he said nothing.

"Sit here, Father." She urged him into his seat and placed a piece of buttered bread in his hand.

For a moment he seemed oblivious to the food. Then slowly he began to eat. His condition had worsened to the point that she wondered if she'd soon have to feed him. She had no idea how she'd manage that.

Takotah already spent half of her day here, and slept here most nights, as well, helping to bathe him and aiding him with his personal needs. If there was one thing Cassie was grateful for in all of this, it was that her father was not aware of the indignities he suffered. Had his body failed and his mind remained, he would have found such ministrations unbearable and degrading.

As her father ate, she told him what news she'd heard. The planters were going to try to repeal the tobacco-inspection act and had even sent representatives to London. One tobacco warehouse had burned to the ground in Williamsburg. The fire had been set on purpose, that much was certain. But no one knew whom to blame. Some thought it was angry planters hoping to flout the inspection law by destroying all the inspection posts. Others blamed renegade slaves, but then they always blamed the slaves. She thought it must be planters. There were more than a few who'd stoop to arson.

When her father finished his first piece of bread, she placed cider in his hand and encouraged him to drink, guiding the cup to his lips. Then she broke off a chunk of cheese and gave that to him. "Rebecca's baby is growing every day. She's as cute as a button."

Cassie felt silly talking when she knew her father could not really understand her, but who knew what word might catch his attention and bring him back? She must keep trying. At first glance he seemed perfectly healthy for a man of fifty-four. He'd grown paler and thinner in the past year, and his hair was now completely white. There was no outward sign of illness—until she looked into his eyes.

Their light was gone. The same blue eyes that had once sparkled down at her with mischief were now dull and blank. It was as if something had leached the life from him, leaving only his body behind.

Takotah believed his spirit had gone to be with his beloved Amanda. If so, then the blame for his condition fell at least in part on Cassie. Had she not fled from her mother's bedside when Takotah needed her most, her mother might still be alive and her father still himself. There'd be no need for lies and elaborate ruses. Life would be so much simpler and happier. Cassie had prayed for his recovery every morning and every night since he'd become ill, but it seemed God had better things to attend to.

She took a half-eaten piece of cheese from her father's hand and began to brush his hair. It was time for his daily walk. For a while, he'd kept his own garden, but that ground lay untilled this summer, overgrown by weeds. Now even walking was hard for him. He didn't seem to see the ground, and walked with the shuffling gait of a man of eighty. But his hand was still warm, and he held hers tightly as if some part of him were trying to reach out to her in the only way he could. That was what she told herself, anyway.

She tied her father's hair back with a leather thong and helped him to his feet. "It's a beautiful day, Father. You've been cooped up in this cabin all night. A bit of sunshine might be just the thing."

An hour later she had settled her father inside again and was heading for Andromeda's stall.

"It seems I'm not your only prisoner."

Cassie gasped and spun around to find Cole leaning against a tree. *"You!"*

Chapter Sixteen

C assie's heart beat so hard she could scarcely find breath to speak. Quick as a cougar Cole reached her, took her wrists in his iron grip, and hauled her up against his chest. "Don't lose your composure, Miss Blakewell. You need to think up a lie and think it up quickly. It is you, not I, who must explain this encounter. How many people know you keep your father imprisoned in this swamp?"

"Let go!"

"I want an explanation, and I want it now!"

"Release me, and you shall have your explanation!" She felt his grip loosen and jerked her wrists free, then took several hurried steps backward, placing enough distance between them that he wouldn't be able to touch her again.

But what could she say? The truth would surely seem a lie, and yet there was no lie she could pass off as the truth. If she told him the truth, he'd have the power to destroy everything her father had worked so hard to build. She could, of course, put him under guard again and make sure he told no one. But if he really was Alec Kenleigh, he'd soon be a free man. She'd have no control over his actions.

"I'm waiting, *Mistress*." His arms crossed over his chest, he looked like a man with all the time in the world. But the grim smile playing across his lips told her his patience was at an end.

"Very well. But you must vow not to repeat what I am about to tell you to anyone."

"I make no promises."

She exhaled, gathering her courage. Hadn't she always known this day would come?

"My father is no prisoner." Her voice quavered. She could not meet Cole's gaze, knowing that his eyes held only contempt. "He ... he became ill shortly after my mother passed on. At first it was little things, like forgetting what he wanted to say. We thought it was merely grief, but before long he was getting lost in our house."

She felt the sting of tears, but did not try to stop them. "I begged him to call for a physician, but he refused, sure he'd be locked in an asylum. When he realized he was getting worse, he built this cabin for himself. He didn't want the other planters to see him. He feared they'd use his illness to take his land. Before leaving the plantation he wrote them a letter telling them he was going abroad for a time and leaving me in charge. He made me promise to keep his secret, to watch over Blakewell's Neck until Jamie was old enough to manage it on his own. It is not as I would have it, but I must keep my promise."

For one agonizing moment Cole said nothing. Then he began to applaud. "Brava, Miss Blakewell. A performance well worth waiting for."

"It is the truth, and you'd best keep it to yourself." Cassie wiped the tears from her face and strode over to Andromeda. "Holding a man in chains goes against everything my father and I believe in, but I'll not hesitate to lock you up if it will save my family."

"I'm sure you wouldn't."

She mounted and rode into the marsh with nary a backward glance. *Damn the man!* Cole Braden had treated her with nothing but scorn and suspicion since she'd first deigned to save his accursed life. Had she really hoped he'd believe her? *Foolish girl,* she thought, ashamed of the fresh tears that filled her eyes and blurred her vision. Well, Cole had followed her here. Let him try to follow her home.

T *he scheming bitch!*
    Whatever Alec had expected to find, he'd not been prepared for this. He wouldn't have believed it had he not seen it with his own eyes. What kind of woman would keep her own father imprisoned, ill and alone, in a fetid swamp? The man needed the attention of a skilled physician, not the company of snakes and water rats. Yet here he was, left behind to rot while his daughter ran his estate as if it were her birthright.

He strode quickly over to the tree where he had secured Aldebaran, mounted, and rode after her. He'd not give Miss Blakewell the satisfaction of leaving him behind as she obviously intended to. She was riding at a near gallop, but he was able to spy her form ahead in the darkness and urged the stallion to quicken his pace. She had just disappeared in front of a stand of trees when Alec heard her mare whinny in distress. For a moment he thought the animal had tripped on an immersed tree root or become mired in a sinkhole. But then the horse reappeared without its rider, reins dangling at its side.

He dug his heels into Aldebaran's flank. "Cassie!"

There was no response.

He bent low over Aldebaran's neck, pushing the horse to his limits, hidden tree roots and sinkholes forgotten. Mud and water spattered his clothing. Low-hanging branches lashed at his face. He neared the stand of trees and at first could see nothing. For a moment he thought she must be playing some kind of trick on him, and he was contemplating what he'd do with her when he got hold of her again. Then he spied locks of red-gold hair floating on the surface of the muddy water.

"Cassie!" He leaped from the stallion's back and pulled her, unconscious, from the knee-deep water. She was bleeding profusely from a gash on the side of her head, and she was not breathing. Without thinking Alec quickly turned her facedown, wrapped his arms just beneath her ribs, and squeezed firmly once, then again. An old sailor he'd met on one of his forbidden forays to London's shipyards had told him he'd once revived a drowned sailor this way, and Alec prayed it would work now. Seconds moved by like hours, and still she did not breathe.

"Come on, damn it! Breathe!"

He squeezed again, harder this time, forcing water from her lungs. At first he thought he had imagined the cough. But then she coughed again, her entire body shaking with the effort. He felt her take a deep, shuddering breath.

He turned her over and pulled her tightly against his chest, his pulse drumming in his ears. She was alive. For a moment he could do nothing but hold her. He stroked the line of her cheek with a finger and offered a prayer of thanksgiving to any god who might be listening. She was alive.

Alive, yes, but badly hurt. He lifted her gently onto Aldebaran's back and climbed into the saddle. He could return to her father's cabin on the island or try to continue in the direction she'd been riding and hope that he didn't lose his way. Without the sun to guide him, he could not be sure where he was heading. If he should get lost out here and end up spending the night, Cassie might die. His decision made, he brought

Aldebaran about and urged the horse to a walk, hoping the mare would follow. She did.

At the cabin he quickly dismounted, leaving the horses to fend for themselves, and carried Cassie inside. He laid her on the small bed that stood in one corner. Ignoring her father, who sat silently in a rocking chair before a rough-hewn table, he rapidly removed first her boots and stockings, then her sodden riding habit, corset, and chemise, tossing the clothing carelessly onto the floor. He'd undressed lots of women before, some just as hastily, but never had he been trying to save a life.

His gaze traveled over Cassie's naked body, looking for injuries. Her chest rose and fell evenly with each breath, though Alec was sure her lungs still held water. Her skin was cold and deathly pale, and dark bruises had begun to form across her lower ribs where he'd squeezed her.

He quickly covered her with the quilt that lay at the foot of the bed and tucked it closely around her. Next he tore a strip of linen from the bedsheet and delicately bound it around the cut on her head. It was no longer bleeding, but it would need to be kept clean. She must have run into a low-hanging branch. Why she, an expert rider familiar with this terrain, had made such a deadly mistake he did not know.

No, he was lying to himself. He knew precisely how it had happened. Even now her red, swollen eyelids told him she'd been crying.

It wasn't his fault, damn it!

Or was it? He had followed her, frightened her, bullied an explanation from her, then accused her of lying.

But she *had* lied to him. Her father was not in England. Her explanation for his presence here was so implausible, Alec was still tempted to laugh. A father went mad, became a recluse, and left his estate to be governed by his daughter? Not bloody likely, even in this godforsaken colony.

No more ridiculous than the tale you're asking her to believe.

Alec closed his eyes and tried in vain to banish the accusing voice that invaded his thoughts. Hadn't he always been able to tell when she was lying? Then he remembered what the cook had said the night little Catherine had been born.

The master was so beside himself with grief when his dear Amanda finally passed on, he never saw how Miss Cassie tortured herself for it. Then when she began to lose the master, too...

Alec looked down at Cassie's sleeping face, remorse cutting through him like a knife. She might lie when it suited her purpose. She might be more headstrong and authoritative than was right for a female. But he had never seen her do anything to hurt anyone in her care. In fact, she'd done the opposite, working in the fields, nursing both slave and servant through illness as if they were members of her own family. He'd witnessed the care she'd given Rebecca the night her babe was born, had seen the torment on her face as she'd watched Rebecca's suffering. That she would deliberately treat her own father with any less concern than she would a bondswoman was inconceivable.

She moaned and stirred in her sleep as if in the midst of a bad dream. He pulled the quilt closer to her chin, allowing his fingers to linger for a moment on her cheek. He'd wanted to believe she was lying to him. It would be so much easier to ignore her if disgust were to replace the desire that tore at his gut day and night. Her outward charm would be eclipsed by unforgivable internal flaws, and he would be free to think of nothing but returning to England. Aye, he wanted to hate her, for if he could not ...

Alec stood and walked to the door. He needed to see to the horses.

London

S ocrates answered the impatient knocking at the front door to find a young lad with bright brown eyes, a street urchin by the look of him, eagerly holding forth a letter in one grimy hand.

"From the colonies, sir." The child stared at his face, a reaction Socrates had learned to endure with good humor.

"Thank you, young man." Socrates pressed several coins into the lad's palm, hoping the money would not be wasted on ale for a father who spent his life in the city's gutters, or laudanum for a mother who worked on her back. It was more than was customary, but Master Alec had always insisted on sharing with those less fortunate, and Socrates would carry on the tradition in his memory. "Buy yourself a good meal and some new clothes."

The boy looked into his hand in disbelief, then smiled. "Yes sir! Thank you, sir!" Then he paused. "Sir, your color ... does it wash off?"

"Certainly not. No more than do your freckles."

The boy smiled shyly and was gone.

Socrates shut the door behind him and glanced down at the letter. It was addressed to the lieutenant, who had just left for the country to visit Elizabeth and the children. Whatever it was, it would have to wait. The lieutenant was in need of a holiday, and Socrates would not ruin his all-too-brief respite with business. He started toward the lieutenant's study, but something drew his gaze back to the letter. Under normal circumstances, Socrates would not have given the missive a second glance before placing it in the hands of its intended recipient. It was not his custom to pry into the affairs of his employer. But this letter was different. Why? It was wrinkled, but that was not uncommon. The youngsters who were hired to carry such dispatches often did not take their errands seriously, smudging communications with dirty fingers, dropping them into mud puddles, crumpling them in pockets. Perhaps its point of origin was what made it seem unique. The Kenleighs rarely received letters from the colonies. Why, even Master Alec, who'd had correspondents across Europe, seldom—

Socrates suddenly felt as if the breath had been knocked out of him. The handwriting! His hands shaking, he turned the letter over again. The crude seal on the back was unfamiliar to him. But the handwriting . . .

It was impossible. Master Alec was dead and buried. Both the lieutenant and Philip had identified his body, or what was left of it.

Socrates sat at the lieutenant's desk and tried to compose himself, his seventy-year-old heart pounding. For fifty years he'd served the head of the Kenleigh household and never once lost his calm. He'd not give in to emotion or wild speculation now.

But he was right. He knew it.

"Socrates, you old buzzard, what have you there?" Master Philip, still in his nightshirt, stood in the hallway, a bottle in one hand, a young woman at his side.

In his preoccupation with the letter, Socrates had not heard him approach.

"A dispatch for your brother-in-law, sir." He masked his excitement. He'd not share his thoughts. Master Philip lived but to taunt him and would no doubt think him daft if he said they'd received a letter from Master Alec. Let him sample the handwriting and draw his own conclusions.

"Give it to me." Philip snatched the letter from Socrates' grasp. "Shall we see who is writing to our dear brother-in-law, Lord Matthew Peg Leg, darling?"

The young woman giggled and smiled up at him through her few remaining teeth.

Philip ripped open the letter, the cold smile on his face daring Socrates to try to stop him. He'd taken to interfering in the lieutenant's affairs ever since he'd decided the lieutenant was making decisions behind his back. Socrates found himself holding his breath, waiting to see Philip's reaction.

No sooner had Philip's eyes touched the parchment than his face began to flush. He hastily folded it and shoved the young woman away from him. "Get out." He turned his back to her and walked across the hall to the drawing room.

Her face paled. "But, sir! My—"

"Get out!" Philip slammed the door behind him.

Socrates heard the key turn.

The girl stood, gaping.

Socrates cleared his throat, unsure of how to proceed. He'd never spoken to a prostitute before, much less paid one. But he'd not let it be said that the Kenleighs did not pay their debts, regardless of how those debts had been incurred. It would besmirch their reputation—and his.

"How much is your . . . wage, Miss?"

"Ten quid, sir." She looked at her feet.

He suspected she was lying but handed her the coin anyway. The young woman curtsied, then turned, and fled, not bothering to close the door behind her.

From the drawing room came a bellow and the sound of breaking glass, followed by silence. Though he was accustomed to Master Philip's temper, this display of rage surprised him. Could he have been mistaken about the handwriting? He'd known Master Alec since he was a boy and had grown to respect him both as an employer and a man. Perhaps he missed him so much that he was imagining things. Age and grief could do horrible things to one's mind.

When Philip appeared an hour later, he was surprisingly sober, subdued. Saying only that he was going out, he quickly dressed and left, not bothering to dine.

Socrates entered the drawing room to find the remains of a fire in the fireplace and, among the ashes, small fragments of parchment. Bending down, he began to poke through the ashes, retrieving what he could. The lieutenant would need to know about this.

A lec raised his eyes from the book he'd been reading to the sleeping figure in the bed. The ardent words of Catullus were growing tedious.

Twice she had awoken, only to lapse into unconsciousness again. Takotah said she was sure Cassie would recover, but he would feel much better if she'd open her eyes and speak to him. He sat down next to her on the bed and felt her forehead, grateful to find she showed no sign of fever.

Takotah had come and gone twice already, once to bring Cassie's father food and water, a second time to tend Cassie's wound and to take the old man with her to the lodge she'd built for herself nearby. Cassie was too weak to move, she'd explained, leading Blakewell out the door behind her.

If Takotah had been surprised or displeased to discover Alec here, she'd kept it to herself. Micah, on the other hand, had been furious. Alec had expected as much and couldn't blame the man. There was no way to deny the fact that he'd followed Cassie and knew of her father's condition. Nor could he deny his part in her accident. Only Takotah's insistence that Alec remain to help her care for Cassie prevented Micah from dragging him back and locking him in chains.

"He has healing hands," she'd said, reminding Micah of the night Rebecca's baby had been born.

Both Micah and Takotah had backed up Cassie's story, Micah alternating effusive praise for Cassie with threats against Alec. Then something had happened to make Micah forget about Alec altogether.

Micah had found the old Scot, Henry, skulking about, apparently lost, in the swamp. Henry had at first insisted he'd been off to look for oysters and lost his way. Then he'd confessed he'd been trying to escape. Warning Henry that they'd send him back to Crichton Hall if he tried to escape again, Micah had taken him back to the plantation and locked him in his cabin as punishment. Alec could still see the worried look on Micah's face and knew that he, too, felt uneasy with the Scot's explanation. Had he seen the island?

Alec forced his gaze back to the book in his hands.

C assie was having the strangest dream. She was at her father's cabin, arguing with Cole. She was angry with him, angry and hurt. What had he said? She must remember. She had to get away from him. She would ride as fast as she could.

She felt a warm, callused hand caress her cheek, and heard herself moan in pain.

"Cassie?"

It was Cole's voice. What was he doing in her room? She must be dreaming. Oh, her head throbbed. She struggled to open her eyes, to clear her vision. It was then she realized she was not in her room, but in her father's cabin.

Cole sat next to her on her father's bed, looking down at her with a worried frown.

"What ... ?" She fought to sit up, to form a coherent question.

"Rest easy, sweet. You hit your head on a branch and nearly drowned. I brought you back here."

"You ... followed me?"

"Aye, I did."

"Damn you." It hadn't been a dream after all.

"How do you feel?"

"My head ... hurts." Cassie gazed about the tiny cabin, her vision blurry and felt herself grow alarmed. Something was not right. If only she could think.

Then it came.

"Where is my father?" Worried, she tried to sit, only to have a thousand glass shards shatter inside her skull. Through a haze of pain she heard herself whimper, felt Cole ease her back onto the pillow.

"Easy, love. Takotah has taken him to her lodge next door. She says you're going to be fine. She wanted you to drink this." He gently lifted her head and pressed a cup against her lips.

Cassie grimaced, overwhelmed by the smell of rum and herbs, but drank, aware that the concoction contained poppy and had powerful pain-relieving properties. "Will you...tell?"

"About your father?"

She nodded.

"I don't know. What you've done, what your father has asked you to do ... It isn't right." His brow furrowed.

"Please, I beg you, don't betray us."

"As you wish, *Mistress*."

But this time when he said it, he did not mock her. She read from the glint in his blue eyes that he was merely teasing.

"When will you stop calling me that?" she asked, her body already growing warm from the potion.

"Calling you what?"

"*Mistress*." Cassie did her best to imitate his husky tone, but couldn't help giggling. The pain in her head was beginning to dull, and she felt strangely euphoric.

"When are you going to stop calling me Cole?"

She struggled to come up with a clever reply but was distracted when she noticed her chemise and stockings draped over her father's rocking chair. In a panic, she felt beneath the covers. She was completely naked.

Cole followed the direction of her gaze with a grin. "I'm afraid that, in the course of saving your life, I found it necessary to undress you. That makes us even."

Cassie's cheeks flamed. How like him to remind her of such a thing! True, she'd seen him unclothed, but that was different. He'd been a stranger then, and it had been her job as the owner of his indenture to care for him. "No doubt you've undressed hundreds of women," she said hotly.

"Thousands." He smiled.

She gaped at him, then realized he was teasing her again. What a silly goose she was! She felt light-headed. Perhaps it was the rum. "What are the women like in London?"

He looked surprised by the question. "They're a self-absorbed lot."

"Are they beautiful?"

"Not as beautiful as some."

The look in his eyes as he gazed down at her made Cassie's heart beat faster. "Kiss me."

Had she just asked him to kiss her? Aye, she had.

Cole traced the outline of her lips with a finger, then sat back in his chair, his hands grasping the book in his lap. "You have no idea how much I'd like to oblige you. But I'm afraid, my sweet, that Takotah's vile brew has gone to your pretty little head."

She sighed, disappointed and thrilled at the same time. He'd called her "my sweet." She stretched and yawned, feeling drowsy but determined not to fall asleep. In the weeks she'd known him the two of them had never had an unguarded conversation. This was so much better than arguing. And she loved his smile. "What are you reading?"

"Catullus."

"Read to me."

"In English or Latin?"

"English, of course." She smiled.

Cole smiled—a rather sad smile, Cassie thought—opened the book, and after a moment's hesitation began to translate. "'Let us live and love, my Lesbia, and pay no attention to the ramblings of bitter old men. Suns may set and rise again, but for us, when our brief light is gone, there is the sleep of one everlasting night. Give me a thousand kisses … '"

Alec stopped, unable to continue reading. He looked over at Cassie. She was asleep again, her eyes closed, her breathing deep and even. He looked back at the page and the next poem. "'*Odi et amo*…I hate, and I love. You may ask why I do so. I do not know, but I feel it and am in torment.'"

He closed the book and gazed at the sleeping woman beside him. Hate? No. But he was in torment.

Dear God, when had he begun to love her?

Chapter Seventeen

"*A*re ye sure ye're fit to make the trip, Missy?" Nan's round face was beaded with perspiration.

It was horribly hot.

"I'll be fine." Cassie accepted Micah's hand and climbed into the stuffy carriage.

In truth, Cassie wasn't sure she should be going. Only two days had passed since her foolish mishap, and she was still afflicted with headaches and dizziness, though both were less severe. But if she sent word to Geoffrey that she had been injured and was not coming, he would come to call and start poking around again. She didn't want that, not after what had happened last time. She had resolved not to allow herself to be caught alone with Geoffrey again. All that talk of marriage had alarmed her, as had his misguided attempt at seduction. She would be polite, she would smile, but she would not be alone with him. She would take no chances.

She lifted a squirming Jamie onto the seat beside her, leaving room for Elly across from them. Cassie had relented and allowed Elly to come along. Only time would tell if she'd come to regret her change of heart. Elly would serve as her dressing maid, at least when it came to helping with her attire. Cassie would tend to her own hair, as brushing it without irritating the cut above her temple would not be easy. That was what she'd told Elly, anyway. In truth, she didn't want all of her hair to be pulled out by the roots.

"We'll make sure to save a few hornworms just for you, Missy." Micah gave her a teasing grin, helping Elly climb in and closed the door behind her.

Cassie laughed at his jest and waved good-bye.

The carriage lurched to a start, rocking over the cobblestones.

Elly, who'd never ridden in a carriage before, clapped with delight. Jamie waved good-bye to his friends, who'd gathered by the well to see him off on his first big adventure, while Daniel sobbed inconsolably at being left behind.

Cassie felt like crying herself. She'd much rather stay home than attend Geoffrey's birthday celebration, even if it meant worming tobacco all day. There was so much to be done here that leaving for three days just to listen to the same people prattling on about the same trivial matters seemed a waste of time. The women would talk about the gowns they planned to wear the night of the ball. They'd talk about which young women were going to marry well, which were not, prompting one of them to ask her why she was not yet wed. Then, in smaller groups and quieter voices, they'd talk about each other. The men, on the other hand, would argue politics until tempers flared. They'd discuss horses, gamble, drink, and argue some more.

The outbuildings of Blakewell's Neck faded from view, and Cassie's heart sank. She wouldn't see Cole for three days.

When Takotah had pronounced her well enough to travel back from the island, he'd helped her mount and had ridden beside her all the way home, watching her as if he feared she'd faint and topple into the water at any moment. But if she had expected the same easy banter she'd shared with him at the cabin to last once they'd reached home, she'd been disappointed. Cole had become a closed book the moment the outbuildings came into view. He'd ridden with her to the stables, and helped her dismount without a word. When Nan and the others had rushed over to greet her, fussing and fretting, he'd vanished.

She hadn't even been able to thank him for saving her life.

"Come back here, young man," Cassie reached for Jamie, who stood against the carriage door, his head stuck precariously out the window. "You don't want to fall out, do you?"

Jamie frowned and would probably have stood his ground had a sudden rut in the road not tossed him into Cassie's lap, making her point for her.

"Will there be calf's head, Missy?" Elly's face was alight with excitement.

"Aye, and joints of venison and beef. Perhaps a suckling pig— though I doubt Master Crichton will feed the servants such fare." Cassie had already explained to Elly that redemptioners and slaves would have their own celebrations outside with their own meals. Though the food would be better than that normally prepared, it would not equal the board in the great house.

"And cakes?"

"Aye, white cakes frosted with almond paste, plum cakes, pies, and puddings, too."

Elly's eyes grew round in amazement, her heart-shaped face glowing. Cassie was suddenly reminded of how young the girl was. Only seventeen and completely alone. It was Elly's youth that had prompted Cassie to buy her indenture. With no parents to watch over her, she'd likely have ended up with a babe in her belly by some thoughtless rake before the first year of her service was out. Cassie hadn't wanted to let that happen. "If you'd like, I will try to bring some food back to my chamber for you."

"Oh, please, Mistress! Thank you!"

Cassie returned her infectious smile. It was easy to see why Zach was so smitten with her. Petite, with long golden hair and delicately carved features, she looked like a porcelain doll. Cassie felt not the least bit dainty, being taller than most women, taller even than many men. Would that Cole looked at her the way Zach looked at Elly. Why Elly did not return the sawyer's affection was a mystery to Cassie. Elly had barely acknowledged his presence when he'd come to see her off this morning.

Jamie had inched his way over to the door again and stood looking out at the passing scenery. Cassie was about to reprimand him when she heard the sound of an approaching rider.

Jamie smiled and squealed. "Debaron!"

Cassie's heart leapt.

"Good day, young sir!"

Abruptly she pulled Jamie aside and reached out the window, tapping on the side of the carriage as a signal to the driver to stop, irritation warring with the pleasure she felt at seeing Cole so unexpectedly. "You seem to have a habit of following me, Mr. Braden."

He gave her a jaunty grin, his white teeth flashing, as Aldebaran pranced restlessly beneath him. "Did you forget that you asked me to ride Aldebaran in tomorrow's race?"

"I never—"

"Must be that blow on the head. I was wondering why you'd left without me."

Cassie glared at him, biting back a retort. She knew full well she'd never asked him to race in her father's stead. What kind of game was he playing?

Cole urged Aldebaran closer to the coach and lowered his voice, speaking for her ears alone. "Fear not, my dear, my intentions are honest. I mean to settle your father's score with Crichton by proving this is the fastest stallion in the county once and for all. Unless you are prepared to shoot me in the back, nothing is going to stop me. I love a good horse race as much as the next man, and this will be one to remember."

For a moment, Cassie could only gape at him. "Are you *mad?* To them you're a lowly convict, or had you forgotten? You'll insult them. They'd never allow it!"

"Leave that to me." His lips curled in a smile.

"You are going to be the death of me, Cole Braden!"

"I certainly hope not." His blue eyes twinkled with amusement.

As uninterested in horse racing as she was, she knew she would enjoy watching Aldebaran win. Two years ago the stallion had beaten every racehorse in the county, and the senior Master Crichton had been clamoring for a chance to even the score ever since, all but accusing her father of cheating. When her father failed to attend last year's race, Master Crichton had viewed it as cowardice and told everyone within earshot that Abraham Blakewell was afraid of losing.

"Very well, but do nothing to cause my family embarrassment, or I will have you dragged home by your ears."

Jamie pushed his way to the window and reached out to pat the stallion's neck.

"Come here, tadpole." Cole pulled Jamie through the window and into the saddle in front of him.

"What—"

"He'll be fine."

With a click of Cole's tongue and a kick from his heels, Aldebaran sprang forward.

When they arrived at Crichton Hall an hour later, Jamie was ready for his nap, having had all the excitement he could manage for one morning. Cassie's head was throbbing terribly, and Elly, unaccustomed to modern conveyances, was feeling queasy.

"Catherine!" Geoffrey called from the doorway.

But his smile vanished the moment he saw Cole, who had tethered Aldebaran to the carriage and was helping Cassie to the ground.

"Geoffrey." Cassie fought to quell a wave of dizziness. How she longed for a cool drink. She willed herself to stand without Cole's support. She didn't want to antagonize Geoffrey by arousing his jealousy.

"Are you well? You look terribly pale."

"Aye. A bit dizzy perhaps."

Cole stood protectively beside her. "She struck her head on a branch two days ago and fell from her horse."

Geoffrey glared at him. "What is this piece of filth doing here?"

"He—"

"I've come to prove once and for all that Aldebaran is the swiftest stallion in Lancaster County."

"My father—"

"You, a convict, race against gentlemen?" Geoffrey's laughter was devoid of warmth or humor.

"Geoffrey! Mr. Braden! Please—"

"I race in Blakewell's stead at his request, unless, of course, you and your father don't feel equal to the challenge, Crichton."

Geoffrey's face became pinched, and a muscle in his cheek began to tic.

Cassie found herself holding her breath. Then it came to her.

"Ooh!" She moaned, allowing her knees to buckle and sagging toward the ground in a false swoon. She'd not let this come to blows.

It was Cole who caught her.

"Get your hands off her, convict!"

"She needs a quiet place to rest." Cole lifted her gently into his arms.

For a moment neither man spoke.

"Very well. This way," Geoffrey said at last.

Cassie heard Jamie begin to cry and call her name. He sounded so small and frightened, she at once regretted having begun this deception. She hadn't considered its effect on him.

"She's going to be fine, tadpole. She's just asleep," Cole said.

"Would you like to help me settle Aldebaran in his stall?"

"Uh-huh," Jamie answered.

"Then wait for me here. I'll be but a minute."

She felt Cole climb the front steps and knew they had passed through the doors into the foyer when the warm sunlight left her face and was replaced by the smell of freshly cut roses and newly washed parquet floors. She knew Crichton Hall well, having played there since she was a small child and was able to discern where Geoffrey was leading them. Up the central staircase they went, then to the right, toward the guest chambers.

She allowed her head to roll so that her cheek fell against Cole's chest. The scent of leather and pine soap tickled her nose. She could hear his heartbeat, could feel the warmth of his skin through the linen of his shirt. Her stolen ride in his arms was nearly over. She heard Geoffrey open the door to one of the guest chambers, then felt Cole lay her gently on the bed.

"She'll need something cool to drink when she awakens," Cole said.

"You're fortunate my concern for Miss Blakewell's safety surpasses my desire to see you punished. Defy me again, convict, and you'll know the meaning of regret!" Geoffrey's voice was ragged with fury. "Now get out!"

"Take care of her, Crichton."

Cassie tensed. Why did Cole insist on provoking Geoffrey? Did he not understand he could come to harm by such insolence? *Oh, curse men!* She had just fainted—in dramatic fashion, too—and the two of them were still vying to insult each other. How much longer could they keep this up?

*W*hen Cassie emerged from her bedchamber an hour later, she felt much better. Her headache was all but gone, and the lemonade that had been sent up from the kitchen had left her feeling refreshed. Even her irritation with Geoffrey and Cole had ebbed somewhat. She'd taken the time to change into her light green muslin gown and had tried in vain to hide the bruise that had spread to her forehead. Thank goodness the cut and stitches were hidden beneath her hair.

She followed the sound of chamber music and conversation downstairs and outside to the veranda, which, thanks to Master Crichton's determination to expand Crichton Hall until it rivaled the governor's mansion, now spanned the rear of the manor. There, bewigged guests—mostly Carters, Pages, and their relations—sat sheltered from the afternoon sun, sipping lemonade, awaiting the arrival of others.

"Catherine." Geoffrey excused himself and strode forward to take her arm in his. "Are you sure you should be up and about, my dear?"

"I'm fine, Geoffrey. Thank you."

"I don't understand why you decided to travel so soon after your accident." He led her out the wide casement doors onto the veranda. "Are you sure you're quite ready?"

"She's crazy as her father," muttered a male voice in the background. Cassie suspected it was one of the Harrison brothers. It was not the first time someone had insulted her or her father in her presence. Her father had often been the butt of unkind remarks.

"You know very well, Geoffrey, that nothing can change my mind once it's made up." She settled herself on a painted wooden settee next to Lucy Carter and smoothed her skirts. "I was determined to attend your birthday celebration, and nothing, certainly not a silly bump on the head, could keep me away."

"Bump on the head? What happened, Cassie, dear?" Lucy asked.

The youngest of Robert "King" Carter's five daughters, Lucy was one of the few young women Cassie looked forward to seeing. She and her elder sister Mary, though both younger than Cassie, had always shown her kindness, never turning up their noses at her less fashionable attire or her unorthodox upbringing. She hadn't seen them more than two or three times a year in the entire time they were growing up, but she considered them true friends. Their mother had died at a very young age, and they had been a source of solace for Cassie after her own mother passed away.

"I struck my head on a branch while riding and was knocked from my horse."

A collective gasp went up from the women. Lucy raised one smooth white hand to her lightly rouged lips in a gesture of dismay. Cassie's own hands were freckled from working in the sun, her nails neither long nor manicured. The difference had never seemed important before. Why should she care now?

"You're damned lucky to be alive, young lady," said King Carter, who sat otherwise engrossed in a game of whist with Geoffrey's father.

"I'm afraid she fainted this afternoon just after she arrived." Geoffrey's words provoked another round of gasps. "She's fortunate I was there, or she might have struck herself again on our front stairs."

"Yes, Geoffrey. Thank you for your gallant kindness." Cassie fought to keep the censure from her voice at Geoffrey's lie. It had been

Cole, not he, who had caught her and carried her indoors, though she was not supposed to know that.

"Does it hurt?" Lucy brushed her cool fingers gently over the bruise on Cassie's temple.

"A little."

"How is your father faring these days?" asked the senior Geoffrey Crichton. "Still looking for new breeding stock?"

She heard someone snicker and forced herself to ignore the double entendre. "He is doing well, though his search is not going as smoothly as he'd hoped."

"Did I mention, Father, that Blakewell sent his convict to race Aldebaran?" said Geoffrey, flicking the lace at his wrists.

Master Crichton's head snapped up from his cards, and he fixed Cassie with a glare. "What's this?"

"He didn't want to be falsely accused of cowardice again." She lifted her chin higher. She'd never liked Geoffrey's father. He'd always frightened her.

Carter laughed. "Sounds to me like the man is tired of your insults."

Master Crichton murmured something Cassie couldn't make out and returned to his cards.

"Hello, I say!" came a voice from inside the manor.

It was the younger Robert Carter, lately of Nomini Hall, and his wife, Priscilla. Lucy squealed with delight and ran in a swish of blue skirts to greet them. Cassie sighed with relief, grateful she was no longer the center of attention.

The afternoon passed without further incident, the remaining guests drifting in slowly: the Braxtons, the Randolphs of Turkey Island, the Fitzhughs, the Lees, the Byrds, the Nicholases, the Ludwells of Green Springs. Cassie spent most of her time getting the news from Lucy and Mary, who had much to report. Judith, their elder sister, was still in mourning, her husband having died suddenly in January. She had remained at home, as custom demanded, with her six children. Lucy and Mary had met Governor Gooch and his sister-in-law, Anne Staunton, in February and found them good-natured and hospitable. Their older brother, Landon, now a handsome young man of twenty, was lately smitten with young Elizabeth Wormley, but no one expected this infatuation to last any longer than the others. Most exciting, Lucy was to wed William Fitzhugh next spring.

Cassie was genuinely happy for her friend and had congratulated her with a hug and a kiss on the cheek. But, rather than feeling uplifted by the good news, Cassie felt her spirits fall. She'd had little to share with them. What could she say? That her father was wasting away before her eyes? That she'd been deceiving them all for more than a year? That she thought night and day of a man society deemed unworthy even of simple compassion?

She picked at her food during dinner. When she went to the nursery to tuck Jamie in for the night, she was so distracted she repeated the same verse of his favorite lullaby until he grew impatient and corrected her. At least he'd had an exciting day, helping Cole with Aldebaran in the stables and playing with the other children in the hayloft.

She kissed Jamie goodnight, then made her way to her chamber.

What was Cole doing now?

Probably adjusting to his first night of sleeping with horses. Whether he was Cole Braden or Alec Kenleigh, his character spoke of a man accustomed to feather beds and fine brandy, not blankets spread over hay and corn whiskey. The image of him bedded down in the stables made her want to laugh.

She opened the door, expecting to find Elly asleep on her pallet. Instead the girl was twirling about in front of the looking glass, lost in a daydream, holding Cassie's finest gown to her chin.

"Oh!" Elly froze and dropped the gown to the floor. Remembering herself, she picked it up and clumsily hung it in the armoire.

"I brought these from the kitchen." Cassie pretended not to have seen and opened her handkerchief on the dressing table. Inside were several morsels from her own plate, including a sliver of roast veal and a piece of sugared white cake.

Elly moved shyly toward the food, then grabbed the entire handkerchief and ate greedily.

"Do you like it?" Cassie sat before the looking glass and pulled the pins from her hair.

"Mmm."

"I'll bring more tomorrow." She gave Elly her warmest smile.

Despite everything Cassie had tried to do for her, Elly still seemed to dislike her. Cassie had no idea why. Perhaps their stay at Crichton Hall would be the beginning of a more comfortable relationship. Cassie certainly hoped so.

Her head had begun to throb again, and she found herself longing for the comfort of her bed. What she needed was a good night's sleep. She ran the brush carefully through her hair. Tomorrow she would awaken refreshed, her spirits restored, her mind unburdened by thoughts of a dark-haired felon.

For Cole Braden was, indeed, a felon, even if his real name turned out to be Alec Kenleigh. He had stolen her heart.

$\mathcal{E}$lly took the last bite of cake and watched from her seat on the windowsill as Miss Cassie brushed her hair and dressed for bed. She'd never tasted anything like this before. It was so sweet—and fluffy, like a cloud.

If she were a wealthy planter's wife, she'd eat cakes like this every day. Though it was kind of Miss Cassie to remember her, Elly could not bring herself to say even one word of thanks. Miss Cassie still thought her a silly servant girl. But Elly was growing tired of being ordered about. Miss Cassie was not as important as she liked everyone to believe.

Nor was she the lady she pretended to be. Elly had seen the Carter sisters this afternoon. They were true gentlewomen, with silk gowns fit for princesses, fair faces, beautifully styled blond hair. Oh, to be one of them! They never walked barefoot in the mud like Miss Cassie, or washed dishes or worked in the fields. So many things were not as Elly had first believed, but her eyes were beginning to open.

She'd thought Blakewell's Neck grand when she had first arrived in Virginia. But Crichton Hall made Miss Cassie's home seem a hovel. With ceilings so high you could not see the cobwebs, polished wooden floors that could have been mirrors, and stairways so tall they seemed to go straight to heaven, Crichton Hall was a palace.

Elly might one day be the mistress of this grand place. Geoffrey loved her now. He'd told her so this afternoon. When she'd gone to fetch lemonade for Miss Cassie, he'd found her and pulled her with him into an empty room. She'd protested at first when he tried to kiss her. But then he'd told her he truly loved her, that he'd loved her since the first time he'd seen her. If the kiss had not made her burn the way Zach's kisses did, it was only because Geoffrey was a gentleman and had not set out to arouse her so. What mattered was that Geoffrey loved her.

$\mathcal{T}$he next morning dawned cool and rainy. Cassie found herself staring impatiently out the drawing room window, while the other women, joined by their daughters, engaged in needlework and listened to Lucy accompany Mary's singing on the harpsichord. Cassie had wanted so badly to go riding this morning. The rain hadn't kept the men from hunting, but the women were expected to stay indoors in such weather. It hardly seemed fair.

"I say, Cassie, haven't you heard a word I've said?"

"I'm sorry, Priscilla. My mind seems to be wandering."

"I said I have more embroidery upstairs if you'd like something to keep your fingers busy."

"No, thank you. I'm afraid my stitches would only spoil your work."

It was the truth. Besides, she hated needlework.

"Did your mother never teach you how to ply the needle?"

"She tried. I'm afraid I wasn't a very attentive pupil."

"Then perhaps you'd like to work with little Anne on her sampler."

Cassie ignored the muffled giggles and smiled at Anne, Priscilla's three-year-old daughter, who looked up from her practice stitches at the sound of her name.

"My sisters-in-law tell me you've refused two offers of marriage." Priscilla's voice took on a superior tone. "May I ask if you're planning on remaining a spinster?"

At Lucy's shocked gasp, the room fell silent.

Cassie felt her face flush.

Priscilla shrugged. "It is unnatural for a woman to remain unwed and childless."

"Unlike some, I find love, not money, the only incentive to marry. I did not love those men, and so I could not marry them. But then I wouldn't expect you to understand, since it was the size of Robert's purse, not his person, you found so attractive." Her pulse racing, Cassie turned and walked quickly from the room, ignoring the stunned look on Priscilla's face.

"Priscilla Churchill Carter, you should be ashamed of yourself!" she heard Lucy exclaim before the drawing room door closed behind her.

Outside, rain fell in a fine mist. Cassie inhaled the fresh air, letting the cool breeze carry away the frustration that boiled inside her. She had no idea what she'd done to provoke Priscilla's nastiness. Lucy had once told her the other women were resentful of her freedom, but Cassie rather doubted that. They seemed to take great pride in their limitations, condemning women who lived any other way, raising their own daughters to suffer the same. Cassie wrapped her shawl over her head to ward off the rain and walked toward the stables. She needed to check on Aldebaran, she told herself, aware at the same time that it was only an excuse. She wanted to see Cole.

She found him brushing the stallion's coat, his sleeves rolled up above the elbow, the ties of his linen shirt left undone. If he was surprised to see her, he did not show it.

"Miss Blakewell." He gave her a perfunctory nod and continued with his work.

"How fares Aldebaran, Mr. Braden?" She scratched the animal's withers.

It seemed strange to speak so formally to the man whom she'd kissed more than once and who'd so recently seen her naked, but with other grooms standing only a few yards away, she could ill afford to do otherwise.

"He's restless."

The stallion snorted and tossed his head as if to concur.

"Have you recovered from yesterday's fainting spell?" He met her gaze, a faint smile on his lips

What did he find funny? "Yes, thank you."

"I had no idea you were such an accomplished actress," he said in a whisper, his smile broadening to a wide grin.

"You *knew*?"

"Aye."

"But you—"

"Played along? Of course. I couldn't let you hit the ground. Besides, it is seldom a man gets to hold a woman as lovely as you in his arms."

Cassie could tell by the warmth in his eyes that he meant what he said.

"What I want to know is whom you thought you were protecting with your timely swoon." He brushed the horse with rhythmic strokes. "If it was me, you have sadly underestimated my abilities. I assure you I am quite capable of handling that popinjay."

The comment was meant to reassure her, she knew, but she felt herself growing irate. "You don't realize the nature of your position, Cole Braden. Geoffrey could easily have you beaten or flogged. I've seen how cruel he and his father can be. You're on their land now. There would be little I could do to stop them."

"So it *was* me you were protecting. You do so hurt my pride." His voice was full of exaggerated self-pity.

One look at the pout on his handsome face, and there was naught she could do but smile. "Men! Their arms may be strong, but their pride is easily wounded."

He turned toward her, his face suddenly grave. "There may come a day, Cassie, when the enmity between Crichton and me turns to violence. When that day comes, don't interfere."

His blue eyes gazed at her unblinking, no hint of humor in their depths.

She felt a shadow pass over her and shivered involuntarily. "Cole, you cannot mean that!"

"There are some things a man must do to remain a man, Cassie. I don't expect you to understand."

"That's good, because, indeed, I don't understand, Mr. Braden! Damn your pride!" She whirled and strode from the stables, feeling worse than when she had entered.

Chapter Eighteen

By the time the hunting party returned later that afternoon, with triumphant whoops and baying hounds, the rain had stopped and the sky had cleared. The women put down their embroidery and moved to the veranda to enjoy refreshments and the company of their husbands, brothers, and sons. Eager to avoid another confrontation, Cassie kept to herself, watching Jamie play with his new friends on the lawn. In the distance, slaves were busy smoothing the fresh quarter-mile track with rakes in preparation for the afternoon's race.

Some of the older boys had cornered an old gander by the barn and were taking turns trying to grab hold of the poor creature. Its pitiful hissing and honking began to attract the attention of all nearby, including Geoffrey and Landon, who had been sharing hunting stories over strong cider.

"Shall we help them?" Landon watched one boy after another back away from the bird, rubbing fresh bruises.

Geoffrey answered by removing his waistcoat and wig and leaping over the railing into the soft grass onto his good leg. It had been so long since Cassie had seen him without his peruke, he looked odd, his blond hair cropped short.

"Oh, Landon, no!" Lucy shook her head as her brother followed suit.

"Leave him be, Lucy," her father chided, playing another round of whist, this time with William Byrd. "Young men need their amusements."

"Yes, but a gander pull, Father?"

Cassie felt her stomach turn. She hadn't seen a gander pull since she was a little girl, but she remembered it well.

By the barn, Geoffrey and Landon had begun to draw an audience.

Even the smaller children had quit playing and gone to watch. Cassie secretly hoped the bird would escape, but it wasn't long before Landon stepped out of the crowd with the gander pinned beneath his arm. In short order the creature was covered from beak to breast with grease and hung by its feet from the branch of a nearby tree. As the bird frantically tried to free itself, beating its wings and shrieking, Geoffrey, Landon, and the older boys mounted horses brought from the stables by slaves and began taking turns riding toward it at a full gallop, trying to grab it by the neck, each attempt greeted with shouts and cheers from the other competitors. The gander beat its wings, twisting this way and that, trying to evade the hands that grabbed for it.

But it would soon tire, and someone would manage to yank off the poor creature's head. The winner's reward for such daring and courage would be roast goose for supper.

"I can't watch this." Lucy turned with a swish of silk skirts and retreated inside the manor.

"Nor I." Cassie turned to follow her.

Then she noticed Jamie holding his hands over his ears in the yard below. The gander's cries were frightening him. She hurried down the stairs toward him, calling his name. A strangled honk and raucous cheers told her that someone had managed to get a firm grip on the bird this time.

"Jamie!"

He did not hear her. His gaze was fixed on the scene before him, his expression one of terror. She followed his gaze to see Geoffrey holding the gander's head aloft, blood streaming down his arm. "Jamie!"

The boy turned and ran toward her, burying his face in her skirts.

She knelt and wrapped her arms around him, holding his head to her breast and stroking his pale curls. "It's all right."

At the sound of horse's hooves, she looked up. Geoffrey dismounted and walked over to her, still holding the gander's head, gore spattered over the lace of his white linen shirt. "Would you like the head, Jamie?"

Jamie did not look up.

The stench of warm blood assailed Cassie, and she fought the urge to gag. "You've upset him enough with your puerile games, Geoffrey. Please take that away."

"I say, boy, you're not crying, are you? It was just an old bird." Geoffrey gave a disgusted snort. "We were going to slaughter it anyway."

"Leave him be." Cassie picked up the shaken child and carried him toward the manor.

"You're raising him to be a milksop!" Geoffrey yelled after her.

It took nearly an hour to calm Jamie and rock him to sleep for his afternoon nap. To his credit, Geoffrey had sent up a puppy, his promised gift for Jamie, with a brief note of apology for Cassie. The tiny, spotted, wriggling ball, which Jamie immediately named Pirate, won his heart instantly and now lay curled up asleep beside him.

By the time Cassie left the nursery, the other guests were drifting toward the racetrack, some of the women in carriages. This was the event the men had been waiting for. One by one they appeared riding or leading their favorite horses.

Cassie forced the butterflies from her stomach. It was unheard of for a gentleman to let a servant race in his stead, much less a convict. Though her father was certainly unconventional, there were some unspoken rules even he would never have broken. This was one of them. Surely Cole would back down without making a scene. If he forced the issue, she feared for both of them. She joined the other women, who were discussing the night ahead.

"You'd best take a quick nap before dinner, Mary, dear," she heard Priscilla say. "If you want to capture young George Braxton's attention, you don't want to look like a wilted daisy."

"I'm sure you're right," Mary replied.

"Isn't that your convict?" Lucy asked in a whisper.

Cassie looked up to see Cole leading Aldebaran across the field toward the racetrack, her heart fluttering at Lucy's choice of words. *Your convict.* "Aye."

"He is devilishly handsome, isn't he?" Lucy whispered with an excited grin.

"Aye, and damnably stubborn."

"Are the rumors about him true?"

"What have you heard?"

It was impossible to keep even the slightest bit of intrigue private in this colony.

"That he claims to be a gentleman spirited away and falsely sold as a convict."

"Aye, it's true."

"Do you believe him?"

Cassie paused. Did she believe him? "Aye."

"Do you think they'll let him enter the race?"

Cassie had no idea. "Do you?"

The two watched as Cole strode with Aldebaran over to the track.

"You're not welcome here, convict." Geoffrey appeared, leading his roan stallion. "This race is for gentlemen."

"Really?" Cole gave Geoffrey a disparaging look. The crowd fell silent as bonneted and bewigged heads turned toward Cole.

Cassie wanted to cover her eyes.

"Very well." Cole turned Aldebaran back toward the stables. "Blakewell wrote in his letter you might do this."

"Do what?" asked Geoffrey.

"Back down."

"Oh, no." Cassie moaned.

A murmur swept through the crowd.

"Look here, convict, no one is backing down—"

"Shut up, boy." Geoffrey's father forced his way through the throng to stand before Cole. "We accept Blakewell's challenge, convict. The winner against Aldebaran. I've called Blakewell a coward more times than I can count. I won't give him the chance to do the same to me."

Cassie heard King Carter guffaw, and realized she'd been holding her breath.

"But, Father—"

"I said, shut up, boy!"

Geoffrey's face grew rigid, but he obeyed.

"Who is that?" Cassie heard a woman whisper.

"Blakewell's convict," someone else answered. "They say he was deported for ravishing women."

"With his looks, it must have been easy work."

"They'd have done better to have hanged him, I say," muttered another.

The first several races passed in a blur. It was clear from the outset that the contest would come down to Geoffrey's stallion and a new horse just purchased by King Carter and ridden by his namesake, as, one by one, all other contenders were eliminated.

"One hundred pounds of Orinoco says my beast leaves yours in the dust," boasted Carter with a good-natured grin.

"One hundred? Bah! Five hundred says you'll lose again," Master Crichton bellowed.

"Very well. Five hundred then."

A frenzy of betting followed as each man in the crowd picked his favorite. The horses were allowed to rest, then taken by their riders to the starting line.

"This is to be a fair race," said William Byrd, who was presiding over the races. "Are we agreed?"

Geoffrey and young Robert nodded.

At the crack of the pistol the horses bolted forward, hooves tossing clods of damp earth into the air. The shouts of the spectators were almost deafening as first one horse, then the other pulled ahead. It was Geoffrey who passed the finish line first by a nose.

"It was luck," Carter handed Master Crichton a bill of lading, a dark frown on his face. "We've not had time to train our animal."

"Luck? It was better horseflesh!" Master Crichton boasted.

Cole had already led Aldebaran to the starting line and stood waiting for Geoffrey's stallion to catch its wind. Cassie felt her heart quicken. She hoped he would win, for her father's sake as well as her own. It would be a just return for all the insults they'd endured.

"Care to place a wager?" Master Crichton asked gruffly.

At first Cassie hadn't realized he was speaking to her.

"Women don't game, Father." Geoffrey gave a nervous laugh.

"He treats his daughter as he would a son," said Crichton. "What say you, girl? A wager?"

"Don't blame Catherine. She is merely her father's chattel," Geoffrey said.

Cassie felt all eyes upon her, and she lifted her chin higher. "One hogshead of Orinoco."

She was no one's chattel.

Gasps and shouts of outrage filled the air.

"She's as crazy as her father!"

"A woman wagering? For shame!"

It was a wager she could ill afford to meet, and she at once regretted her impulsiveness. One hogshead held more than one thousand pounds of tobacco. At most she had half that. If Aldebaran were to lose, she'd be in debt to the Crichtons until the harvest.

Master Crichton glared at her, clearly unhappy at being forced into such a high wager, but he nodded his acceptance. Men began to shout at one another, placing their bets, most of them favoring Geoffrey.

"He is such an odious man!" Lucy whispered. "You should not have let him bully you into this."

"It's too late now." Cassie gave Lucy's hand a squeeze.

Geoffrey rode to the starting line and waited for Cole to mount.

"A fair race." William Byrd raised the pistol. "Agreed?"

Cole nodded.

Geoffrey nodded, scowling.

The pistol fired with a sickening crack. Cassie could not bear to watch, but she felt frozen in place and could not turn away. Her pulse slammed in her ears, drowning out the clamor around her. Though Geoffrey's horse was fastest coming away from the starting line, Cole quickly overtook him and had pulled ahead by half a body length before the halfway mark.

What happened next was a blur. Cassie saw Geoffrey lift the horsewhip, saw his arm slash downward, saw Cole stiffen as the whip tore through his shirt.

"No!" she cried, her voice lost in the din.

Geoffrey raised the whip again and struck, hitting Aldebaran's flank.

The stallion faltered, and for a moment she feared it would stumble. Geoffrey streaked past to retake the lead, looking back over his shoulder as he rode.

Before Cassie could catch her breath, Cole had managed to calm the stallion and was rapidly gaining.

Watching Cole's approach over his left shoulder, Geoffrey attempted to block him by riding to the left, directly into Aldebaran's path.

But Cole was ready. He guided Aldebaran to the right, passing Geoffrey with such an astonishing burst of speed that Geoffrey had no time to react. Cole beat him to the finish line by more than a body length.

Cassie shouted with joy, relief washing through her. But her relief was short-lived.

No sooner had the riders crossed the finish line than Cole, his face a hard mask, leapt from Aldebaran's back and dragged Geoffrey roughly from his saddle, flinging him into the dirt.

"You son of a bitch! If my name were mine again, you'd pay for this!"

"Cole, no!" Cassie fought her way through the throng, afraid Cole was about to do something that would land him in chains—or worse. But by the time she'd reached the finish line, out of breath and in a panic, he had already turned his back on Geoffrey and was walking back toward Aldebaran.

Geoffrey struggled clumsily to rise, his face contorted with rage, his wig askew. "Stop him!"

Except to shake their heads or look away, no one moved. Without looking back, Cole took the stallion's reins and started for the stables.

"Whatever you are, Geoffrey Crichton, you're no gentleman!" Cassie fought the urge to slap him in the face. She turned to follow Cole, but found Master Crichton approaching, his mouth turned down in a grimace. She prepared herself for the upbraiding he was going to give her.

But Master Crichton thrust a bill of lading into Cassie's hand and, without a word, turned and stalked back to his manor.

"Father, did you not see? That piece of filth assaulted me!"

Master Crichton did not even glance in his son's direction.

*A*lec ignored the shocked stares and gasps that followed him. He barely noticed the men and women who stepped hastily aside to let him and Aldebaran pass. Anger boiled his blood, dulling the pain of the wounds on his back. Crichton was lucky to still be in one piece. Alec had come close to smashing his fist into the coward's face. Only the sound of Cassie's voice, frightened and alone in the crowd, had stopped him. He would not shame her or put her at risk.

He entered the stables, passing a group of gaunt children who gazed listlessly up at him through vacant eyes. Like all redemptioners on this estate, they looked ill-used and underfed. Even the dogs looked better tended.

He led Aldebaran to his stall and tied up the reins. Running his hands over the stallion's flank, he was relieved not to find a laceration or welt. He'd never used a whip on the horse, and, as he'd suspected, surprise, not injury, had made Aldebaran falter.

"You beat him anyway, boy." Alec scratched the stallion's withers and patted the velvet of his nose. "I knew you would."

He'd just removed the saddle when Cassie entered. She looked anxious, out of breath. For a moment she said nothing. "Thank you," she said at last.

"For what?" He didn't mean to sound angry.

"For winning." Her lips turned up in an elfin smile that immediately cooled his temper.

Alec lifted the bridle off the stallion's head and hung it on the stall door. "You're welcome."

"I came to tend those welts on your back."

"I'm fine."

"Nonsense!" She stepped between him and Aldebaran, brandishing a jar of salve, a determined light in her eyes. "Glare at me if you wish, but I'm not leaving until your wounds have been cared for."

"Very well." Alec strode to a nearby bench, pulled his shirt over his head, and was surprised at how much it hurt. He heard Cassie's soft gasp, then felt her fingertips gently spread ointment over the broken skin. It stung.

"I'm sorry. I don't want to hurt you."

"You won't." Alec felt her place one hand on his right shoulder to steady herself as she worked. His muscles contracted at her touch.

"Where are the other grooms?" she asked with a feigned air of nonchalance.

"Celebrating, I presume." He heard the gay strains of fiddle music in the distance and knew there would be dancing and drinking long into the night.

"One thing is certain. You're going to return to England with such an interesting assortment of scars, even the most highborn gentleman will find himself eager for a peek." Then she gasped. "Oh, I . . . Forgive me!"

Alec chuckled, shaking his head. "Is it really that bad?"

"Well ... "

"Show me."

He sensed her hesitation, then felt warm fingers glide along his skin.

"Most of them run diagonally here." She traced his scars with her fingertips. "And here."

Then her purpose seemed to change. He felt her fingers slowly move up to his shoulders, then to his neck and into his hair.

He couldn't breathe. If she didn't stop . . .

Abruptly he stood to face her, his gaze locking with hers. Her green eyes looked up at him with undisguised longing.

He traced a finger along the line of her lips. "Mistress. You'd best go."

She grabbed the salve, turned, and fled.

*A*n hour later Cassie sat at the dressing table and brushed the snarls from her hair, vowing that this attempt would be her last. She had tried to braid it three times, each time ending with a tangled mess. Why was she so distracted? It didn't help to have Elly tapping her foot on the floor and sighing. Cassie had asked her to stop, and the girl had—only to begin anew a few moments later. It seemed Elly had grown bored with her new duties already. Cassie wasn't surprised.

"Elly, please!" she said, more harshly than she'd intended.

Elly glared at her, but quit tapping her foot.

Giving up on the braid, Cassie took the length of her hair and piled it in a loose coil on her head, leaving one long ringlet dangling down each side of her face and a few at the nape of her neck. Eschewing the powder that would make her freckled face seem pale, she opened the small jar that held rouge and dabbed a bit on her cheeks.

Why had he sent her away? She watched in the looking glass as her finger traced her lips with rouge, recalling the sensation of his finger there. She supposed she should be grateful. But she wasn't. She'd wanted him to kiss her. Truth be told, she'd wanted more than a kiss. If he got her with child, at least she'd have a part of him when he sailed away to England, for she was now sure he would be leaving. One day soon the letter would come. He would be Cole Braden no longer.

She fought to stifle a growing sense of melancholy. Taking her mother's pearl necklace and earrings from the leather pouch, she fastened them in place. Downstairs, musicians tuned their instruments, and she and the other guests would soon be called to dinner. There was little time.

"If you like, you may join the other servants at the bonfire tonight." She stood and smoothed her skirts.

Nettie had worked night and day to finish her gown in time, shaping it from silk and lace taken from one of her mother's old gowns. Covered with tiny embroidered rosebuds of pink and green on a background of ivory, it was perhaps the loveliest gown she had ever worn.

"Thank you." Elly looked at the floor.

"I'll be sure to bring you something from the table." Cassie took her silk gloves from the dressing table, opened the door to the hallway, and stepped out.

Slaves bustled up and down the furnished corridor, fetching this and that for their masters and mistresses. Cassie went downstairs toward the billiard room, where most of the younger men could be found this time of day. She intended to have a few words with Geoffrey, whether Cole wanted her help or not. What Geoffrey had done today was despicable.

She followed the sound of male voices and found the door to the billiard room open a crack. She hesitated for a moment, unsure whether to knock or simply enter. Young women did not normally venture into areas reserved for male entertainment.

"The bastard had it coming, I tell you!"

Cassie recognized Geoffrey's voice and froze.

"But Geoffrey, you agreed to a fair race. You humiliated not only your father, but also Master Blakewell. You cannot blame your father for being angry." That was Landon.

"Then he cannot blame me for what I plan to do. That whoreson mistreated me in front of our guests. He will pay. Are you with me?"

Cassie felt her pulse quicken.

"Aye," said a voice she did not recognize.

"If it's a good plan," said another. "I don't want that crazy bastard Blakewell raising hell on my father's doorstep when he gets back from England."

"The convict is on our property. All I need is a few witnesses and the help of a willing female."

"A trap?"

Several men laughed.

Cassie felt her stomach turn.

"You'd best concoct your scheme without me," Landon said. "A convict he may be, and an upstart at that, but I've no quarrel with him. If I did, I'd take it up with Blakewell."

With a start Cassie realized Landon was approaching the door.

Quickly she darted for the stairs, but she was too late. By the time she reached the first step, he had already entered the hallway. Pulse racing, she pretended to have just descended.

"Good evening, Landon." She gave him her happiest smile, hoping he wouldn't notice the flush on her face or the trembling of her hands.

Obviously startled, he hastily shut the billiard room door behind him. "Miss Blakewell."

"I believe I'm in need of some cool lemonade. This heat is all but unbearable."

"Shall I fetch you a glass?"

"That would be most kind."

Cole was in danger. Somehow she had to warn him.

Chapter Nineteen

C assie choked down another bite of roast beef and followed it with a swallow of red wine. Would this dinner never end? They'd made it through the *hors d'oeuvres*—oysters laid out in their shells and some kind of fish soup—and were just beginning the first course. An array of fifteen different meat dishes, from calf's head to suckling pig to large joints of venison and beef, were laid out on the table. Cassie had no appetite. Her stomach was too full of butterflies to tolerate food.

"They say he claims to have been spirited away," whispered one of the older matrons—some relation of the Burwells—to the woman beside her.

"No!"

"Aye, and a gentleman at that."

Cole had been the focus of the evening's gossip, though no one had actually ventured to discuss him or the race openly for fear of further shaming the senior Master Crichton. Cassie now found herself in the uncomfortable position of eavesdropping, growing more alarmed by the minute. She had to get to the stables. But how? She had tried to slip away before dinner, but Landon had pestered her for her opinion on the surest way to win Elizabeth Wormley's heart. He'd still been pressing her for advice when dinner was served.

She'd thought of confronting Geoffrey and telling him what she'd overheard, but that might hasten his plans and ruin her chances of sending Cole to safety. She'd thought of revealing Geoffrey's plans to his father. But Geoffrey would surely deny it, and his word was worth much more than hers.

"He certainly has the bearing and manner of a gentleman."

"His comportment this afternoon was unquestionably superior to that of a certain young man."

"And he's as handsome as the devil himself."

Cassie looked up from her plate, her gaze locking for one moment with Geoffrey's. He'd overheard the remark, too. Though he smiled at her—a stiff, forced kind of smile—Cassie read cold fury in his gray eyes. It was said a man and his sanity could quickly be parted over an injury to his pride—real or imagined. Geoffrey was easily the most prideful man she knew.

By the time dessert had been cleared away nearly two hours later, Cassie's nerves were threadbare. Whatever Geoffrey was plotting, he'd have to act soon. It was already dark. Most of the men had withdrawn to the billiard room to smoke and drink brandy, and the women were repairing to their chambers, eager to primp before the dancing began. The orchestra, which had entertained quietly during dinner, was now in the midst of a lively contredanse.

Deliberately falling behind the other women, Cassie fled through the casement doors to the stairs and the garden below. The sound of violins followed her, their peaceful melody a sharp contrast to the staccato of her heart. With only the light of the quarter moon to guide her, she dashed past the rose garden toward the stables.

"I see I've found the fairest flower in the garden."

She gasped and whirled about to find Cole emerging from behind a willow. Despite the gravity of the situation, she felt herself smile at the sight of him. How could she have ever thought this man a felon?

"Cole, you must leave now! Take Aldebaran and ride for home!"

"But I was enjoying the music." A smile played across his lips.

That was in part true. Alec had heard nothing but folk tunes played on crude fiddles for five months and had not realized how much he'd missed chamber music until he'd heard it in the distance.

But he'd come toward the manor not for the love of music, but in the hopes of catching a glimpse of Cassie. And now here she was, as if summoned by his thoughts. Soft ringlets framed her face, making her cheekbones seem impossibly high. Her rouged lips were parted, as if in anticipation of a kiss, red and ripe as cherries. Her gown, of embroidered ivory silk and lace, though not of the latest style, emphasized her curves only too well and would have drawn many a jealous glare from women in London. The fitted bodice, though not cut daringly low, revealed the soft swell of her bosom, and its flared hips, supported from beneath by panniers, as was the fashion, emphasized her slender waist. A single teardrop pearl, suspended from a strand of smaller pearls at her throat, rested in the dark cleft between her breasts. But what struck him most was her eyes. Framed by the soft shadow of her lashes and animated by a compelling combination of anxiety and strength, they held him prisoner.

"Cole, you must listen to me! Geoffrey has plotted to entrap you. He hopes to see you hanged. You must leave for home now!"

"Not just yet."

She started to protest, but he placed a finger over her lips.

"I refuse to hear another word until you grant me the favor of this dance."

"But you must—"

"My lady." He offered her his most gallant bow and took her hand.

Her eyes grew wide with alarm, and she tried to pull her hand away. But he did not release her. Hesitantly she curtsied.

It was a simple quadrille set to an old composition by Lully, and though Alec had danced these steps perhaps a thousand times, he'd never felt them come alive in quite the same way. Enchanted by Cassie's movements, he let his eyes follow her as she circled gracefully to stand beside him, her fingers entwining with his as they took several side steps in unison and greeted a second, imaginary couple. The scent of lavender assailed him. The sight of moonlight and shadow playing on her skin made him yearn to touch her, to taste her. For one moment their gazes met, and he saw in the depths of her eyes a desire to match his own.

Suddenly his feet refused to move. He lifted her chin with a finger. "Why must I leave?"

She was trembling. "Geoffrey has plotted with some of the other young men to frame you—for ravishment, I think. I overheard them say they needed a woman's help."

"I'll not run like a coward."

"Please, Alec, ride at once! I could not bear to see you harmed!"

For a moment he did not fully comprehend what she'd said.

Then it came to him: She'd called him by his real name. She'd called him Alec.

"Very well," he said after a moment, aware he must be smiling like an idiot. "For your sake, Mistress."

"Follow the road south." She pointed. "Stay to the right, and you'll be home in about an hour."

"I remember the way."

"If riders approach, hide in the forest."

"Quit fretting. Go back inside before someone notices your absence."

"Then you'll leave this place?"

"I promise. As soon I see you've gotten indoors safely, I'll mount and ride out fast as the wind." He took her hand and touched it to his lips. "Say it again."

"Say what?"

"My name."

For a moment she looked confused, then a smile tilted the corners of her mouth. "I called you Alec."

"Aye. Do it again."

"Good night, and godspeed, Alec."

*E*lly paced nervously from one side of the library to the other, the eyes in the portraits that hung on the walls seeming to follow her as she walked. Her skin prickled. Candlelight flickered over the gilded bindings of books and off the backs of chairs, creating eerie shadows in the corners. He'd said he'd meet her here when the clock struck nine, but that was twenty minutes ago, or so she reckoned. What was keeping him?

She had no idea what Geoffrey might want to tell her. Her stomach twisted nervously every time she thought about it. She looked about the room for something to use as a looking glass, but found nothing. She'd done her best to look pretty, even taking a bit of Miss Cassie's rouge. Miss Cassie would never notice. Still, there was nothing Elly could do about her gown, an old blue thing she'd been given when she'd arrived.

She glanced up at the portraits again. Could she be imagining their glares? Quickly she looked away, her heart pounding. No matter where she stood, the eyes stared at her, the faces distorted by candlelight into beastly shapes. She had to get out of here. She ran toward the door, only to see its handle begin to turn. She started to scream, but a man's hand was clamped over her mouth.

It was Geoffrey at last.

"Why are you so frightened?" He was smiling.

"The eyes." Weak with relief, she pointed toward the portraits. "I don't like this room."

"Neither do I. Let's go somewhere else, shall we?" Geoffrey looked out into the hallway to be certain no one was watching, then took her by the hand and pulled her after him through the corridor and down the back staircase.

"Where?"

"Shhh! You'll see, my love."

At the bottom of the stairs he stopped and peeked around the corner to be certain the path was clear, then pulled her into a room directly across the hall. It was a bedchamber.

She should not be here with him. This was not proper. "Geoffrey, I don't—"

"Elly, dear—Helena—please forgive me, but my room was the only place I could think of where we could have a few moments alone. I've brought us some of my father's finest Madeira. Have you ever tasted a good Madeira?"

She shook her head. She wasn't even sure what it was.

"Then, my love, you must taste. You needn't worry. I would never do anything to tarnish your reputation. Surely you know that?"

She fought to still the inner voice that told her to flee. Geoffrey was a gentleman, after all. She could trust him.

"Besides, we shall be betrothed soon enough. Then it will be within my power to silence any wagging tongues."

"Geoffrey?" What had he said?

"Haven't I made my intentions clear, Elly, darling? Forgive me. I mean for us to be together." He poured amber liquid into a small crystal glass and handed it to her. "It will take some time to procure my father's permission, of course, but he is not an unreasonable man. On the day he gives us his blessing, I shall purchase your indenture and bring you here to be mistress of Crichton Hall."

"Oh, Geoffrey, yes!" She could scarcely believe her ears.

"Then let us toast our future. To happiness." He raised his glass, then tossed the contents down his throat in one swallow.

"To happiness." Heart soaring, she put the glass to her lips and took a small sip. The liquid was sweet, but it burned her throat as she swallowed.

"No, no. Not like that, my dear. You can't drink to our future with a mere sip. You must swallow it all, as I did."

Elly looked at the contents of her glass, raised it to her lips again, and swallowed it in one gulp. She could not repress a shudder as it seared a path into her belly. Before she could put the glass down, Geoffrey refilled it.

"To your beauty." He refilled his own.

The second glass didn't burn quite as much as the first. By the third and fourth, Elly was quite convinced this drink, whatever it was called, was really quite pleasing. She felt warm all over.

"You are quite lovely, Elly." He stroked her cheek.

"You really think so?"

"Aye." He lifted her chin and kissed her.

She wrapped her arms around him and leaned against him for support, her legs feeling rather unsteady.

"Come, Elly." He guided her across the room, one arm about her waist. "The wine seems to have made you a bit tipsy."

"Wine? I thought it was Mad . . . Madeira."

"Madeira is wine, silly girl."

She heard herself giggle and felt herself being lowered onto something soft. How thoughtful of Geoffrey to realize she was sleepy. She could scarcely keep her eyes open. She felt him lie down beside her, felt his fingers stroke her cheek. "That tickles." She snuggled against him.

His fingers traced a line to her neck and into her hair. "Yes, indeed, Elly, you are a beauty."

Then his lips found her throat. Elly felt him wrestle with the laces of her dress. Through a fog, she realized what he was doing.

"No, Geoffrey." She struggled to push him away. "We cannot."

"Why not?" He captured her hands in one of his and kissed her throat.

"We're not yet married."

"Does it feel good?"

"Aye, but—"

"Then relax and enjoy it." By then his fingers had found her breasts and were stroking her nipples. Then Geoffrey lifted her skirts to her waist and sought out the folds of her sex with his hand.

Oh, Zach, yes.

"Ah, yes, Elly. You want me as much as I want you."

But the voice was Geoffrey's.

She felt him lift her thighs and part them. Some part of her screamed out that she should make him stop. But she could not move, could not summon the right words.

Then she felt a piercing fullness and heard herself cry out.

"Shhh, darling. It will get better." Geoffrey settled his weight between her thighs.

But it didn't. Each thrust brought sharp pain. Elly bit her bottom lip and forced herself to lie still. She hadn't meant for this to happen, but she wanted to please him. His body drove into hers again and again. Then he groaned deeply and sagged limply against her, breathing heavily.

"Don't worry, love." He pulled himself from her and rose to pull up his breeches. "I'm told it only hurts the first time. Now I must get you back to your mistress's rooms so I can get back to my guests. I've got some unfinished business to attend to."

Before she realized it, Elly found herself staring at the walls in Miss Cassie's bedchamber, Geoffrey having vanished without so much as a kiss. Her head throbbed, and she felt sore between her thighs. Geoffrey was going to marry her. He had just made love to her. It was a dream come true.

Why did she feel so miserable and alone?

*C*assie glanced over the shoulder of her dance partner toward the clock in the hallway as he twirled her in that direction. Alec was surely home by now, wasn't he? Another twirl and she was facing the other direction, a wall of gilded mirrors reflecting a churning sea of powdered wigs and brightly colored silks.

Alec Kenleigh. She repeated the name silently, savoring the feel of it. At first she hadn't realized she'd used his real name. It had surprised her, even frightened her.

As Cole Braden he was a man who shared her way of life, who worked with his hands in the sun all day, a man she'd come to love. For love him she did, God save her. There was no way to deny that now.

But as Alec Kenleigh he was a wealthy gentleman, a man from another world who would soon be leaving.

Had he gotten away in time?

"Oh!" She gasped, embarrassed. "I'm sorry."

She'd been so lost in her thoughts she'd tripped over Benjamin Harrison's feet, nearly colliding with his partner.

"Are you feeling well, Cassie?" Charles Braxton asked, his brow furrowed with concern, his arms reaching out to steady her. "Mary told me about your terrible accident."

A kind, well-spoken young man only a few years older than she, he'd danced with her once already this evening. Handsome, with light brown hair, hazel eyes, and patrician features, he was precisely the kind of man she'd hoped to marry—before Alec had arrived.

"I'm sorry, Charles. I fear I'm a bit dizzy." She tried to ignore the pricking of her conscience. Charles did not deserve this. He had never treated her with anything less than courtesy, yet Cassie had been so distracted she had all but ignored him. Now she had fibbed to him, as well.

"Come. Let me fetch you something cool to drink." He guided her across the crowded floor to a vacant chair, one arm wrapped protectively around her shoulders.

"Thank you, Charles. You're quite kind."

With a bow, he disappeared, wending his way toward the other side of the room, where bowls of lemonade and cider, as well as cakes and candied fruits, awaited guests. Tapping her foot distractedly to the music, Cassie watched the dancers whirl and curtsy, weave and bow.

Geoffrey was not among them. He'd disappeared just after she'd warned Alec. She hadn't seen him since. Where was he? Had he seen her with Alec in the garden and gone to ambush him as he rode home?

"Here you are, Cassie." Charles handed her a glass brimming with fresh lemonade.

"Thank you." She gave him her warmest smile.

For a moment they sat in awkward silence.

"How is your father's tobacco crop this season?" He cleared his throat nervously.

"The rains have been good, and, barring disaster, it will be the best in many years." Cassie searched the crowd for Geoffrey.

"How many acres did he plant?" Charles shook his head apologetically. "I'm sorry. You must think me dull to ask such questions. Womenfolk find these things tedious, I know."

"Quite the contrary, Charles. My father and I discuss the details of planting every day, when he's home. I find it most interesting. It is how we colonists survive, after all."

"You are a most unusual woman." Charles smiled.

It was the way he smiled that gave Cassie pause. Was he becoming infatuated with her? Several months ago, she would have welcomed his interest. But now?

"Not all that unusual, I assure you, Charles. I'm as fascinated by silk and frippery as the next woman."

"Pardon me, Catherine, but we must speak at once." Geoffrey appeared from nowhere and took her by the arm, a look of smug satisfaction on his face.

Cassie's heart began to thud sickeningly against her breast. Had she warned Alec too late? Had he been caught? Did he, perhaps, lie injured—worse yet, dead—along the road or somewhere in the forest?

"What is it, Geoffrey?" Sick with dread, she followed him into the hallway, where several of the younger men stood waiting, excitement written plainly on their faces. These were the few who'd agreed to help him entrap Alec, no doubt, and Cassie hated them, each and every one.

"It seems the convict has taken Aldebaran and vanished," Geoffrey announced.

For a moment she was so overcome with relief she could scarcely speak. He was safe! Alec was safe!

"What's this?" bellowed the senior Master Crichton, who had come up behind her in the company of King Carter.

"The convict has vanished, Father, the stallion with him." Geoffrey flicked the lace at his wrists. "We've organized several search parties. With the hounds on his scent, he'll not go far."

Knees shaking, Cassie willed herself to stand and look Geoffrey in the eye. "You'd like to hunt him like an animal, wouldn't you, Geoffrey? Fortunately you won't have that pleasure. I sent him back to Blakewell's Neck hours ago."

The shocked look on Geoffrey's face was almost enough to make Cassie laugh.

"It seems that several young hotheads had planned to do him harm here tonight. To frame him for rape was the plan, wasn't it, Geoffrey, my boy?" King Carter said. "Landon told me all about it. I was going to intervene if it came down to it, but I see Miss Blakewell has already done what was necessary."

"What's this?" Master Crichton glared first at Carter, then his son.

"It's a misunderstanding, I assure you, Father." The muscle in Geoffrey's jaw twitched.

Cassie knew Geoffrey was beyond fury. He'd been bested twice today.

"Yes, a misunderstanding. That's what it is, I'm sure." King Carter's voice said just the opposite.

"Come, Miss Blakewell. I believe Master Crichton and his son have a few matters to discuss." Master Carter took her by the arm and led her toward the dancing.

"A detestable boy, that one. Your father shouldn't leave you to handle such things yourself. It is high time you got yourself a husband, young lady, someone to protect you and look after your interests."

"Yes, of course," Cassie said, only half listening, giddy with relief. "Thank you, sir."

"Is aught amiss, Cassie, dear?" Lucy bustled toward them, fluttering her tiny oval fan, her eyes glittering with excitement.

"Nay, Lucy. Everything is wonderful, simply wonderful."

Geoffrey swallowed the last of the Madeira and threw the bottle into the fireplace, pleased by the sound of shattering glass. That bastard Landon had run to his father and told him everything. Even Catherine had known. There was nothing Geoffrey could do about it, of course. The Carters were untouchable. His father practically worshiped King Carter and would do nothing to displease him.

And Catherine . . .

Geoffrey had seen it in her eyes. Anger. Hatred. More than anything—more than his father's threats or the snobbish, accusing look Carter had leveled at him—the loathing in her eyes tormented him. He loved her. He'd always loved her. Didn't she understand? He was trying to protect her.

Cole Braden might wear gallantry the way a priest wore black, but it was just a disguise. The man was nothing more than a lying convict, a man who sought to steal from his betters. He'd obviously been able to win Cassie's sympathy with his tale of woe, and now Virginia's matrons were prattling on about him as if he were a missing prince of England. But Geoffrey saw through him. They were not really so different, he and Cole Braden. Each wanted something, and was willing to do anything to get it.

But Geoffrey had earned it all by the privilege of his birth. Cole Braden was nothing.

It was nearly dawn. Rising unsteadily from an overstuffed chair, Geoffrey walked to his bed and collapsed into its softness. The musky smell of sex drifted up from his blankets, reminding him of the servant girl he'd deflowered hours earlier. She'd been worth the effort, that one. He felt his loins tighten and found himself wishing he'd spent more time inside her and less time arguing with his father.

The old man had hollered and strutted until Geoffrey was certain his heart would give out. At least he'd hoped it would. The damn hypocrite. Had his plan succeeded, his father would have praised him for it. But appearances were everything. It mattered not one whit what he did, so long as he did not get caught and besmirch the family name. It was a lesson his father had beaten into him since he'd grown old enough to wear breeches.

He had another plan, and this one would not fail. Though Henry had not been successful yet, it was only a matter of time. Accidents happened every day. With freedom and fear as his incentives, Henry promised he'd get the job done. Geoffrey simply had to be patient.

Chapter Twenty

*C*assie carried the bundle of fresh linens toward Jamie's room, where Nettie was busy airing the bedding. In the week since they'd returned from Crichton Hall, it had rained almost continually, and Cassie was determined to take advantage of the sunshine while it lasted. Every window in the house had been thrown open, and the sound of children's laughter rose from the courtyard below. No doubt they were already covered head to toe with mud.

"Here's the last of it." She handed the linens to Nettie and moved on toward her own room, trying not to look into her father's study as she passed.

Alec had been in there all morning reviewing her father's books in an effort, he said, to help. Why she had decided to let him help, she didn't know. She was as adept at ciphering as any man and knew a great deal more about running a tobacco farm than Alec ever would. She'd told him so, only to watch him turn his back and walk away angry.

They'd barely spoken these past days. When they had, the words they'd exchanged had been heated. When she came near, he found reason to go elsewhere. When she smiled at him, he looked away. When she spoke to him, he replied with polite indifference. It seemed a thousand years since he'd asked her to dance with him in the moonlight. What had happened to the affection they'd shared so openly that night?

She knew he did not approve of her running the estate.

"It is not right for a man to hide behind his own daughter," he'd said. "He's forced you to commit forgery and worse, while denying you the joy of a husband and children. Damn his pride! It ought to be one of your father's peers carrying the burden of this estate on his shoulders, not you."

She'd flown into a rage then. "It is man's disdain for woman that makes my task difficult, not the labor itself. What makes you think I want a husband? Perhaps I find more joy digging in the dirt than I would playing wife to some self-important boor who would view me as livestock to be kept and bred."

"This is how you prefer it? Perhaps your father isn't to blame. Perhaps his daughter's unnatural ambitions have brought this about. Simply trying to prove a woman can do it, Cassie?" He'd walked away.

Why couldn't he understand?

She spread the sweet-smelling sheets over her bed, trying once again to put aside the sadness that gnawed at her heart. It was undoubtedly better this way, she told herself, not for the first time. The less they spoke, the less likely she would be to slip in front of one of the servants and forget to call him Cole. Besides, Alec would be receiving his reply from London within the next six weeks by her estimation, and then he would sail out of her life forever. She had to find some way to quit loving him, and now was as good a time as any.

If only it didn't hurt so much.

"Elly!"

It was Nan in the courtyard below. Evidently Elly was missing again.

"Eleanor!"

Elly had not become more tractable since accompanying Cassie to Crichton Hall, rather the reverse. Elly turned up her nose at every chore given her and disappeared for long periods of time without permission. She'd even begun to treat the other servants with disdain and refused to give Zach, who obviously loved her, the time of day.

"That child is going to bring us trouble," Nettie had said only this morning when Elly had once again failed to appear at breakfast.

"Not when I'm done turnin' her over my knee," had been Nan's reply.

As for Nettie, Cassie had also noticed a change. For the first time in years, she seemed genuinely happy, humming while she worked and sharing unguarded smiles with all who passed. It wasn't hard to figure out the reason. Ever since Daniel's bout with the ague, Luke had been a regular visitor at her cabin, carrying firewood, repairing their clapboard roof, doing other chores a husband might do. Nettie fed him each night at her fire and had mended the shirt he'd torn repairing a fence. Daniel adored Luke and followed him about the plantation, chattering like a squirrel. Cassie had kept her observations to herself, sure Nettie would have shared her secret if she'd wanted to.

A child's footsteps sounded on the wooden stairs, followed by the clickety-click of animal claws.

"Stop, you! No!" she heard Nettie cry.

Cassie ran to help, but it was too late.

Sitting in the middle of the newly made bed was Jamie. With him sat a very muddy Pirate, wagging his brown tail, a trail of paw prints running across the floor and up the white linen behind him. Nettie stood, arms akimbo, glaring at the boy with mock severity, a smile tugging at the corners of her mouth.

"What have I told you about bringing Pirate into the house, Benjamin Hamilton Blakewell?" Cassie scolded.

"Sorry." Jamie clearly understood that the use of his full Christian name meant he was in real trouble.

"And you, don't you know that good dogs stay outdoors?" Eager for attention, the puppy leapt off the bed and jumped up onto Cassie's skirts.

She patted its head and scratched it behind its floppy brown ears, struggling to maintain some semblance of anger. Soon the pup would be expecting a seat at the dinner table. "Now scoot along, both of you," she said, trying to keep a stern tone to her voice.

Picking up the puppy, Jamie lugged it, hind paws dragging on the floor, into the hallway.

No sooner had he put Pirate down than the pup scampered up the hallway, first into Cassie's bedroom, where it leaped onto her bed, leaving muddy stains on her clean sheets, then into her father's study.

"Pirate, stop!" Cassie called.

By the time she reached the study, all was in chaos. Nettie was chasing Jamie, who was chasing Pirate, who thought the entire thing a game and was now barking excitedly from beneath the desk. Alec stood in the center of the confusion, a ledger in one hand, a look of mild surprise on his face.

"Jamie, come here at once!" Cassie called, her words all but drowned out by Jamie's giggles and Pirate's yaps. She shrugged her shoulders apologetically at Alec, who gave her a lopsided grin, his blue eyes bright with amusement.

Oh, how she had missed that smile these past several days. She smiled back, unable to stop the flush she felt slowly creeping into her cheeks. How did he manage to do that? With a glance, a word, a smile, he could set her heart aflutter, make her blush as if she were a silly girl of twelve in the throes of her first infatuation.

Breaking eye contact, Alec laid the ledger on the desk, reached down, and picked up Jamie with one arm, the squirming pup with the other.

"What have we here?" he asked, exaggerating the deepness of his rich baritone voice. "Why, it's that dread buccaneer Jamie Blackbeard and his vicious hound Pirate. God save us all!"

"God save us all!" echoed Nettie, shaking her head and turning back toward the bedroom.

They had thought themselves finished with the laundry.

"I'm sorry." Cassie smoothed her muddied skirts.

"No bother." Alec walked through the doorway into the hall, plopping the puppy onto the floor beside him. "I welcome the interruption. It does a man good to stretch his legs now and again."

He flashed her another smile and, lifting Jamie onto his shoulders, bounded down the stairs and out the back door, Pirate at his heels.

By the time Cassie had gathered the newly muddied sheets for laundering and carried them outside, Alec and Jamie were embroiled in an imaginary swordfight, much to the delight of the other children, who gathered to watch.

"Stand down and prepare to be boarded, Blackbeard! You'll not escape the noose this time!" Alec brandished a small stick as if it were a sword.

"You can't catch me!" Jamie also wielded a stick. With a fierce cry that drew muffled laughter from Nan and old Charlie, Jamie attacked.

Alec neatly deflected the blow and began a counterattack, thrusting and parrying with exaggerated effort. "Hold your sword so the blade tilts upward. That's the way," he said, giving his opponent advice. "Now lunge forward. Ward off my thrust. That's it."

Cassie leaned against the porch railing, her arms full of linen, and watched. Leaping about barefoot on the cobblestones, his breeches moving over the shifting muscles of his thighs, his white cotton shirt open to reveal the dark curls of his chest, Alec looked like a pirate himself, and a very virile pirate at that. Try as she might, Cassie could not forget how soft those curls had been under her palms or how hard his thighs had felt when pressed against hers. If only ...

No, it was best she had not lain with him. Aye, it was best this way, for Cassie knew with certainty that if he were to join his body with hers, she'd never be able to stop loving him.

"Avast, buccaneer! You have slain me!" Alec dropped theatrically to his knees. His hands pressed to the mortal wound in his abdomen, he groaned and then, to great applause, fell down dead.

Holding his sword high in the air, Jamie stood triumphantly over the body of his vanquished enemy, while Pirate, excited by the noise and sure that he was the center of attention, barked and leaped in circles, stopping only to favor Alec's face with several sloppy puppy kisses.

Alec roared back to life, lifted Jamie, and swung him about in the air, evoking playful screams from the children and laughter from the adults.

She wasn't going to be the only one devastated when he returned to England, Cassie realized. Jamie would miss him, too.

"That's all for now, tadpole." Alec, put the boy down, tousling his curls.

Cassie reached up to wipe wetness off her cheeks and realized with a start that she was crying. She turned and hastened across the courtyard.

There was work to be done.

*A*lec studied the figures on the page before him, engrossed. He'd always known Cassie was a woman of surprising abilities, but he'd not been prepared for this. The clever ways she'd hit upon to shore up the estate's finances, which could politely be described as unfortunate, were quite impressive.

As far as Alec could tell, Abraham Blakewell had been entirely dependent upon tobacco for his earnings, planting corn only for food. In good years, he'd spent lavishly for a man of his means, buying books, horses, and gifts for his wife and daughter, often going into debt despite a large harvest. In bad years, the debts had simply grown. Until Cassie had taken up her father's duties.

Though she tried to duplicate her father's script when ciphering, her ledger entries were neater, steadier, and contained fewer corrections than his, and Alec had no trouble discerning exactly when she had begun keeping the books. The first thing she'd done was to eliminate unnecessary expenditures. Then she'd begun planting wheat, barley, and hemp, providing the estate with new sources of income, however modest. She'd also begun selling vast amounts of lumber to factors in Williamsburg who, in turn, had sold it to the navy.

This, of course, had forced her to buy more slaves and bondsmen, as plowing fields, milling grain, and felling trees required many strong backs and able hands. Much of her profits thus far had been eaten up by these new expenses. In the end, Alec was sure her strategy would pay off. By his calculations, the estate, which had come perilously close to ruin, would be freed from debt in five to seven years, depending upon the tobacco harvest.

If Blakewell's Neck survived, Jamie would have only his sister to thank.

Alec heard the rustle of skirts in the hallway beyond and forced himself not to look up. It was a new form of torture, working near her like this. He closed his eyes and inhaled, sure that he could mark her scent in the air. For a week now he'd done his best to avoid her, burying himself in any task he could find, working until his muscles ached and welcoming their arguments like a condemned man greeted a last-minute pardon. He simply could not trust himself to be alone with her, especially since she'd destroyed the last barrier he'd thrown between them by using his true name. He wanted her with every fiber of his being, feared whatever self-control he'd possessed had been exhausted. If they were ever alone again ...

Well, they simply could not be alone again, not until he was a free man.

He turned the page, forcing himself to concentrate on the task at hand. Last year's tobacco harvest had been the largest and most profitable in five years. According to her notes she had ordered the same amount planted this year, and—

The sound of approaching footsteps and the soft swish of skirts scattered his thoughts again and drew his gaze involuntarily toward the door. She entered somewhat hesitantly, holding a silver tray laden with food.

"I thought you might be hungry." She placed the tray on the desk.

"Ah, yes. Thank you."

The scent of boiled beef and fresh bread made his mouth water. But that was not what fueled his greater appetite. She'd changed her gown since he'd last seen her—the last one having been spattered liberally with mud—and now wore a green muslin creation almost the color of her eyes. Soft ringlets curled at her temples, begging to be touched. An ivory lace fichu was draped over her shoulders and tucked into the low-cut bodice for modesty's sake, and he found himself wishing he could remove it to expose the soft mounds it concealed. Silently cursing his lack of resolve, he unfolded the napkin and placed it in his lap, willing her to leave him in peace.

She did not budge. Instead she stood, arms crossed, watching him. She was waiting, he realized, for some kind of response from him about her management of the estate.

"You're wondering what I have to say about all this." He motioned to the stack of ledgers on her father's desk.

She nodded, her eyes ablaze with challenge.

He found himself wishing he hadn't been so persistent in taking on this task. Being near her like this was the last thing he needed.

"I must say I'm quite impressed." He vowed to himself to keep his mind strictly on the matter at hand. "You've a thorough understanding of accounting. You've worked hard to find new sources of income, been thrifty with your resources. I doubt there's a man your age in the colony who could have done a better job."

Tension left her face as his praise sank in.

"Thank you." Her eyes beamed.

"I took the liberty of bringing the books up to date. And I found something of interest." He reached for the first ledger on the stack. "I believe your factor in Williamsburg is cheating you."

"Wh . . . what?"

Alec gestured to the chair, motioning for Cassie to sit. He placed the ledger on the desk before her and opened it, turning to the pages he'd marked. "Looking back through your records, I noticed the amount of tobacco lost prior to sale is about ten percent of the crop each year."

"That's quite common."

"Some loss is to be expected, of course—faulty cooperage, overprizing of hogsheads, loading accidents." He reached for another ledger. "But before your father began patronizing your current factor, losses averaged only two percent. That's a dramatic difference."

She bent forward, her eyelashes shadowing her cheeks, and read the entries on the marked pages one by one. Without knowing it, she tormented his senses. Her hair, twisted into a soft coil, teased him with the faint scent of lavender. The heat radiating from her skin warmed his blood. The silky arch of her neck, the creamy swell of her breasts called for his kisses.

"You're right." She lifted her gaze to meet his. "Either we've become careless in building and filling casks, or—"

"He's stealing from you, pilfering eight percent of your crop each year to line his own pockets. Over the years, it adds up to—"

"A small fortune. That bastard!" She stood and turned toward him, determination on her face. "What can I do?"

Alec couldn't help grinning at her foul language. "You can't prove he's stealing, not without witnesses. You can't accuse him without proof. But you can make some inquiries, find a factor you can trust. Perhaps Robert Carter can make a few suggestions."

She nodded.

"Also, I've noticed you've made a considerable investment in slaves and bondsmen of late, mostly slaves. There might be ways to get more work out of the slaves you have rather than buying more."

She looked puzzled and started to speak.

Alec held up his hand. "What if slaves had some incentive to work harder—freedom, for example? What if you allowed them to sell a small portion of what they themselves have grown each season and use that money toward buying their freedom?"

"It's almost impossible to free slaves nowadays. Laws have been passed—"

"Laws that can be circumvented or ignored."

She shook her head. "You don't understand. If we were to set our slaves free, we'd find ourselves financially ruined and run out of Virginia. Besides, it's not safe for free Negroes here. Freedmen have been pulled off the streets of Williamsburg and murdered. If we freed them, where would they go? What would they do?"

"That would be their decision."

"You'd throw them out with no way to survive? How is that compassionate? I don't like slavery any more than you do, Alec."

"Then find a way to do without it." He didn't mean to sound so angry, but he needed to make her understand. He took a deep breath and ran his fingers through his hair. "My father visited Virginia once. He bought a slave, brought him home to England, set him free. Whatever his flaws—and he had many—my father hated slavery. The man he freed stayed on with my family. He learned to be more properly English than King George himself. He became my valet when I was a young man, tortured me with lessons on deportment. He's like an uncle to me."

A faint smile tugged at her lips. "What's his name?"

"Socrates. He'd have my hide if he could see me dressed like this."

Cassie laughed.

"Slavery is wrong, Cassie. It's not enough to say you don't like it. You must do something to end it."

"I don't see how I can. The laws … " Her voice trailed off, but Alec could see she'd at least think about it.

"One other thing. You might want to consider building your own ship."

Her eyes widened in surprise. "A ship?"

"Aye. Think how much you'd save if you didn't have to pay the cost of transport. True, there would be other costs—a captain and crew. But that expense would easily be covered by the fees you could charge to carry other planters' cargo."

Alec could see her mentally performing the math. He saw the question cross her face before she asked it: "How can I possibly undertake something as complicated as the building of a ship?"

"I happen to be on very good terms with a certain shipbuilding firm in London. Top quality. Builds ships for the Royal Navy. I'm told the owner is forever in your debt. I'm sure I can arrange something."

"You would do that for us?"

He touched her cheek, looking into her eyes. "No. I would do it for you."

For a moment she said nothing, her eyes bright with emotion. "Thank you, Alec."

She placed her hand on his chest. Her touch scorched his skin through the cloth of his shirt.

He had it in mind to set her away from him, to return to his seat and resume their conversation. But before he could act, Cassie fell against him, her arms encircling his neck, drawing him down, her lips touching his.

He responded instinctively, holding her tightly against him, kissing her the way he'd been longing to kiss her—deep and hard. With one hand he sought the curve of her back, while the other plundered the softness of her hair. She tasted so good. She felt so good. He heard her whimper, heard himself whisper her name.

Their tongues met, caressed. He felt his body's potent response, and some part of him still capable of rational thought shouted that he should stop this before it went too far. It was yet the middle of the afternoon. The door was wide open, permitting any who passed a full view of their embrace. They were in her father's study, for God's sake.

Yet, he was sorely tempted. He could shut the door, take her on her father's desk. Or carry her across the hall to her own bed. "Cassie," he said hoarsely, "we must stop."

"Come to me tonight, Alec." Her eyes reflected the same desperate longing that burned in him, the soft curves of her body still molded to his. *"Please."*

He groaned, gently pulled her arms from behind his neck, and stepped away from her. "I am trying so damn hard to do the right thing."

"I don't want you to do the right thing."

Alec could see in her eyes that she more than meant what she said.

Without a word, he turned and strode from the room.

Chapter Twenty-one

*C*assie dropped her hairbrush onto her dressing table and fell across her bed, succumbing at last to the torrent of tears she'd held back all evening. She hadn't meant to leap into his arms. She hadn't meant to kiss him. She'd even asked him to come to her bed. What must he think of her now? What should she think of herself? Dear God, what kind of woman was she to long for a man so desperately that she could hurl herself at him like that?

I don't want you to do the right thing.

Had she really said that? Aye, she had. They had names for women who said such things. Did Alec think her whorish? He must. She had thrown herself at him, and he had turned and walked away without a word. And it was just as well. As soon as the letter from England arrived, he would forget her and return to the life he'd been born to. He didn't love her. He'd never given her any indication he felt anything for her beyond physical desire. But wasn't that enough?

Oh, yes. For one night with Alec, she'd gladly give up . . .

What? Jamie's future? Her own safety? Her family's honor?

Alec understood the risks. He knew what was at stake, just as she did, but he hadn't let his desires overrule his better sense. While a part of her wished he weren't so reasonable, she knew he was right. If he ever spoke to her again, she'd find some way to tell him so.

A flash of white light and the rumble of distant thunder signaled an approaching storm. She lifted her head and wiped the tears from her cheeks. She'd gain nothing by weeping.

A sudden gust of humid wind whipped her bedroom curtains about and caused the balcony doors she'd left ajar to slam against the wall, rattling glass and threatening to wake the dead. Rising as if from a dream, she went to bolt the doors shut.

*A*lec took another swig of whiskey, fighting fire with fire. If he could not have her, and he could not forget her, he would drink her out of his mind.

Out of his mind. There was a phrase that fit.

Not a moment had passed today when he had not thought of Cassie. He'd spent the afternoon as far away from her as he could, first taking Aldebaran on an exhausting ride through the forest, then helping Zach, who seemed to be in an equally foul mood, fell trees. No matter how hard he worked, he could not drive her from his thoughts.

I don't want you to do the right thing.

Did she know what she was doing to him? He was trying so damned hard to be a gentleman, trying to behave honorably. But even an honorable man had a breaking point.

Another ragged bolt of lightning split the starless night sky and was answered by a deafening crash of thunder, the weather seeming to reflect the tempest that brewed beneath his skin. The approaching thunderstorm had sent everyone else scurrying indoors earlier than usual, despite the sultry heat, leaving him on the doorstep to his cabin with his own ill temper—and a jug of corn whiskey—for company.

From where he sat, he could see her bedroom, the faint yellow glow of candlelight against the curtains of her balcony doors a sure sign that she, too, was still awake.

It would be so damn easy . . .

Rain began to pour from the black sky in sheets, soaking through his clothes to his skin. He dropped the whiskey jug in the dirt, stood, and pulled off his sodden shirt. Turning his face skyward, he welcomed the cooling onslaught.

*A*nother roll of thunder shook the house.

Was that Jamie crying or just the wind? Cassie picked up the candle, opened her bedroom door, and hurried down the hallway to his room. Jamie had such a fear of thunder and lightning that he'd be terrified if the storm woke him.

Another flash of white. Another deafening rumble. The storm seemed to have settled directly above them, as if it had come to spend its fury on their heads. Rain drummed on the roof and battered the windows, drowning out the sound of Cassie's footsteps and the creaking of the nursery door as she opened it. She held out the candle, letting its warm light fill the little room, and was relieved to see Jamie sound asleep, one little arm thrown over Pirate, whose paws twitched slightly at Cassie's intrusion. Silently, Cassie closed the door and tiptoed back to her own room, shutting her bedroom door behind her.

She had just placed the candle back on her bedside table when another deafening thunderclap shook the house, seeming to bring down the rafters. Wood cracked, and wind ripped through the room, snuffing out the candle.

She whirled about, expecting to find her balcony doors blown open, and froze, a scream stifled in her throat.

Alec.

A jagged bolt of lightning filled the room with blue light, revealing a look of feral intensity on his face. His hair hung in a wet, dripping mass about his shoulders. Water traced rivulets over the bare skin of his chest and abdomen. His breeches clung to his thighs like a second skin. Splinters of wood lay in the puddle at his feet, all that was left of the wooden bar that had bolted her doors. Without speaking or taking his gaze from her face, Alec closed the door behind him, shutting out wind and rain.

"You shouldn't be here." Her voice was little more than a whisper. She looked away, unable to bear his penetrating gaze.

"I've come to take what you offered."

"You . . . you said you wouldn't." Cassie realized she was wearing only her shift and shielded her breasts with her arms.

"I changed my mind." He took a step toward her. "Are you displeased?"

"No. Yes!" She took a step backward. She felt like a fox, and he was the hound. Except she had asked him to come to her. And here he was. What had she done?

"Do you want me to leave?"

" I ... I ... " She could hardly breathe, hardly think with him so near.

He crossed the distance between them in a single graceful stride. "You've no reason to fear me." He gently traced the curve of her cheek with his finger.

"I know that."

"Do you?" His hands cupped her bare shoulders. "You're trembling."

A flash of blue-white. Thunder.

"I am?"

"Aye, love." His fingers traced their way slowly down her arms. "Is it desire, or are you afraid?"

"I don't know." Still she could not look at him. "Maybe both. I … I'm not sure what desire is supposed to feel like."

He tucked a finger under her chin and lifted her gaze to meet his. Taking one of her hands, he placed it over his heart. "It feels like this."

Beneath her palm, she could feel the rapid beating of his heart, a staccato rhythm that matched the one beneath her breast. A small whimper escaped her.

Before she was prepared for it, he pulled her softly against him. His lips closed over hers in a searing kiss, his wetness soaking through to her skin. He smelled of pine and rain, tasted faintly of whiskey, and for one terrifying instant she feared she would be lost. She sagged against him.

Taking her weakness for acquiescence. Alec moaned, pulling her tightly against him. His tongue plundered her mouth, and to Cassie's surprise her tongue responded in kind. But then she felt his hands move beneath her shift, felt them cup the flesh of her bare buttocks, lift her and press her hard against him.

A flash of light. Thunder.

"Alec, please … " An emotion she recognized as fear drew her back. Her hands grasped his and pulled them away. "Stop!"

With obvious difficulty, he released her. His hands cupped her face. "If you want me to go, I will."

"I don't know what I want!" The words were almost a sob. Her entire body shook. "When you touch me, I feel … But … I'm scared."

"I would never hurt you." His thumb traced the fullness of her lower lip.

"I've heard women say it hurts." She looked away again.

"It's true a woman's first time can be painful, but I promise I will be as gentle as I can. I want only to bring you pleasure." He took her hands in his.

"Some say there is no pleasure in it for women."

"I pity them, for I've never known a woman who didn't enjoy it as much as any man." His thumbs drew lazy circles on the insides of her wrists.

"You've deflowered many virgins then?" Even Cassie could hear the note of jealousy in her voice.

"None."

"Then how shall you know what to do?"

To her surprise, he chuckled, his teeth white in the darkness. Then he brushed a stray curl back from her face and pulled her gently into his embrace. He was so warm and so strong, and she felt that perhaps she had been waiting her entire life for this, for him. When his lips took hers again, she surrendered.

"Dear God, Cassie." His voice was rough with emotion. "What have you done to me?"

A flash. A rumble.

She had no answer for him, even had she been able to speak. Transfixed by his scent, by the male feel of him, she could not think, let alone talk. Then his lips traced a line along the most sensitive part of her throat, and she heard herself moan. Her hands moved of their own accord to rest upon his chest. They had come this far before, and her fears began to drift away.

"If you undress me first, there will be less to frighten you," he whispered.

"Undress you?" Her words were a squeak. "I don't think—"

"Aye, undress me." He took her hands in his and led them to the opening of his breeches.

She stared up at him, eyes wide. He was moving too fast. She wasn't ready. But she wasn't a child. She had wanted this, hadn't she? So what was the matter with her?

She looked down. Hands trembling, she struggled to loosen the tie that held his breeches in place. His strong fingers closed reassuringly over hers, stilled her trembling, and guided her motions until, at last, his breeches lay on the floor.

Another stroke of lightning cast his nakedness in momentary high relief. He stood still, making no move to hide himself. She'd seen him unclothed once before, but he'd been unconscious and quite ill. She'd done her best to avert her gaze. Now he stood before her, healthy and strong, his shaft huge and erect against his belly. Her breath ceased, and a tremor of desire tinged with fear rushed through her. She'd never seen a man in this state before, and her gaze fixed on him.

"There's nothing to fear." Alec caressed her cheek.

Then he reached for her, pulling her into his embrace. His arousal pressed full and hard against her, only a thin layer of cloth between them. This time, when he lifted her shift, she didn't object. He released her from his arms only long enough to pull it over her head and cast it aside.

She'd never been completely naked in front of anyone since she was a child. Impulsively she shielded her body from his view.

"Don't." He took her arms, gently drawing them away from her breasts. "You've no reason for shame. You are so incredibly beautiful."

She felt the passion in his voice, sensed his gaze hot upon her, but could not meet it. But then his arms enfolded her, and she could think of nothing else. Her breasts yielded to the hardness of his chest, skin meeting soft skin, flesh against fevered flesh. His shaft was a brand against her belly. His lips closed over hers again, their tongues twining. With one hand he caressed the soft underside of her breast, then his fingers found her nipple. He rubbed it, teased it. She gasped, and the gasp became a moan as the tender bud grew taut under his touch. His hand took her other breast, cupped its fullness, traced lazy circles over its hardening crest with his thumb. Liquid heat flooded her body, pooling deep inside her.

"Oh, Alec." Her breasts felt so full and heavy. Was this what it was like—all this longing, this fever, this desperation? She found herself wanting to touch him the way he was touching her. Hesitantly she slid her hands over the skin of his chest. Her fingers weaved through the mat of soft curls, traced the hard outline of his muscles, skimmed his flat nipples. She heard his breath catch, felt him tense beneath her touch.

He lifted her into his arms, placed her gently on her bed, and lay down beside her. But it no longer felt like her bed. It had become a foreign country, exotic and unfamiliar, and she a traveler. She looked up at the man who had become her guide in this strange land, and the intensity of his gaze made her heart pound.

"Cassie, my sweet." His mouth captured hers again, his lips straying to place fiery kisses across her face and throat. When his lips closed over one taut nipple and drew it into his mouth, she felt her entire body shudder with delight.

Lost in sensation, she felt his tongue tease first one taut bud, then the other, licking, nipping, suckling. The feeling was both shocking and delicious and seemed to shoot straight from her nipples to the aching flesh between her thighs. Clutching handfuls of his wet hair, she twisted beneath him, panting his name. She wanted him to stop. She wanted more. She didn't know what she wanted.

"I've imagined making love to you a thousand times." He blew gently across her breasts.

Cassie gasped as her already sensitive skin, wet from his kisses, tightened against the chill. "Alec, help me!"

The throb between her legs had become an unbearable ache, and she felt her thighs spread of their own accord.

His hand slid in tantalizing, slow circles across her belly, over her inner thighs, and into the thatch of curls that concealed her womanhood.

She gasped and tried to pull away as his fingers found the soft folds of her sex and parted them. She had never imagined anyone touching her there.

He stilled her, caressing her belly. "Let me bring you pleasure. Let me give you what you want."

"Is . . . is that part of it?"

"Aye." He kissed her face, her lips, her breasts. Gently he again delved between her nether lips, stroking her most tender flesh, then began to play with her sensitive bud. She felt her inner passage clench at this new, indescribable sensation. The slow burn he had ignited within her became an unquenchable wildfire, and she arched against his hand, aching for release.

"Oh, please!"

"There's more." He smiled lazily—and slowly slipped a finger inside her.

Spirals of pleasure sprang to life within her at this new torment, and the noises that came from her throat hardly sounded like her at all. Who had she become?

"Mmm. You're so wet, love." He slid first one finger, then two, in and out of her moist sheath, penetrating her deeply. Drawing her inner moisture onto his fingers, he spread it over her sensitive nub until it was slick and his fingers slid quickly and easily over it. Without mercy he caressed her inside and out. "This pleases you, my sweet?"

"Oh, yes!" It was a kind of torture as his fingers slid into her, then withdrew to circle over her swollen bud, then penetrated her again. Her nails dug into the muscles of his back as she strained against him, frantic for what she thought must come next.

He moved over her, pressed her thighs farther apart with his own, and sat back on his haunches. Cassie's breath caught in her throat as his gaze dropped to her most private self, and she felt her entire body turn scarlet. No one had ever seen this part of her. Reflexively she would have drawn her legs together, but he held her fast, his hands stroking her inner thighs.

"You are so beautiful—everywhere." With one hand he caressed her swollen sex until she moaned with pleasure. Then he stretched out above her, took her hands in his, and drew her arms above her head, his weight pressing them into the downy softness of her pillow. His gaze locked with hers as he began to slide the head of his shaft up and down over her throbbing sex. His eyes were dark, their pupils dilated with desire.

But still he did not penetrate her fully. The head of his manhood found her cleft, probed, then withdrew and probed again, pressing against the barrier of her maidenhood.

Pinned beneath him, Cassie felt helpless, ensnared by his sexual and physical power and her own raging passion. Her breath came in ragged gasps.

He spoke her name, his gaze still locked with hers. Then he thrust— and breached her barrier.

She cried out, startled by the sudden sharp pain, her entire body going stiff.

He caught her cry with his lips, murmured endearments against her cheeks, kissed her brow. "It won't hurt again, I promise."

She could feel the tension in his body as he held himself still within her, his ardor barely contained. To her surprise the pain did fade, replaced by a delicious sense of fullness. He felt like iron wrapped in velvet, hard and thick inside her.

Slowly he began to move. Pleasure slowly unfurled in her belly. Lost in him, she gave herself up to the heat of their joining.

His motions were a sweet torment as he rocked against her. Each thrust answered her desire, heightened her need. She had never imagined anything could feel this good, as stroke upon stroke, he filled her. Her hips matched his movements, inspired by some instinct all their own. She heard herself call his name over and over, heard him answer, his voice strained. Her fingers twined tightly with his as her body raced headlong toward some precipice.

She arched toward him as the world exploded into a shower of light. Unimaginable pleasure spread from somewhere deep in her belly through every inch of her body. She cried out as he carried her over the crest and wave after wave of delight washed through her. She felt his body shudder, heard him groan as, with one last powerful thrust, he joined her, spilling his essence inside her.

*A*lec opened his eyes and looked down at the woman who lay asleep, nestled in his arms. One leg tucked intimately between his, her head resting on his chest, the softness of her hair spilling over his arm where he held her, she felt as if she'd been tailored to fit his embrace. He reached down, brushed a stray curl from her cheek, watched her stir, a faint smile playing across her lips. Outside, the storm had quieted, thunder and wind giving way to the soft patter of rain dripping from the eaves into puddles below. The clouds had begun to scatter. The moon and a few stars hung in the dark sky, casting a faint glow through the curtains and across the bed.

After what he'd done, he ought to hate himself. But he didn't. Try as he might, the only feeling he could summon was a deep sense of … contentment. He hesitated to name the emotion, unsure that he'd ever felt this way before. Strange that one woman could touch him so deeply.

What if he'd gotten her pregnant? He was no good to her as Cole Braden. If people believed she was carrying a convict's child, her life—and the child's—would be misery. She'd be shamed, ostracized, perhaps flogged. But surely it was only a matter of weeks, days perhaps, before his name would be restored again. Even if their passion had produced a child tonight, he'd be Alec Kenleigh long before any pregnancy would show. No one would dare ridicule her once he'd given her his name.

He'd meant to love her more slowly. It was her first time. But months of celibacy and endless weeks of wanting her had taken their toll. It had been all he could do not to come before she did. Next time, it would be different.

He closed his eyes and allowed himself to drift off, his nostrils filled with the musk and salt of their lovemaking. He'd been asleep but a moment when he felt her shift in his arms, her cool fingertips tracing a line across his chest. Through half-closed eyelids he watched as she explored his body, unaware he was awake. Her gaze moved from his face to his chest and abdomen with innocent curiosity, finally resting on that part of him that was so new to her. He felt himself begin to grow hard under the heat of her perusal, and felt her breath quicken.

"It knows you're watching." More than a little amused, he tried not to laugh.

She gasped and looked up at him, obviously embarrassed. "I ... I—
"

"You've no reason to be ashamed." He turned so they lay on their sides facing each other. "Much of the joy between a man and a woman lies in the discovery of each other."

He kissed her gently, languidly, stroking the hollow just above her hips. The softness of her breasts pressed against him, and he felt heat rush to his cock.

Evidently emboldened by his words, she began to explore his body openly, her fingers slowly tracing the lines of his shoulders and chest before moving to his abdomen. His muscles contracted in response.

"Do you like this?" she asked.

"Aye." His arousal complete, he watched the play of emotions on Cassie's face as her hands slowly crept lower, curiosity and sexual desire competing with maidenly shyness. For a moment, he thought shyness would prevail. Then he felt her hand close over him, her fingers tentatively exploring his length, forcing a groan from his throat.

She jerked her hand away. "Did I hurt you?"

"Nay." He couldn't help chuckling.

Slowly she took him in her hand again, her inexperienced touch more titillating than that of the most practiced courtesan. "It is wondrous."

"Wondrous?" Alec had always considered himself well endowed, but none of his lovers had used the word *wondrous* before.

"Aye. It is wondrous how a man's wee willie can be so small and soft one moment, then suddenly become so large and hard."

"*Wee* willie?" He choked on the words, torn between laughter and humiliation.

"Aye, wee willie. Have you never heard the term before?"

"Nay! Pray tell, where did you learn it?"

"It's the word my mother used to describe a male's ... nether parts."

Alec saw her cheeks flush. "And I suppose it's the term you use when you speak to Jamie."

"Aye, what else?"

"Poor lad."

"What do you call it?"

"I call it a cock, love. Mmmm."

"Cock." She stroked down the length of him, until his foreskin was drawn taut, then drew her hand up again over the head. "And does it please you when I touch your cock?"

"Aye." She was a fast learner. "Stop."

He removed her hand, afraid it would be over before it began if he let her continue.

"Did that not feel good?"

"I'm afraid, love, it felt too good." He pulled her to rest against his chest.

For a moment, neither of them spoke. From somewhere in the distance came the song of a whippoorwill. *Whip-poor-weel. Whip-poor-weel.*

She met his gaze from beneath thick lashes. "Why did you change your mind and come to my bed?"

"The roof to my cabin was leaking frightfully."

She sat up with an indignant huff but laughed at his jest just the same. "I want the real reason."

"The real reason?" He pulled her back into his arms and planted a kiss on her nose. He paused, uncertain how to express what he felt. "I wanted you more than I wanted to breathe."

"I'm glad." Her smile made his blood run hot.

"You, my love," he said, brushing a wayward curl from her eyes, "are a temptress, a beautiful seductress."

Cassie shifted uncomfortably under his gaze, and Alec realized with some sense of amazement that she did not believe him.

"Your eyes, for example." He paused and kissed each eyelid. "They put emeralds to shame."

She shook off his compliment with a smile and a toss of her head.

"Your lips make a man think of nothing but kissing you." His mouth closed over hers to show her just what kind of kiss he had in mind.

She wriggled against him.

"Your breasts…" He cupped one eager mound and circled its rosy peak with his thumb, "…Are meant for this."

He turned her gently onto her back, holding her arms over her head and capturing one taut bud with his mouth. Slowly he circled her nipple with his tongue, then drew it into his mouth to suckle it before moving to its twin. He heard her whimper, felt her twist beneath him. Her head was thrown back, her eyes closed, her body cast half in shadow and half in moonlight.

Abruptly he stopped.

She whimpered in frustration.

"I suspect that when the gentlemen of London catch their first glimpse of you, they shall become a bunch of randy satyrs and I shall have to spend all my time fighting them off." He turned onto his side and looked down at her, his head propped on one arm.

"London?"

Chapter Twenty-two

*C*assie sat up and looked at him with surprise, her hair in glorious disarray about her shoulders. The tight pink crests of her breasts glistened with moisture where he'd kissed her, and Alec found it terribly difficult to think.

"Aye, London." He laughed, letting his hands glide over the softness of her skin. "You didn't think I'd leave you behind, did you?"

She dropped her gaze, and he saw that was precisely what she'd believed. An image of the young woman his brother had abandoned leaped unbidden to his mind.

He sat up and cupped her face with his hands, sexual play all but forgotten. "Look at me, Cassie."

Slowly she lifted her gaze to his, her eyes full of wariness.

"I will never forsake you. That I promise."

"Alec, I—"

He held a finger to her lips to still her. "I know we've spoken no vows, but I swear before God I will make you my wife as soon as I am able."

She stared at him. "Wife?"

"Aye, my wife. For all we know, you could be carrying my child now." His hand slid down her gently rounded belly to rest over her womb. Her gaze met his again, and for once he could not read the emotion he saw there. Doubt? Fear?

"Kiss me." She leaned forward, brushing her lips against his.

He complied, pressing her gently back onto the pillows, tasting her mouth. Taking the kiss deeper, he stroked the milky undersides of her breasts, kneading their fullness. This time would be different. He would teach her the secrets of her body, and then … He heard her sigh, felt her breath quicken as he lazily stroked first one taut peak, then the other, taking each into his mouth in turn.

Her fingers twisted in his hair, drawing him closer. Her pleasure the source of his own, he caressed the soft curves of her hips and belly, then reached to cup the patch of red-gold curls between her thighs. He pressed the heel of his palm into her woman's mound in a slow, circular motion.

She moaned. "That feels so … so … "

"Good?" He brushed his lips over the sensitive skin of her throat, then teased the whorl of her ear with his tongue.

"Aye!" She lifted her hips to meet the pressure of his hand.

Taunted by her sighs and tortured by the musky scent of her arousal, he delved gently into the inner folds of her sex, maintaining pressure on her mound, and was rewarded with a lusty moan. She was hot and slick, more than ready for him. Still he refrained. He sought and found her swollen bud and, catching it between two outstretched fingers, tugged gently on it until she trembled with pleasure.

"Do you like that, my sweet?"

Her head tossed from side to side on her pillow—the only answer he needed.

"Perhaps you'll like this even better." Alec penetrated her with one finger, two, stroking her gently, deeply, until his fingers were slick with her juices. Then he began to slide them quickly back and forth over that most sensitive spot. Her breathing was almost frantic now, and her thighs spread wider to give him access.

With one hand, she gripped his arm, her nails biting his flesh, while her other hand clutched at the sheets.

"You like that, too, I see. What about this?" Possessed by an appetite all their own, his lips traced a line from her throat to her breasts and down her belly. He felt her shiver and saw goose bumps spread across her creamy skin. He wanted to taste her, to possess her with his tongue and lips. Lowering his mouth to her cleft, he kissed her deeply.

"Alec!"

But her voice when she cried his name held not pleasure, only shock. Her entire body was stiff with surprise.

"Shhh, love." He lifted his head to kiss her belly, careful not to alarm her. Until tonight, she'd been a virgin. Ruled by his own appetites, he feared he was again moving too fast. "Someday you'll ask me to love you with my mouth."

He slowly kissed his way back up her body. When he looked into her eyes again, he knew a thrill of victory. She wanted it even now. Let her wait. Anticipation would make it all the better.

"I need you." Her gaze locked with his, and in their depths Alec saw a hunger to match his own.

"Aye." Raising himself above her, he settled himself between her milk-white thighs. Struggling to hold on to his self-control, he touched the tip of his shaft to her cleft and withdrew. He'd hurt her once. He wouldn't hurt her again. Slowly he entered her again and again, going deeper each time before withdrawing, giving her time to open to his intrusion. She was heaven—so wet and tight. He found himself fighting not to come right away. "Sweet Jesus!"

Slowly, so slowly he moved within her, her soft moans urging him on. He had wondered many times what it would be like to make love to Cassie, to watch her naked and writhing beneath him, but no fantasy could compare with this. She twisted and arched with abandon, whimpering his name, her artless responses more intoxicating than anything he could have imagined. When she wrapped her legs around him, opening her body to him fully, Alec thought he would lose himself.

"Alec, please." Her hands moved over the muscles of his back, gripped his shoulders.

"Come for me, love," he murmured against her cheek. He quickened the pace, felt her muscles tighten in response. "I want to feel you come."

Almost immediately, she cried out, and he felt her body tense, her muscles clenching around him in ecstatic rhythm.

When her peak had passed, he stilled himself within her and waited until he felt her body relax, trailing kisses over her cheeks and forehead. "My beautiful Cassie."

Her eyes fluttered open. "I didn't know it would be like this."

"Ah. But there's more." Holding himself deep within her, he pressed his pelvis against her mound in slow, tantalizing circles. She was wet with the juices of her climax. Her skin was rosy and covered with a sheen of sweat. Her breasts were swollen with passion, and Alec couldn't resist the urge to suckle them.

Drawing on her nipples with his lips, he felt her response begin to build anew. She whimpered and called his name, but he would not release her. Not yet. He angled his pelvis the better to press against her swollen slit, grinding in relentless circles. Her nails dug into his back, and still he would not relent. He wanted to prolong her pleasure, to take her to the brink.

"Oh, Alec, I'm dying!"

Feeling her desperation, Alec suckled harder upon her, nipped her breasts gently with his teeth, and quickened the pace. Around and around he moved, his cock deep inside her. And then he felt it—her sharp intake of breath, the quivering of her belly, the tightness of her muscles as they contracted around him.

She cried out and arched her back, nearly lifting him with her as bliss overtook her a second time.

When her climax had passed, he again held himself still within her and watched as her breathing slowed, nuzzling her throat, kissing her eyelids. "You have no idea how exciting it is to watch you come."

"You watch?" She looked up at him, a shy smile curving the corners of her lips.

"Mmm-hmm." He withdrew from her all the way, still rock hard, and then buried himself again, eliciting a deep moan. "Keep your eyes open this time."

"Again? Oh, Alec, I can't—"

"You can." He kissed her. "You will."

Near the end of his restraint, he reached down and lifted her legs so that they rested on his shoulders. "Trust me," he said at the surprised look on her face. Placing his hands beneath her bottom, he angled her hips so his shaft would stroke the most sensitive part inside her. Then he withdrew again and plunged into her intoxicating warmth. Her hands gripped the muscles of his arms, nails digging into his skin.

Faster, harder, he drove himself into her, his gaze locked with hers. Deeper he plunged, until he could feel her womb. His sac bounced against her bottom with each stroke, his testicles tightening as his own peak drew near. He felt her climax, saw the bliss in her eyes—and his control shattered. Giving in to rapture, he exploded, pouring himself into her as she milked him to ecstasy, giving him final release.

Moments later he kissed the moisture from her brow.

"I believe, my dear," he said when he could speak again, "you have slain me."

*C*assie peered at the tobacco leaf Micah held in his hands, keenly aware of Alec's presence beside her. The color was right—a grayish yellow-green—and when the overseer bent it, the leaf snapped cleanly in two.

"It's time." Micah's brow was beaded with perspiration. He turned and whistled sharply, signaling to the field hands to bring their knives and begin cutting.

Cassie shaded her eyes from the hot August sun, surveying the field, row upon row of tobacco plants extending well into the distance. It was an enormous task that lay ahead of them.

"You'd best begin." She gave Alec a guarded smile, memories of last night's lovemaking fresh in her heart. With so many people around, she could not do what she wanted to do, which was to take his hand and give him a kiss. It was still hard for her to believe these past six weeks of loving had not been a dream.

"As you wish, Mistress," he replied, his eyes telling her he had not forgotten last night either.

"Do be careful," she whispered, watching as he tested the tobacco knife in his hand, getting a feel for its weight. "I wouldn't want you to lop off anything important by accident."

"Thank you for the advice." His face was serious, but his blue eyes sparkled.

She turned and threaded her way through the rows of lush waist-high plants back to the cookhouse, where empty jugs waited to be filled with sweet water and cider. The men would grow thirsty working so hard in this heat and would need something cool to refresh them.

Looking over her shoulder to capture one last discreet glimpse, she saw Alec bent low, slashing the tobacco stalks and tossing them on the ground to wilt in the sun, the muscles of his back shifting as he worked. Pretending he meant nothing to her was sheer torture. So far, their affection for one another seemed to have gone undiscovered by all save Takotah and perhaps Nan.

Takotah had left a pouch of herbs on Cassie's bed one afternoon without saying a word. Only when Cassie opened it and smelled the contents did she realize Takotah's intent. These particular herbs were used to prevent a man's seed from taking root. She had tucked them away, hesitant to use them. Her monthly flux had come and gone as expected last month, and she'd been torn between relief and bitter disappointment at the knowledge that she did not carry his child. He would be leaving so soon.

A shadow passed over her heart at the thought. She was forced to feign indifference by day, but he meant everything to her. She'd lost count of the times they'd made love these past six weeks, meeting secretly by night in the stables, in his cabin, at the cove. Just when she thought he'd taught her all there was to know about love between a man and a woman, he'd show her something new, bringing her unimagined pleasure, satisfying her completely. Except for one thing.

He still hadn't said he loved her. And she, afraid to tell him what lay in her heart, had not been able to speak those words to him, even though they were on her lips every time he smiled or touched her or called her name.

As she rounded the corner of the cookhouse, she made the mistake of looking toward the porch. It was empty. For a moment the sight took her by surprise, but only for a moment. A lump rose to her throat as she remembered.

Old Charlie was gone. The ague had come back in force, the stagnant marsh air fed by the recent rains. This time, it had taken lives. The first to die had been a slave child barely a year old. Charlie had been next, the fever taking him so suddenly Takotah had had no chance to treat him. They'd buried him nearly two weeks ago. Cassie had defied the law that forbade funeral services for slaves and read from the Bible herself. Still, she could not believe he was gone. He'd been with her family since before she was born, had held her on his knee, told her stories, whittled wooden horses for her as he had later whittled wooden ships for Jamie. How she would have gotten through that day without Alec to comfort her, she knew not.

Four others lay ill at the moment, but Takotah expected them to recover. Cassie prayed they would. Summer was nearly past.

Soon the marsh air would cool and lose its vile potency. If only they could all stay healthy until then. The supply of quinquina was running dangerously low.

She opened the door to the cookhouse to the sound of someone retching.

"Did God give ye no sense, child?" she heard Nan ask.

Nan held Elly's head over a copper basin while the girl threw up her breakfast.

"We all know better than to eat strange berries. Is it an early grave yer lookin' for?"

Elly wiped her mouth on the cloth Nan provided, panting for breath, her face unusually pale.

"What did the berries look like?" Alarmed, Cassie felt Elly's forehead for fever. She was cool.

"I'd swear they were blackberries, Mistress." Elly's blue eyes were as round as those of a frightened child. "I'd not have eaten them else."

"Does your stomach hurt?"

"Nay, Mistress. Oooh!" She threw up again.

"Poor lamb." Nan stroked her forehead.

"When did you first start feeling ill?" Cassie was puzzled. Usually eating poisonous plants brought stomach pain, fever, fits, and other symptoms.

"It's been this way every morning this week," Elly said when she caught her breath.

Perplexed, Cassie tried to recall any illnesses that included similar symptoms.

"When was your last flux?" Nan asked gravely.

Cassie gasped, understanding at once the direction Nan's thoughts had taken. This was what she had hoped to prevent.

"When was your last flux?" Nan asked again.

Elly turned beet red. "June."

Nan reached inside Elly's gown and, ignoring the girl's squeak of protest, felt her breasts. "You're not sick, lamb. You're with child." Nan shook her head soberly and bent her heavy form to remove the fouled basin. Its contents would go to the pigs.

"Who is the father?" Cassie demanded.

"A baby!" Elly whispered. She lifted her chin and glared at Cassie in defiance.

"Very well. I think I know the answer." Cassie turned and stormed out of the cookhouse in search of a sawyer who was about to get the tongue-lashing of his life.

Zach had not been himself for weeks. He drank alone until the wee hours of the morning, then got up late each day, his temper foul. Alec had said it must have something to do with Elly. He'd been right. By the time she found him, Zach was working beside Alec, a trail of freshly cut tobacco behind them.

"Zachariah Bowers!" She quickened her stride.

Both Zach and Alec looked up. Cassie suppressed the thrill she felt at seeing Alec again. He stood covered in sweat, his brown skin glistening in the midmorning sun. She could read in his eyes that he was happy to see her, too.

But that was not why she was here.

"When a woman calls your name like that, ye know ye've got trouble," Zach muttered to Alec, who nodded gravely in agreement.

"If it's about the drinkin', Miss Cassie—"

"In a way it is." She fixed him with her harshest gaze. "You may want to give up the whiskey now you're about to become a father."

"A what?" Zach gaped at her. "A father?"

"It is your babe Elly carries in her belly, is it not?" She watched his eyes fill with comprehension.

"Oh, no, Elly. Good Lord!" He dropped to his knees as if struck by a fist.

Whatever reaction Cassie had expected, this was not it.

"Nay, Mistress," he said after a moment, his voice ragged. "The babe is not mine."

She stared at him, bewildered. "Are you sure?"

"Aye. If I'd managed to woo Elly into my bed, I'd remember." He laughed bitterly, steadied himself, and rose to his feet, his eyes clouded with despair.

"I'm sorry. I-I thought … " Cassie stammered, suddenly understanding his recent bad temper and constant drinking. Elly had been ignoring him, had been with someone else. How could Cassie have borne such bad news so tactlessly?

But Zach had already turned back to his work, slashing at the tobacco with the wooden movements of one in a trance.

Cassie shared one last concerned glance with Alec before turning back.

If Zach was not the father, who was?

*A*lec watched Cassie walk back toward the cookhouse, admiring the soft sway of her hips beneath her blue work dress. So Elly was pregnant. He wasn't surprised. But Zach certainly had been. Zach slashed at the tobacco as if it were an enemy. Alec knew there was nothing he could say. In fact, opening his mouth just now might earn him a black eye and a few loose teeth.

A few months ago, he'd have thought Zach a fool for loving a woman who seemed to care nothing for him. But now? All things considered, Alec thought Zach had reacted to the news with a good deal of restraint. How would Alec have behaved had Cassie been with someone else? What if she had lifted her skirts for him, then turned away? Or ignored him completely and gone into the arms of another man? What if she were now carrying another man's child? It was something he didn't even want to imagine.

Allowing himself to get caught up in the rhythm of his work, Alec didn't realize how much time had passed or how thirsty he'd become until Zach tapped him on the shoulder some time later and handed him a jug of cool cider. He stood, stretched his back, and took several deep swallows.

The crack of musketfire split the air.

The jug in Alec's hands shattered.

Chapter Twenty-three

*I*nstinctively, Alec dropped to the ground, pulling Zach with him. "Over there."

He pointed to the edge of the forest, where the shot had come from.

Around them, men's voices called out in alarm.

"Did I hear what I think I heard?" Micah, bent at the waist, made his way down the row.

Alec nodded, looking down the tobacco row at the men crouching for cover. "Is everyone all right?"

They nodded.

"I'm going to have a look." Alec began to rise.

"Are ye daft?" Zach wiped the beads of sweat from his forehead. "Someone just took a shot at ye."

"That's why I'm going to check it out." He stood, his gaze fixed on the dark line of trees ahead.

"I'm coming with ye."

Crouching, Alec and Zach moved swiftly across the field to the forest, followed by Micah and the rest of the men. The ground was covered with a dense blanket of pine needles. There were no footprints Alec could see, but the sharp odor of gunpowder lingered in the air.

"Over there!" It was Henry. He stood at the far end of the search party, pointing off through the trees. "Lads, a fair few, dressed for the hunt. They ran like rabbits when they saw us."

Alec looked in the direction Henry was pointing but saw nothing.

"They'll nae be back." Henry seemed nervous. His face was red from exertion. His brow dripped with sweat. "Just a huntin' accident. Good no one was hurt."

"Back to work," Micah called. The worry on his face told Alec he was far from convinced this was simply an accident, but the tobacco crop called. "We got a mountain of tobacco to cut before sunset."

Alec watched Henry walk back toward the fields. Together with the falling tree and the copperhead in his cabin—he'd found it lurking beneath his blankets and had dragged it outdoors by its tail, the blanket still over its head—this was someone's third attempt to kill him. Whoever was behind this wanted it to look like an accident, but the assassin was getting desperate. Shooting him in broad daylight was bound to raise suspicions.

Alec called, retrieving his tobacco knife from the dirt. "Micah, Zach, I don't want Miss Cassie to hear about this. She has enough to worry about."

Micah nodded and moved off down the row.

Zach eyed him suspiciously. "Don't tell me this isn't the first time somethin' like this—"

"Fine." Alec adjusted his grip on the knife. "I won't tell you."

"You know what this means?" Zach grinned.

"What?"

"I need to watch out for yer scarred hide."

The two men went back to work, one keeping an eye on the forest, the other on a certain Scot.

Women and older children had now come out into the field and were gathering cut tobacco from the ground and hanging the leaves from tobacco sticks along the fence so that they would wilt. There the leaves would remain for three days before being hung in the drying sheds. When Alec had asked why the tobacco was not hung immediately in the sheds, saving time and effort, Cassie had smiled at him as she might a child and told him that allowing the plants to wilt first made it possible for them to pack more into each shed. And then she'd reminded him ever so sweetly that, after the tobacco was harvested, there would still be corn, wheat, and barley to bring in, not to mention apples.

Alec turned his mind back to his work, once again stunned by the depth of his feeling for her. He, the man who had once dismissed notions of love and marriage as one might reject children's fantasies of Father Christmas, was now willing—nay, eager—to go to the altar. No doubt Matthew, who had always predicted this day would come, would find his transformation most amusing.

But something was wrong. Whenever he spoke of marriage or returning to London, Cassie became distant and refused to speak of the future. Perhaps she doubted his sincerity. She had all but admitted believing he would leave her bed without looking back when the time came.

"Believe in me, Cassie," he'd told her this morning. "That's all I ask. I said I would never forsake you, and I meant it."

She had looked away, unable to meet his gaze.

That she could still suspect him hurt more than he was willing to admit. Perhaps she still doubted his identity. Or perhaps she didn't want to marry him at all. She'd expressed her disdain for marriage and the role of a wife more than once. Alec had never considered the possibility that she might refuse to marry him, and he didn't like the way it made him feel.

*C*assie hung the heavy tobacco stick from the fence with a sigh. Sunset danced orange and red around her. Her shoulders and arms ached, and her hands and gown were stained with tobacco juice. She needed a warm bath and a hot meal.

They'd gotten farther today than she'd expected, harvesting a little more than half of the field. God willing, they'd be finished by this time tomorrow. It looked as if it would be their largest harvest ever, but Cassie knew better than to get ahead of herself. There was still so much that could go wrong. Too much rain could make the leaves rot in the sheds. Too little, and they would become brittle and crumble when they were packed. Hogsheads could burst. Warehouses could burn to the ground. Ships could sink. At best, tobacco farming was a risky wager. Perhaps that was why so many gamblers seemed to be drawn to these wild shores.

She wandered back toward the house, the sound of fiddle music drifting her way from the cabins. The smell of roasting meat made her mouth water. She had ordered several hogs slaughtered for tonight's feast. It had been her father's custom to celebrate each night of the tobacco harvest with food, dance, and strong cider, and she had continued that tradition. Everyone had worked hard today. Her people deserved something special.

She reached the cookhouse to find Nan pouring one last kettle of steaming water into the washtub. A fresh gown and chemise had been laid out on the table. The candles had been lit, and the curtains drawn. Cassie thought she had never seen a more welcoming sight.

"Oh, bless you, Nan."

After so many years, Nan seemed able to anticipate her every need.

"Don't thank me. Thank Nettie. She's the one who carried this dratted tub inside."

Cassie looked about, but Nettie had evidently gone to join the celebration.

"She's lookin' for Elly," said the cook, as if reading her mind. "What she can possibly want with that one, I couldn't say, but then, 'tis none of my affair."

Cassie fought back a smile. Nan hated being left out of any secret, especially one with a potential for good gossip. But she was right to wonder. What would Nettie want with Elly? She barely tolerated the girl.

"Enjoy yer bath, lamb, then come have a bite to eat. Ye must be famished." Nan took down her knitted shawl from its peg and closed the door behind her.

Cassie stepped out of her dirty clothes, leaving them in a heap on the floor, and sank into the hot water. It felt so good to be off her feet. She closed her eyes, stretched out, and wiggled her toes, letting the warm water soak the aches from her muscles.

"Are you enjoying your bath, my love?"

She gasped and sat bolt upright, covering her breasts with her arms. Water sloshed onto the floor. "Alec!"

He closed the door behind himself and slid a chair beneath its handle, blocking it.

"What are you doing here? You nearly frightened me to death!" She couldn't help smiling.

"Pardon me." He didn't sound the least bit sorry, his lips spreading in a sensuous grin. He pulled the sweat-stained linen of his shirt over his head and discarded it on the floor. Then he untied his breeches and pulled them down his muscled thighs until he stood naked before her.

"What are you—"

"I'm here to help you with your bath." His voice sounded sincere— and full of mischief. He crossed the room then slid into the tub behind her, stretched his legs out on either side of hers, and pulled her back to rest against the broad expanse of his chest.

"Help?" She was shocked at his boldness, her pulse racing. "What if Nan—"

"Then you shall tell her to go to hell."

She felt him pull the pins from her hair. Its weight fell softly over her right shoulder, across her breasts, and into the water. He gently worked the snarls free, then dipped the bucket in the tub and slowly poured warm water over her hair.

She shivered with delight and relaxed into his touch. He massaged lavender-oil soap through the length of her tresses and into her scalp, his fingers lingering on the sensitive skin at her temples, behind her ears, and at her nape. Her skin tingled.

"Do you like this?"

"Mmmm."

His strong hands dropped to her shoulders and neck and rubbed away the day's tension. When at long last he poured water over her hair again, rinsing the lather away, her eyes were closed and she felt as tranquil as a babe in its mother's arms.

"Are you falling asleep?" His voice was deep and tinged with desire.

Cassie giggled, well aware that putting her to sleep was not his intention. Then she gasped as he began to rub the slippery soap over her breasts. His hands kneaded their fullness, drawing her nipples to taut, aching points. She pressed her breasts deeper into his palms, awed by the delicious sensation of skin sliding silkily over soapy skin.

Then his hands were gone, replaced by the rougher texture of the sponge. She moaned and clutched the sides of the tub as warm water flowed from the sponge over her breasts, rinsing the soap away.

Heaven though it might be, this was out of her control. She wondered what he would do next, uncertainty and anticipation heightening her excitement. But she didn't have to wait long. He began to stroke her belly, his hands moving gradually lower and lower until she was fairly lifting her hips out of the water in expectation of what was to come.

"Shall I wash your woman's petals?"

She giggled at the silliness of the words he'd chosen, but wanted it all the same. "Aye! Touch me."

He lifted her thighs and parted them so that her feet came to rest on either side of his knees. Then his fingers crept down through the curls on her mound and parted her lips, allowing hot water to touch her most delicate flesh. Cassie gasped at the heat and felt delicious warmth spread through her belly. He did not use soap, but slid his fingers between her lips, gently stretching and caressing them until she whimpered in delight.

"You're so swollen, love." His fingers settled on her engorged bud. He stroked her, teased her, until her body trembled with urgency. But just as she neared her peak, he stopped and caressed her inner thighs instead.

She moaned in frustration, her body taut, her sex throbbing with need. He controlled her now like a puppet on strings.

"Up with you, my sweet." He guided her up onto her knees. "We mustn't forget your delightful *derrière*."

For a moment she was puzzled. She didn't speak French. But when he turned her so that she rested on her hands and knees before him, his face directly behind her, her breath caught in her throat. In this position she was so open to him, to his perusal, his touch. Nothing lay hidden.

She felt him pour warm water over her taut skin, felt his hands begin to smooth soap over her bottom and rinse it away, coming nearer and nearer to her woman's cleft. When his fingers finally found her, slipping deep within her, she cried out and rocked back against his touch, spreading her thighs to welcome him.

He kissed and nipped the flesh of her buttocks, his tongue hot as his fingers opened her, stroked her.

Again she neared her peak.

Again he stopped.

"Is there ought else I can do to please you?" He caressed her swollen sex softly, teasingly.

Cassie moaned in desperation. There was something she wanted, but it was something she couldn't name, let alone ask for. He'd started to do it on that first night, but she had stopped him, too shocked to let him continue. It was positively indecent, this act she was imagining. But now…

Oh, God, if only …

She willed herself to say it. "Make love to me with your mouth!"

She heard him groan with satisfaction. "Mmm, yes. But not like this." He stood and helped her to her feet, then scooped her up into his arms and stepped out of the tub.

She trembled with anticipation as she realized what he meant to do. In two strides he'd reached the table and, pushing the butter and honey crocks to the far end, laid her upon the linen tablecloth so that her bottom was even with the table's edge.

"You are so beautiful, love." The intensity of his gaze made Cassie's heart skip a beat. He stood between her thighs, dripping wet and so virile, his shaft hard and erect. Then he draped her legs over his shoulders and sank to his knees.

Cassie closed her eyes, barely able to breathe. She felt him part her outer lips, felt his breath upon her.

"I've waited so long to taste you." Then his lips were on her, kissing her sex deeply.

Cassie began to quiver, shaken by sensations almost too good to bear as he laved her, licked her, pleasured her with his mouth. Just as he had suckled her nipples, he suckled her sensitive bud, drawing on it gently with his lips, flicking it lightly with his tongue. Her fingers clutched his hair, and she heard herself cry out again and again, heard herself call his name. "Oh, Alec! Alec!"

His tongue grew bolder, its caresses firmer, faster. And then he thrust it inside her.

She came. Tremors of ecstasy shot from somewhere deep inside her through every inch of her flesh, making her cry out, until, weak with pleasure, she lay panting.

"How is your bath so far?" He leaned over her and captured her lips with his, probing her mouth with the same tongue that had just given her such ecstasy.

"Mmmm." She could smell and taste herself on his lips—a musky, wild flavor—and her hunger began to build anew. She grew bolder. "I want to taste *you* now."

"Oh, Cassie." The look in his eyes was one of erotic longing. With his arms to steady her, she sat up on the table, then stepped down to stand before him. Candlelight danced over the taut ridges and valleys of his muscles, and she took in the beauty of his body. Impatient to pleasure him, her fingers played with the mat of curls on his chest, then followed the dark line down his belly to the curls below until she gripped his shaft. His muscles tensed and she grew bolder, kneeling before him.

Alec felt her lips brush against him as her tongue began its tentative exploration and feared he would come apart. Brushing wet curls from her face, he entwined his fingers in her hair as she took his cock into her mouth and slowly began to devour him.

He'd thought himself about to go insane when she'd asked him to kiss her, finally allowing him to bury his face in her sweetness. But this … Trying to be gentle, he began to rock his hips to match her rhythm, meeting her hungry kiss, giving her all of him she could take. Her tongue danced circles around the head of his cock. Her lips gripped him, stroked him. He thought of shooting his seed into her sweet mouth, felt his testicles tighten.

"Stop!" He battled desperately for control. This was not what he had planned.

Cassie stood, her green eyes dark with passion. He pulled her to him, feeling the softness of her breasts against his chest. His lips closed fiercely over hers. Their tongues met, sparred, twined.

"I want to come inside you," he whispered hungrily against her throat.

"Aye."

He turned her, bent her over the table before him, spread her thighs, and plunged into her warm, wet sheath, possessing her completely. He reached around with one hand to stroke her and increase her pleasure, while the other caressed the rosy skin of her rounded backside. The scent of her filled his nostrils as he carried her with him toward another climax. Their cries mingled as his thrusts brought them both sweet release.

"I think," she said a while later as she sat snugly in his arms before the embers of the dying cookfire. "I shall have to bathe much, much more often."

"*I* took fifty pounds off that bastard Landon Carter last night in billiards," said Geoffrey, pulling up his breeches and straightening his embroidered vest. "Poor fool. He hasn't got a ruthless bone in his body, yet he fancies himself skilled at wagering."

Elly pulled her skirts down over her thighs, grateful that it was over. Truth was, she didn't enjoy it at all. She only hoped they'd done nothing to hurt the babe. She hadn't told him yet. She wanted to wait for the right moment. She hoped he'd be as happy as she was.

"Pardon?" she asked, realizing that Geoffrey had asked her a question.

"All caught up in your thoughts, are you?" He took an apple from the basket he'd brought with him and sat down in the grass beside her. "What kind of thoughts fit into that pretty little head of yours?"

Elly loved it when he said she was pretty. Should she tell him now?

He didn't give her time. "I asked you whether your mistress is still questioning your absences."

"Nay," she lied, not wanting to endure another lecture about not making Miss Cassie suspicious. She paused. "I've something I want to tell you."

"And what's that, love?" He took another bite of apple.

"I'm going to have your baby." She held her breath.

Geoffrey laughed. "I suppose it was bound to happen sooner or later. Another Crichton bastard."

Bastard? But her baby wouldn't be a bastard. He was going to marry her. He'd said so. "You said you wanted children."

"Yes, but I'm afraid this one won't count. I won't be able to claim it. My father would never allow it."

Elly's pulse began to race. "But you said—"

"Said what?" His eyes were cold.

She could scarcely breathe. "You swore you'd marry me."

"Have you a witness to this oath of mine?" He took several bites of apple and threw the core over his shoulder.

A witness? They'd always met in secret. How could there be a witness? "Geoffrey, you can't mean this. You can't do this to me!"

"I'm afraid, my dear, I already have." He stood and ran a hand gently along her cheek. "Pity. You are a sweet little thing."

"Geoffrey!"

"We can still meet if you'd like. It won't bother me when your belly gets round. But, say, I've somewhere else I've got to be just now. I've no more time today." He strode to his horse, mounted, then turned its head toward the road.

"What am I to do?"

"Get rid of it if you like. But be careful. I've heard that can be dangerous." He urged his horse to a canter and disappeared into the forest.

For a moment Elly was too stunned to feel anything. Then the terrible weight of what had happened crashed in upon her. She fell to her knees, tears coming in great, wrenching sobs, her heart in pieces.

She should have known. She should have known. She'd believed him. She'd trusted him. How could she have been so stupid?

She had no idea how long she cried. It had begun to grow dark.

In the distance someone was calling her name.

Nettie.

Elly would have hidden, but Nettie had already seen her and was walking quickly toward her. Elly waited for Nettie to start yelling at her for running off.

But Nettie said nothing. She stood, arms crossed, looking down at Elly, her expression unreadable. "You got no time for cryin' now, girl. You got a child to think about. Get up on your feet."

Then Nettie held out her hand.

*G*eoffrey left the road and guided his horse to the prearranged meeting place, dismounted, and waited. It would be growing dark soon. He had no desire to find himself in the forest after sunset. A thrashing in the bushes announced Henry's arrival.

"You're late."

"It's nae easy tae get away."

"So?"

"I missed by inches."

"Good Lord, man! How hard can it be to kill one man?" Geoffrey stomped his foot on the ground.

"I had tae run for me life. I almost got caught."

"I asked you to do a simple job for me, Henry. I gave you good reason to do it—freedom. You do remember our arrangement?"

"Aye, sir, but it's nae easy tae get 'im alone these days, him beddin' the mistress and all."

Geoffrey froze. He couldn't have heard Henry correctly. "What did you say?"

"He's gone tae her bed most every night. I've seen 'im sneakin' away from her room afore dawn. They think no one knows, but I've been watchin', like ye told me."

Bile rose in Geoffrey's throat. "Are you certain?"

"Aye, sir. Seen it wi' me own eyes."

"Good work." He slapped Henry on the back hard, wishing he could crack the man's skull. "This changes everything."

"It does?" Henry turned and looked at him, his gaze darting nervously about.

"Aye. You've done well, Henry." Geoffrey turned abruptly, grabbed the man's throat with both hands, and squeezed. "Tell no one what you saw, do you understand me?"

Henry sputtered and choked, grabbed Geoffrey's wrists with his hands, his eyes bulging. He nodded frantically.

Geoffrey squeezed harder, his fingers digging into the ruddy flesh of Henry's neck. "If you speak of it to anyone—anyone!—I will have you flayed to death. You'll live only long enough to grow tired of listening to your own pathetic screams!"

He released Henry with a shove.

The man fell to his knees, hands around his throat, coughing.

Geoffrey paced the clearing, his mind racing. *Damn Braden to hell! And damn Catherine!*

"There's more, sir." Henry stumbled timidly to his feet, rubbing his throat. "I've seen her father."

Geoffrey stopped. "Go on."

"He's on an island, hidden in the marsh. It's nae easy tae find. The man's daft, don't know 'is own daughter."

Geoffrey smiled. "Not in England after all, as I suspected. Listen carefully. Here's what you're going to do."

*T*apping his foot in time to the music, Alec took a small swig of whiskey and passed the jug to Luke, who drank deeply. The big slave's eyes were fixed on Nettie, who was dancing with abandon near the bonfire, her body swaying seductively. It was no secret that the two had become lovers, though Luke still refused to take Nettie to wife. There'd been more than one late-night argument attesting to their difference of opinion on that subject. But seeing the hunger in Luke's eyes, Alec had no doubt Nettie would prevail. The big man stood no chance against those long brown legs and soft brown eyes. Why he suddenly found that so damned amusing, Alec didn't know. Perhaps love had addled his brain.

He spied Cassie in the distance, bouncing baby Catherine in her arms, light from Rebecca's cookfire casting shadows upon her face. It was hell having to stay away from her like this. He'd watched all evening as she had moved from family to family, fire to fire, chatting amiably with slave and servant alike, tasting their food. Her eyes sought him out from time to time, her gaze lingering for a moment before gliding over him with feigned indifference. She was working her way in his direction. It was a game they'd become adept at playing these past weeks.

"Come dance with us, Miss Cassie!" called one of the slave women as Cassie moved toward them.

"Oh, no, I'm sure I couldn't." She shook her head and pulled her shawl tighter around her shoulders.

"Why not? Have you forgotten how, Missy?" teased Nettie. "Or would it not be proper?"

Alec had to fight not to laugh, knowing very well Nettie's taunt would goad Cassie into joining her. Cassie had told him how the two of them had been best friends as children. Despite the gulf that separated them now, he thought he could see a glimpse of that affection still.

"Well, I-I ... " stammered Cassie before dropping her shawl on the ground and kicking off her shoes. "Very well."

Though it took her a moment to catch the beat, soon she was dancing about with them, her head tossed back in carefree laughter, her eyes bright with excitement. It wasn't long before she and Nettie were imitating each other, daring one another with their steps, their hips undulating in a natural rhythm that needed no explanation. Alec felt a tightening in his groin and cursed. He yanked the whiskey jug back from Luke and took a deep swallow, his amusement at Luke's frustration coming back to haunt him. How long did this damn celebration have to last anyway?

He wanted to go to bed now. Cassie's bed, to be precise.

"Missy!" Nan ran toward them as fast as her plump legs could carry her, her face pinched with urgency.

But Cassie was too caught up in the dance to hear her.

"Missy!" Nan motioned frantically.

Cassie waved a greeting to the cook, then, seeing the look on her face, stopped dancing and hurried to her side.

Something had happened.

Alec stood, every nerve in his body alert.

Cassie whirled around, shouted something to him, her face lined with emotion.

The only word he was able to make out was *London.*

Chapter Twenty-four

*T*he letter lay on the kitchen table, its red wax seal glistening in the candlelight, but Cassie could not make herself open it. Nor could she shake the sadness that had gripped her the moment Nan's words had reached her ears. She'd known for weeks that this moment would come, and she'd tried to ready herself. Still, she was not prepared. This letter would restore Alec's name and, with it, his freedom. What would happen after tonight, only God knew.

"You read it first." She tried to sound cheerful and stepped back from the table.

There was no mistaking the excitement glittering in his blue eyes or the joy in the smile on his handsome face. He'd been awaiting this reply for so long. She could not begrudge him his happiness. Instead of grabbing the letter and tearing it open as she had expected he would, he pulled her close and took her chin in his fingertips.

"I'll not abandon you." His blue eyes held such tenderness that she could not keep tears from spilling onto her cheeks.

"Read the letter." She forced a smile.

"I've waited almost four months. Another moment will do no harm." He brought his lips to hers and kissed her gently, slowly, his thumbs caressing the wetness from her cheeks.

She pressed her hands into the hardness of his chest, fighting the urge to wrap her arms around him and cling to him with every last ounce of her strength.

All too soon, his lips released hers, and the moment was gone. She pulled her knitted shawl tightly around her shoulders and watched as he opened the letter and began to read. Candlelight danced silently over the copper kettles and spoons that hung on the cookhouse walls, its homey warmth a sharp contrast to the empty chill that had taken hold of her heart. The bathtub, its water now cold, sat on the floor, a bittersweet reminder of what they'd shared in this same kitchen only a few hours ago.

"Christ!"

Cassie gasped as Alec's fist hit the table with a deafening crash that made the butter crock jump.

"What is it?"

"Bloody hell!" His face was angrier than she'd ever seen it. "It was Philip. Dear God. He's the one."

"Alec?"

"Read," he said in a choked voice, handing her the letter and turning his back to her, his body rigid.

Hardly able to breathe, she forced her eyes to the page.

Sir:

I was distressed to read that you have living among you a convict who claims to be Alec Kenleigh, my esteemed elder brother. I must inform you that my dear brother has been dead these past months, having been murdered by thieves in March of this year while on his way home late at night. I had the most unfortunate duty of identifying his body and am therefore able to assure you that whatever despicable creature you have had the misfortune to take in is not my brother, but the most contemptible of liars.

Having contacted the magistrate at Newgate Prison myself after the arrival of his disturbing missive, I learned that Nicholas Braden is a man of formidable talents when it comes to treachery and deceit. It is said that he earned his berth to the colony by seducing a fortune out from under the daughter of one of our sovereign's peers. The magistrate assures us that Mr. Braden was in chains on the night my brother was so cruelly dispatched. My advice to you, Sir, is to treat this accursed criminal with the utmost caution. Know that his ruse has brought fresh grief to my family. Had we the power, we would see him hanged for this latest affront.

Signed by my hand on this, the twenty-third day of June in the third year of our sovereign, King George II.

Philip Kenleigh

Cassie read through the letter twice, the words swimming before her eyes, blood rushing to her head, her heart pounding like thunder in her ears. "No! This can't be possible!"

The letter slipped from her fingers and fell unheeded to the floor.

Alec was there, saying something, reaching for her.

"Don't touch me!" she heard herself cry, twisting to get away from his grasp.

"Cassie, calm yourself."

"Calm myself?" Her legs were trembling. She could hardly stand. "Calm myself when ... when everything you've ever said to me is a lie?"

"Surely you don't believe—"

"What am I supposed to believe? According to this letter, you cannot possibly be who you say you are."

"Cassie, listen to me—"

"Listen to you? I've listened to you. I've believed you. My God, I've lain with you!"

Suddenly red bricks were rushing up at her.

She felt strong arms catch her and lower her until she sat on the floor, her skirts in a heap around her.

"It is obvious what has happened." Alec's voice was soothing, his hands stroking her hair. "When Nicholas Braden died, his body was left in place of mine. And my brother Philip, behind it all the time, told authorities it was me to have me declared dead."

Nicholas Braden's body left in place of Alec's? Alec's family fooled? His brother to blame? Cassie struggled to make sense of his words. *Yes,* her heart cried, *that must be it!* There had to be an explanation. How else could she explain her feelings for this man? Because if what this letter said was the truth ...

"Leave me." She struggled to push him away, her voice barely audible even to her own ears.

For one moment, she saw in his eyes a desperation to match her own. Then it was gone, hidden behind unforgiving stone.

"Very well. Miss Blakewell." He released her and stood.

Without another word, he was gone.

C assie blew out the candle and fell back onto her pillows, exhausted, listening to the choir of crickets that chirped outside her window. These past seven days had gone by in a fog. She'd buried herself in her chores, working until the light failed, tending those sick with the ague until dawn. She'd hung tobacco in the sheds, harvested the kitchen garden, and gathered herbs for drying. She'd scrubbed every brick in the kitchen and every floorboard in the great house, even hauling the carpets outdoors for beating. Still she could not escape, crying herself to sleep despite her fatigue, only to be consumed by fitful dreams.

Like a sickness in the belly, remorse and fear ate at her day and night.

She knew she had reacted foolishly that night. As soon as she'd regained her senses and thought the situation through, she'd realized what Alec had known right away: It was Nicholas Braden's body that had been found on the street that night and lay rotting in the grave in London. It had to be. Though Cassie would be the first to admit that there was absolutely no evidence to support this supposition, she could not believe otherwise. It was impossible that everything Alec had said and done during these past months had simply been a lie, part of some elaborate plot. His kindness to Jamie and the other children. His hard work and helpfulness. His kisses and gentleness as he made love to her.

No man, no matter how artful, could feign the kind of goodness she had seen in him day after day.

Besides, what could he stand to gain? There was no wealth for him to steal. That much he had seen for himself when he'd reviewed her father's ledgers. Her dowry, modest by Northern Neck standards, would be valuable only in the hands of a planter, which Nicholas Braden certainly was not. Nor could he possibly gain his freedom by seducing her, as neither she nor her father had the power to relieve him of a convict's indenture. And though a lesser man might have used intimacy with her as a means to gain privilege and thereby escape the rigorous toil intended for a convict, he had never shied away from hard labor, often doing the work of two able-bodied men.

He was telling the truth. Of this her heart was certain. She would have asked his forgiveness days ago, but she knew something else, as well.

He was leaving, and she must let him go.

From a distance, she'd watched as he'd taken Aldebaran riding early each morning, staying away a bit longer each day, building the stallion's endurance. Today he'd been gone for nearly four hours. It would not be long now. One morning he would ride out and not return. Flying like the wind on Aldebaran's back, he would ride to the nearest port town and sign on to the first ship leaving for England.

It was within her rights—nay, it was her legal obligation—to place him under guard again, even to shackle him, but she could not. To see him chained like an animal was more than she could bear. Besides, if he did not escape and return to England to prove to his family he was still alive, he'd be forced to endure fourteen long years of servitude. God save her, she loved him and would not see him reduced to that.

To the rest of Virginia society he was now Nicholas Braden for good. The day after the reply had arrived from London, the sheriff had sent a missive to her father, demanding to know what the letter had revealed, eager to put the matter behind him before he and Master Crichton left for Williamsburg for the season. Cassie had taken her time in answering. At first she'd considered lying, but any ruse would eventually be discovered, and she would likely find herself in gaol. Instead she'd written a vague reply, telling the sheriff only that the Kenleigh family believed Alec to be dead. The sheriff had written back the same day to say he considered the matter closed.

Let Alec take the stallion. Let him ride. Fast. If he were caught, he would be hanged.

Cassie put a hand to her belly to still the butterflies. Surely he would make it to port safely. Aldebaran was the fastest horse in the county, if not the colony. And if she was slow to report his escape, giving him most of a day's head start, she could seem to do what the law required of her, while protecting him from capture. Unless...

There were so many things that could go wrong. The stallion could go lame or lose a shoe. Or throw Alec and injure him. Someone might recognize them and give Alec away. What if he failed to find work on a ship before news of his escape reached town?

Though he did not bear a brand, he could never be mistaken for a common seaman. His bearing and gentle features bespoke his social standing as clearly as if it were emblazoned upon his forehead. Would a captain hire him? Would others sense at once that something was amiss? What if he got lost and never made it to port? Though he knew his way around Blakewell's Neck and its forests, he was new in the colony. Did he even know which direction to travel?

Cassie sat upright with a start. She grabbed her robe, sprang from her bed, flung open her bedroom door, and hurried down the darkened hallway toward her father's study. It had to be here somewhere. With only the half moon to light her way, she felt her way along the ledgers on her father's desk, removing one volume after another, searching.

Where was it?

The thud of a book as it hit the floor made her jump. She wanted desperately to avoid waking Nettie—or worse, Pirate, who would surely rouse everyone. It would be for the best if no one knew what she was about to do.

She was about to despair when at last she felt it—thin, unbound, made of rough parchment. Hastily pulling the document out from between two ledgers, she ran quietly to the window just to make sure, unfolding it as she went. Moonlight revealed faint lines drawn long ago in black, red, and blue ink—the curving banks of the Rappahannock, the Piankatank, the York, and the James, and between them jutting arms of land marked with borders designating each planter's estate.

Heading toward the hallway, she hesitated, then turned back and walked over to the bookshelf, careful to avoid creaky floorboards. Standing on her toes, she pulled an old box down from the top shelf, wiped the thick layer of dust from its lid, and turned back toward the door.

Heart racing, she tiptoed down the stairs and noiselessly opened the back door. Looking cautiously about and seeing no one, she stepped into the moonlight and hurried toward the stables. She'd hide the map and the box there for Alec to find first thing in the morning. He'd know what to do with them.

The cobblestones were cold and rough against her feet, and the cool breeze raised goose bumps on her skin. She'd just reached down to open the stable doors when they seemed to open of their own accord and a hand closed over her mouth, silencing her scream. Strong arms pulled her inside and closed the door behind her. She was engulfed in utter darkness.

"What in the name of God are you doing out here?" Alec released her.

"You nearly frightened me out of my wits!" Her pulse still raced.

"You haven't answered my question."

"This is my home, in case you've forgotten. I'm the one who should be asking questions."

"Very well, *Mistress*." There was a chill in his voice.

She heard him take a step, then watched his face emerge from the darkness, illuminated by the orange glow of a candle he'd retrieved from its hiding place beneath an overturned bucket.

His eyes were hard, impenetrable.

"Alec, I ... " *I love you. Please forgive me.* "I brought these. You have greater need of them than I." She held out the map and the box she'd planned to hide in Aldebaran's stall.

Taking them from her with a pensive frown, he opened the box first. The expression of astonishment that came to his face when candlelight revealed the two flintlock pistols within drew a smile to Cassie's face. Oh, how she had missed him this week.

"They are ... *were* my father's."

Placing the box on a nearby bench, he hurriedly opened the map, his eyes examining it quickly before coming to rest gravely on her. "Cassie," he said after a moment, "I cannot take these. If I'm captured—"

"If you're captured, I shall say that you stole them." She spoke with a calm she did not feel.

"I hate to think what my escape might cost you as it is. If you were to be implicated in any way—"

"Please, Alec. Take them." Her words came out a whispered plea.

For a moment he said nothing. Then he gave her a lopsided grin, his gaze soft. "Since they shall see me hanged either way, I don't suppose it would hurt to add theft to my list of crimes."

A wave of pure dread washed through her. "It is nothing to jest about."

Then she knew. His being here tonight meant he was leaving in the morning.

"Tomorrow?" She didn't bother to hide the tears that welled up in her eyes.

"Aye."

"Is there aught else you need? Bread and cheese? A hunting knife, perhaps—"

"And what would the good folk of Blakewell's Neck think to see me riding out laden with provisions? That I was going for a picnic? Nay, love." He shook his head. "You should go now. If anyone were to find you here ... "

Cassie nodded, wanting desperately to reach out and hold him, the ache in her heart overwhelming. "Alec, be safe. I'll not have a moment's peace until I know you are at home and well."

"I'll send word as soon as I reach London."

The tears came in earnest now, pouring down her cheeks, her shoulders shaking as she fought to suppress the sobs that welled up within her. She felt his arms enfold her, pull her close, felt his breath hot on her temple as he whispered reassurances. Burying her face in the linen of his shirt, she clung to him as if to save herself from drowning.

"Shhh, Cassie, love." He wiped the tears from her face. Whether he meant the kiss to comfort her or to bid her farewell, she did not know. Nor did she care. With a whimper she melted against him, eager to banish her grief, if only for a moment.

Their lips touched lightly as Alec held her against him, nibbling her mouth with his own and tenderly kissing her face. Cassie twisted her fingers through his hair, drinking in the taste and feel of him.

"Alec!" She was aware only of his touch as he reached beneath her gown, lifting her breasts and molding them with his work-roughened palms, gently caressing her taut nipples, making her moan, sending a cascade of heat deep into her belly.

Then he lifted her off the ground, carried her to an empty stall, and laid her in the straw beneath him. With trembling hands Cassie opened his breeches and, taking the heaviness of his erection into her hands, guided him into her.

"Love me, Alec." She lifted her hips to meet him, unable to stifle a sigh as he buried himself inside her with one slow thrust, filling her completely. Oh, how she had missed him. How she had needed him.

But he was here now, inside her, stroking her, making her ache for completion. She arched against him, ran her hands over the bunching muscles of his back and buttocks as he moved slowly inside her. He knew just how to move, just how to touch her to drive her mad. Then all at once it was upon her, sweet pleasure spiraling through her body.

He captured her cries with his mouth, but he did not seek his own peak. Not yet. Twice more he brought her pleasure, slowly, tenderly, showing her with each kiss and each caress that she was his. Then, when she knew she could bear no more, he poured himself into her, his body shuddering with release.

*A*lec gave the cinch one final yank, keeping a tight hold on the restless stallion's bridle.

He was worse than a bastard. God forgive him. He'd sworn to himself after Philip's letter arrived that he'd not come inside Cassie again. The chance was too great that he would get her with child. Yet his promise to himself had quickly dissolved into nothing. Before the letter had arrived, he'd reassured himself that their love was safe because his name would be restored long before any pregnancy would show. As matters now stood, at least three months would pass before he could return and take her to wife—if he survived to return at all. He'd known this, yet he'd made love to her anyway—not once, but twice, carrying her from the straw to the warmth of her own bed, where he'd all but lost himself in her, finding it almost impossible to walk away.

He'd left her only after he'd thought her asleep, placing one last kiss on her hair.

"Ride north. To Maryland," she'd whispered. Her voice had been thick with tears.

Aldebaran snorted and stamped his hooves in the straw. The stallion sensed something was afoot.

"You're about to be stolen, old boy."

The stallion jerked his head as if to nod his hearty consent.

"I'm glad you approve."

Tucking the map Cassie had given him into the sleeve of his shirt and secreting the pistols in the folds of the saddle blanket, he led Aldebaran out into the morning air and mounted. The day had dawned clear and cool, sunrise turning the eastern sky a bright pink. Already a few cookfires had been lit, the scent of smoke drifting on the breeze as the women began their morning chores.

He looked past the stables to the row of slave and servant cabins, and beyond that to the harvested fields. In the distance the forest made a ragged, black outline against the sky. Somewhere a babe began to cry, eager for its mother's breast.

Something twisted in his gut. Why should he hesitate to leave this place? It had been his prison for the past five months. England—not Virginia—was his home. Back home his family was mourning him as dead. He could only imagine the grief his sister was suffering.

Philip had planned this and planned it well. But why have him transported to the colony when killing him would have been much easier? Perhaps Philip had felt some guilt, had not wanted to stoop to outright murder. As soon as he was in London, Alec would give Philip the most unpleasant surprise of his life. But before he could do that, he had to make it home.

Urging the horse to a trot, he set his eyes firmly on the forest to the east of the estate. *Ride north,* she'd said. The horse's hooves clicked over the cobblestones of the courtyard. Smoke curled from the cookhouse chimney. Nan was already hard at work.

"Thank God ye're awake!" The voice came, not from the kitchen, but the porch of the great house.

"Miss Cassie told me not to trouble ye." The cook wrung her hands in her apron, her face pinched. "But I know she'd want ye to be by her side at a time like this."

He reined the stallion to a halt. "What has happened?"

"Oh, Mr. Braden, it's Jamie. He's got the ague!"

Chapter Twenty-five

*A*lec leapt to the ground and secured Aldebaran to the porch railing. Bounding onto the porch and through the door, he took the stairs two at a time, stopping just outside the boy's room. Inside, Jamie lay in his little bed, pale and shivering violently, seemingly oblivious to his sister's ministrations as she caressed his tiny forehead. She was humming a lullaby, her voice almost a whisper. She was crying.

"Cassie, is there aught I—"

Startled, she spun about to face him, still clad in her night shift and dressing gown. Her eyes were red and swollen, and he knew that she had been crying long before she'd learned of Jamie's illness. "What are you doing here? I should have thought you well on your way by now."

Turning her back on him, she settled back on the edge of the bed and held a hand to the boy's cheek.

"How is he?" Alec refused to let her bait him. It was fear and grief that made her speak thus to him.

"He's so, so sick." Her shoulders sagged and her head fell. Her voice was choked with tears. "I haven't enough powder for him. Zach came down with the fever last night, too."

Plus the three bondsmen and the slave child Alec had heard about yesterday and Rebecca, whose fever had returned, that made seven who now lay ill.

"No one will begrudge you giving the child what he needs, love. He is your brother and heir to this estate. It is his right."

Cassie shook her head. "I can't save the last for my brother and let the rest suffer and die."

"Then send for more."

Her shoulders shook with a stifled sob, tears pouring silently down her cheeks. "This time of summer there is none left in the colony save that hoarded by wealthy planters, and they'd not share their stores with us, not even for good English coin."

Alec sat next to her and pulled her into his arms, struggling for words. Two of his nieces had contracted the measles once. He'd been quite worried then, but Emily and Victoria had had a skilled physician to care for them, and all the medicines money could buy. This was different. The ague was a killer. The stories of those who'd survived crossing the ocean only to die during their first summer in the colony were legion. While Jamie at least had it to his advantage that he'd been born in this wild land, he was still but a young child.

For a moment, Cassie sagged against him, the warm wetness of her tears seeping through the linen of his shirt. Then, abruptly pulling away, she reached over to tuck the covers tightly under the boy's chin.

"You should go. Soon everyone will awaken."

"Cassie, I—"

"No! Go now, while you still have time! My heart has been torn into enough pieces this night. Seeing you again … it is torment. I cannot bear saying good-bye afresh."

She lifted her gaze to meet his.

"Aye." With that, he turned and strode from the room.

"Get her out of here!"

Elly closed her eyes, pushing back tears. She could not blame him for hating her. It was no less than she deserved.

"Zachariah!" Nan seemed to be fast losing her temper. "If ye don't quiet down and drink this potion as yer good mistress asks, I'll give ye a thrashin' that you'll ne'er forget."

"I'll drink when ye make her go."

Elly watched, gripped by a nameless fear, as Zach sank slowly back onto his pillow, glaring at her and shivering. She'd watched two brothers die from scarlet fever, another from a blow to the skull. She'd watched as her mother died of consumption, her father from drink. She knew well the smell of death, and it had settled in this cabin.

Zach was frightfully sick, and it was her fault. Dark circles marred the hollows beneath his eyes, making his skin seem even more pallid. His blond hair, dark and wet with perspiration, clung to his scalp. Not for the first time this morning, Elly prayed silently.

"Why yer mistress wishes to waste precious medicine on a man like ye when there are better souls to tend is beyond me," Nan was saying. "Now drink. And don't complain about the taste either. Ye have only yerself to blame for this fever, stayin' out in the night air, drinkin' like a fool."

"Shut up, hag." Zach fixed the cook with a frown. He lifted his head to drink, then stopped. "What do ye mean, 'better souls'?"

"She meant nothing," Elly blurted.

Didn't he realize how sick he was? He must drink.

"Ye're lying. But that's nothin' new, is it?" He glowered at Elly, then dismissed her altogether.

She opened her mouth to protest, but found herself staring at her feet, ashamed.

"Who else is sick? Is there not enough powder?" Zach asked Nan again through chattering teeth.

"Elly speaks truly. I meant nothin' other than to say ye are to blame for yer own sufferin'," Nan said. "And if ye don't open yer mouth to drink, I'll get Luke in here to pry it open. I'll not have ye heapin' worry on your mistress's shoulders."

"Do what ye will, but I'll not swallow till I have the truth."

"Ye are a stubborn devil." Nan muttered a few curses. "The truth is, there is precious little powder left, this bein' the last portion. Now, either ye'll drink or I'll wash me hands of ye and dispatch the men to start diggin' yer grave."

A faint smile spread across Zach's pale face. "Ye always did know how to charm a man, Nan. Who else is sick?"

"The same as before ye started troublin' us this mornin', that's who. Now drink!"

"The truth, Nan, for I can see in yer eyes that ye're keepin' somethin' from me."

Nan sighed and shook her head. "All right, but tellin' makes no difference. Ye must still drink."

"Out with it, woman!"

"The mistress awoke early this mornin' to find Jamie shiverin' with fever. Sure and 'tis the ague."

"Lord!" Zach closed his eyes. "And ye'd have given me the last of the powder, savin' none for the child?"

"Jamie has already had one draught. It is your mistress's wish that the last be split between all who are ill and the rest be left to God."

Zach shook his head, his eyebrows drawn together in a frown. "I'll not take medicine from a child. Take that to Jamie."

"I knew ye were goin' to say that, ye bein' such a noble bastard and all." Nan shook her head. "It's a right and worthy thing ye do, Zach. God be wi' ye."

"But, Zach, if you don't … " Elly found herself kneeling next to the bed, clutching his hand.

"I might die? Would that be so bad, Elly, dear?" His eyes were hard, cold. He jerked his hand away.

"Aye," she answered, her own voice a whisper. "Zach, I—"

"You care for me, Elly, sweet? You love me?" He smiled ruefully. "Get out."

Only when she heard herself sob did Elly realize she was crying.

"Come, Elly. It is best if ye take this medicine to the mistress and send Luke with water and linens."

Elly wiped her face with her apron and stood, swallowing her tears. "No. You go, Nan. I'm staying, whether he wants my help or not."

Zach moaned in protest.

Nan started to scold her.

Elly cut them both off. "I'll not leave this cabin until Zach is well."

Surprised at the strength in her own voice, she squared her shoulders and smoothed her apron. She was no child to be ordered about. No one and nothing would make her leave Zach's side.

"Well, he's too weak to argue with ye." With that, Nan turned to go.

"Don't bet on it!" Zach's shout followed her out the door.

*A*ccording to the map Cassie had given him, he should now be well onto Robert Carter's land. Corotoman lay not far ahead. He'd left the road, hoping to save time by cutting through the forest. Somewhere here along the river should be Carter's wharf, busy with men loading and unloading the cargo that had made him his fortune.

Alec gave Aldebaran his head. The stallion found his way over logs, through dense stands of pine, along strands littered with debris left by the retreating tide. Distances in England were nothing compared to the vast spaces that stretched between neighbors here. Already this journey had taken more time than Alec had imagined.

He'd begun to worry he'd somehow gone in the wrong direction, when he saw it in the distance—first a thinning of the trees, then boats nestled in a small natural inlet. Men bustled about, carrying crates and pulling drays laden with hogsheads and other crates. Urging the stallion on, he rode to meet them.

"Ho, there!" came a voice.

Alec reined Aldebaran to a halt and dismounted to see a man running toward him from out on the pier. His clothes were stained with sweat, and, as he drew near, Alec was assailed by the rancid stench of unwashed flesh.

"Ye're Blakewell's convict."

The man, an overseer most likely, appraised Alec with squinting eyes, and without waiting for him to answer, took a pistol from his belt and aimed it at Alec's head.

"Aye. I've come to have a word with Carter on Blakewell's behalf." The man hesitated, his eyes darting from Alec to the map still in Alec's hand to the stallion and back again.

"More likely ye're tryin' to escape. Are ye surprised to find yerself here, convict? Thought maybe this was a port town?"

"If I'd not known this was Corotoman, I'd not have asked to speak with Carter, would I?"

The man paused for a moment, thinking it through. "And what would the likes of ye have to say to me master?"

"Do you always pry into your master's business? I should think he'd find that disagreeable in a servant."

The man licked his sunburned lips nervously. "This way, convict. But keep yer hands where I can see 'em. And if ye try to run, I'll shoot."

Alec accompanied him across the dock toward the outbuildings—drying sheds, a warehouse, enough slave and servant cabins to constitute a sizable village. It was said Carter owned more than two thousand slaves. In the distance, Alec could see the three-story great house, enormous by Virginia standards. Not far from it were the charred remains of the original Corotoman, which Cassie said had burned to the ground two winters past. Though larger even than Crichton Hall, the new house wouldn't have amounted to more than a modest country manse in England.

Stopping in front of one of the warehouses, the man gestured for Alec to stop and disappeared inside. Securing Aldebaran to a nearby wooden railing, Alec waited, aware that more than a few had stopped work to stare at him. Finally the man emerged, holding shackles. Two slaves followed behind him.

Something lurched in Alec's gut, some half-forgotten memory of chains and pain and darkness. Instinct told him to fight, to flee.

"Hold him." The overseer motioned the slaves forward.

Fighting the urge to strike out, Alec shrugged off the slaves and held out his wrists.

"If it makes you feel safer, by all means." He smiled coldly, and the slaves laughed, evidently amused to see the overseer frightened of someone who offered no resistance.

His face red, the overseer fastened one end around Alec's right wrist before locking the other to the wooden railing. The click of the lock and the feel of cold, hard iron against his skin sent chills up Alec's spine.

"Watch him." The overseer turned and vanished behind another warehouse.

The two slaves dropped into conversation, speaking some language Alec had not heard before. Obviously, they were not the least bit concerned he might somehow escape. Sweat trickling down his back, Alec forced himself to relax, leaning against the warehouse to escape the hot sun.

The overseer hadn't been gone long, however, when he reappeared, with Carter trailing behind him. The old man was dressed impeccably despite the heat, his face beaded with perspiration. Carter stared at him with a discerning eye, his gaze coming to rest on the iron shackles.

"Why is this man in manacles?" he asked the overseer, who shifted uncomfortably under his master's gaze.

"He's a convict, master. He wandered out of the forest onto the dock. I thought he might be tryin' to escape and didn't want him runnin' off. He has a map."

"Yes, yes, well, it's not likely that he'd ask for me by name if he hadn't meant to find himself on my land, now, is it? Loose him."

Following his master's instructions, the overseer clumsily produced a key from his vest pocket and released Alec.

"Just why *are* you here?" Carter dismissed the overseer and slaves with an impatient flick of his wrist.

"I came on Blakewell's behalf to purchase a quantity of quinquina powder."

"The ague, eh?"

"Aye."

"And what makes Blakewell think I've enough to spare? My people have been hard hit this season, and I've far more to tend to than he does."

Alec smiled. He'd not play that game. "He's prepared to offer you something quite valuable in return."

"Ah. Of course. And what would that be?"

"He'll lend you Aldebaran to stud."

Carter's eyes widened with amazement. "Perhaps I *should* have you locked up. That's hardly like Blakewell."

"The stakes are high for him this time."

"His daughter is ill?"

"His son. And no powder."

"His only son and heir. That is a problem." Carter considered Alec for a moment, his brown eyes staring unflinchingly into Alec's. "Well, Braden, let's get out of this damnable heat. We've much to discuss."

"Aye. And not much time."

*C*assie bathed Jamie's fevered brow with a cool, damp cloth. He was hot and sweating now, chills having given way to restless thrashing. She'd given him the second draught—the one Zach had refused—less than an hour ago, saying a prayer for Zach as Jamie swallowed the last drop. She'd refused it at first, sending Nan back to Zach's cabin, medicine in hand. But then Nan had returned, saying Zach was as obstinate as ever and had refused to touch the lifesaving concoction.

Moved though she was by Zach's sacrifice, Cassie couldn't help feeling remiss in her care of him. Though one dose would have helped but little, to have no quinquina at all was surely a death sentence. Some died quickly, consumed by fever. Others died slowly, the fever wasting their bodies. Zach knew this. He had chosen to die if it might save her brother. She hadn't stopped him.

"Cassie?" Jamie's eyes fluttered open, and he reached for her, whimpering.

"It's all right, sweet boy. I'm here." She lifted the crying child into her arms, wrapping a blanket around him to ward off chills. A lump caught in her throat to see him so ill …

"I'm hot." He struggled weakly to kick free of the blanket.

"That you are, love. I must keep you covered, else the air will give you chills."

His eyes closed, and for a moment Cassie thought he'd fallen asleep again.

"Where's Pirate?" He lifted his head and looked about for his puppy.

"Outside causing mischief. I didn't want him to wake you." Jamie nestled against her, pressing his face to her breast. His skin was pale, his lips parched and drained of color.

"Tell me a story."

"Aye, but first you must drink some cider. Can you do that for me?"

Jamie nodded.

Cassie held a cup of cool cider to his lips and encouraged him to take several swallows. She laid him back onto his bed and began telling him the story of Robin of the Hood.

Jamie shook his head. "Blackbeard. Tell me the one about Blackbeard."

It was the tale Alec had always told him, and it had replaced that of Robin of the Hood as his favorite.

"I'm afraid I don't know that story well, my sweet."

"Cole knows it."

Cassie suddenly found it hard to speak. "Aye, but he's gone … riding."

"When he comes back, can he tell me a story?"

Hot tears sprang to her eyes. When she'd heard the sound of Aldebaran's hooves disappearing into the distance this morning, she'd thought she would die. Her heart had seemed to shatter, leaving nothing but pain behind her breast. Only Jamie's plight had drawn her mind from Alec.

Why hadn't she told him? She had let Alec ride to what might well be his death without telling him she loved him. The thought pained her more than knowing she'd likely never see him again.

She'd have to report his escape soon. Strange no one had questioned her about his absence. It was well past suppertime.

God, grant him speed and keep him safe.

She'd give him one more hour, then she'd alert the authorities. One hour, maybe two. "He might not be back for a while, sweetling."

She quickly wiped the tears from her cheeks and smiled.

"Will you help me tell the story?"

"Aye."

"There once was a pirate named Blackbeard, who was the scourge of the seas," she began, ringing out a damp cloth and pressing it to his cheeks.

"And the colonies," Jamie added, his voice weak.

"There once was a pirate named Blackbeard, who was the scourge of the seas and the colonies," Cassie corrected herself.

The sound of a horse's hooves and Pirate's excited barking interrupted her. The horse drew nearer, until its steps rang off the cobblestones below. A familiar whinny, a familiar deep voice.

Scarcely able to breathe, Cassie stood. It could not be. Yet ...

Pulse racing, she rushed to the window to see Alec talking with Nan in the courtyard below.

"Fetch Takotah," she heard him say.

But this made no sense. Why had he returned?

She scarcely had time to ponder the question before he bounded up the stairs and stood in the doorway. Cassie stared, unable to believe her eyes. There he was, his shirt stained with sweat, his chest rising and falling as he caught his breath. His gaze caught hers and held it, his blue eyes reflecting the same worry and anguish that had consumed her all day.

"Cole!" Jamie called, a smile lighting his wan face. "Tell me the story about Blackbeard."

"Aye, tadpole." He walked to Jamie's bedside and stroked the boy's curls. Then his gaze returned to Cassie. "I prayed I'd not be too late."

He pressed something into her hands, and Cassie found herself staring mutely at a leather pouch.

"Quinquina."

Cassie stared at him, astonished. "But how? Where?"

"Honestly and fairly, but we'll discuss that later. Right now I hear there are several people, including a wee lad and a stubborn sawyer, in need of this remedy."

Cassie's heart soared as she opened the pouch and found enough powder to cure at least a dozen people. Her knees grew shaky, and she found herself needing to sit down.

Alec stood before her, smiling, steadying her. "Have a care, Mistress. Don't swoon."

"I never thought to see you again." Her voice was a whisper.

He brushed a curl from her cheek. "I could not leave until I knew Jamie was past danger. How is he?"

Cassie glanced over at Jamie, who watched them through heavy lids. "He is weak, but no worse than expected, though I feared that, without more powder, he'd—"

"Shhh, love." Alec touched a finger to her lips "We have all the powder we need. We shall see him well cared for. I shall personally make certain you get some sleep. But now for Blackbeard."

He sat next to Jamie, his voice taking on a deep, dramatic tone.

"Tis said Blackbeard was the scourge of the high seas and a bane to His Majesty's colonies. And a more terrifying pirate there ne'er was. Why, 'twas said he lit his own hair and beard on fire as he stormed the decks of captured ships."

Cassie looked at the pouch in her hands, then stood. God willing, both Jamie and Zach would survive.

Chapter Twenty-six

*W*ithin three days, Jamie had grown hale enough to refuse to eat Nan's chicken broth. Within a week, he was on his feet, though he was too weak yet to run about with the other children. Cassie had stayed by his side throughout the illness. Alec had been there to tell Jamie stories and cheer her when her spirits flagged. When Jamie's fever had finally broken, Alec had taken her to her bed and held her as she fell into an exhausted sleep.

Zach, too, was recovering, though not as quickly. Senseless with fever by the time Alec had arrived with more powder, he'd refused to take the quinquina at first, believing the women meant to trick him into taking Jamie's portion. Only when he was unconscious and so weakened he could not fight them had they been able to force him to drink. Elly had nursed him to health—with some skill, Takotah said—staying by his side night and day until the fever broke.

Only two more had fallen ill since then. Thanks to the additional powder, they had survived. With the summer nearly at an end and the marsh air cooling, Cassie did not expect the ague to return, though one could never be certain. She'd seen it kill in the dead of winter. But the danger was ebbing, and with the harvest nearly complete, an air of near celebration had overtaken Blakewell's Neck. There was cider to make, vegetables to pickle, and buildings to strengthen against the onset of cold weather. All tasks were being taken on with a renewed sense of enthusiasm.

Cassie sat on the steps of the cookhouse, shelling peas and watching blue jays compete with chickens for the corn she'd sprinkled about the courtyard. The scent of approaching autumn tickled her nose. Soon the leaves would change and the days would grow cooler. Autumn had always been her favorite season. Not as rainy as spring nor cold as winter, free of the sticky heat of summer, fall brought with it a feeling of calm and contentment, as the world began to slip slowly into its winter sleep.

"Leave me be, woman!"

It was Zach. He was walking slowly toward the well, Elly beside him.

"You've barely escaped the grave, Zachariah Bowers. I'll not have you up walkin' about when you should be in bed."

Elly was right, of course. Zach was weak, though he tried valiantly to hide it. His face was gaunt and pale, and Cassie could see that walking from his cabin to the courtyard had left him out of breath.

"I'll not have ye telling me what I can and cannot do!"

Cassie turned her eyes back to shelling peas, feeling as if she were intruding on something private. Nan predicted Zach would soon get over his hurts and forgive Elly, despite the fact that she carried another man's child. Cassie silently prayed it would be so, though watching the two of them together, it seemed unlikely. Cassie knew that Takotah had offered to rid Elly of the babe, but Elly had refused, saying the child, though a bastard, would at least love her. In this she'd had Nettie's support. It was most strange that Nettie, who only a few weeks ago could barely stand the bondsmaid, seemed to have become Elly's only friend.

"That's far enough!" Elly sounded truly angry now. "If I must, I'll get Luke to tote you back to your bed like a sack of oats!"

Cassie looked up to see Elly, who was at least a foot shorter than the sawyer, wrap her arm around his waist and turn him back toward the cabins. For a moment Zach accepted her support, clearly sapped of what little strength he'd had. Then he pushed her away.

"I don't need your help."

Elly fell backward onto the cobblestones. She cried out and clutched her belly.

Cassie dropped the bowl of peas and bolted down the cookhouse steps. By the time she'd reached Elly, Zach was already kneeling at her side.

"Curse me! Is it the babe?"

Elly nodded, drawing several deep breaths.

Cassie was astonished that Zach would do such a thing. "I suggest you leave women in peace and seek out a field hand for your sport! Otherwise someone might think you a bully!"

"Aye, and rightly so." His face was pale with remorse, his brown eyes pleading. "I'm sorry, Elly, love. I never meant for you to fall."

"I tripped on my hems." Elly slowly sat up. "It was but a passing pain."

Zach lifted the girl into his arms and stood. "I'll take care of her, Miss Cassie."

Cassie realized her mouth was agape. One minute Zach couldn't bear to be near Elly. The next he was carrying her off like a knight in shining armor.

"But, Zach, you're weak—" Elly protested.

"The day I'm too weak to carry a wee thing like ye is the day they can put me in my grave."

Cassie watched as the sawyer carried Elly toward her cabin, afraid he might collapse and cause them both grave harm, yet not wanting to interfere.

"Oh, I'm hopin' for her, Miss Cassie," said Nettie, who'd come up behind her. "I'm hopin'."

"So am I, Nettie. So am I. I suppose I should make sure she's not bleeding."

"Let me."

Cassie was silent for a moment. She didn't want to pry. "I'm glad she has a friend in you, Nettie."

Nettie met her gaze. "Our sons will be brothers."

"Brothers?"

But Nettie was gone, following Zach to the servant quarters. For the second time in as many minutes, Cassie realized she was standing with her mouth agape.

Frustrated to be left in the dark, she went back to shelling peas, first picking up those she had spilled on the ground. Her gaze drifted to the stables, where Alec, with Jamie's help, was settling Aldebaran with some oats. It was the second time this week he'd traveled to Corotoman with the stallion. He'd traded a foal by Aldebaran for the pouch of quinquina and was making good on his word. Master Carter had been more than eager to take advantage of what he presumed was her father's sudden change of will and had produced not one, but four mares in season he deemed worthy to take the stallion's seed, offering good coin in exchange for the three extra foals.

At first Cassie had been furious with Alec when he'd told her of the arrangement. Her father had refused to breed the stallion, sure such strenuous activity would rob the horse of its speed and stamina. Alec had dismissed this as ridiculous, but Cassie wanted to follow her father's wishes in as many matters as she could. Of course, she hadn't been able to stay angry for long. Alec had risked his life and put his own future aside to save Jamie. Had he been spied riding through the forest by someone who recognized him, he might have been beaten, even killed.

Cassie was happy that he would be staying a bit longer. But it was only a temporary reprieve, and she tried to temper her joy. When he finally rode out, her grief would be as fierce as it had been before, tearing her from the inside out. But she'd not think of that just now. Not today.

Alec had slept in her bed every night since Jamie's recovery, though he'd refused to join his body with hers, instead pleasuring her with his hands and mouth in unimagined ways, driving her wild. It was to spare her the shame of bastardy should anything happen to him, he'd told her. Though she knew she should appreciate his thoughtfulness, she longed for the feel of him inside her. Besides, his precaution was likely too late.

Her monthly flow, which should have come and gone by now, had not yet begun, and her breasts had grown tender and heavy. It was still too early to be certain. She'd been late once or twice before, the first time following a bout of fever, the second her mother's death. She would wait and hope—and tell no one.

She'd finished shelling peas and begun helping Nan scrub potatoes—sharing what Nettie had revealed and gossiping in a rather unbecoming fashion about who might have fathered both little Daniel and Elly's baby—when she heard Jamie's giggles ringing like tiny bells through the courtyard. Alec was giving him a ride on his shoulders.

"Cassie, look!" Jamie called, his cheeks a healthy pink. He reached down and covered Alec's eyes with pudgy palms.

"I cannae see!" Alec wailed dramatically in a Scottish brogue.

Jamie squealed with delight as Alec stumbled forward, pretending to trip and drop him, spilling him over his head and landing him safely on his feet.

"That was a fine trick." Cassie's gaze locked with Alec's in a moment of shared joy at the child's happiness.

His smile warmed her like sunshine.

"Cole let me feed Debaron."

"He did?"

Jamie nodded, curls bouncing. "He said Andromeda is in season and Debaron wants to mate with her."

"He did?" Cassie glared at Alec.

He avoided meeting her gaze, a suppressed smile tugging at the corners of his mouth.

"Aye, and he said I could have the foal."

"Did he now?"

"Traitor," Alec whispered in the boy's ear.

"Jamie, wash up for supper. As for you, sir," she whispered to Alec, "I've a thing or two to say to you. Nan, could you please keep the little one occupied?"

"Aye, Missy." Nan's eyes glittered with laughter that only irritated Cassie further.

"What do you mean sharing such things with a four-year-old child?" Cassie scolded as soon as they were out of earshot of the kitchen. "And don't you think you should ask me before you promise him a foal of his own by my mare?"

"It couldn't be helped."

"Couldn't be helped? Just what does that mean?"

"Come and see." He took her by the arm.

"I don't need to *see* anything. I am waiting for an answer."

He smiled but did not release her, pulling her along beside him.

"Alec! Ooh, you are bullheaded!"

"Hush, woman."

The stable was warm, the rays of the late afternoon sun spilling through the doorway, filling the stalls with light the color of honey. Aldebaran snorted in greeting. From several stalls down came Andromeda's familiar nicker.

"We're here. What would you have me see? Horses? I've seen horses."

"Patience, witch." Alec kissed her on the nose as he walked past her toward Aldebaran's stall.

Cassie felt her anger fade. She knew she should be vexed with him, but he was too charming, too handsome, and she loved him far too much to be irate for long. If anyone was a witch it was he, for surely he had put her under a spell.

Removing the oat bag from Aldebaran's neck, he led the stallion into the feed yard, then returned for the mare.

"Oh, no, you don't! I've not given you leave to … Alec!"

He ignored her.

Cassie rushed to bar his way, pressing her back up against the gate to Andromeda's stall, the mare's velvety muzzle warm on her ear.

Alec stopped before her, his hands resting casually on his hips, a jaunty grin on his face. "Do you mean to block my way, woman?"

"Aye! The mare is mine, and you'll not breed her without my permission."

Alec nodded, then reached out to brush a stray curl from her face, his thumb tracing a line across her lower lip, his gaze fixing on her mouth. "Have I ever told you how beautiful you are?"

His lips took possession of hers, and Cassie's mind went blank as his arms pulled her close. His tongue probed her mouth, and she was only dimly aware he had lifted her off the ground and was carrying her toward the workbench. No sooner had he lowered her to the ground than he released her with a slap on her bottom and strode quickly over to the mare's stall.

"What … ? Oh! Do you think you can fool me with so simple a trick?"

"It worked, didn't it?"

Cassie gave an exasperated sigh and followed him as he led the mare out the broad doors and into the feed yard.

"Now watch." He released the mare.

The stallion's response was immediate. He snorted and whinnied a greeting to the mare, his enormous phallus dropping from its sheath.

"That's what Jamie saw. The boy demanded answers. What would you have me tell him?"

Cassie shifted uncomfortably, a blush creeping into her cheeks.

"I … Well, that is to say … "

The first time she'd seen such a sight, she'd run screaming for her father. It had happened shortly after she'd watched the men slaughter a pig and remove its entrails, and she'd feared that the horse's innards had begun to fall from its belly. Her father had laughed and explained that was the way a stallion greeted a mare. When she'd learned the truth, she'd been mortified. Perhaps telling Jamie the truth now wasn't so bad after all.

"Yes, love?" Alec's blue eyes twinkled with amusement.

"Nothing."

Andromeda tossed her mane and trotted to the other side of the corral.

"It seems she's not interested," Cassie said triumphantly.

"I'd not be too hasty, if I were you. Females are often like that, cold one minute, hot the next."

"And isn't it just like a male to make ardent love to one during the morning and another in the afternoon?"

"Aye, Aldebaran has had a busy day, hasn't he?"

The stallion, undeterred by the mare's shyness, followed, whinnying softly and rubbing the velvet of his muzzle against hers. The mare lifted her tail for a moment, giving proof she was ready to mate.

"What did I say? Just like a female. Cold one minute, hot the next."

"We must stop this." Cassie walked toward the gate.

Alec put his arm around her waist to restrain her, clearly pleased with himself.

"Have you ever seen two horses more suited for each other? Andromeda fits Aldebaran as if she were made for him. When your father bought them, he knew exactly what he was doing."

Cassie shook her head. "He never thought to mate them."

"That's a pity, for the two of them have thought about it for a very long time, I'd wager. Can you imagine being ever near the one you desire, but not being allowed to touch like this?" He kissed her hand. "Or this?" He pressed his lips to her hair, one hand passing lightly over her breast, so lightly Cassie thought she might have imagined it.

Frissons of pleasure shot through her, but Cassie pulled away. This was risky. They could not be seen like this. "They are only horses. I doubt they think much at all. Mating is just instinct for them."

"As it is between men and women." The huskiness of his voice caused Cassie's heart to skip a beat.

"What I mean is that horses derive no higher pleasure from … joining." Cassie felt heat flood her face. "It is but a physical act meant to create offspring."

"Certain of that, are you?"

Andromeda trotted forward, rubbed against the stallion's gleaming chestnut flank as she passed, then made room for him behind her. The stallion snorted loudly, tossing his head, his muscular body rippling with tension. He sniffed at the mare's tail, then reared to mount.

"Will he hurt her?"

"Nay, love. Remember, she's a horse, too, and built to take him."

"Of course she's a horse!" Cassie saw the horses' bodies join, then looked away.

Images flashed through her mind, making her blood run hot: images of Alec making love to her, mounting her in a like fashion. She grew mortified that this common barnyard event should spark such carnal thoughts. Then she felt Alec behind her, one hand caressing her hip through the cotton of her gown as the other came to rest casually on the fence beside hers. His breathing was thick and heavy.

"You realize you're in trouble, don't you?" she whispered, overwhelmed by her need for him.

"In trouble?"

"Aye. You bred my mare against my wishes, convict, and you shall have to be punished for your insolence."

"And who shall carry out this punishment?"

"I shall. Come to my room tonight, and you'll see what I do to servants who defy me."

"Aye, Mistress."

*C*assie stifled a giggle at the thought of what she was about to do. When she'd told Alec she would punish him for defying her, she'd been jesting. Then an idea had begun to form in her mind—a startling, irresistible idea. Over the course of the evening, the idea had become a plan. She'd decided at least a dozen times not to go through with it. It was, she knew, not the sort of thing young ladies from good families did with men—even after they were married. It was positively indecent, which made it all the more enticing. In the end, curiosity—and the desire to give Alec the surprise of his life—had won out over propriety, and she had decided to stick with her plan.

She glanced nervously into her mirror and smiled conspiratorially at her reflection. Her hair was twisted stylishly upon her head, a few curls tumbling down her temples and at her nape. Her cheeks and lips were touched with rouge, her eyes lined with color. She wore the same ivory silk-and-lace gown she'd worn to Geoffrey's birthday party—the one she'd worn when she'd first called Alec by his real name. She looked ready for a ball—except, of course, there was nothing beneath the gown. Nothing.

She smoothed her skirts and looked around the room one last time. He'd arrive any minute. The candles on her bedside table cast a warm glow over the room. The covers of her bed were already turned down. In the middle of the bed lay the only pair of shackles she'd been able to find on the plantation. Though old and unused for years, they still worked. The key hung on a silken cord between her breasts.

The creaking of footfalls on the stairs told her he had come. She smoothed her skirts nervously, her heart pounding. Could she really do this? She felt herself start to smile, but forced it away. A quiet knock came at the door. The handle turned. Alec stepped in and turned to close the door. He looked so handsome, dressed in a clean linen shirt and breeches. She had to fight the urge to rush forward and fall into his arms.

"Cassie, love, I ... " He turned toward her, staring. "You look beauti—"

"You're on time, convict." It took every ounce of determination she had not to smile or giggle. "That's good. It will go easier on you."

Cassie could see in his eyes the moment he understood her game. His look of confusion was replaced by surprise and then amusement before his gaze grew cold and hard. "I'm to be punished, then?"

"I can no longer tolerate your insolence, convict. I mean to teach you a lesson." It was good she had rehearsed her lines. It would have been impossible to say them else. Was she really going through with this?

He leaned against her bedpost nonchalantly, crossing his arms. Defiant and confident, he reminded her so much of the man he'd been when she'd first purchased his indenture. "And what makes you think I'll cooperate, Mistress, when I could just as easily break your pretty neck?"

"You'll find what I have in mind far more pleasant than what you'll receive if you disobey."

"I see." His gaze raked over her body in blatant sexual appraisal, and she shivered in anticipation. "And just what do you have in mind?"

Chapter Twenty-seven

"*U*ndress—slowly."

He raised an eyebrow, then untied his shirt and slowly pulled it over his head. It fell, forgotten, at his feet. Candlelight cast the bronzed muscles of his arms, chest, and abdomen in glorious high relief. He reached for the opening of his breeches and began to untie them, his muscles shifting beneath sun-bronzed skin.

Cassie felt desire flow like warm brandy through her veins. "Slowly, convict."

His gaze locked with hers again as ever so slowly he pulled on the ties, undid his breeches, and let them drop to the floor. He was rock hard, his sex thick and heavy.

She found she could scarcely breathe. "Your hair. Remove the thong."

Not breaking eye contact, he reached back with one hand, and his dark hair slid free, falling just below his shoulders. He looked untamed, fiercely male, and, with his lash scars, not a little dangerous. He stepped toward her.

She stepped back and pointed to the bed. "Stop! The shackles. Lock one end around your right wrist, then pass the chain behind the bedpost, lie down, and lock the other end around your left wrist."

He looked at the bed and saw the shackles. She heard his quick intake of breath and saw a shadow pass over his face. Then it was gone.

"Don't you trust me, fair mistress?" His voice was dark as sin and soft as velvet. His eyes held the allure of every man who'd ever tried to beguile a woman into a false sense of sexual safety.

"Never." She smiled and spoke in a rich, seductive voice she didn't know she had. "But I will have your complete cooperation."

"I see." Naked, he walked to the bed, picked up the shackles, and closed one end around his right wrist. It locked with a click. He sat and moved backward across the bed, then reached behind his head and passed the chain behind one of the bedposts. "What makes you think these chains will protect you?"

"Do it, convict."

He lay down, then reached back to cuff his left wrist. *Click.* He lay diagonally across the bed, completely vulnerable. His arms were stretched over his head. His chest rose and fell with each breath. His rigid sex stood defiantly against his abdomen. His legs, spread slightly, stretched the length of the bed, his feet hanging just over the edge. A tremor passed from Cassie's belly to her sex.

His gaze, cold and menacing, bored through her. "Do you like what you see?"

"Aye, convict. And it's good for you that I do." Almost trembling with excitement, she loosened her bodice until her breasts were visible. Then she moved to the bed and began to caress him, first his feet, then his ankles and calves. Where her hands touched, her lips and tongue soon followed. She heard his breath quicken, felt his muscles tense, and reveled in his response. She worked her way up his muscular legs and over his powerful thighs, but, although she touched the sac that carried his seed, she did not touch his shaft. "You've a remarkable cock, convict."

He groaned in frustration. The chains caught on the bedpost, clinking as he strained against them. "Is this to be my punishment then? To be tortured with kisses, soft hands and words?"

Some part of her she'd never known awoke within her, and she felt herself grow more daring. Like a cat toying with its prey, she stretched across the bed beside him. She ran her fingers teasingly on his abdomen, outlining his erection.

"Your punishment is that you shall see, but you shall not touch. You shall want, but you shall not receive—not until it pleases me."

He groaned again, and she kissed his chest. Her tongue found his flat, brown nipples, and she licked and teased them. Her fingers savored the soft skin and hair of his chest, felt the firm planes and ridges of his muscles. Everything about him was intoxicating—the feel of him, his manly smell, the way his muscles tensed beneath her touch. To have him in her power like this was the most intoxicating thing of all, a heady elixir that heightened her senses and her hunger.

She kissed a path along the valley that ran down the center of his belly, then took his shaft in her hand. She'd learned a few things about pleasuring him since the first time she'd tasted him, and she was going to put them all to good use. Holding him firmly with one hand, she began to tease the head with her tongue, tracing swirling shapes over, around, and under. Then she took him into her mouth and began to move her mouth and hand together up and down his length, laving him with her tongue all the while.

"Sweet Jesus!" His eyes were closed, his brow furrowed. His hands gripped the chains that held him fast. His hips matched her rhythm, and Cassie could tell his climax was near.

She stopped, fondled his sac, and let his passion cool.

"Christ!" His voice was ragged with arousal.

Cassie found herself battling to control her own flaming desire. She'd never been in control before, and the thrill of it was like a powerful wine coursing through her blood. She wanted him inside her, but she could not, would not let herself have him—not yet. She ravished him with her mouth and tongue again and again, taking him to the brink, then stopping. His entire body was taut with unspent passion, and the sounds that came from his throat told her he was as desperate as she. Unable to bear it longer, she lifted her gown and straddled him. She saw his pupils dilate when he felt his skin touch her bare thighs and bottom.

His gaze devoured her. "I want to touch your breasts."

Cassie opened her bodice more, lifted her breasts so that he could see them, and circled her nipples with her thumbs. "No."

His eyes held hot fury and lust. He jerked on his bonds, the muscles of his arms and chest straining, but the chains held fast. "You are cruel."

"But not heartless. I want your cock inside me now. That ought to please you." Cassie rested her hands on his chest to balance her weight, then lifted her hips and carefully guided him inside her.

They moaned almost in unison as their bodies joined. She rode him, grinding against him to pleasure herself. Though she knew it would not be enough to bring him to climax, it was everything she needed. With him thick and hard deep inside her, she quickly felt her peak near and let it wash gloriously over her as her sheath contracted around him.

Her cries of pleasure mixed with his tortured groans, and she knew his anguish was real. She would have to end this game, or at least give him his reward for playing along so nobly.

"Have you learned your lesson, convict?" She reached between her breasts for the key and dangled it before him.

Then a hand clamped over her mouth, and, in a whirl of motion, she found herself facedown on the bed, one arm bent behind her back.

"I tried to warn you, mistress." His voice was harsh. "You should never ask a felon to lock himself up. He might not be trustworthy. Scream, and it will be the last sound you make. Do you understand?"

She nodded gravely, her heart pounding with intense excitement.

He removed his hand from her mouth, and she heard the clinking of chains as he dragged them toward her.

"Don't hurt me!" Her voice quavered with anticipation, and her plea sounded genuine.

"No? If your body provides me with enough pleasure, perhaps I shall spare you. You are a pretty thing. It would be a shame if I had to mar your lovely skin." He took her other arm and brought it behind her back.

She felt the cold touch of iron. Then she heard two distinct clicks—much louder clicks than she'd heard when he'd locked himself up—and knew she was shackled. Her pulse raced. She had not planned this!

"What have we here?"

She felt him lift her skirts and pile them up around her waist, baring her bottom.

"You've got a nice ass, mistress, round and pink." His hands stroked her buttocks, raising goose bumps on her skin. Because she could not see him, she could only guess what he might do next. She felt wonderfully helpless. It was more titillating than she could have imagined.

"I can smell you from here—hot, musky, ready for me."

She felt him move between her thighs, cried out when he forced them wide apart. His fingers found her, penetrated her. She heard herself moan, felt her ardor rise again.

"You're so wet. You must have enjoyed yourself." He stroked her deeply. "Now it's my turn."

Cassie began to struggle. She twisted and tried to inch away from him across the bed.

He laughed and held her legs still beneath his. "You can't fight me, love, though you can amuse me by trying." He pulled her bodice down over her shoulders, then reached beneath her to fondle her breasts. "I'm really going to savor this."

His fingers were rough, but he didn't actually hurt her. Instead he drove her mad. Her nipples grew hard as he rolled them between his fingers. "Oh, please!"

"Not such a lady, after all, Mistress? Want me to take you?"

"Oh, aye!"

She cried out as he plunged into her. Deep and hard he drove into her again and again, his hands grasping her hips. It felt so good. Then he angled himself to strike the most sensitive part inside her, and Cassie felt the world around her shatter. Her cries mixed with his deep groans as he spilled his seed against her womb.

Later, when her dress had been hung carefully in her wardrobe and the shackles had been hidden away, Cassie crawled into his arms and snuggled against the warmth of his chest.

"Were you surprised?" She released the giggle she'd held back all night.

"Aye. I must say I was." He smiled, his face unbearably handsome. He traced the curve of her cheek with his hand. "I didn't realize you were capable of such … fantasy. But now that I know … " He smiled a slow, wicked smile.

"You were never really chained, were you?"

He chuckled. "No. But I let you think I was."

"Why?"

"I wanted to see what you would do. I wasn't disappointed."

Then she remembered. "You were afraid to put the shackles on, weren't you?"

"I have these memories. Just images really, feelings." He stopped, his face clouded.

"I'm sorry. I didn't think—"

He held a finger to her lips to still her, his gaze capturing hers. "They're only memories, love. They could in no way compete with the delight you were offering."

"Then you didn't mind?"

"You can shackle me anytime, Mistress."

A dog yelped.

Wood cracked, crashed to the floor.

Cassie heard herself scream. She sat bolt upright, heart pounding sickeningly against her breast.

It was a nightmare.

"Take the boy and the pup to my carriage. And have a care."

It was no nightmare. This was real.

"Alec!"

Men—six, maybe seven—streamed through the gap where her bedroom door had been. It lay on the floor, splintered. Alec was already out of bed, on his feet, still naked. He'd knocked one man to the ground. The second fell as Alec broke Cassie's dressing table chair across his back. But there were too many of them. Within seconds four men had fallen upon Alec with fists and cudgels, raining blow after blow, driving him to the floor. Henry, the old Scot, was among them, a smug look on his face, his gaze traveling over Cassie's naked body.

"Alec!"

Heedless of her own nakedness, Cassie sprang from the bed to help him, only to feel arms grab her from behind. Twisting and kicking, she fought her attacker, but to no avail.

"You go with me."

Cassie knew that voice. She froze.

"That's better." One of his hands covered her mouth, while the other moved slowly over the skin of her bare belly, making her stomach lurch. "If I hadn't seen this myself, I'd never have believed it. How could you?"

Cassie renewed her struggle, aware of men's eyes upon her, only to be thrown roughly onto her bed.

Geoffrey stood above her, his gaze running over her body, his expression a combination of lust and disgust. "Get dressed."

Shaking uncontrollably, Cassie fumbled for her shift, pulled it hastily over her head, and reached for her dressing gown, her only thought to reach Alec. Pray God he was not badly hurt!

"My father will not stand for this." Her voice shook as badly as her legs. "When he—"

Geoffrey laughed at her. "Your father is a danger to no one save himself."

Cassie felt the blood rush to her head. He knew! But how?

"You thought to fool me with your game, love? You forget how well I know you."

"Where is Jamie?"

And where was Micah? Why had no one come to their aid? This could not be happening!

"He is waiting for us in my carriage, love. I would never harm the boy." Geoffrey turned to his men. "Get him up!"

The men who'd attacked Alec moved apart, two of them pulling Alec to his knees, Henry lifting Alec's head by a handful of hair. Alec was bruised and battered, barely conscious. Blood streamed from a cut on his forehead.

"Oh, God, Alec!" Tears spilled down Cassie's face unheeded. She would have rushed to his side had Geoffrey not pulled her tightly against his chest, his fingers digging painfully into her flesh.

"Get him to his feet," he said to his men. "I want him awake for what comes next."

Geoffrey's henchmen laughed. Henry produced a hunting knife as the others struggled to pull Alec to his feet.

Fear coursed through Cassie's veins like a sickness. "Geoffrey, no! What are you doing?"

"You shall see, my love."

Alec's eyes fluttered open, his gaze sweeping the room before coming to rest softly on her. "Are you hurt?"

"No."

Then Alec's gaze locked on Geoffrey, blue hardening with hatred to steel gray. "Harm her, and I'll watch you die."

Alec's voice was strong, but Cassie could tell he was in pain.

"You're hardly in any position to be making threats, convict. Besides, I've no intention of harming Catherine. She's to be my bride."

Cassie started to object, but was cut off.

"As long as the priest is honest and requires the bride's consent, you'll sleep alone, Crichton."

One of Geoffrey's thugs slammed a fist into Alec's gut, forcing the air from his lungs.

"Leave him alone!" Cassie lunged forward, only to find herself jerked painfully back against Geoffrey's chest. She watched, helpless, as Alec struggled to regain his breath.

He met Geoffrey's gaze, loathing in his eyes. "Do you fear me so greatly you bring seven men to do your bidding, while you attack a woman?"

Geoffrey's fingers dug deeper into Cassie's arms. "A man of my station need not sully his hands with this sort of thing. When I want to butcher a pig, I merely send for the butcher."

He motioned Henry forward.

Cassie screamed and fought to pull free, lashing out at Geoffrey with teeth and nails.

"Be still now, love. It's not as bad as that," Geoffrey captured her arms roughly and crushed her against him. "I'm not going to kill him. You'd pine for him forever, and I've no intention of competing with a ghost. No, he will live, but not as a man. Seeing him years from now, bent, broken, pathetic, you will come to loathe him and rue the day you let him share your bed."

Cassie watched in horror as Henry tested the knife's weight in his hand and moved forward. "Wh-what are you going to do?"

"Geld him."

Chapter Twenty-eight

"God, no!" Cassie's heart slammed so hard in her chest, she feared it would explode.

"Do what you will, Crichton." Alec glared at Geoffrey, his face betraying no fear. "I'll still be more of a man than you."

Before she knew what she was about, Cassie had thrown all her weight against Geoffrey, butting her head into his jaw and knocking him backward onto the floor. Breaking free, she pushed past the men who surrounded Alec and fell to her knees before him, shielding his nakedness behind her.

"No!" Low and guttural, the voice did not sound like her own. "You'll not touch him, else I swear, Geoffrey, I shall but live to do the same to you! You will live your life in fear, I swear it!"

Geoffrey stood slowly, rubbing his jaw. He looked at her, surprise and fury written plainly on his face. For a moment, Cassie was sure he would strike her.

"Hurt her, Crichton, and you're a dead man."

"I think not, convict. You shall live to know that I do with her whatever I please." Geoffrey grabbed a handful of Cassie's hair and yanked her to her feet, jerking her toward him and ignoring Alec's curses. "Flog him."

"Geoffrey, no! You cannot do this!" Propelled down the stairs with one arm wrenched painfully behind her back, Cassie struggled not to trip.

"I can. I will. It is within the bounds of the law for me to see him hanged for seducing you, but I'm afraid that would make him a martyr in your eyes."

"Seducing me? I assure you I lay with him most willingly!"

Geoffrey wrenched her arm until she cried out in pain. "Say that again, and I *will* castrate him," he whispered gruffly in her ear.

"Please, Geoffrey, I beg you not to hurt him. Your men have already beaten him senseless. What can you possibly hope to gain?"

"A measure of satisfaction."

The cruelty of his answer left her momentarily speechless.

"Please, I will do anything you ask, only do not hurt him!"

Geoffrey ignored her pleas, pulled her aside to let his men pass, and instructed them to tie Alec to the well post.

"Alec!" Cassie kicked Geoffrey in the shins, biting the arm he held across her chest. "You bastard!"

Something struck her temple. Pain shot through her skull. The world spun. Her legs gave way.

"Don't make me punish you!"

Cassie struggled to lift her head. For the briefest second, her gaze met Alec's. She saw only fury in his eyes.

I love you! Her lips formed the words in silence.

But it was too late. Geoffrey's thugs forced him out the door and down the porch steps.

Outside stood at least a dozen men, holding torches and brandishing firearms. Just beyond the torchlight, Cassie saw the horrified faces of the plantation's inhabitants—Nan, Nettie, Luke, Micah, Zach, and the others—their features cast half in torchlight and half in shadow. Nan was weeping. Micah was bleeding from a cut on his forehead. Zach had fresh bruises on his face. They'd been roused from their beds—roused then subdued, Cassie realized—to witness this.

Tears stung her eyes, and her head throbbed, but she forced her shoulders back and lifted her chin. She had done nothing of which she was ashamed. She would be strong for them. For Jamie, who was no doubt crying for her in the carriage. Most of all for Alec, who was to be tortured without even the dignity of clothing. Geoffrey pushed her to a spot along the porch railing, one arm around her waist, the other still holding her arm twisted painfully behind her back.

"I want you to have a good view, my dear."

"Sir, the boy is gone!"

Jamie! Cassie's heart leaped. Oh, God, had he escaped? How scared he must be.

"Gone?"

Surely Takotah would find and hide him. Cassie drew deep breaths, relieved at least that the child would not be forced to witness this horror. Alec was his hero.

"Aye, Sir. I turned my head for but a moment, Sir, and he vanished!"

"Takotah," Geoffrey mumbled. "Find the Indian witch!"

The man hesitated, fear written on his face.

"Find the boy, or it will be your hide that suffers the lash next!"

The man fled.

Just then the night was rent by a sharp crack as Geoffrey's henchman began to warm up his arm, the whip snapping in the air. Chills of horror raced along Cassie's spine. Alec's arms were stretched over his head, his wrists tied to the well's wooden frame. Naked, the skin of his back and buttocks bare to torchlight, he looked defenseless.

Tears streamed down Cassie's cheeks as she offered up bits and pieces of every prayer she could remember. "Geoffrey, you must not do this! Don't hurt him! I will go with you, do whatever you ask!"

Geoffrey ignored her completely. "Get on with it!"

This could not be happening! There had never been a flogging at Blakewell's Neck.

"No! Please, Geoffrey, I beg—"

The first crack of the whip against Alec's bare skin tore a scream from Cassie's throat and made her knees buckle. "Alec!"

Geoffrey clamped a hand painfully over her mouth and forced her head up.

"Hush, love! No one has taken the whip to your pretty skin."

There came another sickening crack, another, another, and another, until Cassie's head echoed with her own silenced screams.

*S*earing pain tore at his back. His skin was in flames.

"*Sure and this will take some of the fight out of 'im.*"

"*Aye.*"

Another blow landed between his shoulders, forcing a groan from his throat, drawing cackles from his tormentors. The ground pitched and rolled under his feet. Metal pinched his wrists and ankles. His head throbbed.

Where was he? The floor beneath him heaved. How had he come to be on a ship?

He had been kidnapped. That was it. He remembered now.

Another blow. Agony forced the air from his lungs, made his head spin.

Then he heard a scream.

"Alec!"

It was Cassie. The bastards had her, too.

"Touch her, Crichton, and you're a dead man!"

But Crichton merely laughed.

"No, Geoffrey, please!"

It was Cassie's voice again. But where was she?

Twisting his head, Alec tried to find her. He had to find her. But it was so dark. No matter how hard he tried to see, his eyes could not penetrate the blackness.

Another blow. Alec's mouth filled with the taste of his own blood.

"Don't try to move." It was Takotah. "Drink."

Alec fought to the surface from the depth of his nightmare, struggled to open his eyes. God almighty, he hurt.

He was lying on his stomach. Takotah was lifting his head, placing something cool against his lips. He recognized the taste of laudanum. It would numb the pain. But it would also numb his wits, and there was something he urgently needed to do. If only he could wake. If only he could remember.

He turned his head, refusing to swallow, and pushed Takotah's hand away.

"No."

"You must heal if you wish to help her."

Memories crashed in on him. Men breaking down the bedroom door, Crichton pulling Cassie by her hair, wrenching pain as the lash tore his skin, the taste of blood as he bit his tongue to keep from crying out. The bastard had taken her. Alec had to save her. But how long had it been? Where was he?

Alec forced his eyes open again. He recognized the bed, the bookshelf. It was the cabin on the marsh island.

"How did I get here?"

"I mixed a potion into the guards' cider. When they fell asleep, Luke cut you down and lifted you onto Aldebaran's back, and Micah brought you to me."

"And Jamie?"

"The boy is here. Don't worry about him."

The sound of a child's laughter echoed from somewhere nearby.

Thank God! Jamie was safe.

"What time is it?"

"You've been sleeping for two days."

"Two days?"

Alarm coursed through Alec's veins. God only knew what Cassie had suffered in that time. He tried to rise, only to sink back onto the bed in a haze of pain. His head throbbed. His ribs ached. The flesh on his back burned like fire.

"They're hunting you with dogs. Before you can make the journey, you must be much stronger." Takotah pressed the cup to his lips again. "Rest."

Alec drank reluctantly.

So Crichton was tracking him. Or trying. There was little chance they'd find him here. The marsh surrounding this little island was dense and wet enough to lose even the best tracking dogs. Still, it meant the moment he emerged from the marsh, they'd be able to pick up his scent. They'd know where he was going before he got there.

But Cassie needed him. She needed him now. He could not fail her. He had to think.

*C*assie stared unseeing out the window. The lunch the slave girl had brought her sat untouched. She knew she should eat, for the babe's sake if not her own, but both her stomach and heart were unwilling. She hadn't been able to eat or sleep since she'd been locked in this accursed room two nights ago.

If only she knew Alec was safe. Was he suffering? Had anyone comforted him, tended his wounds? Cassie couldn't even be sure he was still alive. Regardless of what he might say, Geoffrey meant for Alec to die sooner or later. Had he already gotten his way?

Please let Alec be alive.

She shut her eyes to ward off unwelcome memories, but they would not leave her in peace. The bitter crack of the whip as it ripped into

Alec's skin. His body tensing with pain at each blow. Blood flowing down his back.

Alec had been flogged until he collapsed, unconscious. Though Alec must have been in agony, he'd never once cried out, much to Geoffrey's obvious disappointment. When Geoffrey had finally called his man off, Cassie, afraid Alec would succumb to fever or die of shock, had begged Geoffrey to let someone tend his wounds. Geoffrey had refused, then dragged her to his carriage. He'd left Alec hanging unconscious from the well post, his wrists bound, naked. She'd fought Geoffrey, kicked, screamed, but he'd hit her so hard she'd blacked out.

Oh, to be free of these unbearable images! To have witnessed Alec's suffering was unendurable torture. The recollection of it was no easier.

Where was poor, sweet Jamie? They hadn't found him, but what of later? Cassie was sure Takotah had taken him, likely to her father's cabin. He'd be safe there. Still, it was torment to be uncertain and absolutely helpless.

God, please keep them all safe.

A robin landed on the sill outside her window, hopped on its tiny feet, and pecked at some unseen meal before taking flight again. How Cassie envied the birds their wings. If only she could fly away. She'd thought about trying to climb down. Although the vines that reached the third floor were but slender tendrils and could not support her weight, the bricks were scarred from rain and full of pits, giving her lots of places to gain a handhold. From this height, one slip would mean her death. Still, had she not been certain she was carrying Alec's child, she might have taken that chance.

The night she'd arrived, Geoffrey had had several slave women bathe her, scrubbing her skin until it hurt, washing roughly between her legs. To remove the taint of what she'd done, he'd said. Except for those women—and the slave girl who brought her meals and emptied her chamber pot—she'd been allowed contact with no one here. Geoffrey had not yet come to see her himself. For that, at least, Cassie was grateful.

Why had he done this? He said it was to protect her, his bride. Curse him! She'd told him she had no intention of marrying him—ever. He said he loved her, but, like most planters' sons, it was most likely her dowry land he loved. Or perhaps he and his father saw an opportunity in the guardianship of Blakewell's Neck. It would take some time for the senior Master Crichton to gain legal control of the estate, but the moment ink dried on parchment, making him guardian, he'd be free to sell the crops, slaves, and bondservants as he saw fit, and, if he were clever, to profit by it.

Cassie knew Geoffrey had a cruel streak, but never in her worst nightmares would she have thought him capable of such heartlessness. Now all those she loved were paying the price of her mistake, Alec perhaps with his life. Would Geoffrey harm Jamie, too? He was her father's only heir. If he were to die, the entire estate would go to her husband. Was that Geoffrey's goal?

What of the child she carried? She'd not be able to hide her condition for long. Cassie placed a hand protectively over her belly, fear nearly making her retch. God forbid Geoffrey should harm it in anyway. Or wrench the babe newly born from her arms and give it up to be raised by some farmer's wife miles from here. She could not even bear to think of it.

There was no one she could turn to for help. No one—not the sheriff, not the court, not Geoffrey's father—would make Geoffrey pay for what he'd done. In most people's eyes, he would be a hero for having saved a fallen woman from herself and from the convict who had ruined her. Most people would think him daft for still wanting to marry her, a woman who deserved to be cast into the streets.

Tears of grief poured down Cassie's cheeks, the dullness of exhaustion creeping over her mind like a mist. She had no idea how much time had gone by when she heard footsteps coming up the hallway toward her room. Light and close together, they did not belong to Geoffrey. A key turned in the lock, and the slave girl entered, this time carrying a gown and chemise.

"The master say to dress an' come to dinner." The girl laid the dress on the bed, her fingers lingering lovingly on the material.

Cut in the latest fashion of emerald silk and embroidered with tiny golden bees, it was beautiful, but Cassie could not have cared less. "Tell Geoffrey I'll not play his mistress, no matter how beautiful the gown." Cassie wiped the tears from her face. "Nor will I dine with him. I'd as soon sup with swine."

The girl gasped, an expression of horror on her face.

"If I send you back with that message, he'll punish you, won't he?"

The girl did not answer.

"Tell him I'm too ill to dine with him tonight."

The girl hesitated for a moment, her eyes dropping longingly to the gown. She turned and walked out the door. The lock clicked into place behind her.

Cassie stood stiffly and walked to the bed. Every time she'd tried to sleep, she'd been overwhelmed by nightmares, until she'd become afraid to close her eyes. She was so tired. Sweeping the dress and chemise onto the floor in a heap, she crawled under the covers.

*G*eoffrey strode down the hallway toward the miserable servant room he'd locked her in, trying to get control of the rage seething inside him. What did Catherine mean by refusing to dine with him? *Ungrateful little bitch!* He'd done so much for her. He'd risked his father's certain wrath to save her from the man who had defiled her, who was as far beneath her as the dirt she walked on. Then he'd spared the bastard's life, not to mention his manhood, though it was a decision Geoffrey now regretted.

Rather than dying, as the convict was supposed to, he had escaped, thanks to the Indian witch. She'd somehow managed to slip a potion into his men's food or drink, cut the convict's ropes, and spirit him into the forest without being seen, heard, or abetted by anyone. Nor had anyone seen Jamie or his dog. The boy, too, seemed simply to have vanished. No doubt all of them were huddling together on that miserable island somewhere in the marsh. Despite repeated attempts, the stupid Scot hadn't been able to find his way back to their hideout yet. But Geoffrey wouldn't give him a moment's rest until he did. Dogs were searching for them everywhere along the edges of the marsh. It was only a matter of time before one of the hounds picked up their scent and tracked them down.

Geoffrey suspected some of the slaves and bondsmen knew more than they cared to share, but most seemed eager to martyr themselves to protect their mistress's secrets. None of them would admit to having any idea how the convict had escaped, where Jamie was, or where Catherine had hidden her father. Geoffrey knew she'd never tell—not without unpleasant persuasion.

How lucky she was he'd stayed his hand so far. When he'd seen her lying naked with that whoreson, he'd wanted to kill her, to break her neck, to *feel* the life drain from her body. But he'd kept his temper in check, barely laying a finger on her, except when she'd given him no choice. He was even willing to overlook the fact that she'd been bedded by the convict—nay, seduced, he corrected himself, for surely in her right mind she would never have lain with the man.

She ought to feel grateful. He was still going to marry her. There were many young ladies wealthier than she, and with better connections, who would have eagerly married him. But not Catherine. Catherine, who'd spread her legs for a convict, who worked with her slaves and dressed little better, whose father had raised her with no respect for the rules of society. Catherine, who never left his thoughts, night or day.

Instead of being grateful, she'd fought him, shrieking like a madwoman. She refused to eat the food he'd sent up. Now she refused to show herself at dinner. Did she think to rule him by sulking like some pampered bitch? Her life and all she received depended upon his goodwill. She'd do well to remember that.

But he must control his temper. Catherine had strange ideas about how people were supposed to behave, ideas she'd gotten from her addled father. She'd made it abundantly clear two nights ago that she considered him a worthless barbarian. What was it she'd called him? Despicable bastard. Heartless swine. Inhuman piece of shite. Indeed, what hadn't she called him? He'd had to hit her hard to make her cease her caterwauling.

But he didn't want to hit her. He loved her. Didn't she see how good their lives could be together? He'd have to make her see. He'd show her how forgiving and indulgent he could be. He'd give her no excuse for not loving him this time.

Taking a deep breath, Geoffrey unlocked her door and strode into the room to find Catherine sound asleep, her hair a tangled, coppery mass on her pillow. Even with her eyes closed, he could see she'd been crying. Her face was deathly pale, except for the dark circles under her eyes and the purple bruises on her cheeks. Dismissing a stab of regret, Geoffrey reminded himself that she had caused her own misfortune.

He called her name, but she did not awaken. Could it be she was not pouting but truly ill? She certainly looked it. Geoffrey moved to check her forehead for fever and was relieved to find it cool.

It was then he spied a heap of green silk on the floor.

Heat rushed into his gut. "Get up!"

Chapter Twenty-nine

*C*atherine started and sat bolt upright, her eyes round with fear. "I said get up!"

"No." Hatred replaced the fright in her eyes.

Geoffrey grabbed her wrist and yanked her forward onto her knees, drawing a gratifying gasp. "I warn you, do as I say! I've been lenient with you so far, but my patience is at an end."

Abruptly, Geoffrey released her and turned away. She was doing it again. She was goading him, trying to make him lose his temper. He would not let her succeed this time.

"You will get up and dress—now." He picked up the gown from the floor and dropped it on the bed before her.

"And if I refuse? Will you strike me again? Perhaps you'll have me flogged."

Clenching his fists, he turned to face the window, choked back bile. "It is not my wish to strike you."

"No? Then leave me in peace. I'll not primp for you or play your mistress by entertaining you at dinner." Her voice trembled.

"Ah, but you see, Catherine dear, you *are* my mistress." He turned to face her, ignoring the look of defiance on her face, then picked up a panel of silk and brushed it against her cheek. "I had this gown sewn for you by the finest dressmaker in all of Williamsburg. There is an entire wardrobe filled with gowns even lovelier than this one—"

"After hurting those I most love and kidnapping and beating me, you expect to win me with frippery? How little you must think of me and all women! Take your bit of silk and get out!"

Rage surged through Geoffrey's veins. Then an eerie calm crept over him like the slow melt of snow. He didn't have to hurt her to gain her cooperation. "Perhaps some news from home would cheer you."

She lifted her head. "You have word?"

Geoffrey felt a thrill of triumph. Turning away so she could not see his smile, he considered carefully what he should say. Not that it really mattered. She had no way of knowing the truth. "Now, let me see. The new overseer tells me the cook is supervising the cider making and pickling—"

"New overseer? What of Micah?"

"The tobacco seems to be drying quite nicely. I've lent your father's estate the use of two coopers to help with the making of hogsheads. That's quite a harvest, my dear. You are to be congratulated."

"You taunt me! What of Micah? And Jamie?"

Geoffrey knew whose name was next on her tongue, but was pleased she knew better than to speak it. "The blackamoor has been discharged. Don't look so horrified, my love. He is still a free man. I sent him packing northward with his papers in order and all the tobacco he could carry. Aren't you pleased?"

"But what—"

"As for word of the rest, including the *convict*"—Geoffrey spat the word—"I'm afraid you must join me for dinner." Feeling quite satisfied, he turned and stalked from the room, stopping to lock the door behind him.

*C*assie felt like a whore. Dressed like this, in a gown cut so low it was indecent, she must surely look like one. Stopping in front of a gilded looking glass in the hallway, she nearly gasped at her reflection. Though her hair was neatly coifed, its tangles having been brushed and pulled painfully into order by a sullen slave woman, her face was that of a stranger. Gaunt and pale, with deep purple bruises on her cheeks and dark circles under her tear reddened eyes, she looked like a woman haunted by fear—years older, timid and weak.

"Damn you, Geoffrey!" But as quickly as it arose, the anger dissipated, leaving Cassie trembling and as shaken as before. Tears pricked her eyes. She hastily wiped them away. It would do her no good to weep now. Geoffrey was waiting, and she must play his game to the end.

Struggling to pull the neckline of the gown up over the exposed tops of her breasts, she wondered just what he wanted from her this evening. Would her appearance at dinner be enough for him? Would his price for news from home rise even higher? If it did, what would she do?

Would she lie with him?

No, she would not. She could not. Quelling another wave of queasiness, Cassie forced such awful thoughts to the back of her mind. She smoothed her skirts and walked down the central stairs to the dining room.

"There you are, Catherine. Don't you look lovely." Geoffrey rose to greet her as she entered. His gaze moved over her, resting on her breasts. "I knew the color would suit you. Do you like it?"

Cassie realized Geoffrey was awaiting her answer, as if something as unimportant as the color of a gown could mean anything to her now. "Aye."

Speaking to him made her feel a traitor.

Taking the seat he pulled out for her, she unfolded her napkin and placed it in her lap, her fingers knotting nervously around the linen. Steam rose from a tureen of soup and several meat dishes placed neatly around the table on silver platters, their mingled smells turning Cassie's stomach. Candlelight from the enormous brass candelabra flickered off the facets of a crystal goblet a young slave woman was filling with red wine.

"Catherine, are you listening?"

" I ... my mind must have been wandering."

"I said I had the kitchen prepare your favorite—roast beef. I hope it's cooked to your liking."

"I'm sure it will be fine." She lifted the wine to her lips and took a sip. Its sickly sweetness nearly caused her to throw up. She took a deep breath, willing the nausea to subside.

If he noticed her discomfort, he said nothing, picking the most succulent pieces of beef and putting them on her plate like a dutiful host, prattling about the lengths to which he'd gone to ensure the meal was perfect. The pleasant tone of his voice grated on her already frayed nerves.

"The sauce on the lamb is a French recipe my father won from Robert Carter in a card game. The Carters on occasion use a French chef, brought directly from France, I'm told."

She picked numbly at the roast beef, only half hearing Geoffrey's self-aggrandizing account of his latest hunt. Sure she could not keep her food down, she put only the tiniest bite in her mouth and was surprised suddenly to feel quite ravenous. The first bite was followed by a second, and, before she realized it, she had cleaned her plate.

Geoffrey was laughing again, his smug voice intruding into her thoughts.

"I knew you were hungry, my sweet." He shook a finger at her. "Let this be a lesson. When you refuse my generosity, you harm only yourself."

"The inexcusable and horrid events of these past days have left me feeling unwell."

"I see you're feeling better now."

It was plain he did not believe her. He thought she'd refused to eat simply to vex him, but she didn't care. At least the babe was finally getting some nourishment. Little did he know that by forcing her to eat, he was also feeding Alec's child. From that, at least, Cassie drew some satisfaction. She would eat when she could, and eat well, for the sake of her baby.

The slave woman removed her plate and replaced it with another, motioning to the kitchen slaves to serve the second course. Platters of meats were replaced by puddings and pies, bread and butter, sweetmeats and fruit.

"Hurry up, else the pudding will grow cold!" Geoffrey yelled to the slaves. "It is no wonder their race finds itself enslaved, as slow and stupid as they are."

Cassie started to object, but held back her words with a bite of bread. Geoffrey was detestable.

"You find my manner disagreeable, Catherine?"

She said nothing.

"You'd best remember slaves and servants are not coddled here."

Still, she ignored him. There was something about the bread. It was wheat bread. She swallowed, a lump forming in her throat. How had she not recognized it immediately? The taste, the smell—it was Nan's bread, soft and sweet. Had Nan baked it, knowing she would eat it? God, how she missed them all.

Geoffrey rambled on, bragging about having beaten Landon Carter at whist, tallying this month's wins from gaming.

"Stop!" Cassie didn't know she had cried out until she heard her own voice. "I … I'm sorry, Geoffrey. But you promised me word from home if I dined with you, and I am here. Please tell me what I want to know. I've no interest in whist or hunting or anything else you do."

The silence that followed was deafening. Cassie did not need to see Geoffrey's face to know he was angry. She could not believe her ears when he began to chuckle.

"Tsk, tsk. Mind your manners, Catherine, or I'm afraid there won't be much to tell."

A sob caught in her throat, but Cassie vowed not to cry. Not in front of Geoffrey. Not again.

For what seemed an eternity he babbled on, complaining about his father, seeming not to notice she wasn't really listening. She buttered another slice of bread, defeat sitting heavy and gray on her heart. Geoffrey would tell her nothing tonight. She'd been a fool to believe that he would.

"I had my men bring several loaves of old Nan's bread. I thought you might enjoy it." He pointed to the slice she held in her hand. "The cook said you'd be grateful. You are grateful, aren't you?"

She nodded.

I am grateful to you, dear, sweet Nan.

Geoffrey seemed happy with her response and smiled. "You will be happy to learn Jamie was found, safe and sound."

Cassie tried to hide her shock and dismay, but Geoffrey had delivered the news so suddenly. "Wh-where did you find him?"

"Hiding in the stables. Try not to look so disappointed, dear. Surely being safe and sound in his own home is better than knocking about the forest with that painted witch."

"Is he well? Does he ask for me?"

"I said he was safe and sound, did I not?" Geoffrey bit off the end of a pastry and began to chew. After what seemed to Cassie an unbearable silence, he continued. "I seem to recall he has asked about you once or twice. I told him you were well and with me, and that seemed to put an end to it. He runs and plays as young boys do."

Poor Jamie. She'd thought him safe, far from Geoffrey's reach. But Geoffrey held him prisoner, too. How Cassie ached to hold Jamie, to see his sweet smile, to know for certain he was safe.

"I should like to see him," she said, adding, "Please," as an afterthought.

"Perhaps. In a week or two."

"Why not tomorrow? You would have brought him here that night had he not run off."

"True." Geoffrey dabbed the napkin at the corners of his mouth. "But your conduct of late leaves much to be desired. Perhaps in a fortnight you'll have regained my favor. Until then—"

"But he is a child, and I am the only mother he's known."

"Aye, and you've coddled him, as you've coddled everyone else. It will do him good to be out from under your skirts for a time."

A new fear began to seep into Cassie's heart. Geoffrey treated children much the same as he did animals and slaves. "You'll not lift so much as a finger to harm him—"

"As you and he are now my charges, I shall do with you both as I deem fit." Geoffrey clapped his hands and called for a bottle of port.

Cassie found herself unable to breathe, unable to think, strangled by fury and frustrated by her own helplessness.

"Have you ever tasted a good Madeira, my dear? You haven't touched your wine. Here, let's have a glass of this instead. It will settle your nerves."

Cassie ignored the glass he placed in front of her.

"I see you do not like my decision."

"No." She struggled to control both her words and her quavering voice. "I do not. It is cruel, as you are cruel."

"Some would say I've been merciful." He paused to take a sip of port. "You've not asked for word yet of the convict. Has your fickle woman's heart forgotten him already?"

Cassie's breath caught in her throat. "Would you answer me truthfully were I to ask?"

Geoffrey laughed, finished off his port with a gulp, and poured himself another. "For a price."

Cassie felt her chest grow tight. She had known this would happen.

"Tell me how to get through the marsh to your father's island, and I'll tell you whether the convict still lives." His expression was cocksure.

"I'll tell you nothing." So Henry had seen. Her pulse beat an erratic cadence in her breast.

He leaned forward, his fingers brushing her cheek. "In time you will learn to do exactly as I ask. There are those who would suffer otherwise."

"You are contemptible!" Cassie felt rage swell within her, anger keeping hopelessness at bay.

Geoffrey smiled. "Have it your way, dear. His pain will be upon your head."

"Then he lives?" She hated the weakness she heard in her voice.

"For now. But tomorrow?" Geoffrey swallowed his wine, refilled his glass. "Come, my dear, you haven't had a drop."

"I'm afraid I've no taste for wine tonight." *Alec is alive!*

"Oh, come now." Geoffrey moved closer. His gaze dropped to her cleavage, his eyes darkening with desire. "A bit of wine will do you good."

Hoping to deflect his attention, Cassie picked up the small crystal glass and took a sip.

"That's better." Then Geoffrey reached over and began to caress her arm.

Cassie felt her stomach turn and hastily pulled her arm away.

"We could have so much happiness together, Catherine. If only you could overcome this stubbornness, I'm sure you could learn to love me as I love you." He leaned over and tried to kiss her.

Cassie drew back, pushing him away. "No."

His face went rigid, a muscle twitching in his jaw. "You spread your legs for that convict and haven't so much as a kiss for me?"

"I do not love you."

"You loved me once. Don't you remember?"

"I was a child. I did not know the heartless man you would become."

"I only did what you forced me to do." His hand moved to caress her fingers. "In time you will come to see that."

She tried to pull her hand away, but his fingers tightened around hers and held them fast. "There isn't enough time in eternity to forgive what you've done."

For a moment Geoffrey seemed genuinely taken aback. His expression turned into a predatory sneer. "I could take you here, in this room, on the table, and no one would stop me."

"It matters not what you do, here or later. I could not possibly hate you more than I already do."

"You say that because you are angry, but you will grow to like my touch. Women do."

"I will never lie with you willingly, Geoffrey. Each time you touch me, it will be an act of rape."

His face hardened into a grimace. His fingers squeezed her hand painfully. Then he released her with a snort of disgust and stood, turning his back to her. "You are wrong, dear Catherine. It will not be rape. One week hence you will become my wife, and then you will have no say in the matter. When I wish to have you I shall, and the law will smile upon it."

Cassie sprang to her feet. "Whom have you found to perform this sham of a ceremony?"

"A man who understands the value of good coin—and who truly wishes to save you from yourself. He believes you are carrying my child and wishes to spare you shame."

It was on the tip of her tongue to tell him it was not *his* child she carried, but Cassie held back, certain that he would harm her—and the babe. Then the terrible truth dawned: If she did not escape soon, she would have to lie with him in order to convince him the babe was his when her belly began to swell. Her baby's life might depend on it.

She couldn't. She wouldn't. "No! God, no! Damn you, Geoffrey! I will never consent to marry you, not in this life or the next!"

When he turned to face her, he was smiling. "Oh, but you will. The convict will pay the price should you resist."

The room spun. Cassie sank back into her chair, Geoffrey's voice nothing more than a buzz in her ears. Gulping breaths of air, she tried to calm her stomach and clear her head.

"Come now, Catherine, control your womanly hysterics."

But control was impossible. Cassie bent over and lost her dinner on the dining room floor.

*A*lec brushed Aldebaran's coat, trying to ignore the pain that shot across his back with each movement of his arms. His skin was not yet healed, and he hadn't yet regained his full strength, but the fever had broken two nights ago, and Takotah could force him to stay in bed no longer. He'd lost so much time already. God only knew what hell Cassie had been forced to endure these past eight days.

Alec closed his eyes and took a deep breath, willing his heart to become as cold and hard as a blade. He'd be no good to her if he could not control his emotions. Already his feelings had run the gamut from blistering rage to self-loathing. He'd known that loving her could bring her to ruin, and still he'd given in to his need. Whatever she suffered now, she suffered because of him.

He would leave at sunset.

Aldebaran snorted and stomped his feet nervously as a mouse scurried amid the straw and disappeared through a crack in the wall to the fading light beyond.

"Don't tell me you're afraid of mice, old boy." Alec stroked the stallion's silky chestnut coat.

How he wished he could take Aldebaran, but Takotah had urged him to leave the stallion behind, sure the horse would give him away to the dogs. If he wanted to make it to Crichton's lair undetected, he would have to travel by foot, a good day's journey if he stuck to marsh and woodland, as Takotah had advised.

The Indian woman's help had been invaluable. While Alec had lain unconscious with fever, she'd traveled the distance herself and learned from one of Crichton's kitchen slaves that Cassie was being kept prisoner in a room on the third floor. Takotah had drawn a map for him in the sand and shared with him her secrets for eluding the hounds. Then she'd pressed a leather pouch into his hands. Its contents, she told him, would ward off sleep and dull pain.

Alec's plan was simple. He would arrive under cover of night, free Cassie, and be back in the forest before sunrise. Takotah said he need not fear resistance from Crichton's slaves, who were so abused as to loathe their masters. No one would sound the alarm or block his path, but neither would they come to his aid. With any luck, he and Cassie would be safely within this island sanctuary before evening tomorrow. As soon as he had fully recovered, Alec would take her and Jamie north and sail for England.

Alec put aside the curry comb, giving the stallion one final pat on his gleaming flank. Back outside, tendrils of pink-orange sunlight stretched across the dull autumn sky, heralding day's end. Nearby, Jamie was trying to teach Pirate to fetch. The child had been valiantly hiding his fear and sadness over Cassie's abduction, but more than once Alec had heard him whimpering in his sleep, muttering her name.

"Here, boy! Here, Pirate!" Jamie called.

Pirate ran stubbornly in the opposite direction, stick in his mouth, tail awag.

Jamie's lower lip began to quiver, tears spilling down his cheeks.

"He'll come back, tadpole." Alec was certain it was Cassie's absence more than the puppy's stubborn behavior that brought tears to Jamie's eyes.

"No, he won't." Jamie sniffed and wiped the tears from his face with the back of his hand, leaving a muddy streak across one cheek. "Pirate!"

Pirate sniffed a fern, then ran deeper into the pines.

"Try calling him again. This time use a strong voice, one that tells him you're his master and he'd best obey."

For a moment, Jamie looked up at Alec, his green eyes clouded by doubt. Then he lifted his little chin in defiance, his stubborn expression reminding Alec so much of Cassie that, for a moment, Alec felt overwhelmed by the sorrow of missing her.

"Pirate! Come here!" Jamie shouted with fierce determination. The pup turned about and dashed back, ears flopping, stick still in his mouth.

"Now praise him."

"Good doggy." Jamie patted the puppy's head until the animal's entire body wagged in delight. "Did you see, Cole? He came back to me!"

"Aye, Jamie. I saw." Alec ruffled the boy's curls, suppressing the urge to sweep him up in a crushing hug.

I will bring your sister back, tadpole, or I'll die trying.

"He's goin' to be as bullheaded as his sister. Runs in the blood."

Alec turned to see Micah approaching, Cassie's father's pistol box in his hands. Crichton had driven Micah off Blakewell's land, threatening to make him a slave, but Micah had only pretended to leave, traveling north by day, but moving under cover of night back to the safety of this little island. Strange to think this small sliver of sand had become a haven for them all.

"I cleaned and oiled 'em both," Micah said. "Hope you don't need to use 'em, but the powder's good and fresh if you do."

Alec accepted the box with a grateful nod, then cracked the lid to view the two gleaming pistols within.

"You leavin' tonight?"

"Aye."

Dinner seemed to last forever, fish and cornbread sliding tastelessly down Alec's throat, the tension in his body building with each passing moment. They'd all agreed Jamie should be told nothing of his plan to rescue Cassie, lest it fail. The boy chattered gaily as he ate, apparently unaware of the grim faces around him. Introduced to a father he could not remember, Jamie treated the old man with the kindness and concern only a child could show, even crawling into his father's lap to tell him of his latest adventures and imaginings. His father's lack of response didn't seem to discourage him.

"Cole, will you tell me a bedtime story?"

"Not tonight, tadpole."

Disappointment cast shadows in Jamie's eyes, but he did not protest.

Alec suddenly felt like an ass. If not tonight, when? He might never see Jamie again. He glanced out the tiny window, where the last bit of daylight still clung to the sky. There was time.

He lifted the child into his lap. "On second thought, tadpole, tonight is the perfect night for a bedtime story. What do you want to hear?"

"Blackbeard!"

Half an hour later, Alec slogged through frigid, knee-deep marsh water, the cheery light of the cabin vanishing behind him. Mud oozed beneath his feet, threatening to suck off the leather moccasins Takotah had made for him. Driven by a growing sense of urgency, he moved through the mire as quickly as he could, straining to see and hear through the oppressive darkness, to make out the ghostly shapes of trees and rotting stumps, the sounds of unseen night creatures a chorus around him. More than once he slipped, tripping over slick rocks and hidden roots. The chilly water made even his bones ache. His body, weak from days of fever and wounds that hadn't fully healed, struggled to keep up with the demands he made of it.

He had to reach Cassie. He had to get her to safety. Nothing else mattered.

Wet to the waist and numb with cold, he forced discomfort to the back of his mind and reached into the pouch Takotah had given him. He pulled out a leaf, put it in his mouth, and chewed. The bitter taste at first made him choke, but almost immediately he felt warmer, stronger. Pain faded from his thoughts, and he pressed on, driven by one intent, one purpose, until he found himself scrambling uphill onto dry land.

Ahead, the pale silver of moonlight beckoned through a break in the trees.

Then, in the distance, he heard it.

The baying of hounds.

Chapter Thirty

C assie looked out the carriage window, her stomach in painful knots. How she wished she could throw open the door, leap to the ground, and run into the forest. But Geoffrey held her arm fast, his fingers digging possessively into her skin. He would stop her before she'd even laid a finger on the door handle. Besides, he'd made it clear that Alec's life, perhaps even Jamie's, depended upon her obedience. She had no choice but to do as he bade.

She'd always imagined her wedding day would be the happiest day of her life, not the most desperate. But she'd never imagined any of this. She was about to be made Geoffrey's wife, his chattel. The thought nauseated her, chilled her to the bone. She could not conceive of spending even one night in his bed, let alone a lifetime. She could not imagine dining with him each night, sharing holidays or entertaining his guests. She could not bear to think of Alec's child calling him "father." But unbearable as it was, barring a miracle, that was what her future held.

She'd tried to persuade the slave who helped her dress to let her escape, but the woman had become all but hysterical, describing how the master would punish her. Cassie had also considered telling the reverend there was no baby. Except, of course, that she was carrying a child, Alec's child.

Was this God's way of punishing her for the wrongs she had done? She had lied, forged her father's signature, and taken a man to her bed without wedding vows. She had lived more or less as she pleased, ignoring most of the rules church and society forced upon young women. Could she be paying the price now? Cassie thrust the notion from her mind. A God who claimed to love could not be so cruel.

Yet here she was.

Geoffrey had not spoken to her the past week since that horrible night when he'd forced her to dine with him. He'd watched in anger and disgust as she'd thrown up on the floor, taking it as a personal affront. He'd banished her to her room, where she'd spent the week alone, tortured by her fears. What was happening to Alec and Jamie and all those she loved? Did they blame her? Did they hate her? How long could she hide her condition? Would Geoffrey believe the child was his? What would he do to her and the baby if he did not?

She had been dreading this morning as a condemned criminal dreaded the day of execution. That was what it felt like—an execution. But now the day had arrived, beginning before dawn with a turn of the key in the lock. Geoffrey had entered in his dressing gown, ordered her to bathe and dress, and presented her with a gown of rose-colored silk that he intended to be her wedding gown. The feral look in his eyes had stilled her protests before they'd reached her lips. Silently, she'd done as he'd demanded—for her babe's sake and Alec's.

"We are almost there." Geoffrey interrupted her thoughts. "Try to look a bit less glum and more like a bride, my dear. It is your wedding day."

The carriage lumbered around a bend in the road, the forest opening to reveal the familiar façade of St. Mary's White Chapel and a host of outbuildings. Dread flowed ice-cold through Cassie's veins.

God, please don't let this happen!

The carriage drew to a stop at the church steps.

"Come, my dear." Geoffrey alighted, then turned to give her his hand.

Legs trembling, Cassie rejected his offer, clutching the door handle for support instead, and stepping unsteadily to the ground. Reverend Dinwiddie stood in the chapel's doorway, hands clasped together, brow rolled into a thick frown, the ruddy color of his round face standing out against the white of his satin vestments.

"A good morning to you, Reverend." Geoffrey led Cassie up the steps. "I trust you are well."

"Good day, Geoffrey. Catherine." The reverend eyed her disapprovingly.

Geoffrey pressed Cassie through the door ahead of him, his hand firmly on her back. Sunlight streamed weakly through small windows on either side of the chapel, the lone stained-glass window above the altar splashing color across the polished wooden floor. A handful of candles flickered off to one side, each one a prayer for divine intervention. Propelled by Geoffrey, Cassie followed the reverend up the center aisle, repeating her own silent prayer.

"I must say I do not like this, Geoffrey. It pains me to go behind your father's back. He has contributed generously to this church through the years, and I hate to deceive him. Fathers should oversee such decisions, especially when matters of estate are at stake." The reverend's voice echoed through the empty space. "You are your father's sole heir. He would want you to marry a woman of consequence."

Cassie was not insulted by the snub, hearing hope instead in the reverend's words. If Reverend Dinwiddie had misgivings about performing this ceremony, she might be able to talk him out of it. Did she dare take the risk?

"I assure you my father will be most grateful you helped avert a scandal. His gratitude will no doubt take the form of further charity. You might even find yourself with another colored window. Perhaps in the narthex."

"Let us both hope you are right, Geoffrey, or I might be sharply pressed to help secure an annulment. That would no doubt prove most difficult with a child on the way."

Cassie felt blood rush from her head at the mention of her unborn child, the one Geoffrey thought was merely a ruse.

"What is it, dear? Are you feeling unwell?"

Geoffrey's use of endearments and his false concern sickened her.

"You know full well I'm here by force."

He merely smiled.

"Master Geoffrey has already told me of your unwillingness to marry, Catherine, and I must say I'm of a mind with him." Reverend Dinwiddie shuffled through the *Book of Common Prayer* that sat on his lectern. "Your father never taught you your place, and now that indulgence has borne fruit, as it were. Your refusal to be sensible only proves the need for a strong hand to govern you. If you will not be ruled by common sense—as, God knows, few women are—those who know what is best must make decisions for you."

Cassie felt her temper rise. "Is it not against the decrees of the Church to marry a woman against her will?" Her throat was tight, her voice unsteady.

"If the edict were strictly followed, my child, there would be fewer brides and many more bastards. In my experience, it is not uncommon to see an unwilling bride brought in shame to the altar, only to see her return a few months later, babe in arms, contented."

"Then you … you will go ahead with this unholy farce?"

Reverend Dinwiddie looked up from his lectern, fixing her with a stern, rheumy gaze, but said nothing.

Tears spilled over onto Cassie's cheeks, her last hope shattered.

"Did I not say she was willful?" Geoffrey laughed.

Reverend Dinwiddie cleared his throat. "We have come together in the presence of Almighty God to witness the joining together of this man and this woman in holy matrimony …"

Cassie fought back sobs as Reverend Dinwiddie read the words that would consign her to a life of misery, her mind beyond thought, her heart beyond feeling. Tears poured down her cheeks, the world a shifting blur around her.

This cannot be happening!

"Catherine, will you take this man to be your lawful husband, to live together in the covenant of marriage? Will you love him, obey him, comfort and honor him, in sickness and in health, and, forsaking all others, be faithful to him as long as you both shall live?"

The reverend's voice drifted to her ears as if it came from far away. Try though she might, Cassie could not form the words she was expected to say.

Geoffrey's fingers bit painfully into her arm. "Ask her again," he demanded, his face twisted in an angry scowl.

"Yes, ask her again, good Reverend, by all means."

Cassie spun toward the sound of that familiar voice to find Alec leaning casually against the doorjamb. He was covered from head to toe with mud. In one hand he held a pistol, its barrel pointed casually at the floor.

"You!" Geoffrey snarled.

"Alec!"

How could it be? Relief surged through Cassie, leaving her weak, breathless. She would have run to him had Geoffrey not grabbed her around the waist and pulled her in front of him like a shield.

"Did you truly believe you'd get away with this, Crichton?" Alec walked slowly toward them, the pistol now raised and unwavering, his eyes as hard and cold as slate. "You must have known I would come for her as soon as I was able."

"I've had dogs looking for you day and night. You should have made good your escape when you had the chance, convict. Now you're a dead man."

Dogs? Escape? Cassie did not understand, unless ...

Geoffrey had lied!

"There will be no bloodshed in the church!" cried Reverend Dinwiddie, suddenly rediscovering his tongue.

"Let her go, Crichton, or the good reverend will find himself with quite a mess."

"You'd fire and take the risk of killing her? I think not."

Slowly Alec drew back on the hammer, training the pistol at Geoffrey's head. "My father took my education in firearms quite seriously. At this range, I can crack your skull like a melon and not get a drop of blood on her gown."

Cassie's breath froze in her throat. She felt Geoffrey's grip tighten, crushing her. Then she found herself stumbling forward as, with a shove, he released her. She caught her footing, lifted her skirts, and ran to Alec, fresh tears spilling down her cheeks as she buried her face in his chest.

"I don't blame you for wanting her, convict," she heard Geoffrey say. "She does know how to please a man in bed, doesn't she?"

She felt Alec's body grow rigid and started to tell him she was untouched, but was cut off.

"If I thought you had forced yourself on her, Crichton, you'd be dead where you stand." The deep baritone of Alec's voice rumbled in his chest, where Cassie's head rested. He looked down at her. "Are you hurt, sweet?"

"No." She looked up into his blue eyes, scarcely able to believe he was really there.

"Who are you, man?" Reverend Dinwiddie stepped forward, puffing himself up to his full size.

Alec pressed Cassie to safety behind him.

"He is a convict, one of Blakewell's servants, Reverend," Geoffrey answered. "Catherine fancies herself in love with him and even took the man to her bed."

Reverend Dinwiddie looked horrified, appalled.

Cassie lifted her chin, unashamed. "Yes, Reverend, and it is his child, not Geoffrey's, that I carry."

Reverend Dinwiddie gasped.

Geoffrey looked stunned, then disgusted, his lips curling with contempt.

But Alec's reaction so warmed Cassie's heart, she nearly forgot about the other two. His gaze dropped in awe to her belly before coming to rest tenderly on her face. "A baby?"

"Aye."

"Take the little bitch!" Geoffrey shouted. "Leave while you can."

Alec's face hardened. "Cassie, listen carefully," he said, speaking so only she could hear him. "Outside you'll find Crichton's horses unhitched and waiting for us. Ride for the island. I'll be right behind you. If aught should go amiss, seek help from Robert Carter. He's a man I think you can trust."

"But—"

"Go. Now! I don't want you to see this."

"What—"

"Go!"

Cassie lifted her skirts and ran toward the door.

"You and I have a score to settle, Crichton," she heard Alec say.

Terrified of what Alec might do, Cassie found she could go no farther. She whirled around to see him walking menacingly toward Geoffrey, the pistol tucked in his breeches.

Geoffrey took several stumbling steps backward.

Alec slammed his fist into Geoffrey's face, knocking Geoffrey backward until he collided with the wall and sank to the floor, blood pouring from his nose and onto the lace of his jabot.

"Lucky for you we're in a church. But be warned—if you ever set foot on Blakewell's land again or come anywhere near Cassie, I will kill you!"

The last four words were spoken slowly, ominously, their echo filling the little church.

Without a backward glance, Alec turned and strode toward Cassie. He took her by the hand and led her out the door. "Don't you ever do as you're told?"

"I was afraid—"

"That I would kill him? I wish I had."

Geoffrey's horses stood tethered to a tree branch, their tails swishing nervously. The animals wore no saddles, but Cassie had ridden bareback before.

"Where's the driver?" She looked toward the vacant carriage.

"Sleeping off a bump on the head." Alec took the horses' reins. Then, out of the corner of her eye, Cassie saw Geoffrey emerge from the church. He had something in his hand, something that gleamed silver in the sunlight. "Alec!"

Alec whirled about, then thrust Cassie behind him. Her father's pistol magically appeared in his hand, and he fired.

Geoffrey staggered, a pistol falling from his grasp. Clutching with both hands at the gaping hole in his throat, he collapsed on the church steps, his eyes wide, his body arching, twisting in pain.

"Cath—" he choked, reaching for Cassie with one bloody hand. He writhed for a moment. Then, with a jerk, he lay still.

Sickened, Cassie turned away to feel Alec's arms enfold her, his hand pressing her against the warmth of his chest.

"We must ride. Do you have the strength?"

Cassie nodded.

"Let me help you mount."

Cassie reached up and took a handful of the horse's red mane. She felt Alec's hands encircle her waist and lift her until she was able to swing one leg across the horse's back.

The animal shifted nervously beneath her.

"There they are! Stop them!"

Cassie turned to find Reverend Dinwiddie pointing, three men running toward them, one of them struggling clumsily to load a musket as he ran.

"Ride, Cassie! Stop for nothing!" Alec slapped her horse hard on the rump.

The horse sprang forward at a gallop. Fighting to keep from falling, Cassie gripped its flanks tightly with her thighs and held fast to its mane.

"Alec!" She tried to look over her shoulder, struggling to keep her balance.

"Ride!"

A glimpse told her he had made it safely to his horse and was riding after her. Cassie fought to turn her mount's head toward home, the ground passing in a blur beneath her.

She had not yet reached the bend in the road when the sickening crack of gunfire split the air, followed by the scream of a horse. Her heart pounding frantically in her breast, Cassie tried to jerk her mount to a stop, but it reared again, terrified, and she found herself holding on for dear life.

Then, over her shoulder, she saw him. "No!"

Alec lay in the dirt, fighting to free his leg from beneath a dying horse. Blood poured from the bullet hole in its neck. Not far behind him, the man with the musket was reloading, Reverend Dinwiddie and the two others closing in.

Without thinking, Cassie turned her horse about, but she was too late.

No sooner had Alec pulled himself free than the men fell upon him, beating him and yanking him to his feet.

"Alec!"

"Go!" he shouted. "Ride!"

The horse stamped beneath her.

"I won't go without you!"

"You must! Go!"

Through a fog she realized that the man with the musket was still reloading. Terror clutched at her heart. He was planning to shoot Alec on the spot! Then, as the man's gaze met hers, she realized with a gasp that he meant to aim for her.

"Cassie, for God's sake, ride!" For a moment Alec's gaze locked fiercely with hers. Then he turned and threw himself on the man with the musket, dragging his two captors with him.

Cassie spun the gelding about and kicked it to a gallop, tears streaming down her cheeks, Alec's name on her lips. When the musket fired again, as she feared it would, a sob rose from her throat, leaving her bereft of all but heartrending grief. Alec was dead.

Chapter Thirty-one

London

Matthew tapped impatiently on the sturdy oaken door with his cane.

"Come in, please, Lieutenant," said the bespectacled young clerk who opened it. "The magistrate will be here presently."

Matthew entered to find a garishly appointed office. Ornate Oriental carpets covered the floor, their rich claret hues struggling violently with the purple of the velvet draperies and the pink and green of the gilt French chairs. Shelves on both sides of the room held a wealth of leather-bound books, their authors and titles spelled out in gold leaf: Aristotle, Cicero, Dante, Chaucer. Matthew retrieved one volume from the shelf, and realized it had never been opened, when its stiff spine creaked in protest as he turned back its cover. Likely the entire collection was for show. As were, no doubt, the oil paintings on the wall. One featured voluptuous naked women being carried off by rugged men in Roman dress, a poor copy of *The Rape of the Daughters of Leucippus,* by Reubens.

The other, a portrait, seemed to have been painted by the same awkward hand. It tried to be a Dutch masterpiece, but wasn't. It pictured an overdressed man staring with exaggerated severity at the viewer. These were the trappings, Matthew judged, of one who was new to wealth, and Matthew was fairly sure where the money had come from. One could grow very rich running a gaol. No doubt his visit today would cost Matthew a fistful of good coin.

"Ah, Lieutenant Hastings. I see you've discovered my book collection."

Matthew turned to see the very man whose portrait hung on the wall emerging from a back room. He was portly, clad head to toe in silks, brocades, and lace. Though it was clear the man frequented a talented tailor, he had not learned which colors went with which.

"I was just admiring the paintings, Magistrate Woodhull."

The magistrate swelled with pleasure, as Matthew had expected he would.

"I've acquired an artist who can mimic any style, any masterpiece. As soon as I saw his work, I knew I simply had to patronize him." He clasped his hands above his large belly. "One can never have too much refinement in one's life."

"Well said, Magistrate. Your library is worthy of any gentleman." Matthew handed the book he held back to its owner.

"Would you like a brandy?" Woodhull beamed at Matthew's compliments.

"No, thank you. I make it a rule never to mix business and drink."

"A wise rule." Woodhull chuckled. "Though I'd have precious little to do if everyone were as prudent as yourself."

Matthew sat in one of the ornate French chairs, ignoring Woodhull's furtive glances at his wooden leg. He was used to curious looks and staring. "I've come for information about the old man who was brought in the morning after my brother-in-law's murder."

"Oh, there's little to be said about him, Lieutenant. He died of fever within days."

"I was hoping you might be able to help me uncover something that had been overlooked." Without breaking eye contact, Matthew dropped several sovereigns on Woodhull's desk.

"That was a very long time ago, Lieutenant. As much as I'd like to help an honorable gentleman such as—"

Matthew dropped several more.

"I'll send for the guard who was on watch when he came in."

In short order Matthew stood face-to-face with one of the filthiest men he'd ever seen. Dressed in clothes that might have been decent had they been washed, the man's hair—or what was left of it—was greasy and matted. His skin was scarred by pox and covered with grime, and his teeth were rotted so that his breath stank, even from a distance. Matthew was sorely tempted to ask for that brandy after all, just to mask the odor.

"It's just as I told the constable, Sir," said the guard. "The ol' codger said 'e saw two blokes kill a man an' take 'is eyes."

"Is that exactly how he explained it to you?"

The guard looked confused.

"Were those his exact words?"

"Well, Sir," began the guard, his eyes fixed on Matthew's wooden limb. "Pardon me, Sir, but doesn't it 'urt? Your leg?"

"Aye. It hurts every day." Matthew struggled to be patient. "Why don't you tell me everything the old man said from the beginning?"

When the guard was sent back to his duties nearly an hour later, Matthew found himself fighting off disappointment. He'd learned little new. Instead, he had more unanswered questions. Why had the attackers only knocked Alec out to begin with if their purpose had been murder? They'd slit the driver's throat on the spot. Why not Alec's? Why had they carried his unconscious body into an alley? They had already committed one murder in the street. What made them seek privacy to kill Alec and mutilate his corpse?

For months Matthew had had a feeling that not all was as it seemed regarding Alec's murder. First there was the strange brutality of it. Then there was Matthew's mysterious letter from the colonies that Socrates said he'd seen, which Philip had stolen and burnt. Though he had initially dismissed Socrates' conclusion about the handwriting as nothing more than the grief and love of an aging servant, Matthew hadn't been able to put the letter from his mind, nor Philip's refusal to discuss it. He was not given to gaming, but he was willing to wager that Philip was at the center of this somehow. Matthew had paid a man to trail Philip, but the spy had learned little Matthew did not already know.

"Are you sure you wouldn't like that brandy, Lieutenant?" Woodhull raised his own glass in question.

"No, thank you, Magistrate." Using his cane to steady himself, Matthew stood. "I appreciate your helpfulness."

"I must say I was surprised when I received notice that you would be coming today. Your brother-in-law made it quite clear your family wished to put this behind you, despite the letter."

"Letter?"

"Aye, the letter from the colonies. I sent you word of it in June."

"From the colonies? I heard nothing of it." Matthew felt his blood turn hot, but remained calm.

Damn Philip!

"Do you still have the letter? Do you remember what it said, who it was from?"

"It was addressed to me from a colonial sheriff, as I recall. He said there was an indentured convict nearby who claimed to be Alec Kenleigh. Strange your brother-in-law didn't tell you. I think I still have it here somewhere."

Matthew's heart gave a thud. "Then find it, man!"

C assie gazed apprehensively into the mirror, her hands too unsteady to put on the earrings Lucy had lent her. Fears flitted through her mind one after another, never resting.

Had Alec suffered these past six weeks? Had they beaten him? Had they forced him to go without food, to go without blankets in the cold? Were the judges' hearts already hardened? Was it too late?

"Let me help." Lucy took the small pearls from her trembling fingers. "With these earrings and your new gown, you'll look as fresh as a meadow in springtime."

Cassie's gaze brushed distractedly over her own reflection, noticing for the first time the new gown. It was one of the nicest she'd ever worn, cut from silk the color of the sky and trimmed with ivory lace. The seamstress had left enough cloth so the waistline could easily be let out when her condition began to show. Lucy had ordered several new gowns made for her, together with matching slippers and bonnets, and her father had paid without protest. Cassie had been so preoccupied with her grief and worry, she hadn't even thanked them.

"You've been so kind to me, Lucy."

"It's nothing you wouldn't have done for me." Lucy put the pearls on Cassie's earlobes.

Cassie smiled at Lucy's reflection, but she knew Lucy was just being generous. No daughter of King Carter would ever have found herself in this predicament to begin with. Even if she had, Cassie's father did not have the power to do what Lucy's father had done. If not for King Carter, she would likely be sitting in gaol this morning, facing trial for murder and horse theft.

She had arrived at Corotoman late that terrible afternoon, exhausted, in tears, desolate. In private, she'd confided the entire story to Master Carter and Lucy. She'd told them about her father's condition, about the lies she'd told for his sake. She'd told them of her love for Alec, how she knew in her heart he was telling the truth.

She'd told them about Geoffrey, how he'd taken over Blakewell's Neck, found her in bed with Alec, had Alec nearly flogged to death. She'd told them how Geoffrey had tried to force her to marry him, how she was certain Alec was now dead, shot while trying to save her. She'd told them of the child she carried.

She'd told them everything except the location of her father's island.

She had expected that Master Carter would call her a whore and throw her out of his house, or worse, summon the sheriff, but he hadn't. Instead he'd had the horse she'd ridden delivered to Crichton Hall with a note of condolence and several pounds in payment for her use of the animal. He'd instructed Lucy to take Cassie upstairs, help her bathe, and see to it she was properly fed and allowed to sleep undisturbed. Cassie had wept out of deepest grief that night, wept until there were no tears left, Lucy stroking her hair until she'd fallen asleep.

She'd awoken the next morning to the stunning news that Alec was alive and unhurt. The shot she'd heard had been a harmless misfire. But her relief was replaced by new fear when Master Carter told her Alec had been hauled in chains to Williamsburg to await trial for murder. Benumbed by the news, she hadn't been surprised when Sheriff Hollingsworth arrived later to arrest her as an accomplice. She'd been resigned to her fate, only to watch the sheriff ride away without her, the whole question of her role in Geoffrey's death having been settled with Master Carter over a game of whist. The next morning she, Lucy, and Master Carter had boarded a small schooner and set out for Williamsburg to await the day of Alec's trial.

That day had finally come.

"There." Lucy smoothed two wayward curls into place with her gloved hand. "You look absolutely lovely. Shall we go?"

"Aye."

The clack of horses' hooves on cobblestone announced the arrival of the carriage in the courtyard below. Cassie dreaded going out in public. Except for church each Sunday, she'd stayed indoors, away from the tittering crowds of Williamsburg. Even those Sundays had been torture. The whispers, stares and pointing fingers were hard enough to endure, but the sound of clanking chains as the gaoler led in prisoners from the public gaol had been all but unbearable. While the rest of the congregation recited words from the *Book of Common Prayer*, sneaking glances at her over the tops of their Bibles, she'd held her head high, praying silently for another miracle, for comfort and protection for Alec, who sat in fetters some twenty rows behind her.

Though they'd prayed under the same roof, Cassie hadn't been able to catch so much as a glimpse of him. Master Carter had made certain they reached the church early, long before the prisoners arrived, and they'd always sat in the front, far from the rough wooden benches in the back meant for the imprisoned. Nor had he allowed her to send Alec letters. Though Master Carter had himself been to visit Alec in gaol a few times, he'd refused to convey any messages between them. It would not be proper, he'd explained, declining to discuss Alec's plight with her.

But Cassie would see Alec today, for today a jury would decide if he would hang.

She took Lucy's arm, and they made their way downstairs to the courtyard, where footmen helped them into the carriage. Master Carter, who, much to Cassie's surprise, had hired counsel for Alec, had gone to the courthouse ahead of them.

She sank into the plush cushions of royal blue and closed her eyes, commanding herself to be strong. It would be a short journey to the courthouse, around Duke of Gloucester Street to the Capitol. Though the crowd outside the courthouse would be great—she'd heard Master Carter say the excitement of a murder trial had the inns and alehouses packed to overflowing—the townspeople had already done their best to humiliate her. She would survive this. With a lurching motion the carriage rolled forward and rounded the corner onto the street. On the sidewalk, people turned to look up at them with sneers and whispers.

Lucy pulled the shades. "It's much better this way, isn't it?" Her voice was unnaturally cheerful.

"Aye. Thank you."

Cassie hated the stares and whispers as mothers pointed her out to their daughters and warned them to protect their virtue. She hated even more the knowing smiles of men who leered openly at her and shouted obscene offers meant to disgrace her. Today the courtroom would be filled with such people, men and women who had gathered to watch the trial as if it were but a play, Cassie's and Alec's grief and suffering mere diversion.

Though the ride was short, it seemed to stretch on forever. Surely they would have passed Raleigh's Tavern and John Carter's general store by now. Soon they'd pass Unicorn's Horn Apothecary. The wooden sign that hung over its doorstep and displayed the head of a regal white unicorn had fascinated her as a little girl. Her father had taken her there to buy her candy in the years when they'd come to Williamsburg each summer. He'd lifted her high on his shoulders so she could touch the unicorn's carved horn and painted mane.

Where had those happy days gone?

The carriage soon turned to the right and slowed, and she knew they had reached the courthouse. With a sense of dread, she heard the door handle turn. Daylight streamed in, and with it the murmur of the crowd.

"It's time, love." Lucy gave Cassie's hand a reassuring squeeze. Summoning her courage, Cassie took the footman's hand and stepped from the carriage. The crowd fell silent. She felt hundreds of people watching her. Legs shaking, she forced herself to lift her chin and, looking straight ahead, climbed the stairs, clinging tightly to Lucy's arm.

"She's a pretty young thing," whispered one woman.

"What a shame," whispered another.

"Well, I say she got what she deserves."

"She can come sit on my lap," called one man. "I'll cheer her up!"

"Harlot!"

Suddenly, as if set free from a trance by that one vile word, people began to shout at her, hurling insults and obscenities. Tears burned Cassie's eyes. She wanted to flee but forced herself to take each stair slowly, deliberately. She'd done nothing of which she was ashamed.

"Don't listen to them, Cassie!" Lucy held Cassie's arm tightly. "Vultures!"

Cassie thought of Alec's feet climbing these same stairs a short time ago. Had the crowd cursed him? Had he been forced to drag heavy chains? Was he afraid?

Three more steps. Two more. One.

Lucy pushed open the polished oak doors, and they entered the darkened hallway. If Cassie had hoped to escape the crowd indoors, she was sadly disappointed. Stretching out before her was a sea of faces, their eyes turned toward her, their expressions merciless.

Her step faltered, and she felt Lucy's fingers tighten around hers. The taunting and curses began afresh, bodies pressing in so closely against her she felt angry breath against her cheeks as she passed. Could they all truly hate her so much?

She gasped as pain shot through her arm, and looked down in disbelief to find bony fingers pinching her flesh, an old woman with dirty nails glaring up at her as if she were a witch to be burned at the stake.

Lucy rapped the old woman's fingers sharply with her folded fan. "It seems, Cassie my dear, all of Williamsburg has turned out today. I'm surprised good Christian folk would take such delight in others' misfortunes."

Voices drifted into an embarrassed silence. Several heads dropped, gazes falling to the floor.

Cassie took a deep breath and allowed Lucy to lead her to the courtroom, the crowd parting in a guilty shuffling of feet to let them pass. Stopping just inside the doorway to let her eyes adjust to the darkness, Cassie followed Lucy to the seats reserved for them in front. She sat and smoothed her skirts into place, keenly aware that hundreds of eyes stared at her from the gallery above. She realized with a start that those who stood in the hallway and outdoors were the ones who hadn't come early enough to get a seat.

"Here comes Master Crichton." Lucy gave Cassie's hand a squeeze. "He's such a mean, contemptible man."

Cassie heard Master Crichton's footsteps as he walked up the aisle, felt his hateful gaze as he passed and took his seat in the section to their left. She could not bring herself to look at him, but stared straight ahead, her stomach knotted. She could not blame him for hating her. Geoffrey had been his son and heir. Because of her, Geoffrey was now dead. That was how most people saw it, and though she wanted to protest her innocence with every fiber of her being, she couldn't help feeling they were right. Every contemptible thing Geoffrey had done, he'd done because of some misguided impulse he'd called love. He'd followed society's rules. She had shunned them. Now he lay in a grave.

Her thoughts were interrupted as the door to the council's chambers was thrust open and the court crier, a short man with an enormous belly, strutted into the courtroom.

"Oh, yea! Oh, yea! Oh, yea!" The crier struck the floor three times with the base of his staff. "Silence is commanded in court on punishment of imprisonment while His Majesty's governor and council are sitting! All manner of persons that have a plaint to enter or suit to prosecute, let them come forth, and they shall be heard!"

From behind him appeared the court's bewigged magistrates, followed by members of the governor's council and finally by the attorney general and Governor Gooch himself. The governor and his men stiffly took their seats behind the high benches at the front of the room.

A hush fell over the courtroom.

"Bailiff, bring in the jury," the governor said.

The door opened again, and a dozen men, most of them members of the assembly, shuffled to their seats.

The attorney general strode forth into the center of the room, his long red robe almost brushing the wooden floor.

"That's Hugh Drysdale's eldest son, Edward," Lucy whispered.

Cassie nodded, feeling an instant dislike for the man. It was his job to make sure Alec was convicted.

"Honorable Governor, esteemed councilmen, and worthy men of the jury, I have here an indictment against one Nicholas Braden, convict and bondsman, lately of Blakewell's Neck, who calls himself Alec Kenleigh," said Master Drysdale, handing the bailiff several sheets of parchment.

The bailiff passed the documents to the bench, where Governor Gooch, a heavy frown on his face, examined them.

"Bring in the prisoner," ordered Gooch.

"Bring in the prisoner!" repeated the crier.

Chapter Thirty-two

C assie fought not to turn her head as the creak of doors and the tap of footsteps announced Alec's arrival. Unable to breathe, only dimly aware of the clamor Alec's appearance had caused among those seated in the gallery above, she stared down at her clasped hands as his footsteps drew nearer. But as he passed her, it was not his bare feet she saw but silk hose and a gentleman's polished leather shoes, brass buckles shining.

Unable to stop herself, she lifted her gaze slowly to look at him, stifling a gasp. This was not the Alec she knew. Far from the dirty, bruised prisoner she had expected, he stood, proud and tall, dressed not like an indentured servant, but the finest of English gentlemen. Breeches of the darkest blue velvet clung to his thighs, the matching waistcoat accented with gold brocade. Ivory lace was gathered at his throat and wrists. His hair, sleek and dark, was braided into a *ramillie*, held in place by a dark blue velvet ribbon. His face was clean-shaven, his expression unyielding—the face of an astonishingly handsome stranger.

His name a whisper on her lips, she met his gaze, and his blue eyes softened as they looked into hers. Then he was gone, making his way toward the stand reserved for the accused, its platform surrounded by a waist-high barrier of slatted wood.

"Silence in the courtroom!" the governor shouted over the hubbub. "This court shall not become a circus. Anyone disrupting today's hearing will find himself keeping company with rats in the public gaol."

A tense silence fell over the gallery.

"Is the accused aware of the serious charges against him?" asked Gooch.

"I am, Governor."

"If it please Your Honor, I should like to read the allegations to the court so we all might know how serious they truly are," Drysdale said.

"Proceed."

"Nicholas Braden, a convict condemned to fourteen years servitude for the crime of ravishment, stands accused again of ravishment, as well as attempting to escape his rightful master, horse theft, assault on a gentleman, and murder of that same gentleman, the recently departed Master Geoffrey Crichton the Third. What say you to these charges?"

"To all but one, I plead innocent, as I was merely defending myself. As for the charge of ravishment, I am guilty."

An excited chatter arose in the courtroom, and Cassie found herself staring openmouthed in shock. Ravishment? She had lain with him willingly!

"Father had Drysdale include that charge to protect you," Lucy whispered, as if reading her mind.

"But it's not true!" Cassie whispered back.

"Silence!" the governor shouted. "Another interruption and I shall have the sheriff arrest every third person among you."

The din dropped to a whisper.

Cassie's heart sank, and her mind raced to the obvious conclusion. This was how Master Carter had kept the sheriff at bay. Alec had agreed to a lie for her sake. Did he not realize he'd given them everything they needed to hang him?

"You do understand this court need only convict you of one charge to order you hanged?" the governor asked. "If you plead guilty, we need not hold this trial. Because you are already a convicted felon, we could hang you straightaway."

"If I may, Your Honor," said a slight young man Cassie had not noticed before. "I am Master George Ludwell, Esquire, Sir, lately retained by Master Robert Carter to represent Master Kenleigh."

"His name is Braden," Drysdale retorted. "Young Ludwell is trying to confuse us, Governor."

Looking slightly annoyed, the governor waved off Drysdale's concern and motioned for Master Ludwell to continue.

"The defendant does understand the gravity of his pleading guilty but hopes the court will concede to hear this case, as the circumstances behind the charges are most unusual. We believe that after all has been heard, the court will allow Master Kenleigh—"

"Braden!"

"—to plead benefit of clergy on the charge of ravishment."

Everyone began shouting at once—the governor, Master Drysdale, Master Ludwell, Master Crichton, and a gallery full of spectators who'd evidently forgotten the governor's threat.

Cassie stared wide-eyed at Lucy, who smiled, her face alight with excitement.

"You see, dear, there is hope." Lucy gave Cassie a little hug.

Hope. Cassie had not dared to feel hope for so long, she scarcely recognized the emotion. Was there a chance? If he was allowed to plead benefit of clergy, the court could sentence Alec only to being branded on the thumb with a cold iron. But how could they accomplish this?

"Silence!" The shout came not from the governor, but from the court crier, who strode importantly into the center of the courtroom and began beating the base of his staff against the floor. "Silence!"

The clamor slowly subsided.

"Governor, surely you cannot allow this farce to proceed!" The voice was Master Crichton's. "This man killed my son, and now he wants to weasel out of the hangman's noose with far-fetched stories! He's already seen to it that his whore won't hang with him—"

Cassie felt heat rush into her face.

"Master Crichton, contain yourself!" Governor Gooch demanded. The governor eyed the entire courtroom in silence before speaking again. "In the interests of fairness and justice, I will allow this trial to continue, but I must warn you, Ludwell, I will not allow you to make a mockery of the law by presenting evidence that has no basis in fact."

"Understood, Your Honor. Thank you, Sir," Ludwell said.

By noon, any hope Cassie had felt had faded away completely, as witness after witness described the events leading to Geoffrey's death. With each word, Cassie felt the jury's hearts grow harder toward the man she loved. Nicholas Braden, the convict who tried to escape a fourteen-year sentence. Nicholas Braden, the convict who, failing to gain his freedom, seduced his master's daughter and bent her to his will. Nicholas Braden, the convict who ruined a fallen woman's only chance at respectability by breaking up the marriage sacrament and killing the noble-hearted gentleman who'd offered to marry her.

Sheriff Hollingsworth told the court how he'd almost been convinced Alec was telling the truth—until Philip's letter had come from London, proving him a liar. He read the letter to the court, every damning word. Then he read aloud from Nicholas Braden's indenture papers, which claimed Nicholas Braden was a "seducer and defiler of women."

Reverend Dinwiddie, clutching a Bible, testified that Geoffrey had tried to save Cassie from herself, going so far as to offer her child a name it didn't deserve. Exaggerating all the while, he told the court how Alec had disrupted the marriage ceremony and assaulted Geoffrey in the church. Then he told how Alec had shot and killed Geoffrey when Geoffrey, armed with the reverend's pistol, tried to stop Alec from running away with the disgraced bride.

Their testimony hadn't seemed to bother Alec. Cassie had glanced furtively in his direction several times, to find him looking every bit the gentleman in control of his surroundings, his stance and brow relaxed as if he had no worries at all. Cassie did not share his confidence.

The prosecutor's case was simple: Nicholas Braden, a convict, had defiled his master's daughter and was in the process of escaping when he'd killed the man who tried to stop him. All evidence pointed to that conclusion. What could Alec and the inexperienced George Ludwell say to counter such ruinous testimony?

"It is Master Ludwell's turn now," Lucy whispered as Master Drysdale moved to rest his case.

Master Ludwell rose and moved to the center of the room. "I call upon Alec Kenleigh to testify."

"I must protest this ruse!" cried Drysdale. "The man's name is Nicholas Braden, and he should be referred to as such. Calling a rat 'Your Highness' and dressing it in ermine and velvet does not make it a prince."

Guffaws and chuckles filled the courtroom.

The governor nodded, smiling at the quip. "Use the name that the court recognizes, young man," he said with an impatient flick of the wrist.

"Very well, Your Honor, but the issue of this man's identity is central to his defense."

Unlike the others, who'd sat in the witness stand to testify, Alec was forced to remain on his feet in the prisoner's box. "Sir, could you tell the jury your full name?"

"Alec Madison Kenleigh the Third."

Cassie listened, fascinated, as Alec described for Master Ludwell details of his life she'd not heard before. It was disturbing to realize that, in a very real sense, Alec was a stranger to her. He'd been educated at

Eton College as a boy, then gone on to study at Oxford, where he'd excelled in classical languages and mathematics. His father had groomed him from childhood to take over Kenleigh Shipyards, the family shipbuilding business, and had left him a vast estate, which he managed with the help of his brother-in-law, Lt. Matthew Hasting.

"Yes, yes," interrupted Master Drysdale, "this is all very interesting, but have you any proof? While we'd all love to go on listening to this narration, there is this trifling matter of a murder trial to be settled. Hadn't you best present your evidence?"

Cassie was horrified to see members of the jury chuckle.

"Quite right. Quite right," Governor Gooch agreed. "Get on with your argument."

"Very well. Master Kenleigh, can you tell the court how you came to be in this predicament?"

Cassie would later recall that the courtroom was completely silent as Alec, his rich baritone voice filling the chamber, told how he'd been set upon and beaten in the dark, how he'd regained consciousness, confused and disoriented on a ship, how he'd been beaten for trying to free himself and finally awakened to find himself in this strange land, a prisoner.

"How did Miss Blakewell react when you told her this story?"

"She didn't believe me. As I recall, she laughed," Alec said with a smile so charming, Cassie found herself smiling, too. "Still, she summoned the sheriff and allowed me to post a letter to England."

"Are you familiar with the reply that was received from Philip Kenleigh?"

"Aye."

"Can you explain that letter?"

"I've come to believe Philip was behind my abduction." Alec then told of the fight he'd had with his brother that morning long ago and of Philip's threat.

"So Philip wanted you out of the way so he could inherit the estate and be free from restrictions you had imposed. Is that correct?"

"It is the only way to make sense of what happened."

Though she could not see his eyes, Cassie heard sadness in his voice. How horrid it must be to find one's own brother capable of such hate. She listened to Alec tell the part of the tale she knew—how he'd promised not to attempt escape, how he'd worked beside field hands and indentured servants and how he'd taken over care of the horses—and she began to feel hopeful. Surely the jurors would see he was telling the truth. Surely they could tell from his measured speech and manner that he was no miscreant.

"So you kept your word, even passing up a chance to escape," Master Ludwell said, after Alec recounted his riding to Corotoman for quinquina. "Please tell the court what events led to Geoffrey Crichton's death."

But this part of the story was new. Cassie listened in shocked disbelief as Alec described how he had manipulated and seduced her, taking advantage of her father's absence to steal her innocence.

"She was untouched, a virgin unprepared to face male wiles. Unprotected, she stood no chance against a man of my experience," Alec said. "I took advantage of her vulnerability and naiveté to ease my loneliness, and though I regret my actions, I'm fully prepared to take responsibility for Miss Blakewell once the matter of my identity is resolved."

Something twisted in Cassie's heart. The rational part of her mind told her he was only saying these things to protect her. He didn't truly mean them. He hadn't taken advantage of her. He didn't really regret the time he'd spent with her. He felt more than a sense of responsibility for her.

Confused, her heart a jumble of emotion, Cassie listened to Alec recount how Geoffrey had found them in bed together, flogged him, and dragged Cassie against her will to Crichton Hall, and how Alec had waited until he was strong enough to stop a marriage he knew she didn't want.

"I wouldn't see her punished for my lack of scruples," he said. "When Geoffrey Crichton aimed a pistol at me, I fired to protect myself."

"This has all been very fascinating," Master Drysdale said as he strode into the center of the room to cross-examine Alec. "Tell me, Braden, how long did it take you to manufacture this elaborate story?"

"I did not manufacture it. It is the truth."

"Did Miss Blakewell help you with the details? She's quite a liar herself, having kept us all in the dark about her father's condition for so long. We still haven't heard the whole truth on that subject, have we?"

Cassie lifted her chin in defiance, and saw Alec's expression harden.

"Leave Miss Blakewell out of this." The menace in his voice was real.

Master Drysdale turned toward the bench, the tails of his red robe swirling. "I have no questions for the prisoner, Governor. One cannot challenge the veracity of fiction."

The gallery erupted with laughter, and Cassie realized in despair that no one believed Alec. They, like Master Drysdale, were convinced Alec was simply telling stories. Members of the jury were smiling.

"They don't believe him!" she whispered in alarm to Lucy.

"Oh, Cassie, you poor dear!"

The next hour passed in a blur. Master Ludwell called his remaining witness, Murphy, the indentured servant who had traveled to Blakewell's Neck so long ago. Murphy repeated the story he'd told Cassie and the sheriff the previous summer about believing Cole Braden dead, only to find he'd come alive the next morning. But Master Drysdale confused the poor old man and made him look a fool.

"Explain to the court why we should take a convicted felon at his word?" he'd asked at long last.

"I'm tellin' the truth, I am!" Murphy insisted as the gallery howled with laughter.

"You may step down now," Master Drysdale said with a dismissive flick of the wrist.

"I'm sorry, sir. I tried," Murphy said, looking up at Alec and shrugging his shoulders apologetically before being led away.

"Do you have any more witnesses, Master Ludwell, perhaps someone who isn't a felon?" the governor asked, chuckling at his own wit.

"No, Your Honor. I am ready to address the jury."

"Let me testify!"

A hushed silence fell over the courtroom, and Cassie felt all eyes upon her where she stood. "Please, Your Honor, I must speak!"

"Cassie, no!" shouted Alec "You mustn't—"

"I say let her speak," said Master Drysdale, his voice unctuous. "If Miss Blakewell can shed light on this situation, she should be heard."

"Master Ludwell?" The governor eyed the young counselor, who was exchanging furious whispers with Alec.

"I agree with our esteemed attorney general," Master Ludwell said, ignoring the anger in Alec's gaze. "Let Miss Blakewell testify."

Cassie's legs trembled. Slowly, unsteadily, she walked to the bench and took her place in the witness box. Gazing out at the courtroom, she was astonished to see so many unforgiving faces. She glanced in Alec's direction, saw the hard lines of fury on his face and looked away.

"Place your hand on the Bible," the court crier instructed. "Miss Blakewell, do you swear to tell the truth, the whole truth, and nothing but the truth, so help you God?"

"I do."

"Miss Blakewell," Master Ludwell began, "why do you wish to testify today?"

"I want everyone to hear what kind of man Alec Kenleigh truly is." Cassie was surprised to hear strength in her voice. She was surprised she could speak at all. "You all think he's lying, but I know he's telling the truth."

Cassie couldn't help looking at Alec. Though she could tell he was angry with her, she saw nothing but concern in his eyes.

"Go ahead, Miss Blakewell. We're listening."

"When he first regained consciousness, Mr. Kenleigh demanded to know where he was. When I told him he was in Lancaster County, Virginia, he looked like a man who'd gotten the shock of his life. He fainted dead away. I thought it strange at the time, but then he'd been so feverish.

"When he regained his strength, he told me the same story he told all of you here today. I didn't believe him either, but I let him write a letter in exchange for his promise not to attempt escape. It seemed the right thing to do."

"And did Master Kenleigh keep his word?" Master Ludwell's sympathetic eyes bolstered Cassie's confidence.

"Aye, he did. He had many chances to escape. He'd told me he bred racehorses in England, so I put him in charge of my father's stables. It was a test—to see if he truly understood how to work with horses. Even though he exercised the horses each day, riding alone for hours at a time, he always came back."

"You didn't keep him in chains or under guard? Why not?"

"My father does not believe in chaining people as if they were animals, Master Ludwell. Neither do I. But I did have one of the slaves guard Mr. Kenleigh until I came to trust him."

"Why did you decide to trust him?"

"It was obvious after a time that he was a man of honor. He worked as hard as any man I've ever known, harder than most. The other bondsmen and slaves looked to him for guidance. I found myself relying on his good judgment. Even the children adored him."

"I see," said Master Ludwell.

"But there's more. He caught my little brother when he fell into our well and saved his life. Once while riding in the marsh, I hit my head on a branch and fell unconscious into the water. He could have left me to drown. He could have escaped. He didn't. He saved my life. And when we ran out of quinquina and so many were still sick, he rode without my knowledge to Corotoman, risking his own life to trade with Master Carter for more powder. When our bondswoman Rebecca needed a man's strength to help in the birth of her baby, he did what was asked without protest. Besides, why would he continue to protest his innocence if it weren't true?"

"I have seen guilty men insist on their innocence all the way to the gallows, Miss Blakewell," the governor muttered.

"Then perhaps you have seen innocent men hanged, Your Honor."

Repressed laughter snaked through the crowd.

"And all of this convinced you he was telling the truth?"

Cassie looked up at the faces in the gallery. The men's faces were still hard as they leered at her. But the women… The women were beginning to understand. Cassie could see it in on their faces, in their eyes, which had softened and now looked at her not with scorn, but with compassion.

"Aye, and besides … " Cassie took a deep breath and looked over at Alec, her gaze locking with his. "I could not have given myself to a man who would willingly harm another."

Alec looked into the green of Cassie's eyes, the explosive din of the courtroom as quiet as the whisper of grass to his ears. He wondered if he'd ever had as much faith in anyone as she'd just shown in him. Dear God, how he loved her. She had put herself in mortal danger because she thought somehow her feelings for him could convince the jury. But the jury was already convinced. They believed him guilty and would see him hanged.

Oh, Cassie, what have you done?

"Silence! Silence, I say!" the governor thundered.

Master Drysdale approached the witness box. Alec could tell by his predatory expression that he thought to amuse himself with Cassie. Alec felt heat build in his chest, felt his body tense.

"Miss Blakewell, we are all quite moved by your testimony. Aren't we?" Master Drysdale turned to the gallery and arched his eyebrows, drawing laughter from the men. "I know that I'm touched. I'm not sure a woman's desire has ever been used as a defense before. 'Don't hang him, Your Honor. I know he's innocent because I've lain with him.'" Master Drysdale's imitation of a woman's voice drew even more laughter.

Alec saw anger on Cassie's face and smiled. He'd seen that look before.

"I had no idea you were wont to imitate women, Master Drysdale. Do you also at times wear women's clothing?"

The gallery erupted in jocular laughter, and Alec found himself chuckling. Only Drysdale and the magistrates were not amused.

"Miss Blakewell, in truth, you have offered no proof Nicholas Braden is anyone other than Nicholas Braden."

"On the contrary, Master Drysdale, I consider it proof that he did not attempt to escape, although he had any number of chances to do so."

"Ah, yes. There is the matter of Cole Braden's noble behavior. You say he was a man of honor, yet he has admitted to stealing your virtue. Did it occur to you, Miss Blakewell, that this upstanding behavior might have been an act?"

"No, Sir, it did not."

"Did you not realize everything Cole Braden did was a ruse to win your trust—and your maidenhead?"

Alec saw pink creep into Cassie's cheeks and felt his anger begin to build again.

"No, Sir—"

"Did it not occur to you that all of his kisses and words of passion were nothing more than a carefully planned tactic to help him win his freedom?"

"No!"

"He used you, Miss Blakewell. You, a young woman with no male protection. He used you, enjoying himself all the while—"

"No!" Cassie sprang to her feet, then swayed.

Alec saw the color drain from her face. Shoving aside the guards, he leaped over the barrier and caught her as she sank to the floor in a faint.

"Cassie!"

Her face was pale, her body limp.

"Damn you, Drysdale! If you have harmed her or the babe ... "
Alec glared at the man, who held a hand to his mouth in surprise. "Is
there a physician or midwife in the house?"

"I am a doctor," an elderly man called from the back of the room.

Robert Carter stood, dabbing a handkerchief to his graying temple.
"Your Honor, perhaps a recess is in order."

Chapter Thirty-three

"Cassie, can you hear me?"

It was Alec's voice. He sounded worried. There was no reason to worry. She was just sleeping. She couldn't remember the last time she'd felt so warm or so happy. Alec was with her, holding her. If only she could stay asleep forever.

"Perhaps some smelling salts … "

"Stay away from her, Drysdale. You've done quite enough."

Drysdale. He was the attorney general. He wanted Alec to hang.

Dear Lord, the trial!

What had happened?

Cassie struggled to awaken. Her eyelids felt so heavy.

"I think she's coming to." It was Lucy.

"Cassie, can you hear me?"

"Alec? What … ?" She opened her eyes to find several faces looming above her—Master Carter, Lucy, Master Ludwell, the governor, Master Drysdale, and Alec.

Dear, sweet Alec.

"Shh! Easy, love. You mustn't sit up just yet. Rest."

"What happened? Are you free?"

"No, love." Alec gave her a sad smile. "You fainted. The doctor thinks you stood up too fast and were too upset. You need to rest. Are you in pain?"

"N-no." She struggled to remember. She'd been on the stand. She'd testified that she believed him, and … It all came back to her. Tears began to prick her eyes. "Oh, Alec. They won't listen."

"Shh, my sweet. You were very brave. I've known men who wouldn't have had the courage to do what you did."

Alec turned to the governor. "Do you think perhaps you could leave us alone for a moment?"

"Absolutely not!"

"Of course."

Master Drysdale and Master Carter spoke at the same time, exchanging heated glances.

"It's highly irregular, but … " said Governor Gooch. "There's no way for you to escape from this room as long as guards are posted outside the door."

She heard the scuffle of feet, then looked into Alec's eyes.

"You did a very risky thing, Cassie." His blue eyes were gentle. His fingertips stroked her cheek. "You put yourself and our baby in danger."

"But I had to save you."

"I'm not sure anyone can do that now."

"Wh … what do you mean?" Her pulse began to race.

"Listen, Cassie. You must hear me. When we go back into that courtroom, the jury is likely to find me guilty."

She shook her head frantically as the sickening truth beat down on her.

"Aye, my love, and you must face it. This may be our last time together."

"No!" The single word was a wail. How could she face life without him? How could she simply sit by and allow him to be executed like a common criminal? How could she let him go? Tears poured down her cheeks.

He pulled her into his arms and held her close. "I am so sorry to leave you this way. Oh, Cassie, will you ever find it in your heart to forgive me? I knew if I let myself love you, I would bring you nothing but pain. Still, I couldn't stop myself."

Her tears soaked the blue velvet of his waistcoat, her face against his chest, his scent surrounding her like a blanket.

"Hear me, love, while there's still time. Robert Carter has agreed to act as your guardian and to oversee the care of Blakewell's Neck. He has already sent a messenger with a letter and a copy of my new will to my brother-in-law at his estate outside London—"

"No, Alec, please!"

"Cassie, listen! Matthew will be able to prove I was telling the truth. You and the babe will want for nothing. I promise you that. Jamie shall go to the finest English schools, and my sister Elizabeth will love you all as her own. You will never be alone."

Cassie felt as if her heart were shattering into pieces. It couldn't end like this. "You must escape! Run! When the guards open the door, overpower them and run!"

"And give them an excuse to shoot me in the back?" He smiled and gently wiped the tears from her cheek. "I suppose that would be preferable to being hanged. No, love. It's too late for that."

Someone knocked on the door.

"One minute!" called the guard.

"No! Alec, you can't let them do this!" She wrapped her arms around him, pressing herself against his warmth.

"Be strong, love. Trust me."

Cassie felt his lips on her forehead and cheeks.

Taking one of his hands, she placed it on the small, hard curve of her belly. "Wh-what should I name the baby?" she asked, barely able to speak the words.

The look of anguish and regret on his face was like a dagger to her heart. "If it's a boy, I'd be flattered if you'd consider naming him after me."

"And if it's a girl?"

"Oh, God, Cassie!" He pulled her against him and pressed his lips into her hair. "Sarah Elizabeth," he whispered, his voice tight. "After my mother and sister."

"Time's up."

Cassie choked back a sob.

"Come now, Cassie. Where is the strong woman who stood up to an entire colony?" He took a handkerchief from the pocket of his waistcoat and dabbed the tears from her face. He turned her hand over and placed the handkerchief in her palm.

The door was thrown open. Guards marched in, seized Alec, and pulled him from her.

"Alec!" Cassie reached for him, then sank to her knees on the floor.

"I love you, Catherine Blakewell," he called as guards pulled him out the door. "If there is any justice in God's universe, you and I will be together again. You must believe that! Stay with her, Miss Carter. Keep her out of the courtroom."

"Oh, Cassie, darling."

Cassie felt Lucy's arms enfold her, and heard the door shut over the sound of her own sobs.

*S*omething was wrong.

Cassie stopped knitting and listened.

"What is it, love?" Lucy looked up from her needlework.

And then Cassie knew. The hammering had stopped. "They're finished."

Lucy's eyes grew wide. "I'm so sorry!"

She laid aside her stitching and leaned over to put a comforting arm around Cassie's shoulders.

All day the pounding of hammers had echoed through the streets of Williamsburg as carpenters worked to build the gallows that would carry out Alec's death sentence. Now all was still. While Cassie had found the hammering unbearable, the silence was even worse.

Tomorrow morning, Alec would die.

Cassie squeezed her eyes shut against the threat of tears. Was she foolish to still hope for a miracle?

"How I wish Father would finish his business so we could go home!" Lucy rose and walked to the window in a swish of silk. "It cannot be good for either you or the baby to live under such a dark cloud. I know you don't agree with me, Cassie, but it would be better for you to be away from all of this."

Cassie knew her dear friend was trying to shield her, but there was nowhere she could hide. Last night she'd lain awake in her bed, clutching the handkerchief Alec had given her, inhaling his scent, too full of grief and heartbreak even to cry. All morning she'd sat alone in her room, looking out the window into the gray November sky, aching and empty, unable to understand why her body was still alive when she was dead inside.

"I have to stay, Lucy. I have to stay as close to him as I can, until … " She couldn't bring herself to say it. "I owe it to him to be here. Leaving now would be like giving him up for dead. You'd feel the same if it were William."

Lucy blanched, her eyes growing wide for a moment. "Oh, Cassie, I'm so sorry! I hadn't thought ... that is to say ... Of course you want to be near him."

Cassie forced a smile at her friend's stumbling apology and returned to her knitting, her eyes focusing on the tiny red sweater that was taking shape. Knitting was supposed to provide her with a practical way to keep dark thoughts away, or so Lucy said, but Cassie's mind drifted. No doubt Alec, too, could hear that the hammers had stopped. Did he regret loving her? Did he feel forsaken? Would he be able to sleep tonight, knowing what awaited him in the morning? Was he afraid?

When the time came, would he suffer?

Cassie had heard stories about hangings, stories she'd tried in vain to block from her mind since the jury had delivered its verdict of guilty. It was said that most died quickly, their necks snapping like twigs, life fading abruptly into darkness. But she knew that others lingered, writhing and twisting in agony at the end of the rope while they slowly suffocated to the jeering of the crowd.

Try as she might to avoid it, she pictured Alec, dressed in plain linsey-woolsey, climbing the steps to the gallows, his hands bound behind him. Cold in the morning air, head held high, he wouldn't struggle as they slipped the hood over his face, the noose around his neck. Then the hangman would pull the lever and ...

She hadn't told him she loved him.

She'd been so upset at the trial. She'd missed her last chance. She stopped knitting, dropping the sweater into her lap. "Oh, I can't bear this!"

That was when she felt it.

"Ooh!" Her hands dropped to her belly.

"What is it?" asked Lucy, rushing to her side.

"The baby. It ... moved."

"The baby? You felt it?" Lucy's eyes were wide.

"Aye and—ooh, there!"

Cassie guided Lucy's hand onto the small, hard lump of her belly.

"Do you feel that?"

"Nay."

Cassie felt a smile spread over her face.

"Tell me what it feels like." Lucy was smiling, too.

Cassie searched for the right words. It was all so strange and new. "It's like ... like the flutter of butterfly wings."

"Butterfly wings." Lucy laughed.

"Aye, butterfly wings." Cassie laughed, too.

"You see, Cassie. Alec's child quickens within you. He'll always be with you."

"Aye."

A baby. Alec's baby. Warmth crept over Cassie, leaving her silent. She'd known she was with child, but it had all seemed distant, unreal. Now she felt his baby moving inside her. She wished she could tell him, share this moment with him. But it was only one of a thousand he would never know, unless ...

Oh, Alec.

She must do *something*. Surely there was some way to free him. Despair began to wash over her once again. "I think I shall go up to my room and rest now."

Lucy smiled indulgently. Cassie knew she wasn't very good company these days, and Lucy had been more than forgiving.

"Shall I have your dinner sent up?"

"Yes, thank you."

Cassie paused in the doorway. "Lucy, I hope someday I shall be as good a friend to you as you have been to me."

*C*assie tiptoed through the darkened hallway toward the stairs, every creak of the wooden floor seeming to shatter the silence of the sleeping house. Her heart in her throat, she could barely admit to herself what she was about to do. Stepping gingerly, she moved quickly down the stairs, then stopped, her heart pounding deafeningly. The light in Master Carter's study was still lit. She'd thought him in bed hours ago. What could he be doing at this hour? It was well past three o'clock.

She shrank into the shadows, not daring to breathe. Seconds became minutes, and the minutes stretched on for what felt like hours. Still, there came no sound from within. Perhaps he'd fallen asleep at his desk and wouldn't notice her as she slipped by. Or maybe he was reading and would hear her if she so much as moved. Did she dare risk it?

Swallowing her fears, her pulse racing, she took first one step, then two, moving forward ever so slowly. Almost even with the study door now, she peered gingerly within to find the room empty, the candelabra still lit. Heaving a deep sigh of relief, she moved silently to the gun case.

She peered inside and felt her heart sink. The pistol she'd hoped to borrow, so central to her plan, was missing, leaving only heavy muskets. She'd not be able to sneak one of those into the gaol. They were far too long and awkward to hide under her skirts.

She hesitated, her entire plan in ruins. Without the pistol, how would she be able to force the gaoler to give her the keys? How would Alec protect himself once he'd escaped? Dear Lord, what should she do now? Go back upstairs and forget the entire thing? She couldn't do that. If she did, Alec would die. Yet if she tried and failed, he would die anyway, and she would be sent to join him once the baby was born— hanged by the neck until dead. Racked with indecision, she wavered. Then, her hand trembling, she took hold of a musket and pulled it from the rack. Could she pretend she knew how to use it long enough to win Alec's freedom? She lifted it to her shoulder a few times, struggling to balance it, and looked through the sights, as she had seen her father do. The result wasn't exactly graceful, but it would have to do.

Then she spied the hunting knife. Taking it by its polished handle, she lifted it, testing its weight in her hand. A knife she could carry, but could she actually use it? Was she willing to spill a man's blood with it? Uncertain, she faltered, put it back, then took it out again. As long as the gaoler *thought* she meant to spill his blood, it wouldn't matter, she decided, tucking it inside her cloak. Hiding several bundles of powder and shot in her bodice, she silently shut the case and tiptoed toward the back door, feeling very much like the thief she had become.

Strangely, the door was not locked, but Cassie gave that oddity only a passing thought as she slipped outside, grateful that the cloak was heavy enough to shelter her from most of the winter chill. Closing the door behind her, she silently bade Lucy and Master Carter farewell.

You have been so kind to me. Forgive me.

Outside, she breathed easier, her breath a mist in the cold night air. No light shone from above, heavy clouds blocking both moon and stars, seeming to muffle even sound. She moved quickly and silently over the cobblestones toward the gate. She couldn't risk opening the gate itself. It was so large and creaky it would surely give her away. But there was a little door in the gate. She'd seen Master Carter make use of it when he took his after-dinner stroll. Its hinges were no doubt well oiled and would not alert anyone to her plans. Balancing the musket awkwardly under one arm, she turned the handle. Holding her breath, she slowly pulled the door open, gazing into the silent darkness of the street beyond.

Nothing moved. Not a single light shone in the windows on the street. She took a few timid steps, then turned and shut the door behind her. It would take only a few minutes to reach Nicholson Street and the gaol if she ran into no trouble along the way. Clinging to the shadows, she started down the street.

Strong arms shot out of nowhere and held her tight, and a hand clamped over her mouth, silencing her screams.

Chapter Thirty-four

"Takin' a stroll, Miss Cassie?"

Though she could not see his face, Cassie knew the voice.

"Zach?" she whispered in surprise when he let her speak.

"Aye, who else?"

She saw his teeth flash white in the darkness as he smiled.

"I'm so glad to see you!" She gave the sawyer an impulsive hug.

"What's this jabbin' me in the side? Do ye mean to gut me in the street?" Zach searched her, then removed the hunting knife from her waist.

"You're lucky I didn't."

"A hunting knife and a musket, Miss Cassie? Don't tell me ye're off to one of those fancy parties the Carters are so fond of."

Cassie fell silent and sank deeper into the shadows, her breath catching in her throat as footsteps approached from the darkness.

"We're over here," Zach called softly.

Cassie heard a low chuckle and saw a man's form emerge from the darkness across the street. It was Luke.

Then it hit her.

"What are you two doing here?"

"We're keepin' an eye on you." Luke pinned her with a stern gaze.

"What?"

"Aye. Master Carter knew ye'd try something like this sooner or later, so he picked yer father's most trusty men to guard ye." Zach grinned. "That's us, of course."

"How long have you been here lurking about in the streets like criminals?"

"Long enough to know ye shouldn't be out here alone at night. It's not safe," Zach said.

"Then you'll help me? I'm going to the gaol—"

"You're not goin' anywhere, Miss Cassie—except back to bed. Come along."

"But what about Alec?"

"He's no longer your concern," Zach said.

"No longer my—How can you say that?"

Zach reached for the musket.

Cassie made her move. Thrusting the weapon against the men and shoving them both as hard as she could, she darted down the street. But she hadn't gone two steps when strong arms again imprisoned her. She struggled, but couldn't break free from Zach's iron grip.

"Please don't fight me, Miss Cassie," Zach whispered. "You don't have the strength to get away, but you might hurt yerself or yer babe in tryin'."

Cassie sagged against him in defeat. This had been Alec's last chance, her last hope, and it had been destroyed by friends. Zach lifted her chin and forced her to look into his eyes. "Trust us."

Then he swung her rather unceremoniously into his arms and began walking back toward the gate, Luke leading the way, carrying the musket.

It was then that Cassie noticed that both men reeked of whiskey.

Strange. They didn't seem drunk.

They had just shut the small gate door behind them when church bells began to peal, shattering the quiet of the night. "Hurry!" Zach ran toward the back door.

Cassie started to tell Luke the back door was unlocked, but by the time she'd spoken the first word, he'd already shattered the glass with the butt of the musket.

What was happening?

She had no time to ponder it now, as Zach was running through the darkened house, carrying her like a sack of potatoes. Stopping at the foot of the stairs, he deposited her squarely on the floor. Cassie heard footsteps upstairs as the household sprang to life.

"How are we goin' to explain this?" He motioned toward her attire from her heavy boots to her gown to the winter cloak. "Do ye have something on beneath all of this?"

Cassie nodded. "Zach, what's going on?"

"It's best that ye don't ask. Just play along." He began to remove her clothing.

For a moment Cassie was too stunned to say or do anything, but when she realized his aim, she began to undress, bundles of powder and shot tumbling from the bodice of her gown onto the floor, until she stood in nothing but her shift.

"I've heard some women pad their bosoms. Here's proof." Zach grinned, grabbed the powder and shot off the floor, and threw it to Luke.

"What should I do with these?" Cassie asked in a panic, her arms full of clothing. The footsteps were growing nearer.

"Give them to me." Zach took her clothing and stuffed it into a nearby closet. "Muss your hair. Ye've been asleep, remember?" Not sure why she was doing all this, Cassie did as he asked, pulling out her pins and shaking her head, while he stepped into Master Carter's study, tipping over the chairs and scattering papers. Behind them came the sound of more shattering glass, and Cassie whirled to see Luke smash in the front of the gun case, spilling its contents on the floor.

The footsteps from upstairs seemed to be upon them.

"There's only one thing left." Zach came to stand before Luke. Luke smiled and chuckled—and slammed his fist into Zach's face.

Cassie stood speechless.

"God's balls!" Zach staggered, felt his jaw, and smiled. "Ye pack a fair wallop. But now it's my turn."

Then he drove his closed fist into Luke's jaw, nearly knocking the huge man onto his back.

The two then stood face-to-face.

"Do you think that's good enough?" Zach asked.

"It will have to be."

They vanished.

"Cassie! What in heaven is going on?"

Cassie whirled about.

It was Lucy. She stood at the top of the stairs in her nightshift, her eyes wide with fear.

" I…I don't know," Cassie stammered. It was the truth.

"Father?" Lucy called, hurrying down the stairs toward the light of the study. All at once her eyes took in the disorderly state of her father's study and the shattered glass of the gun case, and she screamed.

"Father!"

Cassie rushed to her side.

"Oh, Cassie, where is he? What has happened?"

"I wish I knew." What was going on?

Servants and slaves huddled nearby, their sleepy eyes wide with fear and uncertainty.

Guilt gnawed at Cassie. She very much doubted that these good people were in danger, but she dared not say a word for fear of betraying whatever mysterious plot was afoot.

Suddenly Zach staggered back through the doorway, his eye blackened, his lip bleeding, his clothes torn and reeking of whiskey. "He took 'im!"

"Who?" asked Lucy and Cassie together.

"The convict. He took yer father."

Cassie and Lucy looked at each other in stunned surprise. Cassie felt as if her heart would soar free from her breast. They'd broken him out! She didn't understand how they'd accomplished it or what had been involved, but she knew that Alec was free.

Run, my love, she prayed silently. *Godspeed.*

Lucy looked at Cassie as if expecting some kind of explanation. About to speak, Lucy was interrupted by Bess, the old cook, who had come from the kitchen and was now wielding a skillet in Zach's direction.

"I don't know who you are or what you're doin' here, but you'll not be causin' no mischief, or I'll have at you!"

Cassie choked back a laugh at the absurdity of the sight before her. There stood Zach, pretending to be drunk, his thick arm raised in surrender as he backed away from an old woman with a frying pan.

"Don't worry, Bess. We know this man," Lucy said. "He works for Father."

"Aye, that I do, but sure and I let him down this time. Me and Luke, we were—"

"Drinking?" Lucy asked hotly.

"Aye. And the convict just came out of nowhere. He knocked me down and, well, Luke is ... he's beat up," stammered the sawyer. "The bastard stole two horses! Pardon my speech, ladies."

For a moment, there was silence. Then Lucy stood, transformed from frightened daughter to mistress of the household.

"Bess, please aid these injured men and then make tea. Stella, see to it the fires in the kitchen and sitting room are lit and kept burning, and bring us our robes. It is a cold night." She turned to face Zach. "If there are any men among you who are not in their cups, see to it that Sheriff Connelly is sent for at once and my brothers and sisters are notified. Miss Blakewell and I will be in the sitting room should word of my father arrive."

Slaves and servants scurried into action, carrying out their mistress's commands, as Lucy and Cassie walked hurriedly hand in hand into the sitting room. As soon as the door was closed behind them, they began to talk at once. When neither could understand the other, they both stopped and started over, one at a time.

"Alec would never hurt your father, Lucy. You needn't fear for him on that account, I promise."

"I know that, silly. Do you think Alec escaped on his own, or did Father help him?"

"I think your father helped him. In fact, I'm certain."

"Do tell!"

Cassie hesitated. Telling Lucy the truth would mean confessing the way she had crept from the house as a thief. "Oh, Lucy, please forgive me! I never wanted to betray you."

Cassie poured out the entire story, telling how she'd stolen the musket and the hunting knife and planned either to threaten the gaoler or bribe him with her body if necessary to help Alec escape.

Lucy smiled. "If the musket and knife had saved Alec's life, I'd not have missed them. Besides, we knew you were going to try something like that. But your plan would never have worked, you know."

"How can you be sure?"

"I once overheard Father say the gaoler prefers men!" Lucy whispered, her face alight with mirth.

Cassie gasped in shock, and the two burst into giggles, which had grown into tearful laughter by the time Cassie reached the part of the story where Zach and Luke struck each other.

A young girl entered carrying their dressing robes, followed by a slave carrying tea, and Lucy lowered her head, choking back laughter in what truly sounded like sobs and wiping the tears from her face.

Cassie put her arm around Lucy's shoulders, pretending to comfort her. "There, there, Lucy. You poor thing! Your father will return safe and sound. You'll see."

Of that Cassie was sure. But what of Alec? He'd be shot on sight. The life of a condemned man was not worth the cost of the chains that bound him.

Ride swiftly, my sweet.

The servants left the room. Lucy's gaze met hers, all laughter gone.

"He'll make it. He must."

"Oh, Lucy, pray for him."

Lucy took Cassie's hand, and they sat together in silence. They hadn't sat for long when the sheriff arrived to investigate the kidnapping. It took him nearly an hour to piece together that "Nicholas Braden" had broken into the house and kidnapped Master Carter from his study to guarantee his safe conduct should the tracking party catch up to him.

"He can't have gotten far, of that we're certain. It was silly of him to waste time by coming here. We've got men searching every street and alley, Miss Carter. We'll catch him." Then Sheriff Connelly's gaze fell upon Cassie and hardened. "And when we do, we'll string him from the nearest tree."

"Sheriff Connelly, please keep such talk to yourself." Lucy glared up at him. "We're both far too upset by tonight's unhappy events as it is."

"I'm sorry, Miss Carter. I just can't understand why you and your father would waste your time on the likes of her."

Cassie forced herself to meet the sheriff's hostile gaze, refusing to feel shame.

"Sheriff Connelly!" Lucy snapped. "Leave us."

He gave Lucy a courtly bow, turned on his heel, and was gone.

"Don't listen to him, Cassie," Lucy said. "He's an odious man, cruel and stupid."

By first light, news of the escape had spread through town. Soon townspeople had filled the street outside, hoping to catch a bit of news or to witness some excitement. Zach and Luke, by now magically sober and afraid the crowd might turn ugly, insisted Cassie retire to her room.

The two, sporting matching black eyes, stood sentry in the courtyard, not trusting Master Carter's servants to protect her.

Cassie paced restlessly within her protective prison, grateful her window faced the courtyard, not the street. She was able to look at the sky beyond and count the passing hours without fearing that someone would hurl rocks at her from below.

For weeks she had dreaded the passage of time. Now she rejoiced at each fleeting second. Every minute brought Alec closer to freedom and safety. Lucy told her that search parties had long ago given up on finding Alec within Williamsburg, and men with hounds had been sent to search the countryside. Meanwhile, Master Carter's other sons and daughters had begun to arrive to await news of their father together. Unlike Lucy, they knew little about Alec and believed him to be every bit the dangerous criminal. Lucy could not put them at ease by telling them the truth. To do so would risk exposing the plot and put Alec's life in further danger. Cassie was grateful not to be among them, certain as she was that their feelings for her would be far less generous than those of their sister.

Her luncheon tray arrived. She had no stomach for food. Outside, shadows lengthened into afternoon, gray clouds moving in their slow and silent dance across the sky. The babe in her womb moved restlessly, as if it, too, knew something important was happening. Cassie smiled at the odd new sensation, wondering for the first time whether it was a son or a daughter growing within her. She lay on the bed, stroking the swell of her belly, cherishing the tiny life Alec had planted inside her.

Someone knocked impatiently on the door. Cassie opened her eyes. She'd fallen asleep. Beyond her window, night had fallen. The knock came again.

"Cassie?"

It was Lucy.

Cassie's heart stopped in her breast. *Dear God. Had they captured him?* Fearing the worst, she rushed to the door and pulled it open.

"The governor's here to see you." Lucy's blue eyes were wide with excitement.

"The governor? Why?"

"He's brought someone with him—an Englishman with one leg." Lucy took Cassie by the hand and pulled her down the hallway behind her.

An Englishman with one leg? Cassie's mind raced. Who could it be? She hadn't much time to speculate before she stood face-to-face with

Governor Gooch, who astonished her by bowing his head politely when he saw her.

"Miss Blakewell." He cleared his throat. "May I introduce Lt. Matthew Hasting."

Lt. Matthew Hasting.

Cassie felt wondrous relief flood through her like laudanum. A peg-legged man in uniform stood before her. His eyes were sky blue and gentle as he took her hand in his and brought it to his lips.

"I'm delighted to meet you, Miss Blakewell. I hope I haven't surprised you overmuch in your delicate condition."

"You're … You're … " Cassie whispered.

"Alec's brother-in-law," he finished for her. "Soon to be your brother-in-law, I hope."

Cassie clutched his hand and looked into his kind eyes, too overwhelmed to speak.

"Poor thing. She can scarce believe it," said a woman's voice.

"To think all this time she knew he was telling the truth," said another.

"These past weeks have been the worst of nightmares for her, I'm afraid," Lucy said.

Cassie looked into the lieutenant's eyes, searching for her voice. "We must find Alec!"

"That, my dear, is why I've come."

Chapter Thirty-five

*A*lec pulled his mount to a stop and gazed at the stars through a break in the trees above. He'd never take seeing the sky for granted again.

Hooves approached behind him.

"Gotten us lost, have you?" Carter asked.

"Try to have a little faith."

Alec checked the older man for signs of fatigue or weakness, but found none. Robert Carter was surprisingly fit for a man of his years, despite a persistent cough. He'd not asked to dismount once, and they had been able to cover ground quickly, keeping well ahead of whatever tracking parties had been sent after them.

He urged his horse forward, turning its head slightly to the east. They'd reach the island within the hour. There they'd find a warm meal and a place to sleep waiting for them. With Micah's musket at the ready should anyone approach, they'd spend the night there, then hide themselves on board a small ship manned by Carter's most trustworthy men. They'd sail south at daybreak, leading to a port in the Carolinas, where Alec would buy passage aboard a ship bound for England. It wasn't a foolproof plan, but it was a good one.

Alec guided his gelding through a maze of tangled vegetation behind tree roots, careful not to lose his sense of direction. The marsh was a different place in the winter, the chirping and squeaking of birds and insects hushed. A wet breeze blew over the water, seeping through the greatcoat he'd stolen from the poor surprised gaoler, but Alec found the cold exhilarating. After so many weeks behind bars, it felt good to be in the open. He'd come far closer than he'd wanted to the hangman's noose. He owed Carter a life debt and intended to repay him tenfold as soon as he returned to England.

His time spent with Carter talking horseflesh had given him the measure of the man. Carter was honorable, but he had a stubborn streak. And he enjoyed taking risks. Alec had known Carter would protect Cassie and hadn't been surprised when Carter had shown up at the gaol to make certain he was being treated fairly. Alec had taken advantage of the opportunity to ask Carter for help with his will, explaining that he wanted to make sure Cassie and the baby were well taken care of should he be executed. That had led to Carter's hiring counsel and having Alec fitted for new clothing. The two had begun to talk, and slowly this plan—or wager, as Carter called it—had developed. Carter had agreed to help Alec stage his escape by acting as his hostage, gambling that Alec was who he said he was and would not slit his throat once they were safely away. Alec had wagered the escape would work. At stake were both men's lives—as Carter had said, the greatest wager of all.

Alec wondered again what was happening in Williamsburg. Had Zach and Luke been able to distract the sheriff as planned by making it seem as if he'd broken into Carter's house? Had they been able to keep Cassie safe after the alarm had been sounded? Carter assured him that no one, not even the governor, would dare to remove her from his house. But Alec was not so certain. It was one thing to gamble with his own life. It was something else entirely to gamble with hers and the baby's.

A baby. How strange it was to think that he was going to be a father. A father. Were it not for Matthew, he'd have no idea what that meant. Whereas Alec's father had rarely smiled at him or offered him a word of encouragement, Matthew lavished affection on his children, played with them and read them stories. Alec was determined to be like his brother-in-law, and not the cold, heartless taskmaster his own father had been. He thought of Jamie and Blackbeard and found himself smiling.

How difficult this must all be for Cassie. He and Carter had agreed it was best to keep her in the dark, lest the escape plan fail. Alone and locked up in that house, she must have felt that God had forsaken her. While Alec had scarcely seen the light of day these past weeks, she'd been exposed to all the vilification the townsfolk had to offer. He had watched them stare at her over the tops of their Bibles at church and point fingers at her outside. Women looking at her with scorn, men's glances colored with lust. Cassie had held her chin high, ignoring them all.

And in the courtroom … She'd stood up to the governor, bravely taking the stand and declaring her faith in Alec in no uncertain terms. He wouldn't have thought it possible, but his passion for her had deepened, though he hadn't held her in his arms in more than two months.

"What think you of being a father?" The sound of Alec's voice startled the silence.

"So that's what you're thinking about," Carter said with a chuckle, which quickly became a deep cough. "It's a great thing, though I must say I didn't think much of it at first. All that crying, those foul smells. But I came to enjoy it. I've been a better father to my children by Betty than I was to those Judith bore me. As with most things, one improves with practice."

Alec had gleaned that Judith was Carter's first wife and Betty his second. Only seventeen when she'd married him, Betty had died at age thirty-six, weakened by the birth of their sixth child, leaving her husband a widower for the second time—and the father of ten. And for the first time all day, Alec tasted fear. What if Cassie, too, were taken ill? What if she died in childbed? It was something he'd not considered until now, and the thought that she might perish to birth his child sickened him. He remembered well what Rebecca had endured. Would Cassie die? No, that could not happen. He would not let it. Cassie was strong and healthy, braver and more stubborn than any woman he had ever known. She'd survive. He'd do everything in his power to make sure she survived. He'd hire the best physician. Hell, he'd hire a team of physicians. *Best not to think of such things now*, Alec told himself, determined to brush the worry from his mind. His first task was to make sure Cassie had a husband, their baby a father.

"God forbid you have daughters," Carter said.

"Why do you say that?"

"If they're anything like their mother, you'll have to keep them under lock and key."

Alec couldn't help laughing.

The two men rode onward, the silence interrupted only by occasional fits of coughing. Alec began to worry that Carter was truly ill, though the man had yet to complain. Perhaps Takotah could brew one of her frightful potions and ease his breathing. Ahead in the dark, the trees thinned, and beneath the horses hooves, mud gave way to sand. A shape moved in the darkness—a man holding a musket.

"We're here."

*M*atthew peered through the darkness, watching the young woman who would soon become his sister-in-law. Easily the best rider among them, she sat a horse as if she'd been born to it, her motions blending effortlessly with those of the mare beneath her. Riding slightly ahead of them all, her relentless pace challenging them to keep up, she seemed certain of her direction despite the darkness. If she was tired or cold, she certainly didn't show it.

"I should like to wait until dawn," Governor Gooch said.

"If we do, we'll lose him," she called back over her shoulder. "He'll have left by first light."

"But surely we'll lose our way in the dark."

"Not if you stick with me."

Matthew admired Miss Blakewell's spirit and had grown surprisingly fond of her already. He should have known Alec would fall in love with such a woman. Brave and determined, she was also quite pretty in her own way, and intelligent, too. She was precisely the breath of fresh air Alec needed, not at all the type of grasping, shallow creature he'd met far too often in the ballrooms of London. Though Matthew had not yet had time to hear the entire story of how she and Alec had come together, he knew from his conversation with Governor Gooch that Cassie had braved dishonor and worse by testifying at Alec's trial. As far as Matthew was concerned, her devotion to Alec made her a jewel beyond price.

She had insisted they leave Williamsburg last night as soon as she'd regained her breath, ignoring those who'd wanted to wait until morning before setting out. Men with dogs were still tracking Alec, she argued, and, until they found him, both his life and Robert Carter's were in danger. Her logic had prevailed. Their small party had sailed north to her father's estate, where, after a brief reunion with servants who obviously adored their mistress, they'd set out on horseback.

Their little company was as odd a mixture of people as Matthew had ever seen. Beside him rode the governor and two sheriffs, one called Hollingsworth, who was as big around as a tree, and one called Connelly, who, though young and energetic, was none too bright. Behind them followed the two young Carter lads, Charles and Landon, both full of restlessness and vigor. Beside them rode two men with fresh black eyes, a bondsman Miss Blakewell called Zach and a big slave named Luke. Matthew was grateful for the presence of the latter two, as they'd made it abundantly clear they did not trust anyone with the safekeeping of their mistress and would keep a close eye on them all. There were the governor's hired hands as well, each armed, bringing their number to just over a dozen.

It was not yet dawn. Hardly a star shone in the cold, dark sky. Already they'd followed Miss Blakewell over fields and through a forest, and now she was leading them into what seemed to be a thickly wooded marsh. Towering conifers stretched into the darkness above their heads, their roots a tangle in the muddy, knee-deep water below. Slick mud, dead branches, and vegetation tangled to slow the horses as they fought for footing. But the terrain hadn't hindered her progress. Matthew realized she had ridden this way many times before and knew every tree trunk and branch by heart. Twice now she'd had to stop to allow the rest of them to catch up with her.

"Where on earth is she taking us?" muttered the governor.

"To hell, I'd warrant," grumbled Sheriff Hollingsworth.

"It's not far now," Miss Blakewell assured them, circling back from the darkness to rejoin them.

Elizabeth would adore her, Matthew thought with satisfaction. Lord, how he missed his wife and children. It had been more than six weeks since he'd last seen them. He hadn't explained to Elizabeth his reason for coming here, not wanting to raise her hopes. He'd told her only that it had to do with bringing Alec's killers to justice, though he himself had been all but certain that he'd find Alec alive. The letter that the magistrate at Newgate had shown him, together with the mysterious letter that Philip had intercepted and burned, had convinced Matthew that Alec had been spirited to the colonies against his will, and that Philip was somehow behind it.

When Matthew confronted Philip in private, he had at first denied knowing anything about the letters. But when faced with the signed missive he'd sent to Newgate, Philip had reacted like a cornered man, confessing nothing, but vowing to kill Matthew. Fortunately, he hadn't had time to make good on his threats, as the justice of the peace arrived shortly thereafter to arrest him on the grim charge of conspiracy. When he finally did confess, sick and trembling for lack of drink, the horror of what he'd said had left Matthew shaken. He'd never intended for Alec to be kidnapped, he'd said, laughing. He'd meant him to die. That was what he'd paid the men to do. But they had double-crossed him—and doubled their profits—by selling Alec to a sea captain who'd found himself with a useless corpse instead of a full cargo. They'd paid the ultimate price for their betrayal, for as soon as Philip had discovered their treachery, he'd ordered them killed, as well.

How would Matthew tell Alec about Philip? Telling him he had been betrayed was the one part of this trip that Matthew had been dreading. Elizabeth hadn't taken the news well. As far as she knew, she'd already lost one brother. Losing the other had been devastating for her.

Matthew put his worries aside and looked ahead through the trees to where the sky had begun to lighten. The forest thinned. He felt his horse's step grow steadier. They were now riding on more solid ground. Peering through the ghostly half-light, Matthew thought he saw some kind of clearing.

"The sun is almost up," said Miss Blakewell. "We must hurry."

*A*lec slipped on his boots, eager to get under way. As promised, Takotah had awakened them before first light, leaving steaming mugs of tea and breakfasts of cornmeal mush on the roughened table. Nearby, Carter lapsed into another fit of coughing. It had been a restless night for all of them, but especially for Carter, who to his credit, had not complained. Takotah had given him one her concoctions to help his breathing and relieve the ache in his stiff limbs, and Alec knew he had gotten at least some sleep. As if on cue, Takotah appeared through the door of the little cabin with another steaming mug, which Carter accepted with grateful nod, wrinkling his nose at the smell.

"This just might cure me if it doesn't kill me first."

"You think that's bad." Alec grinned. "You should taste what she gave me."

Accustomed to being teased about her potions, Takotah smiled back, the tattoos on her weathered face seeming to come alive. "It is good to have you home."

Home. Alec liked the sound of that. But he wasn't home yet. Home was still a month-long voyage away—if he managed to survive the next few days.

He poured water from a pitcher into the washbasin and splashed it over his face, grateful for its bracing chill. How strange it had been to arrive here in the dark of night. Micah had emerged like a ghost from the shadows and had seen to their horses. Takotah had ushered them indoors by the fire, where a warm meal awaited them. Never had a simple stew tasted so good, nor a bed felt so soft. Having spent many long weeks sleeping in straw on a dirty, wooden floor, Alec was sure he could have slept on stone.

Best of all had been seeing Jamie again. The boy had been kept away until the meal was finished so as not to disturb them. But as soon as the empty bowls had been cleared, he'd come bounding through the door, Pirate at his heels. The pup had almost reached its full size, and

Alec had found himself juggling a lapful of wiggling boy and overgrown puppy.

"Tell me how you saved Cassie from the bad man," Jamie had demanded, throwing his arms around Alec's neck and giving him a big hug.

"That's a long story, Jamie."

"Where is she? When do I get to see her?"

Alec had seen that these weeks away from his sister had been hard on the child. How he'd wished he'd been able to walk through the door with Cassie in hand, and end this nightmare for all of them. But he hadn't. She was little better than a prisoner in Williamsburg, and the only way he could help her was by leaving her far behind and returning to England. How could he explain that to a child?

"Cassie is safe in Williamsburg now," Alec had told him. "She's staying at Master Carter's home. Do you remember him?"

Jamie had glanced over at Carter and nodded. "She isn't coming here?"

"Not yet, tadpole. But I hope to bring her to you before spring comes."

That would seem an eternity to a child.

"There's no reason for the boy to remain out here, now, is there?" Carter had asked. "Under my roof he'd be in no danger. When you set sail he can come home with me—his father, too, for that matter. Would you like that, boy?"

"Would I get to be with Cassie, and can Pirate come, too?"

Carter eyed the dog with suspicion. "I'm sure you can all find lots of ways to cause trouble and disrupt my household, heaven forbid."

"Can I?" Jamie had looked at Alec pleadingly.

"Aye, tadpole, I don't see why not," Alec had shared a smile with Takotah.

That had been enough to bring the light back into the child's eyes.

"Does he know we're here?" Carter had finally asked, looking at Abraham Blakewell, who sat silently rocking in the corner, staring at nothing.

Alec had looked to Takotah for an answer.

"No."

"Poor fellow. He was a good man."

Alec had tucked Jamie into bed after supper, recounting once again the story of Blackbeard, until the boy had drifted off to sleep.

He would have liked to bid Jamie farewell this morning, but it was far too early to wake him, and it was essential that nothing slow them down. Supplies had been stowed on board the vessel waiting for them at the river. Its crew was awake and ready to cast off.

Alec drank his tea in several gulps, its warmth spreading into his limbs, and quickly ate his cornmeal mush. Flavored with bits of bacon instead of weevils, it was a far sight better than the mush he'd been served in gaol.

Carter was moving slowly, and Alec began to worry that he would delay their journey.

"Don't worry about me," the older man said as if reading his thoughts. "By the time you're ready, I'll be one step ahead of you."

The land baron was true to his word. By the time Alec had finished saddling the horses, Carter was standing outside the cabin, ready for the second day of his grand adventure. From the smile on his round face, it looked as if he were heading off for a day of hunting. "I've never felt better," he said with a robust grin.

The two were about to mount for their ride to the river when Micah dashed toward them, musket in hand.

"At least seven men," he said, worry heavy on his dark brow. "I couldn't see them all, but old Master Crichton is with them, and they're armed."

Chapter Thirty-six

*A*lec felt a surge of energy. How in the hell had they found them this quickly?

"Can we outrun them?" He checked the loaded pistol he'd tucked into his belt.

Micah shook his head.

"Take Takotah and Jamie and hide in the marsh. Don't come out until it's over, no matter what happens."

Micah nodded and was gone.

Alec heard voices, the dull thud of horse hooves on loam as the riders came out of the marsh and onto dry land. They must have traveled north by river and then tracked him all night. It was as if they had known just where he was headed. He'd vastly underestimated the governor's determination to see him hanged.

"Here's where the excitement begins," he whispered.

"Things were beginning to grow a bit dull," Carter muttered.

Reaching down to remove a knife from his boot, Alec slipped the blade into the waistband of his breeches.

From the sound of things, the riders had dismounted and were walking stealthily toward the cabin. It was now or never. "Are you ready?"

"Aye."

Alec wrapped his arm around Carter's throat and pressed the pistol to his temple. His senses heightened, he stepped out into the clearing.

"Back off, or Carter dies!"

"Don't shoot!" Carter choked out. "Do as he says!"

Seven men, including the senior Master Crichton and the old Scot, Henry, stopped in their tracks, visibly startled.

The elder Crichton glared at them, his hatred palpable. "I knew I'd find you here, convict. When he heard you'd escaped, Henry told me about the time he'd followed you here. He said he'd been trying for weeks to find this place for my fool of a son. If Geoffrey had told me what he was doing, you'd be dead already. I visited this island several times with Blakewell long ago when he was still sane. Took me a while to find it again, but find it I did. And just in time."

"Congratulations. But now that you've found me, you're going to turn right back around and ride out of here, or Carter will be only the first to die."

"Listen to him!" Carter pleaded, acting every bit as though he were terrified.

"I see your generosity has come back to haunt you, Robert."

Crichton motioned to one of his men, who handed him a musket. "You thought you could humiliate me by defending the man who murdered my son, but you're going to pay for that now. Which of you should I aim for first?"

"You bastard! How dare you?" Carter's mock fear was transformed into genuine fury. "That's murder!"

Alec suddenly found himself struggling to hold Carter back, one arm still wrapped around the land baron's throat.

"Aye, but who's to say that the convict didn't kill you before we killed him?"

As Crichton lifted the musket and began to take aim, Alec pressed the pistol into Carter's surprised hands and used both arms to thrust him to the side, where he fell to the ground in a cursing heap. At least now Carter would be able to defend himself.

"There's no need for you to kill him. It's really me you want, Crichton."

"There's no need to kill anyone!" The boom of Governor Gooch's voice filled the clearing as the governor himself rode into view beside...

"Cassie?"

"Alec!"

"What's this?" Crichton's musket still pointed at Alec's chest.

The governor dismounted, strode over to Crichton, and yanked the firearm from his hands. "There'll be no killing here this morning. This man was telling the truth."

Alec scarcely heard the bitter cursing that gushed from Crichton's mouth. What had the governor said?

This man was telling the truth.

Cassie had dismounted and was running toward him, calling his name, her arms outstretched.

He swept her into his embrace, crushing her against him, overwhelmed by a rush of fierce emotion. "Cassie!"

"Don't I even get a handshake?"

"Matthew?" Blood rushed to Alec's head. He could scarcely believe his eyes. Surely this was a dream.

"Alec, it's over," he heard Cassie say.

Cassie watched as recognition dawned on Alec's face.

For a moment he neither spoke nor moved. "My God, is it really you?"

"Aye. It's good to see you, too, Alec."

Hot tears coursing down her cheeks, she watched as the two men grasped one another in a fierce embrace.

"Thank God you're alive!" the lieutenant whispered, his voice strained. "We thought we'd lost you."

"What in the hell took you so long?"

"That's a rather long story, I'm afraid."

Then Alec's gaze locked with Cassie's again, and Cassie felt his arms surround her and pull her to him. There was so much to tell him, but words would not come as she held him and buried her face in his chest, her body trembling with unspent emotion.

"You brave, beautiful, wonderful woman." His lips brushed hers in a tender kiss.

Warm and soft, his lips took hers again. And again. Someone nearby cleared his throat.

"Now, now. You'll have lots of time for that later." It was Master Carter.

"Never enough time," Alec whispered for her ears alone. His thumbs wiped the tears from her cheeks. His blue eyes told her as words never could how much he loved her. "Matthew, may I present Miss Catherine Blakewell."

Alec turned and introduced her to the lieutenant as if the two had not yet met.

"I've already had the pleasure of making her lovely acquaintance." The lieutenant bowed, placing a light kiss on the back of her hand. "My family and I are forever in your debt, Miss Blakewell. Should you desire anything, you need but ask."

"Lieutenant." She felt a happy blush rise to her cheeks.

"Please, call me Matthew. We are going to be related by marriage, after all."

"Matthew." Cassie's heart swelled. "And you must call me Cassie."

"It would be my pleasure, Cassie." Then Matthew looked Alec up and down, shaking his head and laughing. "If only Socrates could see you now!"

"Are you suggesting he would find something amiss with my appearance? I'd thought myself quite dashing as an outlaw, really."

Cassie found herself laughing along with them as sunlight broke over the horizon, casting long shadows across the clearing.

"I'm glad to see this is resolved," the governor said somewhat sheepishly.

"Governor Gooch, might I have the pleasure of introducing my esteemed brother-in-law, Alec Madison Kenleigh the Third," Matthew said.

Alec stepped forward and shook the governor's hand.

"Sorry this has been such a rough business," the governor said.

"As long as you're not still planning to hang me, I'm prepared to consider the entire affair settled."

One by one, the other men moved to greet Alec and offer their apologies, all except Master Crichton, who stood off to the side glowering, surrounded by his men.

"What did I tell you, Hollingsworth? I never bet on losing horses." Master Carter gave a hearty laugh. When Sheriff Hollingsworth raised an eyebrow, Carter cleared his throat and added, "Well, almost never."

"Yes, we shall have to discuss this latest wager of yours, Carter," the governor said, looking stern. "None of us realized you were such an accomplished thespian. Your abduction scared the poor gaoler half to death."

"Are you implying … ?" Carter suddenly looked like a schoolboy.

"That you faked the entire thing to help this man escape?"

"You were only pretending, Father?" Landon looked shocked.

"You helped him escape?" Charles grinned.

Both gazed at their father with astonishment and admiration.

Master Carter shifted uncomfortably under the governor's questioning gaze. "Aye, but don't tell your sisters, or they'll never forgive me."

Robust laughter rang through the clearing.

Then Cassie felt hard steel bite into her temple as an arm locked tightly around her throat, cutting off her breath.

"Stay away, convict! She'll be dead before you take a single step!" Master Crichton's heartless voice echoed in her ear. His whiskers burned her cheek as he dragged her backward with him. "Drop your arms! Do it!"

Muskets fell to the sand with a clatter.

Cassie struggled, but it only made her need for air greater.

"Let her go, Crichton." Alec's voice was clear and strong.

"Crichton, are you mad?" the governor asked in disbelief.

"Everyone back away!" Master Crichton's tight grip threatened to crush her throat. "This man killed my son, and I'm going to make sure he pays!"

Cassie needed to breathe. The pain in her throat made her eyes water.

"That's right, Crichton. I killed Geoffrey." Alec's voice was silken. He moved away from the other men, creating a clear target. "I'm right here. Why don't you shoot me and even the score?"

"No! You killed my firstborn, and I'm going to kill yours. I kill her, and the child dies with her."

Cassie desperately needed to breathe.

"Let her go, and you can do whatever you please with me." Alec pulled open his coat and shirt to expose his bare chest. "Here's your target."

Her lungs about to burst, her pulse racing, Cassie watched in horror as Henry, motioned forward by a jerk of his master's head, took aim at Alec.

"You can both die," Master Crichton said.

She needed air. She needed to breathe. Her vision began to fade, dark spots dancing before her eyes. She wanted to fight him, but . . . Was this what it was to die? But her baby! She must breathe! From far away a shot rang out, echoing in her mind so that it sounded like several. She felt herself falling into darkness.

"Cassie?"

She felt strong arms holding her, heard herself choke, gasp. She gulped in sweet, fresh air.

"Thank God," a man muttered from far away.

"Cassie, can you hear me?"

It was Alec. He sounded afraid. But he was never afraid.

She struggled to open her eyes, and Alec's worried face swam into view. "Alec."

His strong arms pulled her close. His lips kissed her forehead. "I thought I'd lost you."

Was he trembling?

"Let's get her indoors," a voice said.

Cassie recognized it as Matthew's.

But what had happened? Master Crichton had been trying to kill her. Henry had fired at Alec. Afraid, she started to look about. There on the ground nearby, lay Henry, with something sticking out of his back, and Master Crichton.

Alec turned her face back toward him to block her view, his hand gentle on her cheek. "It's all right, love. You're safe," he said, then added in a sterner tone to the men behind him, "Move them out of here. I don't want her or Jamie to see this."

"But what … ?" she asked hoarsely. Her throat ached.

Alec lifted her into his arms and carried her to her father's cabin. "Just be grateful that Takotah and Matthew have such good aim."

A smile eased the tension on his face.

"I'm still a bit shaky, thank you," Matthew said. "I hope I never have to do that again."

"I've never seen anyone throw a knife like that before," Master Carter said. "I'll never make fun of her potions again. I promise you that."

Cassie wrapped her arms around Alec's neck, the horror past.

In the distance she heard Jamie's voice. "Is Cassie hurt?"

"She'll be fine, tadpole."

"*O*h, Cassie, you look lovely!" Elizabeth led Cassie to the floor-length mirror that stood in one corner of the room.

Alec had purchased this town house in Williamsburg, and Cassie still hadn't gotten used to all the luxury that surrounded her. The large gilt mirror was another wedding gift from Alec.

"Oh, my!" Cassie looked into the mirror and stared in awe at her reflection. The woman she saw in the glass could not possibly be herself.

Her hair, normally so ill behaved, had been tamed into a smooth coil, tendrils framing her face, cascading down her nape. Her face, touched lightly with powder and rouge at Elizabeth's insistence, looked ... Well, radiant. Even beautiful. The gown, cut from cream silk laced with golden thread and covered with tiny seed pearls, made her look like a princess, the swell of her belly hidden in folds of shimmering cloth. Alec had picked the material himself, dismissing the cost as a trifle when Cassie had protested it was too expensive.

"You make such a beautiful bride," Elizabeth said.

"Thank you, Elizabeth."

"Now for the final touch." Elizabeth draped Cassie's mother's pearls around Cassie's neck and fastened the clasp.

The effect was stunning, the enormous teardrop pearl glistening against her bosom, rising and falling with each breath, its color a precise match with the silk of her gown.

If only she felt as confident as she looked. If only she could put these niggling doubts to rest.

So much had happened these past eight weeks, she could scarcely fathom it all. After that terrible morning on the island, they'd ridden back to Blakewell's Neck, bringing Cassie's father home with them, to find all as it should be. Though Alec had insisted Cassie stay in bed for the next two days, feasting and dancing had followed late into the night. That feeling of festivity had continued with the announcement that Zach and Elly would marry. Cassie had consented to the marriage, of course. They were obviously in love, and Elly, round with a baby Zach had already accepted as his own, had become the most hardworking of bondswomen, finally happy in her new life.

Although her father still responded to no one, Cassie thought he seemed to be eating better, and some of the color had returned to his face. She began to hope that, surrounded by the happy voices of children and people who loved him, he might one day recover. As she watched Takotah care tenderly for him each day, Cassie began to wonder if the reason Takotah had stayed on at Blakewell's Neck wasn't more a matter of love for her father than of life debt.

Only Matthew's news had marred their happiness. Philip had committed suicide days after confessing his role in Alec's ordeal—an ordeal Philip had intended to end with murder, not kidnapping. Alec had taken this news harder than Cassie had expected, blaming himself for not intervening in his brother's life sooner. Philip had been his responsibility, he'd said, and he had failed. Though he tried to hide his grief, Cassie could see the shadows in his eyes.

Governor Gooch had given Alec a full pardon on the charge of ravishment, dismissing the rest as self-defense, and Alec had immediately begun preparations for returning to England. Cassie hadn't had the heart to tell him how desperately sad she felt each time she thought about leaving Virginia behind. There had been so little time to talk these past weeks. But there had been one bit of business Alec had insisted on clearing up before they left Virginia.

"I'm going to make an honest woman of you," he'd said one morning as they lay together in bed. "And a proper wedding it will be, too. I want all of Virginia to know there is no shame in our love." Then he'd surprised her with a pair of emerald-and-diamond earrings, the first of many lavish gifts. "They match the color of your eyes."

Not wanting to set foot near St. Mary's White Chapel again, Cassie had asked for a ceremony in Williamsburg. Alec, needing no explanation, had agreed.

Matthew had immediately sent for Elizabeth and their children, insisting the wedding would have to wait until they arrived. "Elizabeth will make my life a living hell else," he'd explained. "She'll never forgive me for not telling her the truth about my visit here as it is."

The weeks they'd spent waiting for Elizabeth and the children to arrive had been busy. Overnight, Alec was transformed into a gentleman, with matters of estate to attend to. It wasn't so much that he had changed, though the new wardrobe ordered from Williamsburg did make him look like a different man—a rakishly handsome gentleman. It was more the way people responded to him. He was the one everyone at Blakewell's Neck now turned to with problems and questions. Her people's respect for his authority was beyond dispute.

Surprisingly, it hadn't bothered Cassie, who'd just been happy to have him alive. He was now guardian of Blakewell's Neck. It was natural for people to treat him so. Still, he'd gone out of his way to include her in all the decisions he'd made so far, carefully considering her opinion, even changing his own mind a time or two. On the issue of slavery, they still didn't see eye to eye, Alec wanting to abolish its use on Blakewell's Neck entirely, Cassie fearing for the slaves' safety once they were off Blakewell land. Alec had retained a barrister to help find ways around the laws that made it almost impossible to free slaves. Meanwhile, he'd asked for Cassie's blessing in freeing Luke and Nettie, who were now as married as slaves could be, in repayment for Luke's help in saving Alec's life.

Cassie had voiced her fears. Where would Luke and Nettie go? How would they survive? Still, she'd known it was the right thing to do. She'd helped Nettie pack provisions, and Alec had given Luke fifty pounds to help them get started in their new life—enough to make Luke all but swoon.

"When I learn to write, I will write to you," Nettie had promised.

Cassie and Nettie had embraced silently, choking back tears. Jamie and Daniel had wailed. Cassie had watched Luke, Nettie, and Daniel sail toward the Chesapeake on their way north, silently reaffirming her and Alec's promise to find Luke's daughter.

If that farewell had been tearful, it was nothing compared to Elizabeth's arrival last week. Elizabeth, carrying Anne and followed by Emily, Victoria, little Matthew, and Charlotte, had run across the gangplank, and brother and sister were reunited in a fierce embrace, Elizabeth weeping with unrestrained joy as five excited children hopped about waiting for their chance to greet their uncle. An elderly black man Cassie assumed was Socrates brought up the rear, disembarking at a much more dignified pace. When Alec snatched him up in a rough hug, Cassie swore she saw tears in the old man's eyes.

"My husband explained everything in his letter," Elizabeth had said moments later, hugging Cassie. "I don't know how we shall ever thank you, but I love you as a sister already."

Socrates had bowed. "I am at your service, Madam."

Cassie had so much to be grateful for. Why could she not shake this sense of melancholy?

"Is the bride ready?" Elizabeth asked. "It's nearly time."

"Oh, lamb, look at ye." Nan stepped through the doorway, dressed in her Sunday best. Tears filled her eyes, and she began to weep. "If yer mother and father could see ye."

Cassie tried to smile. This was the happiest day of her life. If only she felt happier. She needed to speak with Alec. She needed to know for certain.

"What's troublin' ye, love? Don't think ye can fool old Nan."

"Nothing. I ... " Cassie's voice trailed off. She looked up at Elizabeth and Nan, fighting tears.

"I suspect you've got the wedding day jitters, my dear." Elizabeth took her hand reassuringly. "I was in such a state the day of my wedding, I couldn't get dressed. But Matthew showed up and threatened to carry me off to the church in my shift. When I saw him in his uniform standing at the altar, nothing else mattered."

Cassie managed a smile, but she knew this was more than jitters. She needed to speak with Alec. She needed to know. "Have you seen Alec? I need to talk to him."

"Before the wedding, love?" Nan asked.

"Aye, before."

"He's downstairs having a brandy—" Elizabeth said.

"Thank you!"

Oblivious to the surprised faces behind her, Cassie hurried out the door, silk skirts swishing. She was on her way down the stairs when she saw him standing in the drawing room, brandy in hand. Her heart skipped a beat. Dressed in velvet the color of midnight, ivory lace at his wrists and throat, golden brocade on his vest, he was stunningly handsome.

She saw his head turn, knew the moment he spied her, heard her name on his lips.

"You are the most beautiful thing I've ever seen," he said softly as she came to stand before him.

Matthew and Socrates, who'd been deep in conversation, fell silent as she walked into the room, bowing their heads in silent tribute.

"Alec, I-I ... " she stammered, unsure where to begin. "Before we ... that is, I need to know."

"You need to know what, my sweet?" He reached out to touch a curl, his fingers brushing her cheek.

"In the courtroom, you said you regretted what happened between us." Cassie took a deep breath, her insides knotted. "You said you used me to ease your loneliness and you were willing to take responsibility for me."

Alec started to interrupt, a look of amusement on his face, but Cassie continued, fighting to keep her voice steady.

"I absolve you of any responsibility toward me, Alec Kenleigh. If you wish to leave for England without me, you may. I don't think I'd be very happy there anyway."

Alec's expression darkened. "What makes you think you can absolve me of my responsibilities? You *are* my responsibility, Cassie, along with the baby you're carrying, and you will return with me to England."

"I'm to have no say in the matter?"

"Are you saying you don't want to come with me?"

"Virginia is my home."

"England is mine, and as you're to be my wife, it will be your home, too."

"I'm not your wife yet!"

Cassie turned and fled up the staircase, tears blurring her vision.

*A*lec sat in the carriage, his temper growing fouler by the moment, the cheering crowd on the street passing unseen before his eyes. Beside him, Matthew and Socrates sat reading the papers as if they hadn't a care in the world.

But something was very wrong. In a few minutes, they'd reach the church and Alec would be taking to wife the woman he loved, a woman who apparently didn't want to be with him. She wanted to stay here. He'd known something was bothering her these past few weeks, but he hadn't imagined it was anything like this. He'd thought she loved him, but it seemed she loved life at Blakewell's Neck more.

Come to think of it, she'd never told him she loved him. Not with words. Not once. He'd always assumed she loved him. She'd made love with him, her passion unmatched by the desire of any woman he'd known. She'd stood up to the court, to the entire town of Williamsburg for his sake. She'd put herself at risk to save him. Wasn't that love?

"She makes no sense," Alec said out loud.

"Women aren't known for their rational thinking." Matthew didn't bother to look up from his paper.

"She wants to stay here."

"So we heard."

"Can you believe that?"

"It's hard to imagine anyone would prefer this unruly place to the bustle of London's civilized streets," Socrates said.

"She's going to be my wife. She belongs with me, and my home is in England."

"Absolutely." Both men agreed.

Alec eyed them suspiciously. "Why are you agreeing with me?"

"Because you're right. Anyone can see that." Matthew looked up and folded the paper. "Cassie is going to be your wife, and your home is in England, where your family and your obligations await you. You've been gone for most of a year now, an absence that was not of your own choosing. Of course you want to return as quickly as possible. You have duties, responsibilities."

Alec nodded, glad to be understood. "By this time next week, I'll have set sail, and she'll be by my side. That's my child she's carrying, and I'll not leave them behind."

"Of course you won't. Cassie will come to accept the change with time, no matter how unhappy she is initially. Whatever homesickness she feels will likely vanish the moment she arrives at her first London ball."

Alec shook his head. "She doesn't care for such things."

"Then Elizabeth will have to take her shopping. You know how women are about gowns and frippery. Just think of the interesting women Cassie will meet at teas and embroidery circles."

Alec grunted noncommittally. Cassie wouldn't care much for any of that either.

"There's the child to consider," Socrates said. "What kind of life can a child have here? Your son or daughter should enjoy the same privileges you enjoyed, with the kind of proper education your father provided for you—mathematics, history, Latin, Greek. If it's a son, he'll attend Eton."

Alec shifted in his seat. He'd hated Eton.

"You'll be happy to know I've set your office to rights," Matthew said. "It's just as it was the night you disappeared. Everything is just as you like it. The company needs you, Alec."

"What do you mean?"

"Without you, business continues, of course. But no one can run the firm as well as you or with such dedication—all that work those late nights. No one can manage contracts or His Majesty's insufferable ministers quite as well as you. Not to mention scheming MPs."

The carriage pulled to a stop.

"I must admit how relieved I am." Matthew opened the carriage door and stepped carefully to the ground. "When I first saw you here, I was afraid you'd want to stay. So many people seem drawn to this uncivilized place, with its endless spaces and its rather lax society. I was afraid you'd be one of them, and I'd find myself working for a company with one office in England and one in Virginia."

Alec stepped from the carriage, only dimly aware of the cheering crowd around him. He was glad Matthew and Socrates understood his reasoning and agreed with him. Why, then, did he feel so damned guilty?

Matthew and Socrates watched Alec enter the church ahead of them and shared a conspiratorial grin. It had been easier than they'd imagined. Alec no longer belonged in England, and the sooner he realized that, the better.

*C*assie looked out the carriage window, holding the bouquet of dried roses and lavender tightly in her hands, astonished by the cheering throng in the streets. The fickleness of Williamsburg's good citizens surprised her. Weeks before, she'd been little more than a trollop in their eyes, the object of hatred and scorn. Now she was the heroine in a romantic tale, Alec, whose execution they would have watched with relish, her knight in shining armor. But this was no fairy tale. Cassie had just ruined the ending. She hadn't meant for the words to come out as they had. She hadn't meant to hurt him.

"It will be all right, love." Elizabeth patted Cassie on the arm. "You'll see."

"I've hurt him. I hope he gives me a chance to explain." Cassie's voice quavered with unshed tears.

"He is my brother, and I love him. But he is a man. You mustn't expect too much of him."

The carriage pulled to a stop. The door opened. Cold winter air rushed in. With many helping hands, Cassie alighted. The crowd cheered. Bolstered by their good spirits and happy wishes, she couldn't help smiling. She took a deep breath.

This was her wedding day. Soon she would be Alec's wife. They'd gone through so much to be together. She would let nothing rob her of this joy. Tonight she would apologize—she could think of many good ways to do that, each more shocking than the last. She would let Alec know with each whisper, each kiss, each caress that she'd gladly live in hell if it meant she could be with him.

She lifted her chin and entered the church, her heart thumping wildly. Her breath caught in her throat when she saw him standing tall and proud before the priest. Matthew stood beside to his right, dashing in his dress uniform, and beside him, little Jamie, dressed for the first time in his life as a little gentleman.

Cassie's gaze sought Alec's and held it. He was still angry.

Tonight.

"Are you ready, young woman?"

Master Carter stood inside the entrance, waiting to escort her up the aisle.

"Aye," she said.

Elizabeth, as matron of honor, preceded them.

Guests in the pews stood. Faces turned Cassie's way: Nan, awash in tears. Zach and Elly. Dear Takotah and Micah in the back of the church. Sweet Lucy. Socrates. Governor Gooch. Her father, unaware but there.

Cassie felt she was walking on air as Master Carter took her hand and placed it in Alec's.

Alec's fingers closed warmly around hers. His eyes looked questioningly into hers.

She could see the hurt.

She would show him tonight.

"We have come together in the presence of Almighty God to witness the joining together of this man and this woman in holy matrimony," the priest began.

"Wait."

It was Alec.

Gasps of surprise passed through the church like a breeze.

"Cassie, before we do this, I want to know it's what you really want." His gaze searched hers.

Cassie could see the pain, though he tried to hide it. "Of course it is, Alec. More than anything in the world. What I said earlier—"

"What you said made me think. These past months with you have shown me life is too short and fragile to waste even one moment. I've been so intent on returning to my life in England, I didn't think to ask myself whether that life is really what I want. What I want most, Cassie, is for you to be happy. If that means living in Virginia, we'll live in Virginia."

"Do you … do you really mean that?"

"Aye." He smiled, his eyes so full of caring, Cassie's heart hurt.

Somewhere behind them, Nan sobbed. "Thank the Lord!"

"Then what you said in court about loneliness and regrets and responsibilities ... You're not just marrying me out of a sense of obligation?"

Alec's head fell back and he laughed, the rich sound of his voice echoing through the church. "Is that what's been worrying you?"

Cassie nodded, a tear slipping down her cheek.

He lifted her chin, stroking the tear from her cheek with his thumb. His eyes looked deeply into hers. "What I said in court was said to keep you safe. You're the best thing that's ever happened to me, Cassie, and I don't regret a single moment you and I have spent together. If I had to do it all again, I wouldn't change a thing."

Cassie's heart soared. "I love you, Alec."

"And I you, Mistress."

In the church and beyond, the crowd cheered.

Epilogue

*N*othing could possibly hurt this much.

Cassie gritted her teeth and tried not to cry out as the pain peaked, engulfing her, shaking her apart.

"Strength, Cassie, strength," Takotah crooned.

As the pain slowly passed, Cassie slumped back against Nan, who sat behind the birthing stool supporting her.

"Here, love." Elizabeth held a cup of tea to her lips.

Cassie sipped wearily, barely able to keep her eyes open. "How much longer?"

It had taken so long already. She couldn't bear much more of this.

"The first is always the hardest." Her sister-in-law smiled sympathetically.

"It's hard to say."

"Yer doin' just fine, Missy," Nan said reassuringly. "Just take the pains one at a time."

Cassie felt another pang begin, a belt of agony that wrapped itself around her middle.

Clutching her sister-in-law's hand, she cried out as pain once again swallowed her.

"Don't fight the pain." Takotah stroked Cassie's swollen belly in a downward motion. "You can do this, Cassie."

"Oh, no, I can't! I can't! Please!" Cassie cried, her composure in tatters.

"Yes, you can, Cassie. You are strong. Feel how strong you are," Takotah purred.

"It's fine to scream, love," said Nan.

"Aye, it is," Elizabeth agreed.

Cassie could not have stopped herself even had she wanted to. A frantic cry escaped her lips, ending in a sob as the pain finally began to ebb.

"Where's Alec?" Cassie fought to keep her eyes open. "I'm so afraid."

"I suspect he's giving my husband a very hard time." Elizabeth wiped Cassie's forehead with a cool cloth. "Close your eyes and rest, love. Don't worry about him. Don't worry about anything."

Cassie was already dozing.

*A*lec raised the bottle to his lips and took another drink of corn whiskey, the demons of hell eating at him. From upstairs came another cry. The sound of Cassie's suffering was tearing him to pieces. Her pains had started early this morning, but morning had turned into afternoon, afternoon into evening, and still the baby had not been born.

"Let's go outside. The fresh air will do you good," said Matthew, already more than a little drunk.

"No!"

They'd been trying to get him out of the house for the past three hours, but Alec refused to budge. Let them leave if they wished. They could have all the fresh air they wanted. He would stay right here.

"Ye're a stubborn bastard." Zach glared at him with an unsteady gaze, his words slurred. "I should just drag ye outside like ye did me."

Elly's baby girl had been born six weeks earlier, and it had taken all of Alec's strength to pull Zach from the room so the women could tend to her.

"That was different," Alec mumbled.

"Why?"

"Because it was."

Alec closed his eyes as Cassie cried out again, her anguished scream turning to a whimper, and the whimper fading to silence once again. Her cries had become more frequent and more desperate. Was she dying? He could find no way to silence his fear, no way to chase the demons away.

Suddenly he felt himself being jerked to his feet, Zach at one arm, Matthew at the other.

"Come on," Matthew said. "You're only making it harder on yourself. We're going for a walk."

"No." Alec tried to jerk free.

Perhaps it was the whiskey, but the next thing Alec knew the three of them had toppled to the floor with a loud crash.

"Hell!" he heard Matthew mutter.

"God's balls!" Zach swore.

As they struggled to stand, Elizabeth appeared at the bottom of the stairs, her skirts awhirl, her face a vision of fury.

"Will you gentlemen please control yourselves!" she whispered fiercely. "Your commotion is frightening the poor girl half to death! She's scared enough as it is!"

Just then a heartrending cry pierced the air. "Alec!"

She'd called his name, and before he knew what he was about, Alec had jumped up and raced past the others, taking the stairs two at a time, Elizabeth close behind him. No longer caring what anyone thought, he opened the door and rushed to Cassie's side.

"Quiet, or you'll wake her," Takotah chided.

Cassie sat on the birthing stool, completely naked, her eyes closed, her mouth relaxed, her head resting against Nan's ample breast. Her hair was wet with sweat, and her cheeks were flushed. Takotah sat in front of her, her hand gently resting on Cassie's swollen belly.

"You see, you stubborn goat," Elizabeth whispered. "She's fine."

Never in his life had Alec felt so completely helpless. What could he do? And then he knew.

"I want to hold her." He'd held Rebecca when she'd given birth, pretending to be her husband. Couldn't he do the same for his own wife?

Nan scowled, but motioned for him to come and switch places with her.

"Alec?" Cassie whispered, their movements rousing her.

"Aye, love, I'm here."

"And stinkin' of corn whiskey." Nan deposited her girth at Cassie's side, where she took up a cold cloth and began to bathe Cassie's brow.

Cassie began to moan, her fingers tightening around Alec's hands. "No!" she whimpered.

"Strength, Cassie," said Takotah. "Let your body open so the baby can come out."

Alec felt Cassie arch against him, her body trembling.

"Squeeze my hands and scream like bloody hell if you want to, Cassie. I won't leave you for anything," Alec said.

Cassie cried out, her voice a desperate wail, her nails digging into his palms.

"It will feel better soon," Takotah said. "Can you feel your womb opening?"

Cassie nodded weakly as the pain slid away, relaxing against Alec's chest. "I'm glad you're here."

"So am I." Anything was better than sitting around helplessly and doing nothing. Alec stroked her hair, smoothing the damp strands back from her face. He wished for the world he could take this away from her.

The next pain came quickly. Alec watched Cassie's belly harden, heard her heartbreaking cry. *God, please let it end.*

*C*assie let the pain wash over her, no longer able to think. Again and again it came. Time and again she heard her own voice cry out, heard Alec mutter assurances in her ear, his voice an anchor. As each pain faded, Cassie sank against the strength of his chest, grateful for his presence.

"I love you, Cassie," he murmured in her ear.

When the next pain came it was somehow different. Instead of overwhelming pain, there was pressure and an irresistible urge to push. Unable to withstand her body's instincts, Cassie bore down. The pain was not nearly as bad as before.

"See? It's much better now." Takotah smiled. "When the next pain comes, feel your baby move down."

Cassie tried to do as Takotah instructed, pushing with all her might. Again and again she pushed, Alec's voice and the feel of him behind her giving her courage. Pain began to spread like fire between her thighs, growing worse each time.

"I can see the top of the baby's head. It has lots of dark hair." Takotah pressed a warm cloth against Cassie's sex, bringing her blessed relief. "It won't be long now."

"It's almost over, love," Alec murmured.

When the next pang came, Cassie felt as though she would be split in two. "Oh, God, it hurts!"

"Squeeze my hands, Cassie," Alec said. "Squeeze my hands as hard as you can."

Cassie felt certain she would be torn asunder and let out a ragged scream. Then, suddenly, the pain lessened, and Cassie opened her eyes to find herself looking at her baby's tiny face, its head finally free of her body.

"Oh, Alec!"

But Alec said nothing, and Cassie looked up to see him, eyes wide, staring in amazement into their child's face. Suddenly Cassie was laughing. Or maybe she was crying—she couldn't tell which. And with another push, the pain was gone.

With a whimper and then a howl, Cassie and Alec's son announced his arrival in the world, drawing relieved laughter from Nan and Elizabeth. Takotah gently handed the wet, naked newborn to his mother.

Nan opened the door and shouted down the stairway. "It's a boy! And 'e's a sight more handsome than ye two!"

In awe, Cassie held her baby to her breast, then felt him begin to suck greedily, the new sensation startling her. "He's beautiful." She gazed in wonderment into the little blue eyes that looked back at her, stroking his downy hair.

"Not as beautiful as you."

Tears streaming down her cheeks, Cassie watched as Alec gently took one tiny hand in his. The baby wrapped his little fingers around the tip of Alec's thumb.

"I know we talked about naming him after you, but … " Cassie winced as Takotah pushed on her belly to help deliver the afterbirth. "But I've changed my mind."

Cassie had expected to see disappointment on Alec's face, but found only a gentle smile.

"And just what did you have in mind, my sweet?"

"Nicholas." Cassie looked at the surprised faces around her. "Nicholas Braden Kenleigh."

Alec tossed back his head and laughed. "To tell you the truth, I had begun to grow rather fond of that name."

"I love you, Alec."

Cradling both her and their baby boy against his chest, he kissed her cheek. "And I you, my sweet."

*Watch for the next book in the Kenleigh/Blakewell Family Saga—Nicholas's story—to be reissued by Berkley Sensation on February 5, 2013... **RIDE THE FIRE**.*

*Read on for excerpts from **Carnal Gift,** Book 2 in the Kenleigh-Blakewell Family Saga, and **Surrender**, Book 1 in the MacKinnon's Rangers Series!*

Excerpt:

*B*ríghid clasped her hands tightly in her lap. She would not cry. She would not. She tried to breathe deeply to calm herself, but her breaths came in shudders. Sweet Mary, what was she to do?

They'd ridden forever across the stream, over countless hills and past the sacred hawthorn grove that marked the edge of her world to the *iarla's* manor. She'd been so stiff and sore when they'd arrived she hadn't had the strength to dismount without help. The despicable man whose groping hands she'd fought off for the length of their journey had taken advantage of the situation to fondle her breasts.

"Just give good Edward here a little feel, poppet. That's nice."

His touch and the lecherous grin on his face had left her feeling sick.

She'd been taken to a servant's chamber upstairs where a bath was waiting. Bríghid had known from that moment the *iarla* wanted far more than a word with her. The feeling of sickness in her belly had grown, and she'd felt she could not breathe. A young servant girl, a Dubliner by her speech, had been sent in to help her bathe and dress in fancy clothes that lay on the bed, but Bríghid had refused to cooperate. When the servant had tried to undress her, Bríghid had slapped her and cursed her in Gaelic. The girl's wide eyes as she'd fled the room proved she still understood her mother tongue.

Then the *iarla* himself had arrived, the servant girl behind him. He was tall and thin with features that reminded Bríghid of a Roman, or a rat—small, brown eyes, a long, thin nose and high, harsh cheekbones. He stank of drink and something she thought must be men's perfume.

as all but bald. What little hair he had was clipped own. She had forced herself to meet his gaze, though s repulsed her.

surpassing fair." His cold fingers had traced the outline of What is your name?"

ghid Ní Maelsechnaill." She spoke her name as clearly and y as she could. It was an ancient name, a noble name. Nothing this sider did could besmirch it.

He'd laughed. "That's certainly a mouthful."

"Brigid, my Lord." The servant girl gave Bríghid a look of bitter triumph, a pink palm print still on her cheek.

Bríghid bit back the curse that leapt to mind at hearing her name twisted into loathsome English. Now was not the time.

"Thank you, Alice." The *iarla* smiled to the servant girl, but his hand dropped to caress Bríghid's shoulder. "My friend is quite taken with you, Brigid. I saw how he looked at you this morning."

Whatever Bríghid had expected him to say, it was not this.

"I can see you remember." The *iarla* had smiled. "It was at my friend's request I spared your young rapparee. What is he to you—your lover?"

Bríghid had refused to answer the question directly. The less this *Sasanach* pig knew about her family the better. "I am a maid."

She'd meant to sound unafraid, but her voice quavered.

"Then your brother, or perhaps your cousin?" He'd waited for her reply. "Well, no matter. Thanks to your beauty, your rapparee is safe tonight. Do as you're told, and he'll stay safe."

Then Bríghid had understood. She was to buy her brother's continued freedom with her virginity.

"I expect you to show my friend just how grateful you are. Your willingness is everything." He'd tucked a finger under her chin. "Do you understand?"

Bríghid had choked back tears, looked him in the eye, held her tongue.

Two hours later, bathed and dressed in clothes a whore might have found immodest, her hair twisted atop her head, she sat before the fireplace in a long hallway awaiting the *iarla's* command. A crackling fire had been lit, along with a few candles on the mantelpiece, but neither managed to chase away the shadows that hovered in the corners. Empty chairs lined the walls of the hall, which was so large it could devour the cabin Bríghid called home with room to spare. Carpets the color of blood and decorated with exotic flowers stretched across the wooden floor.

In the next room, the *iarla Sasanach* and the man she was to be given to were eating their supper. Servants bustled in and out of the large, oaken doors carrying platters of meats, tureens of soup, bottles of wine, loaves of bread. No one spared a glance for her.

She was tempted to run, but where could she go? She wasn't sure how to find the door, and surely someone would see her. Even if she did make it outside and into the forest, she would freeze without her cloak. She wasn't even sure which direction would take her home again. And then there was Ruaidhrí. The *iarla* had made it clear that her little brother was safe so long as she did as she was told. She had no choice but to bear whatever horror this night thrust upon her—and to survive.

Never had she felt so helpless, so alone.

Angry shouts came from the room beyond. She couldn't make out most of what was said. Something about the French and war and ships. A servant hurried from the room struggling to balance two trays. When one threatened to topple onto the floor, he placed it on a nearby chair, rushing off to the kitchen with the other.

On the tray sat a knife.

Bríghid's heart beat faster. The tray was a good twenty paces away. If anyone caught her, she'd surely be punished. What good would a knife do her anyway? Did she think she could get away with killing either the *iarla* or his friend? She'd be hanged and her family made to suffer. Besides, could she really take a life?

Then she thought of the man who'd fondled her breast, remembered the sickening feel of his hand on her body, the leer on his face. *Yes.* Without thinking further, she stood, walked as swiftly and silently as she could across the room. The knife lay on the tray, small and silver. She hesitated, took it. She had just taken her seat again and was smoothing her skirts when the servant returned. Without seeming to notice the missing implement, now tucked into the waistline of her petticoats, the servant hoisted the tray and raced back toward the kitchens.

She tugged at the silky cloth of the blue gown they'd made her wear, tried to pull it up over the bared tops of her breasts, which had been shaped into deceivingly large mounds by the corset. The white lace bodice did nothing to conceal her nipples. Her shoulders were all but bare, and the roll of cloth beneath the skirts made her hips and bottom seem larger—and her waist smaller—than they truly were.

She felt naked.

Fears she'd tried to quell uncoiled one after another like snakes in her belly. Would it hurt? Would he keep her for more than one night? Would he plant an English bastard in her belly? Would the good people of Skreen parish accept her when she returned, or would she be forever shamed? With Father Padraíg gone, who would hear her confession and absolve her of so great a dishonor? Would she ever find the husband she so desperately wanted, a man who could love her despite her shame?

Her fingers instinctively reached for her throat. But they'd taken her cross, the little iron cross of St. Brighid, after whom she was named. She had worn it around her neck suspended on a leather thong since she was a child, and it had always made her feel protected. Now it was gone, and her grandmother's brooch with it. Shaped like a twisting dragon with open jaws and garnet eyes that gleamed red, the brooch was the most precious thing she owned. It had passed for generations from mother to daughter, staying within the Maelsechnaill female line. Now Brighid had lost it.

"Sé do bheath' a Mhuire, atá lán de ghrásta, tá an Tiarna leat ..." The prayer spilled from her lips of its own accord. *Hail Mary, full of grace, the Lord is with Thee...*

Light poured into the hallway, and a servant motioned for Brighid to come.

"No!" The word was a whisper, a plea. Brighid stood on trembling legs and forced herself to take a step toward the doorway. *For Ruaidhrí.* Another step. *For Finn.* And another. *For poor little Aidan.*

Her fingers rose to her waist, felt the hardness of the knife. She'd been foolish to take it. She'd never be able to use it.

Just in case.

In the doorway, her steps faltered.

He stood on the far side of an enormous, dark table, staring at her just like before. Again Brighid found she could not breathe. His gaze met hers and held it. His green eyes, cold and hard, seemed to see inside her.

Brighid looked away, instinctively lifting her arms to shield her breasts.

"This is Brigid. She's a bit shy, Jamie, but I've no doubt you can cure her of that affliction. The ladies at Turlington's always had good things to say about your abilities." The *iarla* rose from his chair and strode toward her. His hands grasped her shoulders, and he forced her further into the room. "When she heard how you'd intervened on the young rapparee's behalf, she wanted to thank you personally. Isn't that so, Brigid, my dear?"

Brighid tried to speak but could not.

The man the *iarla* had called Jamie was still looking at her, a brandy snifter in his hand. He drained his glass, put it down, his gaze never leaving her.

The *iarla* fingered the ribbons of her bodice. "You always did have an eye for the most beautiful women. She's yours, if you want her."

"A gift?" The man's eyebrows rose, his gaze shifting at last to the *iarla*.

"Consider her a renewed pledge of friendship. I would set things aright between us. You know as well as I things have been strained since you arrived. We scarcely agree on anything it seems. I want things to be the way they were years ago."

"I see. How ... thoughtful."

"I must say, if you don't want her, I certainly do." The *iarla* pulled slowly on the ribbons of her bodice until they came undone and the lace parted. "What do you say we unwrap your pretty package now and share what delights she has to offer?"

Brighid felt the heat of both men's gazes on her bared breasts. She heard herself whimper, stifled the sound. They were going to rape her together right here. Now. In this room.

The man with the green eyes rounded the table so quickly she gasped. Before she could take a step backwards, he stood before her and began to remove his frock.

Icy dread flowed through her veins.

The *iarla* reached for the fall of his breeches, began to free himself. "You can take her maidenhead, of course. I did offer her to you."

Brighid felt her legs begin to shake. There was a ringing in her ears. This could not be happening.

"Sorry, Sheff, old friend." The man draped his frock over her shoulders, covering her nakedness. "I prefer to have my sport in private."

The *iarla* froze in the midst of unbuttoning his breeches and gave a disappointed groan. "Come now. She's far too fair a flower to be plucked by only one man, and my cock is rock hard."

Brighid shuddered at the vileness of his words, tried not to hear them.

The fair-haired lord placed his hands around her waist and propelled her through the door. "Be that as it may, I'm of no mind to share her tonight. She's been in my thoughts all day, and I intend to savor her."

Strong hands guided her down the long hallway to a staircase on the other side. The man was very tall and walked quickly, and Brighid was forced to hurry beside him, taking two strides for every one of his.

The *iarla Sasanach* followed. "You are a cruel man, Jamie. I suppose I shall have to wait until you've gone back to England for my taste of her?"

The other lord laughed. "That depends. If she's as fair as she seems, I shall find it hard to part with her."

They talked about her as if she were nothing, a possession to be used as they saw fit, with no wishes, no life of her own, her body a toy. Her rage—and her dread—grew. Would she be used then traded from one to the other? Would she be spirited to England never to see her family again?

"So now you threaten to steal her from my service?" The *iarla* sounded both indignant and amused.

"You did say she was a gift, did you not?"

"Aye, but I didn't mean for you to take her from under my roof."

They climbed two flights of stairs to another long hallway, this one lined with doors. The man stopped in front of one of the doors and opened it. Light from several candelabras filled the room. Inside stood an enormous canopied bed with thick, carved posts that jutted toward the ceiling.

Brighid's stomach twisted in a painful knot. She took an involuntary step backward, collided with the hard body of the Englishman behind her.

I will not cry.

"Good night, Sheff." The man forced her inside, turned to the *iarla.* "Thank you for the lovely dinner—and the delightful gift."

He started to close the door, but the *iarla* stopped him with the squared tip of his black leather shoe.

"Friends then?"

"Friends." With a smile, the man closed the door.

Brighid was alone with him.

For a moment, he stood, arm around her waist, head cocked as if to listen. "Damn!" He swore under his breath and left her side to blow out the candles.

The room fell into shadow. A log settled in the fireplace, sent up sparks.

Bríghid started at the sound, clutched the frock tighter around her.

"I won't hurt you, Brigid." His features were lit by light from the fire as he came to her. Long lashes framed his eyes. His skin was bronzed, his cheekbones high, his chin strong. His honey-colored hair had been gathered in a ribbon at the nape of his neck. His curls might have given him a boyish look were he not so tall and his shoulders so broad.

"Th-that's not my name." She fought to still her trembling.

He pried the cloth of his frock from her fingers, slipped it from her shoulders. His gaze fixed upon her. "Then what is your name?"

She shielded her breasts, tried to lift her chin. "Bríghid. Bríghid Ní Maelsechnaill."

To Bríghid's surprise, he carefully repeated what she'd said, though his tongue stumbled a bit over her ancestral name. "My name is Jamie Blakewell, Bríghid. And I won't hurt you."

"So you say."

"By the end of this night, you will know I mean what I say."

Surrender

Book 1 in the MacKinnon's Rangers series
Available Now

*I*t seemed to Annie she'd just fallen asleep, when Iain nudged her awake again. Her body achy, her mind dulled by fatigue and hunger, she sat up and saw that it was not long past dawn. Had she ever been this tired? What she wouldn't give for just one more hour of sleep! Or a hot bath. Or porridge and a cup of tea.

How could Iain look so alert and vigorous when she felt listless and painfully weary? They were alive only because of his labors. 'Twas he who'd borne her through the forest on his back, he who'd rowed the boat through two dark nights, he who'd kept watch while she'd slept. 'Twas he who should be worn with fatigue.

Humbled by her own weakness, she sat up straighter, tried to force the cobwebs from her mind. The least she could do was to press herself as hard as he pressed himself and to endure without complaint. She was no squeamish, spiritless lass, and although she might not have been born to this rugged life, she had her wits and at least some courage.

If she'd understood him, they had most of a day's journey before them over land to Fort Edward. She could endure another day.

Iain handed her the leather pouch of cornmeal. "Bide here a wee."

Then he headed off toward the lake with the tin bucket in his hand.

She took a handful of cornmeal, chewed it, and washed it into her empty stomach with a mouthful of cold water from his water skin.

It had been a long night. Wary after their encounter with the French ships the night before and determined not to fail Iain again, shed made certain to stay awake and had watched the darkness glide past, reluctant even to breathe.

Yet, he'd seemed angry, his voice gruff the few times he'd spoken, his face hard. Perhaps he was in a temper over the things she'd said earlier about Culloden and the war. Or maybe he was still vexed with her for giving them away to the French on the ship. Or perhaps it was the poisoned rum, though that certainly had not been her fault.

You take more lookin' after than a bairn.

She'd wanted to be helpful and had offered to take up the other set of oars and row, but he'd shaken his head.

"A pair of oars in your hands would make a bloody din."

She'd felt ashamed to know he was likely right. And so the perilous, long watch of the night had passed in frosty silence, with Annie feeling useless and angry and afraid.

Oh, how he confused her! One moment he held her and comforted her to help her nightmares pass. The next he belittled her, humiliated her.

At least he hadn't kissed her again.

Why hadn't he kissed her again?

Each time she thought of it, her heart seemed to trip. The hot feel of his lips against hers. The scorching shock of his tongue in her mouth. The hard press of his body.

Oh, Annie, I knew you would taste sweet.

The memory of his words made her breath catch in her throat, and she realized she'd taken pleasure in it. She'd taken pleasure in his kiss.

Even as the truth of it came to her, she rejected it. She'd been asleep and caught up in a dream when he'd stolen that kiss from her. 'Twas a deception of her dream that she'd enjoyed it. How could she, who'd been raised a lady, find any pleasure in kissing a traitor, a rough Ranger, a Highland barbarian?

She looked up and saw the man who bedeviled her thoughts walking toward her. The shadow of beard on his chin had grown thicker and darker, and his black hair still hung, long and unbound, lending him a wild appearance. His shirt had come open at the throat, revealing a wedge of dark curls. She remembered what he'd looked like without his shirt, how it had felt to be held against that chest, and her breath caught again.

He moved almost silently, his motions sure, agile and smooth despite his size. He was, she realized, quite graceful. The very idea surprised her. Male grace was a quality she'd never thought of beyond the ballroom; either a man could dance a quadrille with skill and without stepping on her feet or he could not. But here was another kind of grace altogether — an untrained grace, an instinctive grace, an animal grace.

He set the bucket down before her, then knelt beside his pack and took out the soap and cloth she'd seen yesterday, together with the little jar of salve. "The cold water will soothe your feet. Wash them if you like and put on more salve."

Surprised by his thoughtfulness, Annie took the cloth from his hand. "Thank you."

Be quick about it. I'm goin' scoutin'." He rose and strode silently into the forest.

She felt the water with her fingers, found it ice cold. She removed the moccasins, exposing her battered feet. Then she dipped the cloth in the water, squeezed it out and rubbed the soap against it. Although she had every intention of washing her feet, she found herself pressing the cloth to her face instead.

She almost moaned. It felt wonderful. The cold water made her skin tingle, washed away the grime, brought her back to life. Careful not to waste a drop, she washed her face, then her throat, water running in icy rivulets down her neck and beneath her gown. Next, she washed her feet and ankles.

But it wasn't enough.

She glanced about her to make certain Iain was nowhere near. Then she sat up on her knees, let the bearskin coat fall to the ground and slipped her gown and shift down her shoulders to her waist. All she needed was a few moments.

She'd never been naked in the open air like this, and a part of her could scarce believe she was doing something so reckless. She dipped the cloth into the bucket, squeezed it, then stared in astonishment at her own body. Purple bruises stained her skin, caused by her tumble down the embankment. One of her breasts was scratched, and there was an angry red welt above her right hip. Death had made its mark on her.

She shivered.

Eager to put it all behind her, she washed quickly, first her breasts and belly, then her arms and shoulders. The breeze raised bumps on her wet skin, but the cold water soothed her bruises. As dirt and mud and dried blood washed away, she began to feel like herself again.

"You'd tempt a saint, lass. But I am no' a saint."

Annie gasped and covered her breasts with her arms.

He stood not ten feet away, the butt of his rifle resting on the ground, his hand around the barrel, his gaze sliding blatantly over her.

"Y-you ought no' be watchin'!"

"You ought no' be naked."

Iain was surprised he could speak. At his first sight of her kneeling bare-breasted and wet-skinned, the breath had rushed from his lungs. His thoughts had scattered like ashes in a gust of wind. He'd found himself rooted to the spot, his cock painfully hard, his anger and frustration from the past few days merging into sharp sexual need.

Even scratched and bruised, she was bonnie. Her cheeks glowed pink with shame, her apple-green eyes wide with a maid's innocent wariness. Her breasts were round and full, their rosy tips pinched from the cold. Her skin was creamy, her shoulders soft and curved.

Iain had been raised to treat women gently, but he did not feel gentle just now. His mother's Viking blood burned in him, ancient and hot, urging him to fist his hands in her hair and bear her onto her back, to claim her in the most primitive way a man could, to plant his seed inside her again and again.

One arm still shielding her breasts, she fumbled for her shift and gown.

"Leave them off."

She stared up at him, clearly alarmed, and reached again for her gown.

"I said leave them." He closed the distance between them, knelt down beside her, only one thought on his mind: He had to touch her.

Her breathing was ragged, and she trembled. Her eyes were huge and round.

He reached out, took her wrists in his hands, and drew them one at a time to his lips, exposing her. "Dinnae hide your loveliness from me, lass."

Then he feasted on the sight of her. Her creamy breasts rose and fell with each rapid breath, their weight enough to fill his hands. Her puckered nipples looked as if a man had already sucked them to tight, wet peaks. One was marred by an angry red scratch. Behind her breastbone, her heart beat fluttered like that of a wild bird.

Desire lanced through him, sent a bolt of heat to his already aching groin, made it hard for him to breathe. He wanted to cup the weight of her breasts in his hands, to taste her, to draw her nipples into his mouth and tease them with his tongue and teeth.

He ducked down, pressed his lips to the scratch, kissed it.

She gasped, and her body jerked as if his lips had been a brand. "P-please dinnae—"

Lust roared in his ears like the raging thrum of a heartbeat. His cock strained against the leather of his breeches, claiming the right to mate. "You've naugh' to fear from me, Annie."

'Twas an outright lie. If she knew what he was thinking, she'd likely slap him soundly—or scream and run.

You're a bastard, MacKinnon. Can you no' see the lass is an innocent and sore afraid?

Fighting to defeat his need for her, he released her wrists, picked up the cloth and dipped it in the bucket. "Turn 'round. I'll wash your back."

Covering her breasts again, she seemed to hesitate, then did as he asked.

He squeezed out the cloth, lifted the heavy weight of her tangled hair over her shoulder, and pressed the wet cloth to her skin. He heard her tiny intake of breath, felt her shiver, saw the rapid beating of her pulse against the column of her throat.

And the fire inside him grew hotter.

For more on the MacKinnon's Rangers series, visit Pamela Clare's website.

About the Author

USA Today best-selling author Pamela Clare began her writing career as a columnist and investigative reporter and eventually became the first woman editor-in-chief of two different newspapers. Along the way, she and her team won numerous state and national honors, including the National Journalism Award for Public Service. In 2011, Clare was awarded the Keeper of the Flame Lifetime Achievement Award. A single mother with two sons, she writes historical romance and contemporary romantic suspense at the foot of the beautiful Rocky Mountains. Visit her website at www.pamelaclare.com.

Also by Pamela Clare

Historical Romance

Kenleigh-Blakewell Family Trilogy
Sweet Release (Book 1)
Carnal Gift (Book 2)
Ride the Fire (Book 3)

MacKinnon's Rangers series
Surrender (Book 1)
Untamed (Book 2)
Defiant (Book 3)

Romantic Suspense

The I-Team Series
Extreme Exposure (Book 1)
Heaven Can't Wait: An I-Team novella (Book 1.5)
Hard Evidence (Book 2)
Unlawful Contact (Book 3)
Naked Edge (Book 4)
Breaking Point (Book 5)
Skin Deep: An I-Team After Hours novella (Book 5.5)
First Strike: The Erotic Prequel to Striking Distance (Book 5.9)
Striking Distance (Book 6)

Contemporary Romance

Colorado High Country Series
Barely Breathing (Book 1)

90205235R00239

Made in the USA
San Bernardino, CA
08 October 2018